The BLUE-HAIRED BOMBSHELL

JOHN ZAKOUR

DAW BOOKS, INC.

DONALD A. WOLLHEIM, FOUNDER

375 Hudson Street, New York, NY 10014

**ELIZABETH R. WOLLHEIM
SHEILA E. GILBERT
PUBLISHERS**

http://www.dawbooks.com

First Paperback Printing, December 2007
1 2 3 4 5 6 7 8 9

DAW TRADEMARK REGISTERED
U.S. PAT. AND TM. OFF. AND FOREIGN COUNTRIES
—MARCA REGISTRADA
HECHO EN U.S.A.

PRINTED IN THE U.S.A.

Acknowledgments

Once again my thanks to Betsy Wolheim at DAW for giving me a chance to write this and the next two books. Thanks Betsy. I also would like to thank Debra Euler and Joshua Starr at DAW for all the help they gave me on this book.

Of course I'd need to thank my agent Joshua for doing all those things agents do. I also need thank my ex-co-writer Larry Ganem, I will always be grateful for Larry for helping me get this series rolling. I hope I improve with each new book.

Finally, I have to thank all the people that contributed (directly or indirectly) to characters in this book: Olga, Carolina, Natalia, Mariela, Mireya, Carlos, Carlos, Andres, Tang, Shannon, Michelle, Mary Martha, Mary, Steve, Harris, Tom, Ron, Elena, April and others I probably forgot. (Don't worry, Jay, you'll be getting your own character soon.)

Chapter 1

The vine twisted itself around my neck, squeezing tighter and tighter. No way I was going to let the holographic epitaph on my tombstone read:

ZACHARY NIXON JOHNSON
AUGUST 15, 2022–DECEMBER 1, 2062
THE LAST PI ON EARTH
WHACKED BY A PLANT

To make matters worse, I hadn't even had my morning cup of joe yet.

"Come to my lab and pick up your new gun," my good buddy Dr. Randy Pool had said. He never bothered to mention that he'd added an arboretum to his lab and populated it with killer plants. That's what I get for hanging out with mad mega-geniuses.

My holographic assistant, HARV, appeared before me. Looking down his nose at me and shaking his head, he said, "Well, this is another fine mess you've gotten yourself into."

"Me! You should have warned me that Randy's lab was being overrun by killer plants!"

HARV shook his balding artificial head again. "Zach, one, these are plants. They can't exactly run. Two, since Randy modified his computer systems, I no longer have complete access. Randy built me, so he is the one person who can construct defenses to keep me out. It's really quite impressive." HARV paused for a nano in order to let me process what he had said. "Three, they are defensive plants. So technically they are just defending themselves—it's what they do. If you read your e-mail from Dr. Pool you'd know this . . ."

I tugged on the vine that had a death grip on my throat. DOS it was strong! "They're defending themselves quite well," I told HARV.

HARV nodded in agreement. "Yes. They are very good at what they do."

Another vine grappled onto my left ankle, snaking up my leg.

"Can you help?" I asked, struggling to pull the vine off me.

HARV shrugged. "Being a hologram, I'm not exactly built to get physical. Though I am working on it."

HARV is wired directly into my brain through a lens in my optic nerve. It wasn't a pleasant experience to go through and it hasn't always been a joyride sharing my brain with him. Still, there are instances when having him hardwired to me is advantageous. I thought this should have been one of those times.

"In the past, you've allowed me to amplify and use the electromagnetic energy from my body as a weapon."

"True," HARV agreed. "But the new computer modifications Randy has done to his lab are also limiting our interface."

Okay, maybe this wasn't going to be one of those times. This meant HARV was able to critique my performance but not help in the least. Randy always insists that I'm his test pilot; right now I felt more like his crash test dummy.

"I can give you the weakness of the grape plant that this plant is based on though," HARV said. HARV won't admit it, but he has a deep-seated longing to be useful. HARV's eyes blinked for a few nanos. "They are very susceptible to cold."

"Great! Can you lower the temperature in the building?" I asked.

"Yes," HARV said.

Finally, a small spark of hope.

"Of course, I can only lower the temperature five degrees, not nearly enough to make a difference," HARV added, smothering that spark.

That made it clear that HARV wasn't going to be much help. Time to search for other options. I looked around. I was in the arboretum of my more than slightly eccentric, mad scientist buddy Doctor Randy Pool's lab. Until a few moments ago I had no idea that the lab even had an arboretum. Randy was mainly an electronic and virtual kind of guy. I didn't know he even had an interest in botany.

Like everything else in Randy's lab, the arboretum was first class, over the top and through the roof, with a touch of geek. It was a room domed in clear Plexiglas. When I say room, I mean BIG room, at least as large as my house. Not sure how I hadn't noticed this before. There was a nice, paved path traversing the room that was lined with vines and dotted with benches to sit on. Holographic birds (at least I assumed they were holograms) flew back and forth as crickets chirped in the background. I knew the crickets weren't real, as they were chirping the top 400 hits from the last hundred years. (Hearing crickets chirp

"Hound Dog" is almost as surreal as being attacked by a plant.) Unlike the main area of Randy's lab, this area was designed to be quiet and serene. This was meant to be a nice place for one to sit and collect their thoughts. Except, of course, for the killer grapevines. Though I was fairly certain these weren't the norm.

I glanced around the room. Randy was there, but he'd be no help as he was completely entwined by a vine. The vine had him so wrapped up I could barely make out his red hair peeking through the top of the plant. Another plant had a tall, blue-haired Asian woman in its clutches. Even with her mostly entangled in plant vines, I could tell she was easy on the eyes. From the blue hair I knew she was probably from the Moon. A Mooner, as we call them here on Earth. The woman was struggling, but to no avail.

I needed to do something and do it fast. If I had my gun I could pop it into my hand and blow the plants away. (Now that's something I never thought I'd say.) Of course, if I had my gun I wouldn't be here. The reason I was visiting Randy today was to pick up my gun, as he had just finished its latest firmware upgrade. I've never been a fan of guns. They are noisy and can be messy. Still, this was one of those times that reinforced why I like to carry a high-powered Colt 4500 up my sleeve. Sometimes it bothered me that I felt so insecure without a weapon up my sleeve. Of course, now I could see why.

Another vine wrapped around my other leg. That reminded me that while I was without my gun I had supplemented my weapons with a handy, good old-fashioned knife I kept in a right ankle holster. (I find I'm much happier if I don't ponder very long over the fact that I always need to have an extra weapon on me. I won't even start to touch on the fact that my underwear is reinforced with buckyball-enhanced carbon steel.)

HARV looked at me. "You're thinking about your love for weapons again, aren't you?"

"It's more a *need,* not a love," I said.

HARV pointed to my right leg. "You probably should go for your knife before the vine goes for your arms. You're just fortunate that vines haven't been designed to deal with such well-armed opponents yet."

That didn't make a lot of sense to me, but then again neither did the entire concept of attack plants. I stretched my left arm down toward my right ankle while trying to pull my leg up away from the vine. I had to give Randy props; he had engineered these plants to be quite strong. I was glad my girlfriend Electra had been making me practice yoga with her lately. It may not be the most manly way for a tough guy to pass the time, but the added flexibility was coming in handy. (Plus Electra, being a champion kickboxer, could beat the stuffing out of me. So if she says something is good for me, I don't question her.)

Despite my added flexibility, my knife still remained a couple of centimeters from my extended grasp. I took a deep breath and stretched my arm out as far as I could. I extended my fingers. I felt the tendons in my hands tightening. I was less than half a centimeter away, but that half centimeter might as well have been half a kilometer. Out of reach was out of reach. As the plant tightened its grip on my throat, I was starting to think I was out of luck.

Offed by a plant . . . never thought that was how I was going to go. On the bright side, all the hit men, assassins, killer bots, and mutant thugs who tried to do me in in the past were going to be *really* embarrassed when they heard a grapevine sent me to my maker. At least I could take a little consolation in that.

Just as I thought all was lost, something unexpected happened. My knife popped up from my ankle holster into my outstretched hand.

"That was me," HARV said. "I magnetized the left wrist portion of your underarm."

"What do you know, you are a useful supercomputer after all," I kidded HARV.

My first move was to grab the part of the vine nearest my neck with my right hand, pulling it to make it nice and rigid. I slit it. I slipped the dead vine off my throat and threw it to the ground. It felt good to breathe freely again. It felt even better to be wielding the knife. I'm not thrilled with what that says about me.

"I thought Randy's new computer system was limiting you?" I said, bending over to slit the vine from around my right leg.

"It was," HARV said. "But I found a workaround."

With my right leg now free, I turned toward my left. The vine swung at me with a free tendril. I caught the swinging tendril with my right hand before it could do any damage. Pulling the vine toward me, I cut it when it became taut. The plant may have caught me off guard the first time. That wasn't going to happen again. I haven't lived this long, doing what I do, by falling for the same trick twice.

Like my old mentor would always say, *"Fool me once, shame on you, fool me twice and I'll be dead."* Okay, she wasn't a good poet, but that lady could handle her whiskey.

I bent down and sliced the vine off my left leg. I was free to spring into action. I noticed that the vines were in motorized pots. I hit the top of the pot with a sidekick, knocking it over. I wanted to make sure this plant wasn't going to be coming after me.

Brandishing my knife, I raced toward my trapped friend and his shapely cohort. I made a snap decision to free Randy first. I know they usually say ladies first, but Randy was not only closer, he was struggling much harder. Besides, Randy may be overly eccentric, but he's one of the greatest minds on Earth. The world needed him. It eased my psyche that for her part, the woman didn't seem worried at all. I would bet my 1986 Mets poster that the woman was more able to take care of herself in this situation than Randy was.

Moving to free Randy, I noticed out of the corner of my right eye that the potted grapevines in the back of the room that had been acting like grapevines should act were now heading toward me. When I woke up this morning, if someone had bet me ten credits that I was going to be chased by grapes today, I probably would have taken them up on it. When you're a P.I., there are times you need to gamble. I like to think that when the computer chips are down I know exactly when to hold 'em, when to fold 'em, and when to go for my gun.

The plants were rolling toward me and gaining ground. I didn't turn around. I didn't have to. I heard them progressing toward me, their vines snapping on the ground as they closed in. This called for a little strategy on my part. I was going to have to outsmart the plants. Quite frankly, if I couldn't outthink a plant, I didn't deserve my next birthday.

I stopped cold in my tracks. Not because I was scared—I wanted to throw the plants off. Sure enough, they rolled right on by me, one on each side. I could have sworn one of them flipped me the bird as it rolled past then skidded to a stop. Not giving the plants time to react, I dove between them with my arms outstretched like I was an old-fashioned plane. I hit them each high on the bases, clotheslining them and knocking them to the ground.

"You shouldn't dive like that with a knife in your hand," HARV lectured inside my head.

"Yes, Mother," I said.

I sprung up to my feet and ran toward Randy.

Reaching him, I grabbed the vine that had a pythonlike grip on his throat and slit it. Randy pulled the excess grape parts away from his throat.

"Are you DOSing crazy!" Randy screamed at me, his pale skin now as red as his hair.

Not exactly the thanks I was expecting. I realized he had been struggling to free himself so he could stop me from slicing up his plants, not because he was worried about his own health.

"Uh, maybe," I said.

"Plants stand down," Randy said in a firm, yet still geeky (and angry) voice.

The plant released its grip on Randy. I looked over at Randy's companion; she was also now free.

Randy dusted himself off, glaring at me all the while. "Don't you read the e-mails I send?"

I shook my head. "I skim them."

Randy stomped a foot on the ground and threw his arms up in the air. "You *skim* them . . ." he mocked.

"You do send me a lot of e-mail," I said.

Randy rolled his eyes. "I've only sent you twenty-three messages this week."

"Yeah, but Randy, it's only Tuesday."

"Every message I send you is of the utmost importance."

"I agree," HARV said, appearing from the room's holographic projector. HARV was always one to bend over backward to take Randy's side. I was surprised he wasn't attached to Randy's butt right now.

"Randy, you send me more e-mail than my mother and people trying to sell me natural male enhancement combined . . ."

Randy put his hands on his hips. "Well, your mother hasn't inserted a multimillion-credit, super-highly-advanced cognitive computer into your brain, has she?"

"No, of course not," I said.

Randy continued his rant. "As for those other people, I won't even justify that with a comment. Though you probably could use some help in that area."

I pointed to the tall Asian woman as I told Randy, "Remember I like to keep HARV being attached to my brain as a *secret*."

Randy rolled his eyes. "Please, Zach," he spat. "Melda here knows all about all my greatest inventions. I trust her completely. She's working with me on guard plants for the Moon," Randy said, staring at Melda the entire time. With his head turned away from me, I noticed for the first time that in middle of Randy's gangly red hair there was a barren patch. If Randy didn't take measures to stop it, in a few years his head would look like HARV's. I shook my head, trying not to think about that any longer.

"Guard plants for the Moon . . ." I said.

"I combined the simple grape plant with some nanotech. And voilà! The plants can sense an intruder's intentions and then subdue them until further security personnel arrive. Melda thinks they make a great low-cost alternative to bots. They are functional and ornamental. Melda says they are some of my best work." Randy took a deep breath, a shallow breath and then sighed, spitting a bit. "We were in the final stages of testing how long they can hold an intruder when you so rudely interrupted."

Melda walked over to me and extended her hand. "You must be Zachary Nixon Johnson," she said.

I took her hand, gladly ignoring Randy. "If I'm not then the wrong person is wearing my trench coat and fedora."

"Gross." HARV said in my head.

Melda smiled. "Ah, Randy says you have quite the wit." She was a tall, striking woman. I would have thought her blue hair would have looked awkward on her dark Asian skin, but the combination somehow worked. I knew this woman could probably twist Randy around her little finger without even trying. Who knows what she could do to him if she put some effort into it?

"Well, I'd probably be dead a thousand times over if it wasn't for Randy's inventions," I said.

Melda's smile widened. "Yes, he says that often, too. We are hoping that we can implement some of his genius on the Moon."

Randy gave Melda a toothy grin, then blushed. "Melda's not only beautiful and a great judge of character, but she's also a brilliant scientist." Randy was crushing on her bad, and this couldn't be good. He turned to me. "Melda really thinks that all the work I did for you is especially ingenious."

I sighed. Randy may have been one of the greatest minds on Earth but he was also a first-class, no-holds-barred geek. A pretty face on a great body could make him babble like a drunk actor accepting an award. Randy's eyes filled with admiration as he looked at Melda. I could only hope she was as worthy of his respect as he believed. Randy forced himself to remove his gaze from Melda (who was doing a yoga stretch) and return his attention to me.

"Why are you here, Zach?"

"One of your e-mails mentioned my gun was ready."

Randy stood there staring at me. His wide eyes became narrow in concentration.

"My gun, the one I keep up my sleeve," I coaxed. "I dropped it off last week."

Randy's eyes shot back open again. "Ah, yes, that gun. It's ready now." Randy pointed down the path. "It's in my main lab."

"Funny thing is, last week all you *had* was the main lab."

Randy looked at me. "That's not funny at all."

"I agree," HARV said, always the brownnoser.

HARV looked at me. "Dr. Pool had the arboretum built five days ago."

"It's mostly a prefab," Randy said. "It's amazing what you can do if have some extra credits and lots of robo-builders."

"I wouldn't know," I said.

"Follow me and I'll give you your new gun," Randy said, motioning forward like an old stagecoach driver preparing to head West. Randy turned to Melda. "You'll want to see this, too. It's way groovy."

As we walked, I thought about how Randy had recently come into that wealth of extra credits. One his inventions, the PIHI-Pod, had hit it ultra-big. The PIHI-Pod, which is short (but not that short) for Portable Interactive Holographic Interface Personally Optimized Device, is basically a mass-market, less powerful version of HARV. It is a small device that users wear on their ears or the sides of their heads, wherever they prefer. A PIHI-Pod senses a person's thoughts and transmits holographic information and entertainment to him, based on his current needs and likes. It comes in many styles and shapes, none of them being either too big or all that much to look at, but that doesn't stop it from being today's "in" thing.

The scary thing about PIHI-Pods (besides people trying to drive and watch them at the same time) is that I know for a fact that Randy's research was funded by all the biggest conglomerates in the world: Entercorp, Htech, and ExShell. To make matters worse, they are sold exclusively by UltraMegaHyper-Mart. To bring matters to the point I don't even want to think about thinking about, they are also fully endorsed by the World Council as a way to instantly deliver important information to everybody. . . . I've come to accept a world filled with constant DNA scans and full body light-X-rays as part of everyday modern life. DOS, I've even learned to take advantage of these when I needed an extra bit of data to crack a case. But there's something about the government and big corps having direct access to people's minds that scares me. . . . A lot.

Randy is constantly assuring me that only good can come from PIHI-Pods. The devices simply read people's needs and transmit relevant information to them. The devices can't be used to program people. They are also not recording people's thoughts and sending them thought-appropriate advertisements. . . . At least not yet. I knew it would be just a matter of time before some greedy marketing exec started spamming people's brains. HARV insists I'm just paranoid. In my game a little paranoia can go a long way toward keeping you alive.

Chapter 2

We entered Randy's main facility. It was much cleaner and far less chaotic than normal. Yep, Randy was putting on his best face for Melda. No good could come of that. Randy worked best when he let chaos guide and inspire him. Necessity may be the mother of invention, but chaos is what drives the necessity.

One advantage of having HARV wired directly to my brain is that we can actually think back and forth to each other. That's something PIHI-Pods can't do. While Randy led us towards a lab bench, HARV and I conversed mentally.

"HARV, I need as much info as you can give me on this Melda."

"Right," HARV thought back. *"She was born on the Moon in 2024. She was the first baby born there."*

I waited for more. There wasn't any.

"And?" I prompted.

"It's very interesting that she was the first baby born on the Moon," HARV offered.

"You're stalling, HARV."

More mental silence. HARV was having problems
and neither of us liked that.

Finally, HARV said slowly, *"I'm not stalling. Nice
weather we're having. How about those Mets?"*

HARV may be the most advanced cognitive processor on Earth but he wasn't very good at stalling. It
was something he didn't have any experience with.

"Her birthday is August fifteenth," HARV offered.

"Great, now I know when to send her a holo-card."

"You don't have to be mean about it," HARV said.
*"The Earth and the Moon don't actually share a lot
of data."*

HARV didn't need to tell me that. The Moon Colony was established around 2023, not long after humans and aliens made initial contact. At first, things
were all peachy keen with the Earth and the Moon,
with the latter acting as a huge science research lab
and greeting center for aliens. The Moon also served
as an asteroid deflection point for Earth. Earth and
Moon cooperated to build a giant reflector beam that
would defend both the Moon and mostly the Earth
from any impending asteroid crashes. Both sides got
along well for a while, but that was just the drunken
honeymoon before the reality and then the greed set
in.

First, the aliens decided they didn't want a lot to
do with us, certainly not to the point where they need
to interact with us on a regular basis. (The main reason for this is that aliens think we smell funky.) Right
off the bat the Moon lost one of its main functions.
The World Council, being as sharp and thrifty as they
are, figured they needed another use for the colony.
They found one. They declared that the Moon would
be used to store "materials no longer deemed suitable
for the Earth." In other words, we'd give them our
toxic waste.

The Moon protested, saying they were meant to be

an oasis for research and alien contact, not a trash receptacle. The Earth's counterargument was: we have nuclear weapons—so there! The Moon really had no choice but to accept our waste. From there the relationship went downhill. Both sides still coexist, but the Earth makes it clear that the Moon only exists because the Earth allows it to. For the most part, the Moon accepted that relationship.

That is, until a few years ago, when a guy named Boris "Bo" Sputnik became Head Administrator of the Moon. Sputnik was quite the rebel. He pushed the World Council to set the Moon free and make it an independent colony. He promised they would still house our trash and protect us from being smashed by an asteroid, but he wanted to set his people free.

To their credit (and my surprise) the World Council has voted on the "Free the Moon Resolution" a couple of times. Each time, the resolution has been defeated. If memory served me right, a new vote was coming up soon.

"Have you got anything for me yet?" I asked HARV.

The word *NO* flashed in front of my eyes. I always knew when HARV was frustrated, as he would stop talking.

That wasn't a good omen at all. Sure the Moon's computer systems were generally closed to the Earth's computer systems but that had never stopped HARV before. He was an e-expert at cracking through the toughest firewalls, even the latest intelligent e-laser walls.

"I'll keep working on it while you talk to Dr. Pool," HARV said.

Sure enough, we had reached the lab table that my gun was on. I turned my attention back to Randy. It was always best to pay close attention to Randy when he was in close proximity to a firearm.

Randy smiled smugly as he reached for the gun. To my surprise, his hand passed over my gun and instead, picked up a clear plastic rod. Randy showed us the rod proudly.

"This is the new Colt 2062."

I shook my head. I pointed to my gun. "No, it's not. That is."

Randy shook his head. "No," he said. "That's the old Colt 4500."

He held the tube up to my face. "This! This is the state of personal weapons to come!"

I shook my head again. "No, it's not."

"Yes, it is," Randy said.

"Yes, it is," HARV echoed.

Randy pulled the tube away from me and displayed it in an open hand for Melda to see. She reached over and touched it.

"Nice," Melda said. "And I'm not one to usually like weapons."

"It's not a weapon," I insisted.

Randy tossed me the tube. I caught it. It felt like a cross between old Silly Putty, older PVC tubing, and the classic Nintendo Wii controller. I liked the feel. It felt good, though I wasn't going to admit that. Besides, a weapon should feel *right* in the hand, not good.

"It's tied into your brain waves and DNA," Randy said proudly. (Like that was a good thing).

"Wow," Melda said, with a look of admiration in her eyes. I didn't know if the look was real or if she was just playing Randy.

"It can fire bolts of energy ranging from stun to disintegrate," Randy boasted. "You can even use the energy from your own body to charge it more."

"And that's a good thing because?" I asked.

Randy walked over, smiled, and patted me on the

shoulder. It was very uncharacteristic of Randy. He's not a big fan of touching.

"Trust me, Zach, it is."

"Trust him, Zach, it is," HARV reiterated.

"The energy bolts will even lock on to your target's bio signature and track it. And it is self-generating so it charges while you move. It's virtually limitless in its power." Randy's grin was so wide he probably could have swallowed an old-fashioned truck tire.

Having an unlimited supply of tracking bolts and destructive energy unquestionably had its appeal.

"I like good old-fashioned lead bullets," I said. "Sure they can be messy, but killing should never be clean and easy." I never want to get to the point where I take killing for granted.

I didn't think it was possible but Randy's smile widened. "I knew you'd say that."

"Well, you are a mad genius," I told him.

"True," he acknowledged with a nod.

"True," HARV agreed.

"True," Melda said, under her breath but loud enough for us all to hear.

Randy's smile grew even wider. "The Colt 2062 is also loaded with five thousand rounds of new and improved nano lead bullets. The bullets expand and can even split and explode after leaving the barrel."

"Only five thousand rounds?" I said.

"That should be more than sufficient, Zach." Randy stared at me. "Zach, you hold in your hand the most powerful hand weapon ever invented. Also, when interfaced with HARV and your underarmor, it can generate a shield. Plus it can fire a mini-tractor beam."

"Yeah, but does it do windows?" I joked.

Randy thought for a nano. "I'm sure on the correct setting you could blast windows clean."

I played with the tubular Colt 2062 in hand; moving it around to get a good feel for it.

"It doesn't even have a sight."

Randy shook his head. "The sight is intelligent and on demand."

"Huh?"

Randy held his arm out and made a vertical motion. "Lift your arm up like you want to fire it."

I moved my arm upward, aiming the tube. A targeting sight morphed up from the opposite end of the cylinder. Another computer-generated sight appeared in front of my eye.

"The virtual sight also works with HARV's holo interface," Randy beamed like a proud dad.

"Where's the trigger?" I asked.

Randy put his head in his hands. "A trigger! How last week," he said. He looked up from his hands. "Just squeeze the handle and it will fire."

"Really?"

Randy bobbed his head up and down. "Really."

"What keeps me from firing it by mistake?"

"Software, Zach. Software. Very intelligent, situation appropriate, software. It all works with HARV."

"What if HARV is out of commission?"

"That won't happen," Randy and HARV said in unison.

"Just humor me."

"The gun has a manual override that will still interface directly with your brain," they both said. "Just think type of ordnance then squeeze and it will fire. Besides the standard penetrating and exploding ammo, the nano bullets can also morph into glue, paint, or web." Randy paused for a nano, like he so often did when he knew he had something to say but didn't remember what. This time, though, there was something different about the silence. Randy put a finger to his mouth.

"What aren't you telling me?" I asked.

"GUS activate," Randy said looking at my new weapon.

The weapon glowed.

"Okay, it's a flashlight too. . . . That's kind of cool," I conceded.

The words, "Now operational," came from my gun.

"Okay, so it talks," I said. "Not sure if the world really needs another talking gun."

Randy shook his head and hands and most of his body at me. "It doesn't talk. It *thinks!* The Gun's User System, or GUS, is the gun's AI."

"It thinks?" I asked, not bothering to point out that the acronym was really stretching it.

"It thinks," HARV said, not thrilled that he wasn't the only cognitive processor in the room.

"It thinks," Melda said, under her breath.

"Yes, it thinks," Randy said.

"I certainly do!" GUS said proudly.

"Why do I need a thinking gun?" I asked.

"Why *don't* you need a thinking gun!" Randy answered.

HARV turned a shade of red I'd never seen him turn before. "Yes, why *does* he need a thinking gun?" HARV asked, hands on hips, not even pretending to be close to happy.

Randy looked at HARV. "GUS is a backup fail-safe," Randy said. "Just in case."

"Yep!" GUS said, in a chipper tone.

"GUS can make sure the Colt 2062 never falls into the wrong hands."

That was a good point. Of course, with a hand weapon this powerful I wasn't sure there was such a thing as the *right* hands.

"If I am separated from you Mr. Johnson, I can find you by rolling myself up and well, rolling . . ."

HARV rolled his eyes. "Mr. Johnson, what a suck-up."

I had to give Randy kudos. It seemed to be an impressive weapon, at least in theory. Which led me to my next question.

"Has it ever been tested?"

"In theory, yes."

"Is this like the theory that if you put 200,000 monkeys in a room with an old-fashioned word processor one of them would bang out the next hit holographic movie?"

"Along those lines, yes," Randy said, as straight-faced as I've ever seen him. Randy burst out laughing. Melda and HARV joined in, too. I got the feeling they were laughing *at* me, not with me.

Randy turned to Melda. "Laymen can be so simple some times. It would take at least 940,892 monkeys to make a hit holographic movie. With a mere 200,000, you'd be lucky to get a hit HV show."

"So you in fact have no idea if it actually works?" I said.

Randy crossed his arms and looked at me. HARV did the same. Melda just looked on politely; she didn't know me well enough to ridicule me yet. (She may have been laughing on the inside—it's hard to tell.)

"No," Randy said meekly. "How could I? It's synched to your DNA and brain patterns. This is the first time I've ever activated GUS."

"Can I at least test it?"

A sly smile spread across Randy's face. "I thought you'd never ever ask. Targets zero-zero-one, zero-one-zero, zero-one-one, one-zero-zero activate!" Randy shouted.

I looked around the room. Four targets had fallen from the ceiling, one along each wall. Since we were in the middle of the lab and it was quite a large lab, each target was at least two hundred meters away.

Randy pointed at each of the targets. "Fire away!" he said.

"Here, in your lab?"

"It's a very well-built lab," Randy stated, calmly. "Plus, the bullets or energy bolts self-destruct if they miss their target. So fire at will."

"Which one is Will?" I asked, jokingly.

Randy pointed to the clay duck target moving back and forth along the north wall. "I named the duck Will."

I should have known better than to joke with a scientist. I extended my arm, aiming my gun. The site popped up. I took a deep breath. I concentrated on the duck target darting left and right, up and down.

"I'm ready when you are," GUS chirped.

I put the gun down. I turned to Randy. "Can I do this one myself?" I asked him.

Randy shrugged. "Of course, just think GUS off." Randy turned to Melda. "Zach is a little slow sometimes." He pointed to his forehead then whispered (though I could still hear him), "One too many shots to the head."

Out of the corner of my eye I saw HARV nodding in agreement. I turned my attention back to the target. I thought, *GUS off*. I picked up the target with my left eye. Adjusting my gun, I pulled, well, *squeezed* the trigger. It had a nice feel to it.

My gun made no sound. I felt no recoil, but the target exploded. I watched pieces of simulated clay falling to the ground like a really ugly snow storm. I looked at Randy, he had the smile of a proud father.

"I miss the sound and the recoil," I said, even if I had to admit I saw the advantages of not having either.

"Sound and recoil are both programmable options if you feel like being macho. In fact, you can have

sound and or recoil without firing anything if you
wish," Randy said.

"Wow, you've really thought of everything," Melda
said both hands under her chin.

"Pretty much," Randy agreed. "Just to prove it . . ."

Randy ducked down under one of the lab benches.
He motioned to Melda to do the same. I got a bad
feeling about this. "Targets, attack Zach," Randy
ordered.

I didn't have to look to know that the targets from
the south, east, and west walls were heading toward
me. Yep, with friends like mine, I didn't need half the
enemies I had. Only *I* could turn from target-shooter
to target. I spun clockwise, not sure why other than it
just felt more natural. That and from my positioning
in the room, the target on the east side would reach
me first.

I was thinking without thinking, activating GUS. A
targeting cursor appeared in front of my eye. I picked
up the east target, its clay pigeon zooming in on me.
I aimed my gun. The pigeon split into five small pigeons, each making a beeline for me. I pulled the
trigger five times, adjusting my arm ever so slightly
for each shot. It was more of a reflex than a thought.
Each of the five attacking pigeons shattered. Their
remains fell to the ground like holiday confetti. In
fact, I think it really was confetti.

I turned my body and my attention to the targets
coming at me from the south wall. These were actually
disk-shaped targets with bull's-eyes on them. Of
course, they were flying at me like a ninja's throwing
stars. They were coming down on me fast from every
conceivable angle.

"I suggest a wide-area, low-yield energy blast,"
HARV said in my brain.

"What a super idea!" GUS chipped in.

I thought, aimed, and fired all in one fluid motion.

The attacking targets fell to the ground as if they hit an invisible wall.

Throwing myself to the ground, I felt the last target (or targets) whiz past me. Rolling for cover, I stopped in the prone position, peeking up to try to catch a glimpse of the last target. I saw the target was a series of baseball-shaped objects. They had shot past me, but figured it out and were now heading back at me. If they made contact with me they wouldn't kill me, but they would certainly sting a hell of a lot. Randy thought you needed pain for gain in scientific progress. Of course, the pain was always mine.

"Computer tracking, on," I yelled to HARV and GUS.

"How do you know there's computer tracking?" HARV asked out loud.

"Tracking activated with pleasure," GUS beamed.

"Suck-up," HARV said to GUS.

Rolling over to my back, I sat up. The targeting cursor appeared in front of my eye again, but this time with an arrow pointing left. Sliding my arm to the left the word *FIRE* flashed in front of my eyes. I pulled the trigger. One baseball-type object exploded. The cursor appeared with an arrow pointing right. I adjusted my gun every so slightly until the word "FIRE" appeared again. Squeezing the trigger, I caught the third and last ball coming at me from a bit farther right. I adjusted my gun and blasted it. The target was so close to me when I hit it that I was dusted with its debris.

I stood up, shaking target remains off of me. I turned to see Randy was already standing and smiling ear to ear. DOS, his smile practically ran over onto Melda. Randy helped Melda up from behind the table with one hand, while clapping on his chest with his other hand.

"Excellent job, GUS, HARV, and you, too, Zach," Randy said.

"Thank you," HARV said.

"Incredible," Melda said.

"Ah, Zach did the hard part," GUS added.

"He did not," HARV contradicted.

"I know. I'm just trying to make Zach feel good about himself," GUS whispered.

Randy walked over to me. If he had been any more pleased with himself he'd be patting himself on the back with both hands and nominating himself for a Nobel Prize.

"So Zach, does the GUS enhanced Colt 2062 pass its field test?"

I took out a series of intelligent targets in under a minute with a weapon I hadn't even seen until ten minutes ago. It certainly was intuitive. I had to give Randy props, just not out loud.

"Pretty impressive. Isn't it?" Randy said looking more excited than a kid on Holiday morning.

"It'll do. For now."

I popped the Colt 2062 up my sleeve. It felt good there.

"I'm still going to keep my knife and a good old-fashioned magnum or something similar around, just in case."

Randy smiled. "Zach, you're so old-fashioned. But if it makes you happy that's fine."

HARV rolled up his sleeve and looked at his watch. "Zach, if you're going to make your breakfast appointment with Electra at the Lombard Street Bistro I suggest we leave now."

I turned to Randy. "Do you have anything else for me to test?"

"Zach, I just gave you the most sophisticated personal weapon in human history. I've connected you with the most advanced cognitive processor on the known planets. What more could you possibly want? At least for the next few months."

"The winning lottery numbers would be nice."

Randy shook his head. "You don't want to miss your breakfast out with Electra."

I tipped my fedora to Melda. "It was a pleasure meeting you."

She bowed. "The pleasure was all mine."

"How long will be you be on Earth for?" I asked.

"A day or two longer."

"I hope we meet again," I said, mostly being polite.

"Somehow, Mr. Johnson, I'm sure we will. I'm sure we will," Melda said with a pleasant smile.

I don't know why, but that smile sent a shiver down my spine.

Chapter 3

A couple of years ago, I could have driven from Randy's lab near the pier to The Lombard Bistro in less than ten minutes. This was because not only did I enjoy driving my slightly modified 1973 cherry red Mustang convertible fast, but back then I had the roads pretty much to myself. I only had to share them with a bunch of grannies who refused to use hovercrafts, teleporters, or the most scary of all, public transportation.

Land-based travel had fallen out of favor with the general populace. It was too slow for today's fast paced lives. That was fine by me. I didn't mind having the roads to myself.

That all changed almost overnight. First, there was the first teleporting accident in history. Ten UltraMega-aHyperMart insurance salesmen got stuck in stasis for ten hours. None of them were killed, but they were all inconvenienced and missed their sales quotas for the day. For a salesman, that's a fate much worse than death.

Much as it pains me, I also contributed to the rise

of cars by taking ex-teen-pop-star, now World Council Member, Sexy Sprockets for a ride on the ground. Sexy is both an old client and, for some reason unbeknownst to me, now one of the most powerful and influential people on the planet. Not because she's one of the twelve main World Council members mind you, but because she's a retired (at twenty) ex-pop-princess. Though she prefers to refer to herself as ex-pop-princess-sex-goddess-current-coolest-World-Council-member-in-da-world. I have no idea how she gets that on her business card.

Sexy found the ride completely stimulating (she actually used the word *orgasmic*, but Electra would kill me in the most painful way possible if she heard that). Sexy was so jazzed by the experience that she announced on a worldwide HV State of the World Address that, and I quote, "Ground-based cars are so *way past* absolute zero they are smokin' red hot!" I, being over thirty, had no idea what she meant. Others did though.

Thanks to mass media (over) promotion and robotic mass production, land-based cars became an instant hit again. Most people couldn't even remember why we left the ground in the first place. Some will now deny that they ever even used a hover.

I just shake my head and moan that I now have to share the roads with throngs of others. The 2060s cars are all fly-by-wire and have the same basic sleek bullet on wheels shape. All the newer cars are computer controlled so the "drivers" are more riders than anything else. ExShell and Htech, makers of most of today's cars, justify this "same as the next guy" look by claiming that cars come in millions of downloadable and customizable colors for the car body, wheels, and windshields. They also state the driving experience is limitlessly customizable as the car's users have complete control over the internal experience: the sounds the car makes, the holographic displays on the windows, and the type of coffee it serves.

I take some solace in the fact that my car isn't almost totally computer-driven and that it has style and class. It was just like the ones my ancestors drove nearly a hundred years ago.

HARV appeared in my car's dash. Okay, maybe not EXACTLY like the ones they drove. Back then, this car wouldn't have a computer interface and be solar powered, but outside of those two tiny concessions to the modern world, that was it.

HARV pointed to the left, "I've checked with the traffic satellites, you should take Reagan Avenue."

I shook my head no. "Sorry, can't do."

HARV sighed in my screen. He dropped his forehead to his hand. I saw a lot of me in that move. "Zach, I don't believe you won't drive on a street because of its name. After all, he was one of the finest presidents in history."

I pushed down on the accelerator.

"You're going too fast," HARV scolded.

I eased off the gas slightly. "I just think Clinton deserves his own street, too. After all, he was a great president."

HARV rolled his eyes. "Please, he was the *third* best politician in his own immediate family."

"Oh, come on HARV. He was a man's man *and* a lady's man."

HARV's eyes stopped rolling and started spinning. It was unsettling but you learn to live with these things when you have a computer wired to your brain. "That's your criteria for a good president? How about adding spiffy dresser to the list?"

"Not my only criteria, but I just like the guy. He's like the Elvis of presidents."

HARV just looked at me through the screen. He

looked at his watch. "We should be at the bistro in a few minutes. I suggest we don't talk so you can concentrate on the road. The traffic is very heavy these days."

HARV disappeared from my screen. I drove on in peace to meet Electra.

I arrived at the top of Lombard Bistro only ten minutes late, which is pretty much a record for me. The bistro was a quaint little outdoor place that still employed only human waiters and waitresses. To make matters more noteworthy, all of the employees were on roller skates. I'm not sure who thought of the idea of putting a restaurant on top of one of the highest streets in the world and then top it off by putting all your employees on wheels. It did make the place interesting.

I found Electra sitting at a table in the middle of the floor, sipping on an ice water.

"Sorry, I'm late," I said, bending over to give her a kiss.

She kissed me back.

"With you, amor, ten minutes late is early."

A pigtailed waitress in a plaid micromini skidded over to our table. Electra lifted up her water, catching it from spilling.

"Sorry, I'm new," the waitress said, sheepishly. She handed me a menu. Yep, they even had old-fashioned paper menus here.

I waved it away. "I'll just have bacon and eggs and coffee. . . . Lots of coffee."

She looked at me. "Real bacon or simulated soy bacon?"

I looked at her. I pointed to myself. These days, folks dress in many eclectic ways. This is the anything *goes* era. To look at me though, you knew I wasn't into the latest dress fads. I'm an old-fashioned guy, despite the computer attached to my brain and the high-powered mini army I kept up my sleeve.

The waitress studied me. "You're not wearing a PIHI-Pod, you need a shave, and your face has some lines in it," she said, obviously not bucking for a big tip. She looked at my head. "And you're wearing a really funny old hat," she said, totally killing her chance at a tip.

"It's called a fedora," I told her.

She shrugged. "I bet you want the real bacon."

I touched my nose. "Vingo."

"Real eggs or soy eggs?" the waitress asked.

"I'm still me."

She touched her order pad. "I'll put you down for real eggs."

"Smart girl."

"I'm not just a waitress, I'm also an actress," she said proudly.

"These days nobody is just a waitress," I told her.

"Real coffee or soy-coffee?"

I just looked at her. That didn't even warrant an answer.

"I'll put you down for the real coffee," she said, punching her order pad. She looked up at me. "That's three credits extra."

"I'll splurge."

The waitress turned to Electra. "And you, ma'am?"

"The fruit platter of the day with more ice water."

"Very good choice," she said.

The waitress skated off. Electra turned her attention back to me. "So, problems at Randy's?"

I took a sip of water. "I got attacked by a couple of plants."

Electra smirked. "Fine. Don't tell me."

I get that reaction a lot. My life reads like some

sort of eight-credit pulp story. "Randy is hanging out with some tall, exotic woman from the Moon."

Electra raised an eyebrow. Electra's a class-A surgeon, brilliant in every sense of the word, but she loves a good piece of cheese as much as the next person. "Really? What does she want with Randy?"

"She's there observing his methods," I said. "Of course, he's crushing badly on her. It's not going to end well."

Electra shook her head. "Geeks and babes, it's the age-old story.

My eyes lit up. "The trip was pretty beneficial though." I flipped my wrist. The Colt 2062 popped into my hand.

Electra eyed it. "So now you carry your HV remote around with you." She sat back in her chair. "I'm scared."

I moved the Colt closer to her face. "It's not a remote or a joystick. It's my new gun."

"Really?" Electra said, her eyes catching fire. (Electra has a thing for weapons. I try not to think about it too much).

"Really," GUS said.

Electra looked at me. "Your gun talks."

"Tell me about it . . ."

"I'm the Gun's User System! You can call me GUS!"

Electra lowered her eyes and sat back in her chair. "Your talking gun has a name," she said.

"Such is my life," I said. "It's very chipper."

"Sure am!" GUS said.

I heard HARV moan inside my brain.

"HARV hates it, therefore GUS is growing on me."

"Thanks!" GUS said.

Electra simply laughed. "For the man who has everything, a talking gun."

Electra took the Colt 2062 from my hand.

"With an electronic conscience," I added.

"You're kidding?" she said.

"I wish I was."

Electra steadied the gun in her hand. "It has a nice feel to it. I assume it will only fire for you."

I nodded.

"So there was a woman from the Moon with Randy?" Electra said, finally concentrating on something other than my new weapon.

"Yes."

"That's an interesting coincidence," she said.

"How so?"

She reached into her pocket and pulled out her personal paper computer. She unfolded it in front of me. She pressed a button. She read the message. "We are honored to invite you to the Moon for the 1st Annual Amigo Relating Culture or ARC Conference. The purpose of this worlds-altering event is gather the greatest five thousand minds on Earth to share culture and ideas with their friends on the Moon."

Electra was beaming. "Do you believe it? They say I'm one of the five thousand most influential people."

"I'm not surprised."

A chill ran down my spine. First the Moon woman; then the fancy new gun. Now Electra is going to the Moon. This was beginning to feel like I was going to hit one of those stretches I seem to get into every year, where the universe and I have a love-hate relationship going on. It will fall into my lap to save the universe (well, at least my small part of the universe) while the powers that be throw everything they've got at me to stop me.

We heard a scream coming from across the street. "My baby!"

I turned toward the cry to see a shapely lady looking on in horror as the baby carriage she must have been pushing was careening down the street.

I grabbed the Colt 2062 from Electra and rushed into action. HARV came back online as I darted into the street. The carriage was rolling straight down so I decided to cut a diagonal path through the traffic to close the gap between the carriage and myself as quickly as possible.

"You know, this would never have happened if the new San Fran City Council hadn't decided to straighten out Lombard street for aesthetic reasons," HARV noted.

HARV was correct, but not all that useful, as is often the case.

"I'm pumping more blood to your legs so you can run faster," HARV said. "I'm also tracking all the cars on the street now so hopefully you won't get splattered all over the pavement."

Without a doubt, rushing across a busy street during morning rush hour wasn't the brightest thing I've ever done in my life. Sadly though, it was far from the dumbest. As for the difficulty level of dodging traffic, it was par for the course of my life.

I stopped a nano. A green bullet-shaped car whizzed past. The driver flipped me off. Racing forward, I caught a red bullet-shaped car coming at me out of the corner of my right eye. I calculated that if I increased my speed a touch I would be able to get past him without getting squished. Rushing onward, I breathed a sigh of relief as I squeaked past.

Funny, I never knew that all the time I spent playing the ancient classic video game Frogger would turn out to be life training. I knew my mom was wrong when she insisted playing that game would be bad for me.

Weaving and bobbing in and out of traffic, I dodged a yellow bullet-shaped (you see the pattern here) car. I was grazed by an orange glowing car, but my underarm took most of the damage. I was just humiliated that out of all the cars to get hit by it would have to be the orange one.

Despite my best efforts, I was still only halfway across the street and only through one direction of traffic. I was closer to the carriage lurching downhill but still not close enough. No way I was going to reach it in time. It was a sheer miracle that the carriage hadn't tipped over yet. There couldn't have been much time left. I needed to act fast.

I stopped in the middle of the street. A purple rocket-shaped car swerved past me. The driver didn't seem to notice. I lifted up my Colt 2062.

"I'm going to need the tractor beam, GUS," I shouted.

"Splendid idea!" GUS shouted back.

I aimed. Problem was, I couldn't get a clear shot with all the traffic zooming by.

"HARV, stop the traffic," I screamed in my mind.

"That would be illegal, Zach."

"Explain the situation to the cars' computer auto-mated pilot systems. I'm sure they'll understand. It's a baby, HARV!"

"Message relayed to the CAP systems."

I glanced around. All the cars on the street had slowed down and were pulling over.

I adjusted the Colt 2062 in my arm. "Let's lock and, well, lock," I told GUS.

"Got it!" GUS said.

I squeezed the trigger pointing at the carriage all the while continuing forward. The carriage came to an abrupt halt. The baby in the carriage went flying upward.

"For every action there is an equal and opposite reaction," HARV lectured.

"Newton's Second Law," GUS chipped in.

Out of pure reflex I pushed the trigger on the Colt

2062 again, releasing the carriage. As the carriage continued its unguided stroll down Lombard Street, I aimed at the flying baby. I squeezed the trigger again. The baby stopped falling and hung there suspended in mid air.

"I deduced that you wanted to catch, not destroy, the occupant of the carriage," GUS said.

"Good deduction, GUS," I said.

"He's a wonder," HARV said, cynically.

I worked my way across the street, positioning myself right under the wrapped baby. By this time the mother and her camera crew (which I just noticed) had also made it down the hill.

"My baby! My baby!" the woman cried.

I motioned for her to stay back and to give me room. I had the Colt 2062 pointing upward. I needed to cut the power then catch the baby.

"Just turn the handle right," HARV coached in my brain. *"It will allow the baby to fall slowly."*

I moved my wrist ever so slightly to the right. The baby started to lower. Moving my wrist a little more right, the baby lowered more. I turned my wrist even more.

"Too much!" HARV shouted in my brain.

The baby started to plummet. I dove to the ground, hands extended, much like a wide receiver lunging for a football. I hit the ground with a thud, never letting my eyes leave the baby. Extending my arms out I caught the baby a couple of centimeters from the ground.

I pulled the baby toward me. He (or she) licked me. Yes, licked me. The baby was either really ugly or a dog.

The young woman, who I now totally recognized as mass media darling Madrid Ramada, came rushing over to me.

"You did it! You did it! You saved my baby!" Ma-

drid cried. She grabbed the baby—I mean dog—from
my arms and started kissing it on the lips. She turned
to me and kissed me on the cheek. I wasn't sure if I
was offended or glad.

Madrid Ramada is one of those famous people who
is famous just because she is famous. If the media
wasn't constantly harping on her every move she
would have no claim to fame at all, except for being
born rich. Yet in a sort of Catch-222 of fame effect,
the media couldn't get enough of her which, in turn,
fueled more and more coverage about who she was
dating, who she wasn't dating, what size dress she
wore, and what type of deodorant she used. You name
it, the press (and therefore the mass populace) wanted
to know.

She's constantly being hawked by her own imper-
sonal personal press corp.

Madrid took a step back and sized me up. "I know
you," she said.

I tipped my fedora. "Zachary Nixon Johnson, Ms.
Ramada."

She eyed me. "How do I know you?"

"I made a bit of press a couple of times when I
saved the world as we know it."

She shook her head. She removed her gold sunglasses to get a less rose-colored look at me. "No, it's
from something really important."

I let out a little groan. "I took Sexy Sprockets for
a ride in my Mustang once."

She looked at me. "Everybody has taken Sexy for
a ride *on* their Mustang."

I pointed to my car parked across the street. "It's
not a euphemism. I really *did* take Sexy for a ride, *in*
my classic car."

Madrid put the sunglasses back on. She looked
toward my car. She pushed a button on the top of the
glasses. I assumed it was a zoom lens. She smiled.

"That's right. Sexy was one of my dearest friends. How could I forget about you taking her for a ride?"

"I also saved her life," I added.

"Yes, I suppose that's important, too." She looked at me. "So, Mr. Johnson what do you want for saving my baby?"

"Nothing. It's part of the job."

Madrid looked at her wrist communicator. "Oh, I get it. You want to have sex with me." She pushed a button on her sleeve. "I'm free from 2:15 until 2:45."

"Ah . . ."

"That's not what he meant, bitch," Electra said.

Cameras started snapping, recorders started rolling. Madrid glared at Electra then backed down. "Dr. Gevada," she said. Madrid shrunk back.

I looked at Electra while pointing at Madrid. "You two know each other?"

Electra eyed Madrid carefully. "A few years ago, I helped her make something smaller and a couple things big—"

"No need to go into boring details," Madrid said waving her arms.

She walked up and put her arms around Electra and I. Flashes started popping.

"E here and I are old friends," Madrid said. She turned to me. "I just want to thank you Zach for saving my baby. You are truly one of the last noble men."

A meek little assistant ran up to Madrid. "Ms. Ramada, you are due for your fitting in five minutes. You know how huffy Ronaldo gets if you're late."

Madrid exhaled softly. "I swear that man is a bigger diva then I am."

With those words Madrid and her posse strutted off. Electra and I kissed.

"You operated on her?" I asked.

Electra smiled. "It funded two wards on my clinic."

That's my girl, always seeing the big picture. Electra and I kissed again. She looked at her watch. (Being my girlfriend she even wore an old-fashioned analog watch.) "Speaking of the clinic, I'm late."

"See you before you head to the Moon?" I asked.

"Of course," she said with a wink.

She headed off to the hospital and I set off to my office.

Chapter 4

As I neared my office on the bay, I noticed a throng of people assembled just outside my door. Examining them, I noticed they were mostly teenage girls.

"They can't be waiting for me," I said, pulling my car into its parking spot.

Instantly spotting me, the girls stormed the car, banging on it, and screaming things like:

"He's here! He's old, but dreamy for an old guy!"

"I want a piece of his shirt."

"I want a piece of his pants!"

"I want a piece of his hair!"

"I want a piece of his ass!"

HARV appeared in my dash. "Your saving of Madrid's dog, Baby, has been PIHI-Podcast all over the world. The major news networks are calling it a true act of courage."

While the girls continued to pound on my car, I sat there thinking. If this was how they showed admiration, I'd hate to see how this mob reacted when it was angry.

"You do have a gun," HARV suggested.

"I can't go shooting a mob of teenage girls," I said.

"I do have a heavy stun mode!" GUS said, chipper as always.

"Nah, not the good guy thing to do. I can see the lawsuits already."

"Well, you can't just stay in your car," HARV said.

For the moment, I didn't see why not. In my life I've faced high-paid assassins, killer ninjas, mutants of all shapes and sizes, giant elves, a mad gorilla, battle bots, attack dogs, tons of guard bots, angry androids, and a bevy of superhuman females. DOS, today alone I've wrestled with killer plants, been targeted by targets, and dodged oncoming traffic to save a dog. Yet I never felt as helpless as I did at this moment.

I needed help and I needed it quick. The knocking on the car and the chanting was rising to a fever pitch. Then it stopped. I gazed through the window at the girls, their eyes were glassed over.

"Carol," I said to myself.

My assistant Carol was in the office and had taken charge. The girls surrounding my car had dropped to all fours. They started baaing. I saw Carol coming out of the office door, smiling. Carol was a younger, just as beautiful version of her aunt Electra, except with even more of a temper. Carol was also a class I level 6 psionic, or psi for short, making her one of the most powerful minds on the planet. I won't go into great detail about the psi rating system (since it was thought up by bureaucrats, it's overly complicated). Suffice to say, class I level 6 is way good. Carol could do things with her brain that average joes and janes only dreamed of. She may not have been a god among men, but she was almost as close as you could get—almost.

Carol walked up to my car and opened my door.

"Because they act like sheep, I make them think they are sheep," Carol said.

We walked through the hordes of teens mentally

turned to sheep and into my office. I shut the door behind us and activated the office's defense shielding. I pointed outside.

"Send them home, please," I said to Carol.

"On all fours?"

"Any way you want," I said walking from her reception area into my main office.

There, in my office, was a shapely woman sitting with her legs crossed on my desk. She had two large goons in suits, one standing on each side of the door. There was also a rotund man slinking around behind her.

I popped my weapon into my hand and slashed the goon on the right across the face with it. He went crashing to the ground.

"As you can see, I also make an excellent billy club," GUS said proudly.

The thug to the left tried to grab me but Carol caught him with a telekinetic blow to his stomach, doubling him over.

"Sorry, Tió," she said rushing into the room. "All the teenybopper baaing must have clouded my psi senses."

I pointed my gun at the woman sitting on my desk.

"What's the meaning of this?" I growled.

The man behind her approached me slowly, keeping his hands where I could see them. He was a big man, but he was more round than muscular. He didn't look like your standard hired muscle. I kept my gun trained on him as he approached.

"Please, Mr. Johnson, this is not what you think it is," he said voice crackling in fear. "Let me introduce ourselves." He slowly and cautiously touched his wrist holo-communicator. The image of a business card appeared.

It read: CARLOS WOLF, PERSONAL ASSISTANT TO MARIA C. PEREZ, UNIVERSAL INSURANCE COMPANY.

"You're from my insurance company?"

Maria nodded. "Yes," she said proudly.

The word *CONFIRMED* flashed in front of my eyes. So she was who she claimed to be.

"You know, I kind of think I prefer the standard h-mail telling me you've raised my premiums."

Maria pointed at me. She was an older woman but still not too hard on the eyes. "I'm sure your computer has confirmed who my assistant and I are, so you may lower your weapon."

"I don't know, with my premiums so high, I'm still kind of tempted to shoot you," I said.

Without warning my gun jerked from my hand and flew into Maria.

"What the . . . !" Carol said. "She's a psi! How come I didn't pick that up?"

"My gun won't work for anybody but me," I told Maria.

She looked at Carol. "Sit down and be quiet until I tell you to speak," she ordered.

Carol obediently sat down, legs crossed, thumb in her mouth.

Maria looked at me. "I don't need weapons, Mr. Johnson."

"So I see."

"She caught Carol off guard so she must be at least class I level 6," HARV said to me. *"Tread lightly, Zach. Killer thugs have nothing on insurance company salespeople."*

Maria released my gun. It floated back to me. She was definitely not afraid of me.

"You did a really stupid thing today, Mr. Johnson."

"You're going to have to be more specific."

"How true," HARV said.

"You rushed into traffic to save a dog."

"One, I didn't know it was a dog. Two, I knew the

cars were computer controlled, so the odds of me being hit were slim."

Maria smiled at me. "Mr. Johnson, there's no need to be defensive. While we as your insurance provider certainly don't condone your actions, the masses found them quite appealing."

"Your point being?"

"We would like you to be our official spokesperson. Your catch phrase will be, *'If they insure me, they'll insure anybody'!*"

"Catchy and true," HARV laughed.

"You're kidding!" I told her.

Maria pointed at me. The mere gesture pushed me back and pinned me to wall. She strutted over to me. She lifted her finger up. I rose up off the ground. She dangled her finger under my nose.

"Do I look like I'm fooling around?" she said. "Your choice is simple. Do the nice dignified ad or bark our jingle naked."

"Hi, this is Zachary Nixon Johnson, if World Insurance insures me they'll insure anybody," I said in my peppiest voice.

Maria lowered me to the ground. "Very good." She snapped her fingers. Carlos moved forward, pulling a paper-thin computer from his back pocket. He unraveled the computer to show me the contract.

"Trust me, it's fair," Maria said. "Just give us your DNA print."

I touched the screen with my thumb.

Carlos turned the paper computer over, looked at it, and smiled.

"Very good," Maria said. She glanced over at the two guys Carol and I had clobbered. "Wake up!" she ordered.

The two guys started to move. "Follow me out on your knees."

Maria gave me a polite wave. She left, followed by Carlos, followed by the men crawling behind her. The woman had style. As she walked by Carol she gave her a pat on the head. "Back to normal, little one."

Carol stood up and shook her head. "That was annoying . . ."

"Welcome to my world, my dear. Welcome to my world."

"Hmm," HARV said. "You have a call coming in."

"Who is it?" I asked.

"Sexy."

"Sprockets?"

"Do you know anybody else named Sexy?"

"Take a message, buddy."

"She says she needs to see you urgently."

I squeezed my nose with my thumb and index finger. "She's probably just jealous that I saved Madrid's dog."

"That would match her MO," HARV agreed. "I also screened over one hundred messages for you."

"Why so many?"

"Check your wallscreen."

I looked at the images scrolling across my wallscreen. Most of them were of me, diving to catch the little poodle. I was the flavor of the nano all right. I needed a break. I couldn't handle much more of today, today.

"HARV, can you bury my home address?"

"Of course," HARV said.

"I want to go home and make sure I'm not mobbed by the press or fans . . ."

"Don't worry Zach, as is par for the course, I'm already many steps ahead of you."

"You are?"

"I removed your home address from all databases the nano you caught that puppy."

"I don't care what I say about you, you're all right, HARV."

"Yes, I am well aware of that."

I went to grab my coat and hat. I realized I hadn't even had time to take them off. I couldn't have HARV scramble the address of my office. After all, I'm a P.I. I need clients to be able to find me. Now my house, *that* was off limits. In the old days, they used to have unlisted telephone numbers; thanks to HARV, I would have an unlisted address. I liked it that way. I figured that anybody who I'd want to see me already knew where I lived.

I looked out the one-way windows of my office. Another swarm of girls was gathering. I peeked over at Carol. She had her head on her desk and was moaning. Carol was much more used to being the disher not the dishee. In the long run, this little slice of humble pie would do her well; but like economists like to say, in the long run, we're all dead. For the short run, Carol wouldn't be much good to help me get by this crowd.

I needed to be stealthy. One of the advantages of having HARV drilled into my brain is I have a built-in holo-projector. HARV can use the lens in my eye that bonds us to project holograms. I needed a cover. Somebody that the teenage girls and the press would want nothing to do with. . . .

It hit me. "Make me look like Krazy Karl, the used-hover salesman."

HARV appeared before me and smirked. "Yes, I imagine that would get the job done."

Even when hovercrafts were at their peak of popularity, used ones weren't all that popular. These days when items can be made so quickly nobody wants somebody else's throwaways. To further lower his appeal, Karzy Karl was more round than tall and had a

cheesy-looking handlebar mustache. To bottom it all
out, he had what might possibly be the worst slogan
ever: Our used hovers are so cheap we're practically
paying you to take them.

The hover disguise washed over me, making me feel
a bit dirty. I surmised that meant it was working.

Opening my office door, I could feel the rush of
anticipation from the crowd. They clamored, "Here
he comes!"

They saw me, well, the *holo*-me. There was a collective groan from the crowd. They parted for me to pass
through. Many of them shielded their eyes.

I walked over to my car. Most of the crowd had
turned away from me and were back to concentrating
on my office. I got in my car. I started it up.

I overheard somebody say, "Wow, he must have
sold his fancy old car to Krazy Karl. Gross . . ."

With that, I drove off.

Chapter 5

Pulling up to my modest home, I was pleased to see it wasn't surrounded by press or fly-by-the-moment fans. Yep, that's one of the big advantages of today's paperless, computer-driven society. If it's not in a computer, nobody knows it exists. Better yet, if you have a computer to manipulate the system, there's a lot you can get away with.

I entered my house and plopped down on my couch. It was just lunchtime and already I had had a very full day. DOS, the "adventures" I had today were enough to fill up the average joe's event meter for a lifetime. But for me, of course, the events of today were just another slightly busy Tuesday.

I kicked my feet up on the ottoman. It rolled over toward me. I leaned back in the couch.

"Ceiling screen on," I said.

"You'll get a kink in your neck," HARV warned.

"Just do it," I ordered.

My ceiling lit up with pictures and information. Unfortunately, most of it was about me. At least twelve channels were rerunning my catch of the dog. The

ART channel was giving my life story. The cooking channel had a special, "Zach Johnson's Favorite Meals." In between shows my commercial for World Insurance ran.

HARV appeared on the couch next to me.

"Don't worry, between the public's limited attention span, your annoying commercial, and the fact that the public thinks Krazy Karl bought your car, you can't last as the flavor of the nano much longer."

"I hope not," I said. "I truly hope not."

I heard a knock on my door. Actually, it was more of a banging, a rapid banging. That couldn't be good. I reached under a coach cushion and drew my good old-fashioned Colt .44 I keep there just in case. The .44 may not have nearly the firepower of the 2062 but it looked like a gun and therefore carried more intimidation factor.

"Who's at the door?" I asked HARV.

"You're not going to believe it."

"Try me."

"It's Sexy Sprockets and her bodyguards."

"What?"

"IT'S SEXY SPROCKETS AND HER BODY-GUARDS," HARV shouted.

I popped my old gun back into my ankle holster. I stood up and headed to the door. There stood Sexy Sprockets in all her glory. Behind Sexy was her personal bodyguard, Shannon Cannon. Behind them were at least five people in black battle armor.

"Zach, thank Gates you're home," Sexy said walking into my house. Shannon Cannon followed her in then secured the door behind her.

"Sexy, how did you find me? My house is unlisted."

Sexy smiled at me. "Remember, you brought me here once during my rock star days."

"I remember. I'm just shocked you could find the place."

"I'm not half as dumb as people think I am." Sexy walked into my living room and sat down on my couch. She looked up at me and smiled. "I am so glad that I saw that insurance ad you're in. That reminded me that you are probably the one person I know who can help."

"Sexy, you're being more confusing than normal."

Shannon walked over and placed her hand on Sexy's shoulder. It was the first time I noticed Shannon had dyed her hair blue. That meant she was a Moon supporter—a Moonie. Shannon glared at me.

"Can't you see Sexy is scared?"

I had to admit Sexy did look more unnerved than I had ever seen her. I wasn't sure I wanted to know what the DOS could scare Sexy. After all, she was an ex-teen-pop-rock-star. She had seen a lot. This is the girl who once bungee jumped naked off the Golden Gate Bridge on a dare. This was the girl who remastered the Elvis song "In the Ghetto" as a techno-pop-dance-love song. This was the girl who traveled with a mutant superpowered bodyguard and many other heavily-armed protectors.

"What the DOS are you scared of, Sexy?" I asked, despite my better judgment.

She looked up at me, barely holding back her nerves. "Threa Thompson," she shuddered.

Now that was something I wasn't expecting. Threa is one of the three remaining Thompson Quads. She and her sisters Ona and Twoa may be the most physically and mentally powerful beings on Earth. Ona was a wealthy businesswoman. Twoa was a superhero. (No, I'm not making that up.) Threa called herself a fairy princess, and who claimed to live in a magical realm. I helped the three of them stop their sister Foraa (who, believe it or not, had been crazier than all of them put together) from destroying the world. If Threa really was angry with Sexy, I understood

Sexy being scared. The Thompson sisters were not to be taken lightly. I once saw Ona reduce her board of directors to helpless doorstops with a glance. Twoa has been known to overpower ninja death squads simply by removing her shoes. The thing is, Threa had always been the most easygoing of the sisters. Sure she threatened to rearrange my molecular structure once when I killed one of her trolls (not as unusual as you may think). But for the most part she was as level-headed as a superwoman who professes to be a fairy princess can be.

"Why are you scared of Threa?" I asked.

"Apparently she's never paid a province income tax."

"Why doesn't that surprise me?"

"Zach, she's worth close to a hundred million credits but she claims to live in a mysterious realm beyond our dimension, which is preposterous."

"I don't know. Have you ever met Threa?"

"No, I've only been threatened by her. She refuses to pay her taxes. So when I sent a warning to her, my lawyer came back on all fours, with a tail, and barking. He managed to bark out that if I insist on forcing Threa to pay taxes in New California, she'll turn me into a toad." Sexy looked up at me sheepishly. "I don't know if she means a real toad or just make me think I'm a toad, but neither is high on my list. You know how hard it would be to do Council stuff and date and stuff if I was a frog?"

"Threa likes to talk. I'm sure it was an idle threat."

Almost on cue, there was a loud crashing noise. We all turned toward the noise to see two of Sexy's armor-clad bodyguards flying through my door, smashing it into hundreds of pieces.

DOS, that was a real wood door! Of course, I had bigger problems than the door, as three more guards followed their coworkers into my house. They all entered in pretty much the same manner, flying through the air and crashing to the floor, out cold.

Shannon leaped in front of Sexy. I popped my Colt 2062 into my hand.

Sexy eyed my strange weapon. "Really Zach, this is no time for HV."

We heard a *bomp bomp bomp* clanging toward my door. A large, bald head peeked in. When I say large, I mean this was a head the size of a normal man. The head ducked down and the body it was attached to lumbered into the room. The ceilings in my house are over four and a half meters high, but he still scraped his head.

"An ogre!" I spat.

"Zach, this has nothing to do with wild sex parties," Sexy said, trying to sound intelligent.

"That's *orgy*," Shannon corrected.

"Oh, right," Sexy said, sinking back behind us.

I sized up the Ogre. The only thing more noticeable than his girth was his disfiguration. His nose was bent in more places than I could count and stretched down his face, overlapping his mouth. The teeth his mouth did have were sharp and jagged. He vaguely reminded me of the cavemen I saw in museums, only three times as large and even more macabre.

To complete the caveman ensemble, he was dressed only in a fur rag and carrying a large wooden club.

"Oh, that club so does *not* go with that outfit," Sexy observed.

"That was an antique door," I shouted at the intruder.

The Ogre looked at my door lying smashed on the floor. He looked at the dent in my door frame. He scratched his head.

"Ah, sorry, Mr. Johnson," he said in a high pitched squeal. "Mistress Threa has no quarrel with you. I am sure she will make remuneration."

The Ogre pointed a long, bent, index finger at Sexy.

His fingernails looked like claws. "*You* are the one she wishes to speak to."

Sexy peaked out from behind her cover of Shannon and I. "Make an appointment with my assistant's assistant's assistant, and I'll squeeze her in next year."

The Ogre shook his head. I swore I heard rocks clanking around. "The Mistress does not work that way."

He took a step forward.

I pointed my gun at him.

"Sexy is under my protection now," I said.

"Screw that," Shannon said, standing straight and throwing out her rather impressive chest. "Sexy is under *my* protection."

Shannon focused her glare on the Ogre. I was all too familiar with that look. She was blasting him with mental energy.

The Ogre for his part knew this and was amused by it. He bit off a fingernail and spat it at Shannon.

"Oh, gross to the meg," Sexy mumbled clinging onto my leg.

"Ogres are immune to mental attacks," the Ogre smirked.

"Let's see how you handle this," Shannon said. She drew a deep breath, looked at the Ogre, then exhaled on him, hitting him with her toxic breath.

The Ogre inhaled and smile. "Please, I'm an ogre. We live for toxic things like that."

Shannon took a karate stance. "Let's see what you've got, big man," she taunted.

It didn't take my keen P.I. intellect to know how this was going to turn out. Shannon may have been a very powerful mutant psi, but she was out of her league when dealing with something from the mind of any of the Thompson sisters.

The Ogre moved forward on Shannon. Shannon hit

him with a sidekick in his oversized beer (well, more likely ale) belly. If the Ogre felt it he didn't show it. The Ogre put his palm on Shannon's shoulder. Shannon crumbled to the ground, out colder than Pluto in winter.

"The Vulcan nerve pinch?" I said to the Ogre.

He shrugged. "There isn't much to do in Threa's realm so I watch a lot of ancient TV."

The Ogre moved towards us. I had to give him credit; he had style, in a vulgar and geeky sort of way. The thing was, I couldn't let him harm Sexy.

I aimed my weapon at him. The laser sights turned on, locking on his head and chest.

"I'm betting you're not immune to high-powered weaponry," I said.

He nodded. "You'd win that bet."

The next move caught me totally off guard. The Ogre swiped at me with his club, knocking the Colt 2062 out of my hand and sending it flying across the room. Moving quicker than I thought he'd be capable of, the Ogre went to give me the Vulcan nerve pinch. I anticipated his move, ducking under his massive hand. He swung backward at me though, swatting me across the room.

I hit the ground and rolled up. Luckily he, like so many of my opponents in the past, had underestimated me. He thought that swat would knock me out cold. I'm a lot tougher than people think. (Of course the carbon-reinforced underarmor helps too.)

The Ogre was now ignoring me, concentrating solely on Sexy. That was his first mistake of the fight. I reached down to my ankle holster, grabbing my good old Colt .44. (It wasn't a true Colt .44, it was a modernized version, but it still looked cool and it got the job done.) Not wanting to give him a chance to react, I lifted it up and pulled the trigger.

My gun made a very satisfying *BOOM*. The bullet hit the Ogre square in the back. He exploded into a cascade of bubbles.

"Now *that* was different," I said.

HARV appeared next to me for the first time since the fight began.

"Where the DOS were you when the chips were down?"

"The Ogre emits some sort of computer dampening field. I was working my way around it."

I walked over to Sexy and helped her up. I gave her one of my patented "everything will be cool" smiles.

"See, that wasn't so bad, was it?"

HARV tapped me on the shoulder, which wasn't that easy for him to do since he was a hologram. If he was expending the energy needed to do this then something was up. HARV pointed out my living room bay window. Three more ogres had appeared. These had long hair and saggy breasts. They were females.

"I compute that they are mad because you destroyed their mate," HARV said.

I opened up my hand. "Yo, GUS come to me," I ordered.

My Colt 2062 sprang to e-life from across the room. "With pleasure!" GUS sang. The Colt 2062 rose from the floor and floated across the room into my hand.

"Cool weapon," Sexy said. "You going to blast them? I like blasting them."

That's when it occurred to me. If Sexy, an ex-teen-pop-star turned world politician, liked the idea, there had to be something wrong with it. Threa had nearly unlimited mental, physical, and financial resources. If I got in a pissing contest with her she'd drown me. There had to be a better way. I remembered something!

Grabbing Sexy by the hand, I pulled her into the

hallway. We raced down the hall into my master bedroom. I slammed the door behind me.

Sexy smiled. "Why, Zach, I'm flattered, but I'm a big fancy-pants politician now. I can't just jump into bed with you," she said, pulling off her shirt and hopping onto my bed. "We have to issue a statement denying it first."

I headed to my dresser, pulling out the bottom drawer. I began shifting through the contents.

"You know," HARV said. "If you bought a modern dresser you would always know where everything was. And you'd never have to manually open a drawer."

"Yeah, well, I need the workout," I said, tossing items left and right. "Oh, and Sexy put your shirt back on," I said. Sexy may have been beautiful and nubile beyond compare, but I was in a committed relationship. Besides, even if I wasn't, I wouldn't do it with a politician.

"You could tell me what you are looking for," HARV said. "I do have a much better memory than you."

There was no need for HARV's assistance as I found what I was searching for. I pulled it out and showed it to HARV. It was a simple metal bell attached to a pink stick of wood.

Sexy sighed. "Okay, he's lost it."

"Hardly," I said. "This bell was given to me by Threa after I stopped her sister Foraa from sucking the world down a black hole."

"Yeah, that would have been a real bummer," Sexy agreed. "At least on my case, you only needed to save a good portion of the northern hemisphere."

I rang the bell.

There was a flash of light.

Threa appeared in the room in all her glory.

Threa looked at me in shock. Sexy looked at me in more shock. She leaped off my bed.

"How dare you call me!" Threa said.

"How dare you call *her*, my archenemy," Sexy barked.

When I say, barked, I mean barked. Sexy was now on all fours, barking away. I looked at Threa. She had a smile of satisfaction on her face.

Threa patted me on the shoulder (kind of like she would a pet). She smiled. "Ah, I see your plan now Zachary. Bring me right to my enemy."

"That wasn't my plan," I insisted.

Sexy was now contentedly licking Threa's feet.

"It should have been your plan. Because I like it." Threa patted me on the head again. "Good, Zach. Good, Zach."

"Threa, I brought you here to call off your ogres and to appeal to your logical side."

Threa looked at me. "Wow, nobody's ever tried that before . . ."

"To get you to call off your ogres?"

"No, appealing to my logical side."

I took a deep breath. Threa Thompson was one of the most powerful beings in existence. I was pretty certain my new high-powered weapon would, at the very least, cause her pain. But chances were great that if I tried to use it, Threa would stop me and I'd be joining Sexy, licking Threa's free foot. Logic was my only hope.

"Threa, I know you are powerful beyond compare," I said playing with her ego some, "but even you can't take on the entire world."

Threa put a finger to her mouth. "I don't want to take on the entire world, just the World Council."

"They have a lot of resources to throw at you," I noted.

She put her hands on her hips. "I have a lot of resources too. I'm lady and mistress of my own realm."

Time to shift gears and appeal to her sensitive side. *"HARV, how much is Threa worth?"*

"Roughly 127,898,001 credits," HARV thought.

"Threa you're worth over one hundred millions credits," I said.

Threa was now rubbing Sexy on her tummy. "What's your point?"

"My point is, if you *donated* a percentage of that to the World Council as say, taxes, that money could go to help this world."

Threa straightened herself up. "I'm not a huge fan of this world. It's kind of a mean world. Look how badly they treat the Moon."

For the first time, I noticed Threa had blue hair. She was a Moonie.

"But by giving money you could help set an example that the World Council can learn from."

"Zach, they are politicians. Do you really think they can learn anything?"

"There's always hope, Threa."

Threa took a step back. "Lead by example . . . It's crazy enough that it just might work. I'll take it under advisement." She looked behind her at Sexy, now contently sniffing Threa's butt. Sexy rolled back in the universal doggie "I surrender" position.

"She is a cute pooch," Threa said. "Tell her she has nothing to fear from me or my minions. At least for now!"

"Got it," I said.

Threa held out her open hand. She wanted me to place something in that hand, but I had no idea what. She started tapping her foot.

"Threa, I have no idea what you want," I said.

HARV appeared next to me and bowed to Threa.

"Threa, it's always a pleasure to process your image," HARV said.

Threa held out her other hand to him. He kissed it.

"The pleasure is mine, HARV," Threa said giving him a polite little curtsy.

It was a bit offputting that my computer was smoother than I was.

HARV turned his head toward me while his body was still facing Threa. This was one of the times HARV really took advantage of the fact that he was a hologram.

"Give her back the bell," HARV told me.

"Really?" I said. I'm not sure why, but I hid the bell behind my back.

"Zach, she's not going to forget about it just because she can't see it. She's a powerful fairy princess, not an ostrich."

"You really want your bell back?" I asked Threa, though truth be told, I wasn't sure why I would want to keep it.

Threa bobbed her head a couple of times. "I said you may summon me once with that. You have. Now I need it back."

I placed the bell in Threa's hand. She smiled, then disappeared in a puff of smoke.

HARV shook his head. "She must have some personal teleporter I can't detect."

Sexy stood up and shook her head. "What happened?" She stuck out her tongue. "And why do I taste feet?"

I guided Sexy out of my bedroom. "I talked to Threa. Things are going to be okay now," I assured her.

No sooner did I get Sexy and her crew out of there than I saw Electra's BMW hover coming in for a landing.

"HARV, what time is it?" I asked as the hover landed.

"Here?"

"No, on the Moon!"

"Well the Moon uses Beijing time so it would be . . ."

"*Here* HARV, in New Frisco."

"Four PM. You would think you wouldn't be so lazy and you'd move your wrist to look at your communicator," HARV huffed.

Electra got out of the car and kissed me.

"What brings you home so early, mi amor?"

Electra took my hand as we walked toward my house. "I had to get out of there. The press was making me crazy asking so many asinine questions about you."

We walked into the house. "Don't worry, I'm sure tomorrow some Elvis impersonator clone will rescue a cat from a tree, knocking me out of the headlines."

"Yes, Gates forbid they talk about real news like the Moon's newest bid for independence."

"People can't affect that, my dear. If there's nothing they can affect then they only want to hear about trivial stuff."

Electra looked around at the bots rebuilding my door, my door's supports and cleaning up the mess. "What happened here?"

"Same old, same old," I said.

Electra smiled at me. She thought better about asking anything else. "It's for the better," she said. "I need to pack so I can get to the conference early tomorrow."

Chapter 6

To be on the safe side, Electra and I both slept in my home's underground shelter, but the night passed without incident. Electra woke bright and early to pack. I slept a bit while she packed but met her in the kitchen for breakfast before she headed off.

When I joined Electra at the table she was already halfway through the grapefruit and coffee. The morning news was scrolling by on the wallscreen.

"Am I still the flavor of the day?" I asked sitting down across from her.

HARV appeared at the head of the table. He had a sly look in his eye.

Electra shook her head. "Nope, some Elvis impersonator clone in Vegas saved a poodle trapped in a tree."

The maidbot rolled up and deposited a piece of bacon and some eggs on my plate. I munched on the bacon. I turned to HARV.

"Okay, now that can't be a coincidence," I told him.

HARV smirked. He was so high on himself I was surprised he didn't float off the chair. "I set it up," he said proudly. "You've already collected your payment for the insurance ad. Plus Sexy deposited a five thousand credit payment to your account for your help with her ugly little matter."

"So my fifteen nanos of fame are over," I said watching images of the Elvis impersonator clone climbing the tree toward the poor pooch.

I noticed Electra was watching another window. Vixen News was showing a debate between one of their bikini model anchors and a World Public Broadcasting man wearing a suit he looked like he was born in. The two were discussing the pros and cons of a free Moon.

"Zoom in on Vixen News," I ordered the wallscreen.

The Vixen News window expanded to show the woman and man sitting facing each other. No table, no desk, no nada.

"Oh, please Morgan," the Vixen News "reporter" spat. "If we give the Moon their freedom then next thing City in Sky will want theirs. Next, Mars Base will want theirs. It will be complete and utter anarchy."

The man rolled his eyes. "I would expect talk like that from a bimbo whose bustline is ten points bigger than her IQ-two score."

"Ah, I just love a good debate," I said.

HARV and Electra both shushed me.

"This is important," they both clanged in unison.

They looked at each other and smiled. It's very surreal to see your computer and fiancée exchanging a telling glance. I tilted my head.

"If you guys want I can leave . . ."

HARV rolled his eyes. "Typical Zach, if it's not a ball score then he's not interested."

"Not true," Electra said, though from the tone of her voice I knew she wasn't rushing to my defense. "He also cares about classic cars."

"Excellent point," HARV agreed. "Gates forbid he pay attention to something important that is happening in today's world."

"Oh, come on. I've saved the world as we know it at least four times. I'm interested in the world as much as you two."

They both just looked at me, hands on hips.

"Okay, maybe not as much as you two, but more than the average joe or jane."

HARV put a finger up and started twirling it in the air. "Big whoop. You of all people should know that the average man and woman on the street only care about what the mass media, mega-monster machine manufactures for them to care about."

"Mass, media, mega, monster, machine, HARV? I think I have to fine you ten credits for illegal alliteration."

HARV crossed his arms and huffed. "Don't change the subject with me, Zachary Nixon Johnson."

"Has my mom been reprogramming you?" I asked.

HARV looked Electra square in the eyes. "You sure you want to marry him? I think you can do better."

Electra tilted her head to the side looking at me. "He's not much, but I love him."

HARV shook his head. "Proving that even the best of humans are flawed. I'm just glad I'm not human. Being a cognitive processor I think about many things that aren't just bubblegum for the brain . . ."

"HARV, you don't think, *really* think . . . You *simulate* thinking," I goaded.

"You're getting defensive because you know I'm right," HARV smirked.

HARV was right. We do tend to be a rather shallow species at times. I believe it's actually a defense mechanism. We are constantly bombarded with so much information we certainly can't process it all and we can't affect very much of it. That's why we only choose to notice the most important life-threatening events—that guy has a laser and he's pointing it at me, the bomb is ticking away, Electra is about to lose her temper. Or we pay attention to the most trivial of events—sports scores and what the hot star of the nano is wearing or dating or not wearing and not dating. We pay attention to that which can kill us or that which entertains us. Everything in between is filtered out.

HARV pointed at the screen. "What happens on the Moon is important. I'm sure the other planets are watching Earth carefully. The Moon isn't just a suburb of Earth any longer. Some Mooners are showing genetic differences from Earthlings. Almost one in five hundred of them is born a psi, compared to the one in a million here on Earth. They are a new branch of *homo sapiens*, superior in all but numbers, but you treat them like second-class beings."

"HARV, I treat everybody the same," I said.

HARV rolled his eyes. "When I say you, I don't mean you, I mean humanity in general."

I patted HARV on his shoulder, even though he didn't really have a shoulder. "You can't generalize like that, HARV."

"Enough you two," Electra ordered. "Yes, HARV, some of us are shallow. Some of us fear change. Hence, they are worried about the Mooners—and psis for that matter. Others of us hope and pray these changes will lead to a better world—or worlds—for us all. All in all though, it's so much easier to wonder about what the Elvis clones are up to."

I smiled at her. That's why I love her so much. Electra has the ability to take a complicated matter and summarize it so even a supercomputer can understand it.

I bent over and gave her a kiss. "That's why you're the smartest human or machine in the room."

"Damn straight," she said. She pointed at the screen. "Still, this is an important issue. More people need to think about it. If more people stand up, maybe the World Council will let the Moon go."

"When was the last time the World Council ever listened to anything, Electra?" It was true. It's like once they get elected they become deaf and dumb.

Electra stood up. She pointed at me. "You should make sure Sexy votes for Moon freedom this time."

I looked over at HARV; his head bobbed in agreement.

"You want me to use my influence on Sexy to influence her vote?" I asked.

Electra moved over to me and kissed me. "Just state the case. Let her decide. Tell her you like her lip gloss." Electra looked at her watch. "I'd better get to the shuttle port," she said. "This way I can play my own part in Earth/Moon relationships."

I grabbed her arm gently. "You sure you want to go through with this? I'm getting a bad vibe."

She turned her head toward me. "That's sweet of you to worry. But I'll be fine. I'm a big girl who can take care of herself."

To drive home her point she used her free hand to grab the arm I was holding her with and used it to throw me over her shoulder. The moment I hit the ground I remembered why I loved Electra. Yes, I probably need therapy.

Electra bent over and kissed me. "See you in three days, mi amor."

"Be safe," I said.

HARV just snickered.

Chapter 7

It didn't take long for Electra to pack her things. She was as excited as I had seen in her in years about this conference. I was happy for her but something about her impending trip was eating at my gut. The scary thing was I didn't know what or why.

I was sitting in my living room watching the holo-sports highlights when Electra walked in the room carrying an old-fashioned suitcase. (Electra insisted that modern, anti-grav suitcases make us lazy and weak.)

"You should offer to carry her suitcase to the hover," HARV suggested.

I shook my head no.

"The last time a man offered to carry my suitcase, I broke his arm," Electra said walking past us.

I nodded to HARV. I may not be the smartest joe in the world but I know my woman.

"You should have known that," I told HARV as I stood up to walk Electra out.

"Oh, I did," HARV said. "I was just hoping you didn't. I wanted to see how Electra would react."

Ignoring HARV, I headed outside with Electra.

"I'll miss you," I said.

"I'll drop you an e-mail when I get there."

We reached the car. She kissed me. She pulled back a bit and looked at me. "What's wrong, Zach?"

"Still getting a weird feeling about this . . ." I said.

"Zach, the shuttle to the Moon is perfectly safe. I don't think there's ever been a crash. The food is even good."

"It's not the means of travel," I said. "I'm just worried about you on the Moon."

We reached Electra's hover. The door opened.

"Zach, I've been to the Moon on a couple of occasions to teach at their hospital. It's a great place. I didn't get exposure to a lot of people, but those I met were very nice."

"Maybe, but the Earth and the Moon aren't getting along all that well these days."

Electra got in the hover. "So? The Earth would never attack the Moon and the Moon doesn't even have weapons."

"Maybe this conference is a trick to get valuable Earth citizens to the Moon to hold as hostages."

Electra just looked at me. "You know you're paranoid."

"That's why I'm still alive."

Electra smiled at me. "But I'm not you. The universe isn't out to get me."

She leaned forward and kissed me. She waved goodbye to me, giving me the cue to step away from the hover.

About twenty minutes after Electra left, I headed to my office. I drove slow. I was in no hurry to get there, just in case there happened to be any press stragglers hanging around. Who knows, maybe somebody wanted to do a "Where are they now?" story about me.

"HARV, are there any reporters snooping around the office?" I asked.

HARV appeared in my dash. "Nope. You are literally yesterday's news."

I was slightly relieved and perhaps slightly disappointed, though I was determined not to show it.

"Well, back to my normal life," I told him.

HARV snickered. It's unnerving to hear a supercomputer snicker. "Zach, with you there is no such thing as normal."

"Good point."

I parked my car next to my office and went in. Carol was sitting at her desk.

"Morning, Carol," I said.

No reply.

I looked at her and noticed she wasn't moving. I popped my gun into my hand. My first concern was Carol's health.

"HARV how come you didn't tell me Carol was in trouble?" I barked.

HARV's hologram appeared next to me. "Zach, she was fine less than a nano ago."

I gently pressed my index finger on Carol's neck, searching for a pulse. I found one. I breathed easier. I waved my hand in front of her eyes. They didn't blink.

"She appears to be psionically frozen," HARV said.

Carol was a very powerful psi. Anybody who put her out of commission had to be at least as powerful.

"She'll live," I heard a familiar voice call from my office. I headed toward that voice. I knew I knew it, but I couldn't wrap my brain around it.

"HARV, who's in my office?" I asked.

"Can't tell," he shrugged. "They're disabled the video cameras."

"Any guesses on who it might be?" I said, gun in hand, moving closer to the office.

Hugging the wall, I peered through the open door into my office. There, sitting at my desk, was Shannon Cannon. She looked a bit distraught. I assumed she was still recovering from her bout with the Ogre.

I walked into my office with my Colt 2062 trained right on Shannon's ample chest. Shannon was looking at everything in the office but me.

"I assume you're the one who put Carol on psi-ice," I said.

Shannon simply nodded. "She'll come around in an hour or two," she said to me without actually focusing on me.

I stopped about two meters from her. "To what do I owe the pleasure?" I asked.

Shannon looked unkempt. Her hair was out of place and she had a very nervous demeanor, far different than the cold and calculating bombshell I was accustomed to.

"Sexy is dead," Shannon said, not looking at me.

"What?"

Shannon shook her head. "Reduced to ashes under my watch, my guard."

Shannon put her head in her hand and started weeping. I was at a loss over what to do. The comforting side of me wanted to put my arms around her and tell her it would be all right, even though I wasn't sure it would be. My cautious side warned that this lady was one of the most deadly beings on Earth. She could overpower a band of samurai with her breath. I needed to shoot her now and let the police deal with her. My cautious side can be a bit overprotective but I'm still alive, so that's a good thing.

"What are you talking about?"

Shannon looked at me, her eyes unblinking as if they had been glued open. "We were preparing for a highly sensitive meeting. Sexy and fellow councilpeople Carl Weathers and Russ Tree were preparing for a very high level, ultra hush-hush conference," she stopped. Her eyes welled with water. She dropped her head to the table and sobbed, "They're all dust now, dead, dead dust . . ."

I felt Shannon's pain from across the room. This was no act. This was a woman who trained all of life for solely one task—a task she had just failed at. I moved up to her, not putting my weapon away but pulling my finger off the trigger.

I put my arm around her and asked, "What happened?"

Shannon looked up at me. Mascara running down her face made her look like a deranged rodeo clown. "I have very little idea. I went for my scheduled potty break. Even superhuman mutant psi bodyguards need to relieve themselves on a regular basis. I came back just in time to see Sexy reduced to a pile of dust before my eyes. She had already killed all the others: Weathers, Tree, their personal security, their security back up, the guardbots . . ."

"I get the picture. You said 'she.' So you got a look at the killer?"

Shannon gazed at me, though I wasn't really sure she saw me. "She was a tall wisp of a woman, like she was made of energy itself." Shannon stopped for a moment, staring blankly into space. "I don't know how she got in. I couldn't stop her. Everything I did went right through her. It's like she was a ghost meant to be seen only by me." She stopped again, thinking about what all this meant. "She could have killed me. Easily. She wanted me alive to take the fall . . ."

If Shannon wasn't lying or delusional (or both) what she said made sense. If some superassassin really had just murdered three of the twelve most influential politicians on Earth, she had herself a patsy in Shannon.

"Surely security footage will verify what you say?"

Shannon shook her head. I checked. "All security in that room was short-circuited while I was out . . ." She took a deep breath. "That's why I know they'll be coming after me. I'm the only survivor, so in their eyes I have to be the killer. It doesn't help my case that I have been known to generate blasts of energy from my body."

"Yeah, I can see where that might count against you."

She put her hand gently on mine. "You have to believe me, Zach. I would never do anything like this . . . Not to my charges."

I looked at her. I didn't know why, but I believed her.

"HARV, how close are the police?" I asked.

He replied, "Talk fast, real fast."

"You said Sexy, Weathers, and Tree were preparing for a very important meeting. Who was it with?"

Shannon shook her head. "That's top secret, classified, level XYZ-999. I could tell you but I'd have to kill you first."

I looked out the window. Police heavy cruiser hovers were landing in full force.

"Why did you come to me?"

"They are going to put me away. I need you to find the real killer, of course." She put her other hand over mine as I watched scores of heavily armored police and guard bots pour out of the hovers. "You've got to trust me, Zach."

I locked my eyes on hers. "Trust runs down a two-way street. If I'm going to help I need you to tell me who they were meeting with—without killing me."

"HARV, put up the office's defenses," I ordered.

"Zach, against the police?"

"Just put up the energy shields. I want to make sure they don't shoot us before I'm even on the case."

HARV sighed.

"Who was the meeting with Shannon?"

"Boris Sputnik and his delegation," she said.

"Boris Sputnik, the Head Administrator from the Moon?" I asked.

"How many other Boris Sputniks do you know?" Shannon asked.

"You have to forgive Zach. He can be a bit slow sometimes," HARV said, mere nanos before the police started blasting through one of my office walls.

Chapter 8

Shannon shot up and threw her arms around me. She kissed me hard on the lips. "Don't worry, Zach, they'll never take us alive," she said, squeezing me closer to her.

I forced an arm free and pointed a finger up. "First, there is no *us*," I said.

"I always thought we were kindred spirits, both fighting for what we believe is right," Shannon said.

I get that reaction a lot from crazy superhuman females. It must be my aftershave. We could hear the police banging and firing away at the force field guarding my office walls. It wouldn't be long until they got through.

"Second," I said, holding up another finger. "If they kill me or take me in, then there will be nobody left to prove your innocence."

Shannon eased her grip on me. "Sorry, got caught up in the moment."

Police burst into my office, far too many for me to count. Shannon tossed me to the floor split-nanos before they opened fire.

"Remember, we want her alive," I heard the commanding voice of my old buddy Captain Tony Rickey order from the back. The fact that Tony was leading, well, bringing up the rear, of this charge gave me hope that there was hope.

I darted under my desk for cover.

"Remember, Cannon's the true threat here," Tony reminded his men. "Focus all fire on her."

The storm police did as told. In unison, they aimed their heavy energy rifles and fired a concentrated blast at Shannon. They were heavily armed and armored, protected from head to toe in plexiarmor. Shannon had been preparing for them though, waiting there with her hands clasped together, energy dancing around her interlaced fingers. Shannon slowly pulled her hands apart, energy cascading around her finely manicured fingertips. As her hands spread farther and farther apart, the energy pulsated more and more, growing stronger and stronger.

When the blasts from the police hit her, they were totally absorbed by Shannon's own energy. Shannon spread her arms open wide, like a butterfly bursting free of a cocoon, sending a huge blast of energy at the first wave of police, driving them all to the ground.

The second wave quickly rolled in . . . Shannon inhaled, then exhaled on them. Despite the fact the police were wearing protective helmets, her toxic breath still did them in.

"Retreat!" captain Rickey ordered. "Retreat!"

Shannon looked down at me and smiled. Surveying the twenty or thirty fallen policemen littering my office, her smile widened.

"How come the police's toxic filters didn't stop Shannon's breath?" I asked HARV.

"The exact chemical makeup of her breath is top secret," HARV said. "The police don't have nearly the clearance needed. They had to guess. They guessed wrong."

I stood up, trying to take advantage of the police who were regrouping.

From outside, Captain Rickey's voice came booming at us. "Zach, this is Tony. You and Shannon have one minute to come out before we raze the building."

Looking out the window I could see at least three hundred police barricaded behind their squad hovers, all with weapons trained on the building.

"They have five robotic gunship hovers just one minute out," HARV said.

"Shannon, you have to give yourself up," I coaxed. "It's the only way."

"Never," she said. "I've lost my charge. I have no reason to live. I only want you to save my name after I am gone."

She turned toward the window, facing the throng of police, arms open.

"Come and get me," she screamed.

The police hovers opened fire on the window, but the shots were repelled. Right then and there, I was glad that blast-proof window salesbot convinced me to go with the most expensive option.

"Zach, the police are arming old-fashioned heavy missiles," HARV told me a split nano before one of the missiles crashed into the window. The force of the explosion knocked me down.

"Thanks for the warning, buddy," I grumbled. The window and Shannon both survived the initial blast.

"The window can't take another hit like that," HARV said.

"Tell Tony I have the situation under control," I told HARV.

"You want me to lie to one your oldest friends?" HARV said.

"Just do it," I barked.

"Fine. Tony says you have two minutes. He also

says his superiors want him to use the contained nuclear option if this fails."

Great, no pressure there. I stood up and popped my Colt 2062 into my hand.

"I have a message from GUS," HARV said over our link.

"Ah, patch him through, I guess," I thought back.

"Greetings!" GUS high-pitched voice echoed inside of my head. *"I find this quite an unusual means of communication."*

"You're not alone. GUS, get to the point."

"I have just completed downloading new billy-club software that might prove most useful . . ."

"Why do I need software to hit somebody across the head with you?" I asked.

"The new improvements allow me to calculate the rate of impact and increase my mass at the striking area at the exact moment of impact. I will then follow up by injecting this subject with a million volts of electricity."

"You have twenty seconds to react," HARV said.

I walked up behind Shannon. She was paying me no mind, training all of her attention on the surrounding police.

I pulled back GUS. I whacked Shannon on the side of her head. She crashed to the ground.

"HARV, tell Tony I have Shannon," I said.

"Too late," HARV answered.

I dropped to the ground on top of Shannon a split-nano before a rocket exploded through my window.

Chapter 9

"Tony says, 'Sorry about that and we'll pay for any damages,'" HARV said as I pushed myself up off the ground.

I was covered in debris from my office, well, from what *was* my office. Just then it hit me. "Carol!" I shouted.

I pushed through some rubble, fighting my way toward Carol's reception area. HARV appeared in front of me, showing that my office holo-projectors were still functioning.

"Carol's safe," HARV said. "Tony's men evacuated her before they hit the place."

Tony entered with three police android officers, weapons still drawn.

I pointed to Shannon lying on the floor, out cold. "She won't give you any more trouble." I said.

"Sorry about the mess," Tony said. "Some of my men and droids get a little trigger happy."

"DOS, Tony! Your men have taken shots at me for jaywalking before."

"Yeah, they are under orders to cut that out," Tony said.

"But firing on my office when you have forty of your own men and machines down in here . . ."

"We were monitoring them over their battle armor. We knew they would survive the blast. We also knew Shannon would survive with no problem."

"And me?"

Tony patted me on the back. "Zach, cockroaches envy your survival skills."

Tony surveyed the damage. "The good news is that after reviewing the video of your conversations with Shannon, it doesn't look like you're under arrest."

I have given Tony a lot of grief in my time but never have I destroyed his office.

"Gee thanks."

Tony patted me on the shoulder. We watched as the gray-skinned police droid's bots secured Shannon's hands and feet and head with metallic-looking braces. "It looks like you were just an innocent pawn in Shannon Cannon's sick game."

"I don't think it's a game. She believes she's being framed."

"Then she's the only one. Zach, I've seen the footage from the security cameras. One minute, she's in the room. She leaves the room, the cameras go blank. Next thing we know she's standing over the ashes of her victims."

"So you don't see her kill anybody?"

"No, Zach, but it would have taken an ultra-mega-high level of clearance and sophistication to disable the cameras like she did."

"Why bring the cameras back online just to damn herself?"

"She screwed up," Tony said.

"Not buying it," I said, though I had no idea why.

"Zach, you're letting that face and body cloud your judgment."

"She said she caught a glimpse of a blue-haired woman in the room," I insisted.

"Yeah, our profilers have heard that one. They concluded she was really seeing herself in a sad attempt to justify what she did. Think about it, Zach. This blue-haired woman has some of the same powers Shannon does."

"But what's her motive?"

"She's crazy," Tony said.

I raised an eyebrow.

"She's a Moonie, Zach. She's been a very open supporter of the Moon's freedom. What better way to show your support than to murder three of the council members who voted against—or were planning to vote against—freedom?"

"I'm not buying it yet," I said.

"You don't have to buy it, Zach, and we're not trying to sell it."

"What's going to happen when the press gets a whiff of this story?" I asked.

Tony shrugged. "Decisions like that are made above my pay grade."

It occurred to me. The press should have been down here already. Obviously, the SF police force "media handling machine" was in full swing.

"Just curious, Tony. How'd you keep the press away?"

Tony smiled. "We leaked a story about a Madonna clone seen hovering over the UltraHyperMart Golden Gate Bridge with an Oprah clone. They were hand in hand. The Oprah clone was even mooning onlookers."

Yeah, the press would be all over a story like that. I had to give Tony props, the police had covered this up well . . . so far.

"You know, sooner rather than later the press is going to jump on this story," I said.

Tony nodded. "True, this is the first time in history three World Council members were killed together."

"Not because of that," I said. "But because Sexy is an ex-pop-star, Weathers an ex-pro-athlete . . ."

". . . and Tree was having an extramartial affair with his android," Tony said. "I know, Zach, the media will eat this up. Once they figure it out." Tony pointed at me. "You're not going to help them."

I shook my head no. I knew if I was going to investigate this case the less the media found out the better.

"Good," Tony said with a happy stomp of his foot. Tony held out his hand. "On behalf of the people of New Frisco, I want to thank you for bringing in this dangerous character."

I shook his hand.

"Have HARV contact my office about reimbursing you for your office."

Tony slapped me on the back. "You did good, Zach. You did good."

Thing is, I wasn't so sure.

I checked up on Carol. She was a bit shaken but more embarrassed that Shannon had caught her off guard than anything else. I gave her the rest of the day off, which she appreciated.

I surveyed the damage to my office. It was bad. All my wallscreens had been shattered. The holo-projector on the ceiling was dented and my floors were covered in dust and blood. The good news was my classic oak desk, wooden chair, and coatrack were dirty but steady as ever. HARV assured me that the maintenancebots and repairbots assured him that the new parts were easy to fix. They would have my office up and running again in two days, three tops.

I decided to head home.

Chapter 10

Soon as I got home I set up shop. That's the great thing about living in the hyperinformation age—my place of work can be anywhere I am. It doesn't have to be down on the docks in the rustic dive I called an office. Sure the old oak desk, wooden chair, and coatrack are great for setting the ambience and getting clients in the proper frame of mind. The thing is, once on the case, it didn't matter where I hung my hat or worked. My home was as good a place as any.

I kicked my legs up on my coffee table and sat back on the couch. It was unquestionably more comfortable here.

HARV appeared next to me, pointing at my feet. "That's a coffee table, not a hassock."

I sat up straighter, not really sure why. HARV wasn't the boss of me. I also didn't know why I was on the case, especially since the case looked solved. Shannon Cannon went nuclear. Case closed. That's how the police saw it. Word had all too quickly leaked to the press and public and that's how they saw it. The press was going crazy speculating on all the reasons why Shannon snapped. Was it just because she was a Moonie? Was she Sexy's jealous lover? Was she the jealous lover of all three council members? The press was convinced it had be somehow sex-related. The press always thought it was sex-related—mostly because it usually was.

The public was so distraught over Sexy's death that thousands of her fans and voters had an underwear-only candlelight vigil for her, even though it was mid-day. Sexy would have wanted it that way.

Much as I fought it, I also felt a sense of loss. Sexy wasn't my favorite person in the world. DOS, she wasn't even my favorite client. She was spoiled, arro-gant, egotistical, and not all that bright. Yet, in her own weird way, she was endearing. I was going to miss her, probably more than her fan base would. They were sure to forget her as soon as the next hot starlet auctioned her best bra to earn the money to run for office. For me, it wasn't going to be that easy. I would have to pay homage to Sexy in my own way. I was going to track down her killer. The P.I. in me needed to bring the guilty party in, for Sexy and for myself.

"HARV, I need all the footage you can get me from the surveillance cameras in Sexy's office."

I was expecting HARV to put up a fight or at the very least bitch about having to do it.

"Done," HARV said without so much as a lecture.

I looked up. "Done? That's it?"

"I know you, Zach. You're on a crusade. You won't stop—no, you *can't* stop until you find whatever it is you're looking for."

"I'm looking for the real killer," I said.

"Whatever," HARV shrugged. "I am smart enough to know it's not worth fighting with you about."

"You obtained the video pretty easily," I said.

"I used Sexy's password to get access. Things are

in such chaos there I knew they wouldn't have time to take down Sexy's account. Once I guessed her password, it was easy."

"Nice job, buddy."

HARV looked at me for a few nanos. I knew he was processing if he should tell me something.

"What is it, HARV?"

He lowered his head, "Her password was Zach."

Gates and DOS, that hit me hard. I've been kicked in the groin by a renegade mutant mule (long, painful story) and this hurt more.

I started watching the video, replaying it over and over, hoping to catch some clue. Every time it was the same—Sexy, Weathers, and Tree sitting at a big table, discussing this and that, as their many aides ran to and fro like good little worker ants. All this going on under the watchful eyes of twenty security people. Shannon gets up to take her leave. The cameras go dead.

I watched in 2-D from every angle. I watched in 3D from every angle. I zoomed in. I zoomed out. I tried infrared and energy scans. Every time I failed to find anything that would help me.

All the while, HARV stood by my side, analyzing far more angles than I could even dream up.

"We need more eyes," I told HARV.

"Carol?"

"No, she needs to rest today."

"Randy?"

"Not now. His head is stuck up on the Moon, well more on the Moon lady's ass."

"Tony?"

"Yeah, right."

I moved my hand in just the right way to make my Colt 2062 pop into my hand.

"I do not detect any hostiles," GUS chirped.

"You're kidding," HARV sighed, stamping his foot.

I held the Colt 2062 out so GUS could survey the situation. "What do you see here?" I asked.

GUS whirled then spouted, "Sexy Sprocket's office. The recent scene of her murder."

"Very good," I said.

"Please," HARV moaned. "The toaster could have figured that out."

"HARV and I have been looking through the vids for a clue to who the killer is."

"Have you viewed the data through an electromagnetic filter?" GUS asked.

"Of course," HARV said, rolling his eyes, actually spinning his eyes.

"Newer cloaking armor uses shifted microwave energy to create the invisible effect. Have you tried shifting the electromagnetic filter through different hertz?"

Silence. More silence.

"Ah, HARV, I think he was talking to you."

"I didn't try that," HARV said.

"Then do it," I said.

The images started rolling by in superfast motion, over and over again. If HARV was changing anything, I couldn't tell. I used the time to go over Shannon's résumé to see if there was anything of interest. Then . . .

"Vingo!" HARV shouted.

He replayed the footage again. This time, with an arrow pointing to the middle of the room. A form appeared, a ghost of a shape, but a shape nonetheless.

"So that's our killer," I said.

"Certainly," HARV said.

"Yes, I compute the odds of a random, cloaked person coming into the room to be one million to one against," GUS said.

"Can we get a clearer view of the intruder?"

Again, silence.

"I'm going to need help," HARV said.

I held GUS out. "We've got GUS."

"Sure do!" GUS said.

"I'm going to need more help," HARV said. "Randy's help."

I shook my head. "I don't think Randy will be much help as long as that Melda woman is with him. Besides, I don't want her in on this." I didn't trust her.

"That is no longer an issue," HARV said. "Melda has left Randy's office."

"Why?"

"Randy kissed her."

"Oh, never good."

"She slapped him, made him think he was a pig, then packed up and headed out. He just stopped oinking. He's very distraught though."

"Great," I said.

HARV glared at me. If GUS could glare he probably would have also been.

"I'm just saying Randy could probably use a nice, fun project to get his mind off Melda."

"True," HARV agreed. "Though he may prove once and for all this is Shannon."

"My gut tells me it's not her."

"Yeah, well your gut's not admissible in court," HARV said. He paused for a nano. "I've given Randy the data. He says he'll have something for you in six hours."

I stood up. "That gives me time to do a little background checking."

"Where you going?" HARV asked.

"Background check on Shannon Cannon. I need to see if she could snap."

I grabbed my coat and headed for the door.

"How you going to do that?" HARV asked.

"You're the supercomputer. You figure it out."

HARV's eyes blinked. "Madam Desma's School for Talented Girls," he said.

I touched my nose. "Vingo."

"I need you to see if you can track down Threa," I said.

HARV appeared in front of me, scratching his head. "You don't really think Threa is responsible for this, do you?"

"She had a bone to pick with Sexy. Whoever did this was well connected and had a lot of power. Threa fits the bill."

"I'll try to contact her, but murder isn't her style."

HARV was right. The killings didn't match Threa's MO. Still, she was a crazy superwoman whose sister once tried to destroy the Earth. I wasn't going to rule her out simply because I was a little worried that she might turn me into a frog.

Chapter 11

Madame Desma's School For Talented Girls was located on the outskirts of town. The building itself was an old, elegant, redbrick Victorian mansion that was at least two hundred years old. The mansion sat on top of a small hill that overlooked many acres of finely manicured rolling grounds. As I drove up the long brick driveway that lead to the manor, the grounds were filled with girls or young women engaged in various activities. Some were playing what I believed to be badminton, others were sitting in circles reading, a few were playing violins, some were practicing the martial arts and a few were just sitting, sunbathing.

HARV looked at me looking at them.

"If some of them were having pillow fights in their nighties this would pretty much be your adolescent boy's dream come true."

I smiled in agreement.

I entered the building and followed the sounds of music into a large room. There, I found Madame

Desma holding a violin as she stood in front of five eager-looking girls who were holding violins at their sides. These weren't electric or virtual violins, by the way—they were good old-fashioned wooden ones. They had to be almost as old and as valuable as my car.

Desma positioned the violin under her chin. She started to play a lively tune. Surprisingly enough, it sounded like a fiddle.

"Hey, that sounds like a fiddle," I said.

"That's because a violin and a fiddle are the same thing," HARV said inside my head. *"It just depends on how you play them."* Though I couldn't see him, I was sure HARV was shaking his head in disbelief at my naïveté.

Desma immediately stopped playing and turned to me. She smiled. She turned back to her girls.

"Ladies, we have a surprise special guest, Zachary Nixon Johnson."

The girls all gave me polite little claps. I could tell from the looks on their faces they weren't thrilled about having their lesson interrupted.

Desma walked over to me and extended her hand. She was a pleasant looking woman in her early thirties, with short curly black hair. She had the look of a woman who would be equally as comfortable in a concert hall as she would be on a sports field, or for that matter, fixing her own hover or car. No matter what time of the day I saw her, she always had a freshly pressed look.

"So what brings you to my neck of the woods, cos?" Desma asked.

Oh, yeah, she was my cousin once removed (whatever the DOS that means) on my mom's side. She was the only psi in the family that I was aware of.

"You're the psi."

Her brown eyes locked on mine. A faint smile appeared on her face. She frowned. "Come into my office," she said hurriedly.

Desma took me by the hand and led me out of the practice room to the main hall then up a twisting staircase. We walked up the stairs in silence until we crossed paths with a tall, slim woman with dark blue hair coming down the stairway. She was wearing a purple suit dress that appeared as if it was cloned for her. She looked at me and I could feel her glance. I shuddered. Not sure if it was a good shudder or a bad one, but definitely a noticeable one. She didn't have the strong Asian features of the other Mooner females I had met and was fairer than they were. Yet I knew she was a Mooner.

"Ms. Desma," she said with a slight tip of her head. "Sir," she said to me with another tip.

"Elena," Desma replied.

I just mumbled, continuing to climb the stairs.

"Quite pretty isn't she?" Desma said with a nudge.

"I hadn't noticed. I'm engaged . . ."

"True, but not dead, cos."

"She is a looker. From the Moon. Right?"

Desma nodded. "The Moon psis and Earth psis are trying an exchange program."

We reached the top of the stairs. (There were a LOT of stairs.) Desma led me down a hallway to the left.

"She is here with the contingent from the Moon?" I asked.

"You ask a lot of questions."

"Comes with the job."

Desma smiled. "No, she's been here longer. I get the impression, a very strong impression, that she's not a fan of Mr. Sputnik."

We reached a door. I followed Desma into the room

behind the door. It was a small conference room with a little table in the middle and bookshelves with actual books lining the walls.

"Have you taught her much?" I asked.

Desma sat and grinned. "DOS, no. She's teaching me. She's a class I level 8 psi."

I sat kitty-corner to my cousin. I've been exposed to a lot of psis in my time, but never one rated so highly. The Thompson sisters were probably at least that powerful but nobody was ever able to test them successfully. Those girls value their privacy.

"Class I level 8," I repeated.

"Good cos, glad to see your short-term memory works."

While I had to get back on the case, I was fascinated by a psi of this power level.

"So what can she do?" I asked.

"Anything she wants," Desma said with a hint of a smile. "Anything she wants."

"I need more than that," I coaxed.

"Suffice it to say, if she told you to drop dead, you would. Happily." Desma thought for a nano. "Even that computer you have strapped to your brain probably wouldn't help. She'd be the perfect assassin. Luckily, she'd never kill anybody."

"Why do you say that?"

Desma turned her head. "Truthfully, I don't know. Let's hope I'm right or we're all in trouble." She took a nano or two to collect her thoughts. "Now, I assume we're here to talk about Ms. Cannon?" She said in her most professional voice.

Desma pointed to a bottle of brandy and a couple of glasses on the end of table. I hadn't noticed them before. I probably should have.

"Thirsty?" she asked.

"I'm on the job."

"It's over a hundred years old," she coaxed.

I shrugged. "Spam that then. Not like this is a paying job."

Desma made a delicate hand gesture toward the bottle and glasses. Rising off the table, they floated down to us. Desma twisted her hand. The bottle top popped off and was held suspended in midair. She put her elbow on the table then her head in her hand. The smooth, red liquid started flowing down the side of the first glass. I showed her two fingers. The brandy rose in the glass until it was about the height of those fingers. The bottle tilted upward slowly, not dripping a drop. The bottle levitated to the remaining glass, tipping its spout just enough. Liquid filled the void from the bottle to glass, seeping into the glass until it was topped off. The bottle straightened and gently touched down on the table. All the while, Desma's eyes never left mine.

She picked her glass and held it up. "Cheers."

"Impressive," I told her. Lots of psis can do the brute force action, but the subtle moves take a lot of control.

"It's impolite not to return the cheers," she told me.

I touched my glass to hers. "Cheers."

"You're probably the only normal in the world I feel comfortable doing that in front of."

I took a sip, it was smooth with four *oohs* . . . "Let's just say I'm not that normal."

She smiled, more with her eyes than her mouth. "Good point. At least there are thousands of us psis. You're the only person in the world sharing his brain with a supercomputer." She took a sip.

This was about all HARV could stand. He appeared before Desma, transmitting himself from my eye lens. (He didn't seem to mind that he had a table between his top and bottom sections.) "What about me?" HARV asked. "I'm the only supercomputer in the world forced to share its processing power with a human. It's like I'm a fine race car, capable of exceptional speed, power, and precision, except I'm saddled with an amateur driver." HARV spun his head toward me. "No offense, Zach."

"Taken," I said, though I was ignored.

"Yes, HARV. I can only begin to imagine the suffering he's caused you," Desma said.

HARV rolled his eyes. "Oh, the stories I could tell . . ."

"Do you mind if we get to the case?" I asked.

HARV turned the top half of his body toward me. "You know, Zach, some of us are capable of doing more than one thing at once."

"Well, I'm not," I said. I looked through HARV, literally. "Shannon Cannon was a student here. Correct?"

Desma nodded. "Yes, she was a fine, devoted student. A great mix of mutant and natural psi."

"I know she's capable of killing, but would she turn on her charge?" I asked.

"No," Desma said without hesitation. "She was totally loyal to Sexy. She even listened to her music."

"Wow, that is going beyond the call of duty," I said, scratching my head.

HARV chimed in. "I've looked at Shannon's online psych profile and I agree . . . Shannon would never harm Sexy."

"I assume the police are treating this like an open and shut case," Desma said. "Just blame the crazy mutant psi . . ."

I thought about the situation. I tried to put myself in the police's shoes. "It's convenient and fitting and easy. So you can't blame 'em."

"And the evidence does point to a superassassin who knew the building," HARV added.

Desma shook her head. "The assassin would be

near impossible to find if they had a massive man, woman, or bot hunt, but they aren't even looking."

Yeah, the future didn't look bright for Shannon. She had nobody in her corner and everybody lining up to chain her, toss her in a cell, and erase the key codes. I was her only hope. Lucky for her I was good at what I do.

I stood up. "Looks like I better find the police a couple of other suspects . . ."

Chapter 12

I left Desma's and hit the open road. HARV informed me that it would be twenty-four more hours before my office was repaired so for now, the road was my office.

I knew in my gut that Shannon wasn't the one who offed Sexy and the others. But, as HARV always liked to point out, no judge in their right mind would listen to my gut.

The police wouldn't be out looking for other potential killers. They had a perfectly good suspect in custody. She had the means, she had the power, she had the motive. At least, according to my buddy Tony. Shannon did it to protest the three council members voting against the Moon's freedom. She was a mutant psi killer who snapped. The media was eating it up. No way the police would upset the apple cart here.

If anybody was going to find the true killer that anybody would be me. All I needed was a viable suspect.

"HARV, put me in contact with Threa," I said driving through the countryside.

"Threa is in Incognito," HARV said. "Quite literally. That's what she calls her fairy realm. She is not accepting calls or visitors."

I needed to track Threa down, STASAP (sooner than as soon as possible). "Connect me with Ona," I ordered HARV.

Ona Thompson may have been the richest, most powerful, most sexy woman in the world, but she was still an ex-client who owed me. She should be able to get me in contact with Threa.

It wasn't long before Ona's picture filled my dash viewscreen. She was in some sort of dojo, wearing a scantily cut karate uniform. Ona was surrounded by at least twenty angry-looking people, all also wearing karate uniforms.

Ona glanced up at the camera. "Oh, hi, Zach. You caught me during my midday workout. I will be with you in a nano."

"Don't hurry on my account," I said, even though I really wanted her to hurry. My experience with Ona had taught me it's best not to push her.

I watched with great anticipation as the karate people swarmed her, engulfing her in a sea of white uniforms and kicks and punches. The twenty of them just whaled away on their foil for a good minute. Suddenly, they all stopped cold. Their eyes rolled to the back of their heads. They all spun around 360 degrees. They all fell over on their backs, but with their legs up. They weren't knocked out, they were whimpering. They reminded me of beaten puppies. Ona was, of course, standing in the middle of them, without a hair out of place.

Ona looked at me. "I promised them a bonus if any of them could last two minutes with me. I wanted to give them a sporting chance."

"How nice of you," I said.

"I feel it's important to treat my employees with respect," Ona said, wiping the tiniest bit of sweat from her brow. "It builds morale."

"Now what can I do for you, Zach?"

"I need to find your sister Threa."

Ona grimaced. "Now, why would anybody with half a brain, even a tenth of brain, seek out Threa?" She thought for a nano. "This involves Sexy and the Council murders, doesn't it?"

"She's a person of interest," I said.

"Not to the police," Ona replied.

"To me."

"Zach, you should forget about Threa," Ona warned. "She may be crazy but she'd never harm anybody. Or at least not kill them."

"Yesterday I fought some of her ogres that she sent after Sexy."

Ona lowered her eyes. It was a subtle sign but I caught it nevertheless. "Yes, that does seem like Threa's style."

"So I need to talk to her."

Ona turned away from the camera, I assume to look at a clock. "Fine, I'll take it under advisement."

"What does that mean?"

My screen went blank. HARV's face filled the void. "When she wants to talk, she'll find you," he said.

"What the DOS does that mean?" I said.

"You have bigger potential problems right now," HARV said.

"Why?"

HARV pointed behind me, "There's been a black sedan following you for the last two kilometers."

I turned and looked over my shoulder. (I didn't have to keep my eyes on the road since HARV was driving.) There it was, bearing down on me, a big black box of a sedan. It looked like a coffin on wheels with a dome on top. The holo-license read: PIS4U. It was DickCo.

The Dicks at DickCo were my archrivals. They stand for everything I can't stand: big business, glitz, and sizzle over steak. They are a corporation of Dicks for hire. They have a low price tag and lower morals. There's no job they won't take and broadcast it over their own reality network.

"Should I outrun them?" HARV asked.

I shook my head and pointed to the side of the road. "Can't risk a speeding violation. I need the police to like me right now," I said.

HARV slanted his head. "Not possible."

"Hate me *less* then."

"I'm pulling over."

HARV pulled the car over to the side. The black coffinlike sedan slid in behind us. I sighed and got out of the car.

The dome on the sedan popped up. Four people, three men and one woman, slid out. I recognized the man, sort of. He was Sidney Whoop, one of DickCo's top guns. But the Sidney I knew was clean shaven, except for a little mustache, and a fancy dresser. He considered himself a class act. This Sidney had long hair and a scruffy beard. His normal custom-made suit and jacket had been replaced by a ripped T-shirt and a leather jacket. He was flanked by two goons with bald heads who might as well have been the same guy. They were backup muscle, nothing more, nothing less. They were in T-shirts and torn blue jeans and had chains and handcuffs hanging over their belts.

Bringing up the rear was a blond-haired babe. I could see the ambition in her cold blue eyes. She was dressed in tight black leather. This lady had more curves than the last geometry test I had taken. Only her curves looked a lot more fun. I was betting she was a psi.

"Nice outfit," I said to Sidney as he moved toward me.

He held up his arms, modeling for me as he walked. "Like it? We're doing bounty hunter month . . ."

Sidney was good. We've tangled on a few occasions. The scoreboard reads in my favor but it's far from a blowout.

"So to what do I owe the pleasure?" I asked.

"Just here to talk, Zach. I promise." Sidney said with his hand on his heart.

"What?" one of the goons squawked. "Talk? This is Zachary Nixon Johnson. This guy is our claim to fame."

Sidney shook his head. "The boss just wants to talk."

The two goons moved forward. "Talk is for patsies! This is Zachary Nixon Johnson," one of them repeated.

"Let's IRS him over," the other said.

They both started heading toward me. I looked at Sidney. His brows were raised and his mouth quivering some. He wasn't expecting this. I glanced at the girl. One perfectly shaped eyebrow was raised and she was smiling. She was behind this.

"I've got a message coming into your brain," HARV said. "It's from the blonde, Stacy; she says, 'Have fun.'"

So, the blonde was pulling the strings and the goons were just performing chimps. Two hover-cams rose from the sedan, their lights blinking red, indicating they were recording.

The goons pulled their chains and approached. Sidney made a step forward in protest but Stacy touched him on his shoulder and he stopped. This was going to be just me and the big boys.

They each pounded a meaty fist into an open hand. They smirked as they drew nearer.

"This is going to be fun," they both grumbled. (Two thugs, one brain—DickCo probably got them at a discount rate. That's the thing about DickCo—they don't really care about solving the case, just making a buck.)

I slid slightly to the left, stationing myself right between them. I had quite the surprise up my sleeve for them.

"You boys are going to fight fair now, aren't you?" I asked more as a distraction than anything else.

"We got you outmuscled and outnumbered. You're old and slow. We don't need to cheat," one of them laughed.

"We just need to break a few bones, gain us some rep points," the other said. He slid a barely visible neck side to side, making a crunching noise.

"Your moms must be so proud," I said.

They were so close to me I could smell their breath. It was much more pleasant than I would have thought. Still, pleasant breath or not, I was going to have to put them down, hard and fast. I didn't like the idea of two one-bit goons thinking I was ripe for the picking.

I played it coy, bending down to feign tying my shoe, like I didn't notice their advance on me. I wasn't looking at the goons, but HARV was tracking them via my wrist communicator so I knew exactly when they would be in striking distance. I grabbed a handful of dirt and gravel as the thugs closed to within striking distance. I needed to make sure I was the one who would be doing the striking. I straightened slowly as they advanced quickly. I tossed the dirt in their faces.

They halted their attack and starting rubbing their eyes frantically while mumbling something about how dirty outfits look poor on camera. I flicked my wrist in just that right way to make my trusty Colt 2062 pop into my hand. I didn't shoot though, no fun or flair in that. Instead, I spun the weapon in my hand so I was gripping it in the middle. I punched forward with my gun hand aiming for the spot right between the now befuddled goons. As my fist approached them the sides of the weapon expanded outward, turning my firearm into a staff—a very hard staff. I clocked both the offending thugs in the jaw, one with the right side of the staff the other with the left.

They both buckled over backward, smashing into the roadside. I held GUS with both hands ready to use it as a bat if needed. It wasn't. The two were out colder than New Moscow in mid February. Fooled by the age-old fake tie-your-shoe, dirt-in-the-face trick. DOS, my old third grade teacher Sister D wouldn't even fall for that—Gates knows I tried. It just goes to show that DickCo was really trolling the bottom the barrel for their talent.

"Sorry, Johnson," Sidney said. "They're nonunion workers. The union thugs are just so pricey. We have to cut corners these days."

I looked past Sidney to Stacy the psi. "Happy?" I said.

"Not really," Sidney said not knowing I wasn't talking to him. "Is it too much to ask for backups who are happy being backups? None of these new guys are team players anymore. They don't know how to take orders."

"They were taking orders, just not from you," I said.

Sidney turned to Stacy. "Stacy, what the freaking DOS were you doing?"

Stacy had a subtle smile on her face. She pointed to the thugs. They lifted off the ground and started floating to the hover. "You have your orders . . . I have mine," she said. "The boss lady wanted some clips we can use in a training video on how not to approach Zachary Nixon Johnson."

Yes, this was an ambitious woman. I was going to have to watch out for her in the future.

"So what's the message, Sidney?"

"The boss lady wants to meet you in one hour at Madam Ti Chi's Restaurant on Arnold Ave."

"The boss lady?"

"Ona Thompson," HARV said in my brain.

"Ona Thompson," Sidney and Stacy both said.

"Oh, that's right, Ona's EnterCorp owns you guys," I said thinking out loud. "Why didn't Ona just tell me that herself?"

"She's so rich and powerful she never does anything herself," Stacy said.

"And when she says jump, we jump and jump and jump," Sidney said. He pointed at me. "If you know what's good for you, you'll be there."

I arrived at Madam Ti Chi's during the heart of the lunch hour. I had never eaten there but I heard the food was great. It must have been as the place held at least three hundred and if there was an empty seat in the house it was hard to find.

An older Asian woman, who I assumed was Madam Ti Chi, greeted me at the door with a polite bow. She was short and slightly wrinkled; she could have been anywhere from 60 to 160. She had a tiny microphone next to her mouth and an earpiece clipped to her left ear lobe. At first I thought it was PIHI-Pod then I realized it had to be a translational computer.

The women spoke in the microphone and the words "Greetings, Mr. Johnson," came out of the microphone. She motioned to the back of the room. "Follow me," she said.

She led. I followed. "Please pardon the use of a translator computer," the woman said through the translator as we weaved through the crowd. "I have so many customers from so many places I find it only fair that I speak to them all through my translator."

"Not a problem," I said.

She stopped at a small table for two near the back corner. There was already food on the table. One place setting had chicken and broccoli and rice, the other sushi of some sort. The woman pointed to a chair next to the chicken dish.

"You sit here," she said. "The other will be here soon."

I looked at the place setting. Chicken and broccoli was my favorite. This had certainly been arranged. I sat down.

"Hmm," HARV said inside my head. *"I'm detecting an energy surge."*

"A good surge or a bad one?" I thought.

"Energy is neither good nor bad," HARV said.

"Is it dangerous?" I thought.

"Depends," HARV snickered. I absolutely hate it when he snickers.

There was a commotion in the restaurant. I looked around and every other person, whether they be patron, waitress, or even kitchen staff, had stood up and were filing out of the building. It was like a weird zombie Chinese fire drill.

"Should I leave?" I asked HARV.

"No," said a nearby voice. I turned toward that voice to see Ona had materialized in the chair opposite me in all her splendor. Ona stood over two meters tall and had golden skin with just a hint of purple in it. You would have thought it would be unappealing, but instead it was oh-so-sensual. Her platinum blond hair was draped just over her shoulders. She had a body to make a goddess envious. She was wearing a clothlike miniskirt that looked like she borrowed it from Betty Rubble. On anybody else it would have been silly but on her, stunning. I had no idea what color her eyes were, as rumor was that anybody who looked her in the eyes was instantly transfixed.

"You really know how to make an entrance," I told her.

"I bought one of Santana Clausa's personal teleporters," she said. "There are times when it's useful being the richest being on the planet," she said, munching on sushi.

"I can imagine."

She shook her head. "No, you can't." She pointed at my dish. "Eat your food. You're going to need your strength for where I'm taking you."

I was afraid to ask, but I did anyhow. "So, where you taking me?"

"To Threa's realm."

"So you believe me that she may be involved?"

Ona looked down, grabbing a Chinese roll. "I owe you a favor, Zach. You're the only person ever to save me. Let's leave it at that."

Wise advice a smart man would have taken. "What if Threa is involved?" I pressed.

"That would be bad," Ona said. "My sister may be a loon but she's a powerful loon. I don't think she's behind this but I have to check it out."

I took a bite of the chicken. "Glad you can help."

Ona took a sip of wine. "I must admit this isn't totally altruistic on my part." She held her glass up for me to toast. I did.

"You're a businesswoman. I'm not surprised."

We both took sips of our drinks.

She looked up at me from hers. "I may be more than that in the near future."

"More than a billionaire superbabe?"

"I've been asked to replace Sexy on the WC."

"What?" I choked, spitting out my drink.

"The World Council has a policy of replacing assassinated members with new members of very similar values. They figured it would cut down on killings." She took another sip. "Since I'm nearly invulnerable, they figure that will cut down on attacks."

I looked at her. "So your sole qualifications are that you think like Sexy Sprockets and are hard to kill?"

"Yeah, kind of scary."

Kind of didn't even come close to describing the level of scariness.

Ona pointed to my plate. "Finish your broccoli. You're going to need your strength."

I speared a broccoli floret. I took a moment to take in the ironic aspects of it. "Yes, *Mom.*"

She smiled lightly. "Chew your food at least thirty-two times."

I did as I was told. After all, I didn't want to accidentally choke to death without giving Threa a chance to kill me. I chewed then swallowed. In most cases that's hardly noteworthy, but in this case I knew it might be the last time I performed those simple actions.

Ona stood up and looked at me.

"Ready to roll?" I asked.

"You're such a strange little man," she said.

She snapped her fingers.

Chapter 13

The next thing I knew Ona and I were standing on a path in the middle of a lush green tropical forest. A butterfly floated by. I had been to Threa's realm before, but it was different this time, less gothic and D&D-like than I remembered it.

"Look alive," Ona said as we started walking up the path. "You never know what's in Threa's demented mind."

"So is this place real?" I asked.

Ona shrugged. "Real enough. It's a mix of holograms with some genetic and psionic creations tossed in."

"That's what I was thinking," I said.

"You were not," HARV protested in my brain.

We walked on for a few minutes. It was peaceful and serene. I knew it couldn't last long.

"It's quiet," Ona said. "Too quiet."

"Is that a bad sign?" I asked.

"Nah, I just always wanted to say that," Ona winked.

HARV appeared between us. "Ms. Ona," he said

as politely as HARV is able. "I need something more quantifiable than a mix of holograms with some genetic and psionic creations."

"Sorry," she said as we forged forward. "I need a being that can handle one of my orgasms without needing to be hospitalized." She shrugged. "Not even superbeings and supercomputers always get what they want."

We kept walking, luckily in silence. After a few minutes I popped my Colt 2062 into my hand. It just felt like the right thing to do.

"A bit edgy, Zach," Ona said.

"He pulls out that silly little thing whenever he's feeling inadequate," HARV said.

"Just being cautious," I told them, "I've got a bad feeling . . ."

"Oh, good, glad to see your actions are based on such empirical concepts," HARV said, eyes raised and rolling.

The next thing I saw spooked me. There, standing in front of us, were over one thousand humanoid-shaped shadows. Saying they were *eerie* would be as much of an understatement as noting that World Council budget planning premeetings are boring.

"Halt!" the gaggle of shadow beings decreed at once. "The mistress will not be disturbed," they all said, not quite in unison. It was like each of them said it about a nano before the next, making the statement echo thousands of times.

"See, this is why I drew my weapon," I said to Ona and HARV.

HARV put a hand to his eyes and leaned forward as if to get a bitter glimpse. "These are like nothing I have ever processed."

"They are a half-baked concoction from Threa's brain and lab, part real, part surreal. Part of all the things that scare humans: demons, darkness, depression, vampires, ghosts, clowns, taxes, career politicians, and telemarketers."

"Oh, good. I was afraid it was going to be something weird," I said.

"They have no true form, just partial substance. Threa cooks them up in a hurry when she needs a legion of easy to maintain minions."

"How often does she need a legion of minions?" HARV asked, truly curious.

"More often than you would think."

The living darkness crept toward us. It sent a chill up my spine and not in a good way.

"So these things aren't technically alive?" I asked.

Ona thought for a nano or two. "Depends on your definition of alive. Threa thinks they are alive. Twoa and I disagree. They certainly don't have individual will or consciousness, if you want to go spiritual on me." Ona thought for a nano more, then added, "They do give great foot massages though."

Hearing that they were not alive was all I needed. I held out the Colt 2062. "GUS, I'm going to need a wide distribution blast."

"Ah, check, I guess," GUS said far less enthusiastically than normal.

"What's the problem, buddy?"

"He can't get a read on them," HARV said.

"Ah, check," GUS said.

I figured I'd blast them the old-fashioned way, without computer targeting. I squeezed the trigger sending a powerful beam of energy at the mob. The energy harmlessly passed through them, not even slowing their approach.

"They aren't quite there, so you can't hurt them with actual weapons," Ona said.

"Just lovely," I said a split nano before one of the creatures tagged me in the jaw.

I recoiled in pain. "Gates and DOS that hurt!" I shouted.

Ona had her own problems as the multitude of dark blob creatures had engulfed her. Ona screamed and spun, flinging the first round of attackers off of her.

"I hate this," she spat. "Since they don't really exist you can't use real weapons on them."

"We need to do something fast," I said.

Another mob of dark mass had swollen over Ona, covering her up to her neck. "Yeah, you're telling me," she said. "You're just lucky they don't consider you much of a threat."

"Yeah, but that was their mistake," I said.

Two more dark shapes were bearing down on me. I held out an open hand towards HARV. "HARV, holographic sword, now!" I shouted.

HARV crossed his arms and stood there. "What, you can't even ask with a complete sentence? Just because you're being attacked by dark humanoid masses doesn't give you an excuse to be uncivilized."

The masses grabbed me, tackling me to the ground. All the while I left my arm extended and my hand open. "HARV, will you please give me a holographic sword?"

HARV smiled. "See, now that wasn't so hard. It's always important to be polite."

A glowing, long sword appeared in my open hand. I hacked at the black shadow blobs. They screamed in pain as they split and disappeared.

I stood up and held the sword out. This was going to be fun. I moved forward, slashing and hacking as I advanced. The nice thing about wielding a holographic sword was I couldn't hurt myself with it. That allowed me to go crazy.

I sliced my way forward for at least a half a kilometer. Since my sword weighed nothing, it was easy. It actually gave me a feeling of empowerment I hadn't felt in a long time. Obviously, I had some issues. In a way this was good therapy. As I hacked, Ona and HARV followed behind, critiquing me.

"It's about time he's finally doing some work," HARV said.

"I think he's enjoying himself," Ona said.

"He's a very simple man," HARV added.

Finally, I managed to cut my way through the horde that wasn't really quite there, enabling me to get close enough to see Threa. She was just sitting in a pasture, legs crossed, hovering off the ground with her eyes closed, meditating.

Ona looked at her sister, shook her head while rolling her eyes. Ona walked up to Threa, made a fist and clunked her over the head with it. This got her attention.

Threa's eyes shot open, her arm shot up. "Who in the name of the goddess dares disturb me? I will turn them into doormats." Threa focused in on me. "Zachary Nixon Johnson, I always considered you an ally."

Ona tapped Threa on the shoulder. Threa turned to see her sister. "Oh, I should have known it was you."

Ona hit Threa with a left hook that sent her flying over HARV and me. Threa hit the ground, left a dent in it, and popped up, ready for a fight.

"Why in the name of me did you do that?" she shouted, fists clinched and smoke coming out of her ears.

"Just making sure we had your attention," Ona said, ripping off what little sleeves she had.

"Oh, you've got it in spades," Threa said, moving forward and rolling up the sleeves of her gown.

"And they say no family is normal," HARV said.

The two titanic women stormed toward each other. Obviously I wasn't the only one with issues.

"I should record this," HARV said. "It would be the number one download for days."

I couldn't let these two go at it. As fun as it might have been to watch, it wasn't going to help my case in any way.

Moving forward, I positioned myself between them, holding my arms out in some foolish hope that that would be enough to keep them apart. Continuing forward, they ignored me. I was caught between them in something that was both terrifying and strangely erotic. Yep, I definitely have issues.

Both ladies curled their hands into fists. "These are actual targets," GUS said meekly in my head.

I popped the Colt 2062 back into my hand, positioning it between the two ladies. "High energy blasts from both ends!" I ordered.

Energy ripped from my gun, launching both Ona and Threa into the air for at least fifty meters. I smiled. They hit the ground, once again the ground taking the worst of it. They bounced up. They both started to laugh.

"Wow, Zach, can't you let a couple of sisters have some fun?" Ona said.

"That little toy of yours packs a punch," Threa said.

HARV patted me on the shoulder. "Just be glad they enjoyed the experience."

The two superwoman approached me, their outfits, such as they were, ripped to shreds. But neither of them had all that much clothing on to begin with.

"So, what brings you to my realm?" Threa asked.

"Sexy Sprockets," I started to say.

Threa turned bloodred. Fire starting pouring out of any open orifices she had. "How dare you mention that whore in my realm!" she shouted.

". . . is dead." I finished.

Threa exhaled. The fire fizzled out. Threa hung her

head. "Ah, that's too bad. As whores go she was a good one."

"Sexy and two other council members, Weathers and Tree, were killed today," I said looking Threa dead in the eye. Well, a bit in the breasts, but mostly in the eyes. Unlike these superdames I'm only human. Right?

Threa took a step back. "You think I'm responsible?"

"The thought had crossed my mind," I said.

"I told him I was pretty sure it wasn't you," Ona said as meekly as I've ever heard her say anything.

Threa took a step forward, fist curled, she looked right through me. "Pretty sure?"

Ona shrugged. "Sis, with you one can never be totally sure. You are a bit of a flake."

Threa dropped back a step again. "How true." She thought for a few nanos. "Killing people is *so* not my style. And I had nothing against Weathers and Tree. I've only met them two or three times."

I looked at Threa. Her features had dropped some. She was certainly distressed. I'm not sure if she was more upset about the deaths or being accused.

"Where did the murders occur?" Threa asked.

"She really has been in another world," HARV mumbled.

"In the New Frisco World Council office building," I said.

Threa tossed her hair over her shoulder. "But the security there had to be top-notch."

"It was. The killer took them out too," I said.

Threa's eyes opened wide. "Then you know it wasn't me. I would never hurt the little oppressed people."

Ona nodded. "That's true."

The look of sincerity on Threa's face was utterly convincing. If she was the killer, she was an even better liar.

"Sorry for bothering you, Threa," I said, with a tip of my fedora.

"We still on for lunch on Tuesday, sis?" Ona asked.

"You bet, but you're paying."

Ona snapped her fingers. We were back in the restaurant. I wasn't sure if we really had left.

Chapter 14

Soon as I got home, I plopped down on the couch and starting crunching data with HARV. I couldn't totally rule out Shannon and Threa as suspects. A good P.I. never totally rules out a loon. Still, between my instincts and what I knew about the two women, I was fairly certain neither of them was the killer. The killer was somebody who would gain from killing Sexy, Weathers, and Tree. There had to be something that linked the dead trio besides the fact they all had names that could double as adjectives or nouns.

HARV and I pored over the data. Never in the history of history had three people been so different. The only attributes they seemed to share were a love of the limelight and of wasting the taxpayers' money. They each had ten times as many press conferences and photo ops as they had votes on council resolutions.

Out of the three hundred resolutions the three of them had voted on, they all agreed on only one, the resolution to give themselves a 25 percent cost-of-high-living raise. I was getting nowhere, slow.

Randy had so far been no help on reviewing the video of the crime scene. It seems he got caught up watching an old *Battlestar Galatica* marathon. The entire series was remixed in 3-D. Randy couldn't resist. I gave him props for his taste, if not his timing. Randy didn't see the rush. After all, the police were sure they had the guilty party in custody.

After some coaxing and more bribing, Randy assured me he'd get right on it. I continued sifting through the voting records. I always thought all politicians were basically the same person wrapped in a slightly different package. I was wrong. While these three certainly shared the same vapid personality and the dogmatic belief that they were always right, that was about all they shared. They all had different "pet" issues, all of them equally shallow. Sexy was a big supporter of pets' rights. The only resolution she initiated during her tenure on the council was an amendment to block an amendment to consider a proposal to bring back cat eating. Sexy's big motto was *Cats are for hugging, not hunger*.

Weathers, an ex-athlete who had replaced his late wife Stormy (who, unbeknownst to most of the world, had tried to destroy most of the world) liked to think of himself as the champion of the little guy. Of course, to a politician the definition of *little guy* is millionaire, as opposed to billionaire. He was a defender of pro-athletes' rights. These rights included lifelong extra medical coverage, tax breaks on endorsements, and two get-out-of-jail-frees for punching members of the media. I kind of liked the last one.

Tree was a different sort. He had spent the last thirty years on the World Council. He was a lifelong politician which meant he scared me the most. Reviewing the public record videos of him, a blind man could see that he held Sexy and Weathers in disdain. Here's a man who worked all his life as a politician,

yet he always took a backseat to his come-lately col-
leagues like Sexy and Weathers. As far as I knew (and
HARV confirmed) he was never even considered for
head of the council. His pet policy was a policy that
politicians shouldn't have pet policies. He would introduce it every year and every year he would be the
only one to vote for it.

"The three of them were so different, yet they were
all going to meet about the Moon," I said to HARV.

"The official record is they were trying to convince
the Moon to accept more waste products from Earth."

"That had to be a hard sell," I said. "What were
their views on Moon freedom?"

"It's the one thing they almost agreed on. Tree always voted against the Moon's freedom. Sexy had
voted once against and once for freedom."

"And Weathers?"

"He hasn't had an actual vote yet, but his late wife
was always for a free Moon and he hasn't done anything to go against his late wife's views," HARV said.

"Until now," a voice said from across the room.

I spun toward the voice. My gun was already in my
hand by the time I was facing the body associated
with the voice. It was Elena.

"How'd you get in here?" I asked.

"Like your cousin said, I am class 1 level 8. There
is very little I can't do," she said gliding toward me.

"Yeah, well, I've got a front door that's great for
knocking on."

She rolled her eyes. (I get that a lot.) "Put the gun
down," she ordered. "If I wanted you dead, you
would be . . ."

I lowered my gun. I had no choice.

Elena walked forward and sat down on the couch
next to me. She was still wearing the purple outfit
from earlier in the day, and this time I noticed the
ensemble was complete with purple heels. Not many

women could have pulled of the look; she did it with ease.

"Tree is an old fart, totally against Moon freedom," she said.

"I knew that, but the other two?"

"Weathers hated Boris Sputnik—he knew Sputnik always had a thing for his wife," Elena said. "Shannon had convinced Sexy to vote for Moon freedom this time, but then Weathers convinced her not to."

I could see Weathers hating Sputnik. I remember Electra mentioning that Sputnik always seemed very friendly with her during her trips to the moon. The question was, how'd Weathers get Sexy to change her mind about her vote?

"How'd Weathers get to Sexy?" I asked.

"He was to marry her," Elena said. "He convinced her he would dump his current love, and then they would be Earth's new power couple."

I knew Sexy well; this wasn't a big surprise. She'd date a talking cucumber if she thought it would brighten her limelight. "So the three of them would have voted against the Moon's freedom."

"That's what Weathers believed and that's what Sputnik believed. But truthfully, with Sexy you can never be sure. Shannon was certain she was just using Weathers for the hype. She believes Sexy would eventually vote for freedom no matter what Weathers did," she paused for a moment, to let me catch up. "Shannon would never ever harm Sexy."

"That's what I keep hearing. So you're saying they were killed by Moon sympathizers?"

Elena raised an eyebrow. "I'm not saying anything, I'm just noting that I am not the only powerful psi on the Moon."

"How do I know you didn't kill them all?" I asked.

"Well, for one thing if she were the killer she probably would have killed you by now," HARV said.

"I'm not a killer," she paused for a nano. "I might make you think you're a plant for the rest of your life, but I wouldn't kill. I'd even water you on occasion."

Once again, I was being asked to take a beautiful woman at her word. Once again, I believed her. The thing was, just because I believed her didn't mean others would.

"Do you have any proof?" I asked.

"None that would stand up in the court of law, or even of public opinion."

"Got any proof that Weathers would have voted against freedom and was trying to get Sexy to do the same?"

"Ask his girlfriend," she said.

"Who's that?"

"BB Star," she said.

I wasn't surprised. Weathers certainly liked to run with the big girls.

Chapter 15

"HARV, tell BB I need to talk to her now," I said.

"BB is one of the richest women in the world. She runs a huge conglom. Why would she drop everything to talk to you?"

"Because my computer records might become public if she didn't."

HARV smiled. "Ah, blackmail. I love it."

Being one of the good guys, I'm not a huge fan of blackmail, though I'd much rather be the blackmailer than the blackmailee. But there are times when you've got to play hardball to get the job done.

BB Star is president and CEO of ExShell, the corporation that sells us the sun. She was also one of my first big clients. Most of the world knows her as an eccentric ex-stripper who married a billionaire and inherited his fortune and company after he died. She's a recluse who hardly ventures out of her luxury penthouse office.

What very few people know is that the actual BB Star is happily living under her grandmother's name in New Florida, while her actual grandmother has been regenerated and is stripping under a different alias in New Vegas. Trust me, this family almost makes the Thompson Quads look functional. The BB who runs the company is actually a superpowered android who contains the actual BB's memory imprints. It's a long story but a good one if you have the time. Right now, I didn't. I needed questions answered before I even asked them.

BB's image appeared in my living room. She was as blonde and commanding as ever. "Zachary, to what do I owe the honor?" she asked. She looked around the room. "Hanging out with Mooners now?"

"She's a friend," I said.

BB tilted her head away from the camera, "I'd be careful with the friends you choose," she muttered.

"Speaking of friends, I'd like to talk to you about your friend, BB."

She looked blankly into the camera. "I have no friends, only acquaintances," she said, bile dripping from her words.

"From what I understand Carl Weathers was one of your special acquaintances," I countered.

Dead silence, telling me I was dead on. Her eyes dropped. "Carl was a friend. He will be missed," she said.

The day was getting late. I didn't have time to dick around the bush. "Was he going to leave you for Sexy?"

"It was just a ploy for him to get what he wanted," she said. "After he married Sexy he'd come back to me."

"So he wanted to be council chairman?" I asked.

"He wanted to come out from under his dead wife's shadow," she said. "What better way than becoming the most popular politician in the world?"

"I'm sorry for your loss," I told her.

She stared coldly into the camera. "I'll get over it," she said. She pushed a button. Her image disappeared.

"Hmmm, interesting . . . so we may have something to tie the three politicians together," I said.

Elena touched me gently on the shoulder. "Sputnik can't be trusted," she said. "Now sleep," she said softly.

Chapter 16

I came to maybe fifteen minutes later and Elena was gone. I knew where I had to go. I got up and looked at the clock. It said it was 5 P.M. It was a crazy day and it wasn't close to being over yet.

"HARV, call Carol and tell her I need her to meet me at the New Frisco UltraMax Security Prison," I said.

"Ah, why?" HARV asked.

"I need to talk to Shannon one last time to completely rule her out before I accuse the Head Administrator of the Moon of killing the council members."

HARV nodded. "Probably wise. But how do you plan on doing it?"

"Cover me with a hologram of Captain Rickey," I said.

HARV just looked at me, hands on hips. "That's illegal you know."

"I just need to talk to Shannon. I'm not breaking her out."

HARV sighed. "I'm not going to visit with you when you are in jail," he threatened.

"Great. I'll finally be able to get some peace and quiet."

I headed toward my garage. So as to not raise any suspicions I was going to let HARV hover me onto the barge to the prison.

"Uh-oh," HARV said, "you have a call coming in from Desma."

"Patch her through in 2-D over my wrist communicator," I said.

Desma's face appeared on the screen. She looked different than I had ever seen her, her eyes were half shut and her hair looked like her cats had just finished playing with it.

"Is that you, cos?" I asked.

She blinked her eyes a couple of times as if she was using sheer willpower to force them to open wider. She failed. She put her arms down on her desk and dropped her head into them. She looked up.

"I think that little bitch Elena put the mind thingy on me . . ." she moaned.

"The mind thingy?"

Desma yawned, but only her mouth moved. It was weird. I had never seen my cousin in such disarray. "She picked your home address out of my mind, then put me under." She clinched her fist. "Oh, so much for psi unity . . ."

"She just wanted to warn me about Boris Sputnik," I said.

"Well, I need to warn you about her warning you about him . . ." Desma said. I could almost see the room spinning around her. "I need to tell you . . ."

She stopped talking and gazed into the screen.

After a couple of moments of strange silence, I prompted, "Tell me?"

"Oh, I thought it was your turn to talk. I didn't want to be rude," Desma said.

"Tell me what?" I asked.

She stared up at the ceiling and smiled. "I have pretty ceilings."

"Yes, but what about Elena?" I asked.

Desma turned her attention back to me. "You can't really trust her. She hates Sputnik." Desma smiled. "Sput-nik, sput-nik, spuut-niik, that's a funny word, sput-nick. Must be Greek."

"It's Russian," I said.

Desma looked at me like I was guru on top of the mountain. She smacked herself on top of the head. "That's right, Russian! You're so smart. That's why she hates him—she believes he betrayed Mother Russia."

Elena wouldn't be the only Russian to feel that way. Many thought once Sputnik took over the Moon he basically laid down and died and let the Chinese and Americans do most of the work and gather all the glory.

"A lot of Russians think Sputnik dropped the ball," I said.

Desma was now looking at her hand moving up and down. "Yeah, well, I only know I get weird, freaky, far-out vibes from her . . ."

"I don't see her as the mass murder type."

Desma smiled at me through the screen. "Cos, she's a beautiful woman. Even if she wasn't an ultra-powerful psi, you wouldn't see her as a murderer until a few minutes after she stabbed you in the heart." She paused, then added, "Nothing personal, but you're a sap." She looked up at the screen. "Now if you don't mind I'm going back to sleep."

Desma dropped her head to her desk. The screen went blank.

"Just great," HARV said, hands on hips (he was doing that a lot lately— it kind of reminded me of my mom when she's angry). "The more time we spend on the case the harder it gets to crack."

I ignored HARV and continued my way to the garage. I needed to talk to Shannon. I hoped that after our conversation I would be able to remove her from my list of suspects and I'd get some clue as to who the killer was.

Chapter 17

The New SF UltraMax Super Security prison was
housed on the island of Alcatraz. It was literally built
on top of the old prison. When it was decided that
the province of New Caly needed a new high-tech
prison, Alcatraz seemed to be the perfect spot. After
all, it was secluded and already housed a prison. Problem was some psychologists somewhere decided that
the old building was so ugly that prisoners couldn't
feel good about themselves unless they could feel
good about their prison. Therefore, it was decided to
upgrade the old prison.

After spending millions of credits on pre-prep-plans
and pre-plans, it was determined that it was technically
impossible to improve the old prison without spending
more than it would cost to build a brand new prison.
After a few years of debate between the World Council and Province Council it was decided that yes, they
would build a new prison on top of the old.

Everybody was happy with this except for the histo-
rians who claimed that the old prison was a classic

modern relic that shed insight on a rough time in human history and we couldn't destroy it without hurting ourselves. This sparked more debate, focus groups, and consulting firms. Finally, after years of study and billions of credits, the new facility was built on top of the old one and suspended in midair by hover disks. When all was said and done the government managed to build a five hundred million credit facility for roughly ten billion credits.

Probably the strangest result of all this politicking was that the facility was actually quite secure. You can only get to the island by boat. Once on the island, you can only get to the prison by taking a special elevator. The entire place was a no-teleport zone, which I had no problems with.

Carol met me at the boat dock for the ferry to Alcatraz. It was early evening and the ferry was crowded with security personnel from the night shift getting ready to go on duty. They were all dressed in white body armor from head to foot, giving them the appearance they were all cloned from the same well-built guy, even the ladies.

So far, between Carol's psi powers, HARV's holograms, and my sheer dumb luck, nobody had questioned that I was police captain Tony Rickey. I was hoping we'd be able to take advantage of the shift change and sneak in without too much hassle.

"Think like a cop," HARV said.

As the ferry crossed over to the prison I recited all the different types of donuts in my mind: crullers, cream-filled, jelly, chocolate . . .

The ferry docked and I followed the security personnel onto an automated ramp that led through a body scanner.

"Ah, HARV," I thought. *"Are you sure we'll get through the body scanner okay?"*

"Of course," HARV assured me. *"I've interacted with its software to offset the physical differences between you and Captain Rickey."*

"What about the Colt?" I asked.

"Do you mean your weapon or a young horse?" HARV asked.

"My weapon, of course."

"I assumed that, but I wanted to be sure. No problems, it's scanner cloaked," HARV said. I wasn't sure if that was still a bit of a bug in his programming or if it was an attempt to make a pun—a bad one.

"Are you sure?" I asked.

"Will be, in about 12 seconds . . ."

I held my breath as I scrolled through the tunnel-like body scanner. After I completed the pass, two of the guards pulled me to the side.

"Sorry, Captain Rickey," one of the stone-faced men said. "We need to frisk you."

"Frisk me?"

The other guard nodded. "Standard procedure for non-scheduled visitors."

I stepped off the ramp. One of the guards pointed to a table. "Arms out and spread 'em."

I placed my arms on the table. The second guard started patting me down, bottom to top. I fought back the urge to say, "Don't spend too much time in the middle." I've learned never to give the friskers a hard time.

When he reached my midsection he worked his way up my arm and stopped.

"What's up the arm?" he asked.

My only choice was to show them the Colt 2062 and hope to talk my way out of it. The Colt popped into my hand. I showed it to the guards without looking at it.

"Sweet," one of the guards said.

The other smiled and nodded.

I looked at the Colt. It looked like a good old-fashioned billy club. *"Holo-cover,"* HARV whispered in my brain.

"It's in case the subject doesn't fully cooperate," I said.

"Well, officially we have to frown on that," one of the guards said.

The two nudged each other like schoolboys on the playground. "Of course, unofficially . . ." The two winked at me. It was a bit off-putting, but I played along.

I pointed to Carol, "That's why I brought my own psi along. I plan to get the information any way I can."

The guys pointed to the elevator door. "Pass."

I moved into the elevator with Carol close behind me, along with five security personnel.

A message popped into my mind, *"I'm not talking because it's taking all of my focus to keep these guards from asking too many questions. They are wearing psi scramblers. I can't control them, but at least I can keep them from thinking very hard."*

"That was from Carol," HARV said in my brain.

"I know," I said out loud, without thinking.

"What do you know, Captain?" one of the guards asked.

I hesitated for a nano. "I know I won't have any problem getting a room to interrogate the prisoner."

"No, of course not," the guard said. He touched a button on his helmet. "Move Cannon to room 1A," he said into a mike. He waited for a nano. He smiled. "They're moving her now."

"Thanks," I told him. DOS, life is sure easier when the security squads are on your side.

The elevator came to a halt, the door opened, and I followed the guards out. The place was cold and sterile, yet not in a gloomy way. It was like some architect decided that mixing a mental hospital with a day-care center would yield the perfect jail. In a way, the look worked.

A couple of guards came up to me and saluted. A guy could get used to this.

"Don't get too used to this," HARV and Carol both said inside my head. DOS, they knew me well.

"We are here to escort you to the prisoner," one of the guards said clicking his feet when he was done.

"Lead the way," I said, pointing forward.

I followed the guards through the entryway and down a long cement corridor. They led me to a high-tech looking door with a slit in it.

I looked through the slot; Shannon was sitting at a table, her hands and feet wrapped in muscle inhibitor bands. She was also wearing a helmet covered in circuitry. My guess was it was the latest in psi-stopping hardware.

The guards punched a few numbers into a panel by the door.

"We're out here if you need us," one of the guards said.

The door opened. I entered the room. I looked up. There were cameras all around. This was going to be tricky.

Shannon's eyes narrowed when she saw me. "I already told you all I know, copper," she said.

I pointed at her, "Sit down and shut up," I shouted.

She looked up at me. "I already am sitting."

"Good, then just shut up," I said.

Shannon shot Carol an angry glance. "Why do you have the mind bitch with you?"

"None of your business," I said out loud. *"Carol, tell her who I am,"* I thought.

"She called me a bitch," Carol thought back to me.

"Carol," I thought. *"Focus, please."*

"Fine," she thought back. Carol locked her eyes with Shannon.

"She says if she had her powers we'd both be in trouble," Carol said for all to hear. *"She thinks it's a trick,"* Carol thought back to me.

"I need you to talk, no tricks!" I said, sitting across from her. *"Tell her not to worry, I'm not an ogre with a Vulcan nerve pinch,"* I thought.

"What?" Carol thought back.

"Just think it, Carol," I thought back. I knew Shannon would have been too ashamed of that incident to ever admit it to anybody else.

"She believes you," Carol mentally told me.

"Are you still claiming to be innocent?" I asked.

"I am innocent," Shannon said very loudly.

"She's thinking the same thing," Carol told me.

"Her heart rate and brain scan patterns say she's not lying," HARV said. *"Which if she wasn't a psi, would be telling, but in her case she may just be a perfect liar."*

"I don't believe you," I said out loud. *"I want to believe you,"* I thought.

Carol relayed the message. *"DOS,"* Carol said, holding her head. *"It's hard blasting through her inhibitor."*

"Is there anything else you can tell me?" I asked.

"I've been thinking long and hard about what happened," she said. "I think I've seen the tall blue-skinned woman who attacked them before with Sputnik's people."

"Sure you have," a very familiar voice said from behind us.

"Oh shit!" I turned and there stood the real captain Rickey, along with twenty guards.

"Zach, what am I going to do with you?" Tony asked. The hologram cloaking me faded away.

* * *

Tony and his men walked us out of the room. Tony was silent as they were escorting us out of the prison. Occasionally he'd look my way and just shake his head. It was one of the longer walks of my life.

We were on the barge back to the mainland when Tony spoke. He focused his concentration on Carol. "I expect this from Zach, but not you."

"Just doing my job," Carol said. That's my girl.

HARV appeared next to us, dressed in a formal suit and holding an old leather briefcase. "Actually, Officer Rickey, Carol did nothing wrong. There are no laws preventing somebody from causing somebody to think one person is somebody else, even an officer of the law."

I knew HARV was right. Thank Gates that our legal system has been so slow catching up with the advent of psis in society.

"Well, what Zach did had to be illegal," Tony said.

HARV rolled his eyes in disdain. It was a look usually reserved for me. "If you review all recordings, Zach never claimed he was you. He can't help what other people assume."

Tony scratched his head. "Even if I was buying this, Zach still didn't have to play along."

"Zach didn't have any control," HARV said. "I was trying to get him in trouble, so I forced him to wear that hologram."

"Why would you do that?" Tony asked.

"I was just testing Zach to see how he'd react." HARV held out his arms. "So I'm the guilty one, take me away!" he said dramatically.

I was secure in the knowledge that the intelligent machine and hologram laws were even more outdated than the psi laws.

Tony focused on me. "I have to admit they are loyal."

"That because they know I'm right."

"Even if he wasn't right, he has the law on his side," HARV added.

Tony groaned. Now he was finally getting to see why HARV is an acronym for Highly Annoying Really Verbal. "That still gives you no right to impersonate a police officer."

"I was testing the system," I said quickly.

"That's your defense, Zach?"

"For now." I took a breath to figure out how I wanted to run with this. Tony was one of my oldest friends, but I wasn't about to go to jail over this, especially when I knew I was right. "What will the media say when they learn that a simple dick easily got into a high security prison? Besides she is innocent."

Tony looked up at the sky, apparently looking for some sort of inspiration, or maybe just for patience. "What makes you think she's innocent? The fact that she's a hot blonde with big breasts?"

"Well that doesn't hurt," I said. "But I don't get the guilty vibe from her?"

"The guilty vibe?" Tony asked. I heard a few of his men scoffing in the background.

I know it sounded a bit crazy, but truth was, you don't survive as long as I have doing what I do unless you can sense the good guys, the bad guys, and the ones in between. It's a gift I have and part of the reason why I still have my original legs and organs.

"Zach thinks he's gifted with a special P.I. sense, like Spiderman," HARV said.

"It's true," Carol added, with a slight groan.

Tony put his hand to his forehead. "I know. But 'Zach thinks she's innocent' won't hold up in court. DMV, many judges would give her the chair based on that alone."

"I've always wondered what DMV stands for and why it's used as a curse word." Carol said.

"You could research it," HARV said.

"I don't wonder that hard."

HARV pointed at me. "I'm sure he knows."

Carol rolled her eyes. "I'm sure he does too, but I don't want a twenty minute dissertation about how great things were in the old days."

"DMV really doesn't roll off the tongue, but I don't like to say *hell* in mixed company," Tony said. "I've heard it's quite fitting."

"Guys, can we please get back to the case?" I pleaded.

"Oh, that's right, I'm thinking about arresting you," Tony said.

"Not *that* part of the case," I said. "Let's talk about Shannon being innocent. You heard her say she thinks the killer was a Mooner."

"Of course she says that. Our profilers have concluded that she was seeing her own image as a way to justify the crime she was committing," Tony said.

"And you think I'm the one who's wacko," I said.

Tony started to turn red; he does that a lot, mostly when I'm around. "Listen, Zach, I'm getting a lot of heat on this one. My bosses want this case wrapped up. Unless you can give me something legit to go on, I'm considering it wrapped up."

"Excuse me," HARV said. "I have an incoming call from Dr. Pool."

"Not now, HARV, I'm busy tying to avoid being arrested by my best friend," I said.

"Zach, friends don't use holograms to impersonate friends and break into high security prisons."

"You should write that on a holo-card," I said.

Tony turned brighter red. "That does it . . ."

HARV appeared between us. "I think you both better shut up and listen."

HARV's image morphed into Randy's in his lab.

"Hi, Zach! Hi, Tony," he said. "How come I never get to go on the cool boat trips?"

"Randy, I'm about to be arrested here," I said.

Randy's eyes focused. He started looking around

the room. "Now what was I going to say?" he frowned.

"You tested the video from the council chambers," HARV hinted.

Randy's frown morphed into a smile. "Ah, the video. I ran it through many, many, many more filters."

He paused, either for effect or because he forgot what he was going to say. Either way, it was annoying.

"And?" I prompted.

"Oh, yes, I've concluded a body did appear in the room right before the cameras went dead. The body was cloaked and out of phase but I did some magnetic shifting to get a rough image."

Randy's image morphed to the setting of the council chambers. It was filled with busy workers moving to and fro. There was a crack of energy in the middle of the room. That energy took the shape of a tall, shapely woman. Then everything went black.

"See," Randy said, proudly.

"How do we know that wasn't Cannon?" Tony said like a dog with a bone.

"I have video of her in the bathroom at the time. They have cameras everywhere in that building," Randy said.

"How do we know it wasn't a hologram?" Tony asked.

"She left a deposit in the bathroom's, ah, human waste disposal device," Randy said.

"And you know this how?" I asked.

"They save EVERYTHING in that building," Randy said. "I did an analysis on her, well, deposit and it was hers. Shannon Cannon was definitely in the bathroom when the attack started."

"How come your people don't know about the poop?" I asked Tony.

He shook his head. "When a case looks like such a

slam dunk we don't poke around toilets, Zach," he said, a bit more defensively than he probably hoped.

"Come on, Tony," I coaxed. "Even you have to see there is another possible suspect here."

Tony just stood there.

"Superpowered, female, and tall . . . Sounds like it could be a Mooner," I said.

"Sounds like it could be Elena," HARV said in my brain.

Tony put both hands on his head and started to squeeze. "Damn, DOS, damn, DOS," he said. When Tony got angry he sometimes reverted to old-fashioned swearing. "Goddamn, this is not going to be easy. It's going to take me at least twenty-four hours to get clearance just to consider being allowed to talk to them."

"So I'm free to go?" I said.

Tony just glared at me. I had made his job much harder. But we both knew I had done the right thing. Now it was his turn.

"You're under house arrest for at least forty-eight hours," Tony said.

Considering the circumstances, I couldn't complain.

Tony turned to Carol. "It's your job to watch him. Make sure he stays clean."

"I have a date tonight," Carol protested.

"Not if you're in jail," Tony said.

Okay, so now I had both Tony and Carol angry with me but I was free from jail. There was also the first break on the case. I had to consider that a good thing.

Chapter 18

After Carol broke her date, she and I drove to my house in my car. Her car followed us home on auto-pilot.

I was glad Tony had let me off the hook, at least for now. I was also happy that there was a now a good chance that Shannon Cannon was innocent. I don't know why I cared but I did.

I was even happier that Carol had forgiven me for breaking up her date. Turned out she wasn't that thrilled with the guy to begin with. He had begged her to go out with him. It was only the first date and the poor sucker had no idea she was a psi. She was sure that once he found out, he'd go from being infatuated with her to being terrified of her. Melt one ex-boyfriend's car and it kind of sticks with you for a while.

With Electra on the Moon, Carol and I planned a nice, quiet evening of take-out Chinese and watching old credit-for-view movies in 2-D, the way they were meant to be viewed. We watched *The Princess Bride*.

I had to explain some of the humor to Carol but all in all, I believe she enjoyed it.

We watched, ate, and talked into the evening. It was nice to be able to just hang out without having to worry about work or saving the world. Midnight came and we both hit the sack. All might not have been perfect with the world, but I had opened up the police's eyes to Shannon being innocent. Plus nobody was trying to kill me, so I was content.

The peace and tranquility that had become my life lasted until 3 A.M.

"Tió, wake up," Carol said shaking me from my bed.

I shot up to a sitting position. I went for the good old-fashioned Colt .44 I keep under the mattress.

"What is it? Somebody breaking in?"

"No, of course not," Carol said. "I could handle that."

"In that case, what are you doing in my bedroom, at . . ."

"3:02:54 A.M.," HARV said.

"At 3:02 A.M.," I said.

"It's now 3:03," HARV corrected.

Carol pulled me out of bed, not seeming to mind or notice that I was only in my boxers. (I guess I should have been happy that this was one of the nights I decided against sleeping in my birthday suit.) "We have to go, now, before they get away," Carol said. She pointed to my closet and a shirt and pair of pants floated out.

"Carol, what are you talking about?" I demanded.

"The assembly from the Moon is leaving," she said.

"They can't leave—Tony is getting a search warrant," I said.

Carol shook her head. "They are leaving before it's issued."

"They can do that?"

"They have interplanetary immunity," HARV said. "They can come and go as they please."

"How are we supposed to stop them then?" I asked.

Carol handed me my shirt, "We're not going to stop them. We're going to follow them."

"To the Moon?" I said.

"Think of it as a way to visit Aunt Electra," Carol said.

In my years of working with Carol I've never seen her this worked up, and that includes the time when she turned into a superpsi and almost destroyed the world herself. Even if I didn't want to go, I knew I had to. Not just for Carol, but for the world. Something wasn't sitting right with this Moon crowd and I needed to get to the bottom of it.

"How do you know everything isn't kosher?" I asked, though deep down I could feel it, too.

"Some Mooner psi named Elena. She's so powerful, her mental SOS is ripping through my defenses like a laser through butter." Carol grabbed me by the arm. "We have to get to the shuttle port and get on that flight to the Moon."

HARV appeared. "That won't be easy. Due to the conference and the incident, the Moon is closed to all outsiders."

"We'll worry about those details when we get there," Carol said.

HARV looked at me. "She's been hanging around you too long."

"Give me three minutes to change," I said.

"I'll give you two," she replied.

I got dressed and Carol and I headed over to the shuttle port. As we drove through the night we made our plans on how to get on the shuttle. My cover was that I missed my girlfriend Electra and wanted to see her. Carol's was she had an urge to visit and interact with the psis on the Moon.

We figured they probably wouldn't be too keen with a couple of last minute Earthers tagging along. We had a plan of action for that, too. We'd complain and make a fuss, a really loud fuss. Chances were, the Moon delegation wanted to make a quiet and hasty retreat. They weren't going to hassle us that much. I surmised that they would rather let us on the flight than risk slowing down the flight. My logic being that their logic would be that once they had us on their turf, the Moon, they could control us better.

"So that's the extent of your plan, to whine like girls until they let you on the shuttle?" HARV said after I filled him in.

"Hey, I *am* a girl," Carol said.

"I'm pointing most of my criticism at Zach," HARV said.

"I'm betting anything it will get us on that shuttle," I said.

"Yeah, but what then?" HARV asked. "What happens when we get to the Moon?"

"The plan is still forming in my mind," I said.

HARV exhaled and rolled his eyes (literally 360 degrees). "The sad thing is," HARV sighed, "this is actually one of your more elaborate plans."

The shuttle port, like most of the newer buildings, was a tall dome that sat on the outskirts of town where the airport used to be. The shuttle port also doubled as a central public teleporting area. It was kind of interesting how New Frisco was the only place on Earth that had a combined shuttle / teleport port. How did New Frisco become a city of power in the world?

Back in the old days, the early 2000s, Frisco was considered a nice artsy and trendy (i.e. expensive) city, but it always took a backseat to other major cities when it came to actually getting work done. Then, after 2022, when the aliens first landed on Earth, Frisco became a booming center of not just art but commerce and science and government. I wasn't really sure why. After all, the aliens landed in Kansas. Yet somehow after the aliens revealed themselves to us, Frisco boomed.

HARV had a couple of theories about this, which shouldn't be surprising as HARV has at least a couple of theories about everything. I guess when all you do is think all day it leaves you a lot of time to come up with ideas.

HARV's theory on Frisco was actually two pronged: First the aliens had a lot of scouts in Frisco posing as humans. HARV surmised that aliens (being intelligent as they were) tended to be drawn to the artistic nature of early Frisco. The other part of the theory dealt with the human aspect. The same qualities that attracted the aliens to Frisco were many of the same that attracted a large gay community to the area. HARV had concluded (and had some stats to back him up) that gay people get more things done than straight people. HARV attributed this to the fact that gay couples almost always have fewer children than straight couples, and therefore they are less tired and less distracted. As HARV put it, conceiving children through sex is a lot more fun and less time consuming than going through courtrooms and adopting. So heterosexual couples would naturally have more children in the short run which in turn would tire them out more in the long run. Thus, it was only natural that Frisco would excel in this brave new world.

I wasn't sure I agreed with HARV. I enjoyed arguing with him, though. It kept my brain fresh. I did have to admit though, he may have had a point.

We got to the shuttle port, parked the car, and headed inside. The place was fairly empty. A quick glance around the desk area showed that for every Earther manning a position, there was a corresponding Mooner. An Earther and a Mooner at the check-in desk. An Earther and Mooner (and a really big guardbot) patrolling the door to the flight area.

HARV informed me that we had actually beaten Sputnik and his entourage to the check-in area. They had just pulled into the parking garage and were at least three minutes behind us. That's one of the advantages of traveling without an entourage (or luggage): you can move faster.

I walked up to the ticket counter. The Earther employee greeted me. She was a small, older woman with her hair done in an old-fashioned bun. She looked out of place in a shuttle port to the Moon.

"Good evening, sir," she said with a kind smile. "Welcome to the shuttle port, the fastest, most efficient, and only way to go to the Moon."

"Nice motto," I said.

"Do you have a reservation?" the lady with a bun asked.

"I have a lot of reservations," I replied. "Space travel seems so sci-fi-ish."

She smiled at me. "Shuttle trips to the Moon are perfectly safe," she said smile never leaving her face.

"I'd like two tickets for the 6 A.M. flight please," I said.

The woman passed her hand over her control screen. "Very good sir, I'll just need your and your traveling companion's DNA scans."

The employee held up a thumb scanner for me. I placed my thumb on it. A 3-D image of myself appeared above the lady's control panel.

"Ah, Zachary Nixon Johnson," the lady said. "It appears you have enough credits to purchase this trip."

The Mooner employee looked over at my image.

She looked at me. She was a short, middle-aged Asian-looking woman. "I'm sorry Mr. Johnson," she said. "That flight is full."

The Earther worker punched a few buttons on her display. "Ah, no . . ."

The Mooner looked into her eyes. The Earth woman's eyes glazed over. "Oops, my big boo-boo," she said. "That flight is full."

I heard the message "the flight is full, go home now," in my brain. I ignored it.

Carol, on the other hand, didn't. She leaned forward. "You're going to have to do better than that," she said, directing her comment at the Mooner.

My image floating about the screen morphed into HARV's. He pointed at the Mooner woman. "I'm Mr. Johnson's personal computer aide," he said. "I have analyzed your reservations. The shuttle holds four hundred passengers and you have only booked ninety-nine spaces." HARV's image morphed to a layout of the inside of the shuttle cabin. Each of the empty seats was glowing and flashing "available."

HARV leaned over like he was reading the Moon lady's name tag. "Now, Miss Osborne, that would mean that there are actually three hundred and one seats available. Being a supercomputer I'm quite good at math."

Miss Osborne was a bit taken aback. She obviously wasn't used to having her mental commands rebuffed or arguing with a holographic supercomputer. By this time, I noticed Sputnik and his entourage had entered the building. That meant it was showtime.

"Have you done the e-paperwork needed to make the trip to the Moon?" Miss Osborne asked.

She was grasping at random bits and she knew it. She was just hoping that we didn't know it. Of course, we knew that Earthers needed no paperwork to go to the Moon. It was totally open to all of us. It was quite a source of contention with Mooners that they needed to be cleared to come to Earth, yet any joe could go there. Even if I didn't have HARV hooked to my brain I would have known this. Osborne must have known we knew this, but she had to try.

"Ah, yes, good point," she said, putting a finger in her collar to loosen it. "I forgot the Earth to Moon equality act hasn't passed council yet."

"Sputnik is watching," HARV said in my head. That meant it was time to really pour it on.

I pounded on the desk. "Listen, I am a tax-paying citizen of Earth," I shouted. "Not only that, a couple of days ago I was a famous spokesperson. I demand to be let aboard this flight!"

I paused for a nano to weigh the crowd's reaction. There wasn't much yet so I pushed some more.

"Perhaps I should call my friends in the media? I'm sure *World Right Now*, *Instant Buzz*, and *News 2 Know* would love to hear about this!" I ranted. "Maybe I'll call my good buddy, Captain Tony Rickey of the New Frisco police force. I'm sure he'd love to hear about this abuse of my citizen of Earth rights."

This caught Sputnik's attention. He whispered something into the ears of his traveling companions. Just then I realized his entourage was made up almost totally of females. Out of the ninety-or-so members of his party, only four of them were males. It was mostly a blue-haired, Asian-seeming harem. I noticed Melda was directly behind Sputnik, along with another woman who looked like a younger version of Melda.

Sputnik moved forward. He was average height but quite stocky. His hair was blond with streaks of gray and blue, eyes a steely gray, but nothing very notable about his face except for his handlebar mustache and his goatee. He looked like a cross between a game show host, used hover salesman, and coffeehouse poet.

He held out his hand to me. "Why Mr. Johnson, how nice to finally meet," he said.

"He is so lying," HARV and Carol both said inside my brain, though I didn't need their kibitzing in this case.

"The pleasure is all mine," I said.

"Gee, Zach, you could at least try to lie better," both HARV and Carol said in my brain.

Sputnik released my hand. I fought back the urge to wipe my hand on the side of my pants. "So, Mr. Johnson . . ."

"Call me Zach," I said, trying to play nice.

"So, Mr. Johnson," he continued. "Why do you wish to go the Moon?"

"Always wanted to go there. Never had the time. I figure now's the time, with my girlfriend there for this conference."

Sputnik looked at me for a moment. One of his companions whispered something into his ear. He smiled.

"Ah, yes, the lovely Electra Gevada, she is attending the ARC conference. I plan on addressing them tomorrow," Sputnik said.

"I'll give Electra your regards then," I said.

"Really, Mr. Johnson, wouldn't you prefer to visit our lovely Moon at a much less busy time?" Sputnik asked.

"Nope."

Melda moved forward with the younger version of herself trailing just behind.

"Mr. Johnson, how nice to meet again," she said.

Sputnik shot her a glance. It was subtle look but I caught it nonetheless. He didn't know that I had had contact with Melda before. He wasn't happy. I just wasn't sure if he was upset about the meeting or the not knowing.

Melda focused her attention on Sputnik. "Dear, Mr. Johnson and I met while I was working on a project with Dr. Pool. Zach and Dr. Pool are old friends. Zach saved us from a couple of plants. We didn't need saving but it was a bold gesture anyhow."

"Yes, I'm in constant contact with Randy as well as my good buddy, Captain Tony Rickey."

Melda locked eyes with Sputnik. There was some silence—she was sending him a mental message.

"Perhaps you would like my computer to call them now?" I offered. "I'm sure they'd love to talk to you, Mr. Sputnik." I pushed a button on my wrist communicator and HARV appeared before Sputnik and Melda.

"I would gladly make the connections," HARV said.

"This is Mr. Johnson's personal holographic assistant," Melda told Sputnik. "He is very advanced."

"Yes, I am constantly on and nearly impossible to override," HARV bragged. Normally I'm not a big fan of HARV tooting his own horn, but in this case it helped make sure that Sputnik and his ladies didn't try anything.

Sputnik broke his eye contact with Melda. He turned toward me then walked past me and around HARV to stand directly in front of Ms. Osborne. "Give Mr. Johnson and his lovely traveling companion Ms. Gevada a complimentary flight on my account," he said.

Ms. Osborne lowered her eyes and looked at her control panel. "Of course." She touched a couple of buttons.

I turned my attention to Sputnik. "So, you know Carol?" I said.

Sputnik grinned slightly and touched Carol on the cheek. "Of course. We on the Moon are very interested in psionic individuals. My people tell me she is in the top 2 percent of Earth psis. Very impressive."

"Thanks," Carol said. "More like the top 1 percent of psis," she corrected.

"More like the top 5 percent if you count the Moon," the younger woman traveling with Sputnik noted.

Sputnik turned and smiled. This was a true smile, not a crocodilian political one. He held out his hand. The girl approached. She was slightly shorter than Melda but no less stunning; you could tell the two were either related or commonly cloned.

"Mr. Johnson, Ms. Gevada, I'd like you to meet my daughter Lea," Sputnik said.

Interesting . . . I was sure Melda was the mother, but Sputnik wasn't giving her any recognition. *"Typical human male,"* HARV ranted inside my brain. *"Takes credit for everything."*

Lea moved past me as if I wasn't there. She was intent on making her point to Carol. "On the Moon we psis are allowed—no *encouraged*—to practice openly. It lets our powers flourish. You'll like it there," she said to Carol.

I wasn't sure if that was a statement or an order.

"My daughter is quite spirited and quite a promoter of our cause," Sputnik couldn't have been glowing anymore if he had just swallowed uranium.

Lea took a step back, now focusing on me. She held out her hand up to my face. I assumed she wanted me to kiss it so I did.

"You will like the Moon also," she said, though this time it was more of a command. She looked up at me. *"Just don't stay too long or cause any problems,"* she said without moving her lips.

Her words passed right through my mental defenses directly into my subconscious. Before they could sink their claws in though another voice rang through. *"Don't listen to the little false princess,"* the voice said. *"She's so conditioned by her father she can't tell her ass from a donkey."* The voice was familiar. It was Elena.

I looked up through the crowd of Mooners. Sure enough, Elena was bringing up the back of the line, just behind two gorillas carrying luggage.

"Don't fret, I'm sure I'll enjoy my stay," I said.

I gave a polite tip of my fedora to Sputnik and his ladies. With that, Carol and I headed toward security so we could board the shuttle.

Security was going to be the next obstacle. After all, I was traveling with a weapon up my sleeve. Sure it was a very hard to detect weapon. Plus HARV assured me that security to the Moon was extremely low. For some reason Earth Gov didn't feel the need to provide a lot of security. Still, I hadn't exactly made a lot of friends here and I thought security (being Mooners) would be tough on me.

I walked up to the door leading to the concourse. A blue-clad security guard, a big box of a man, stepped out in front of me. "Are you traveling with any weapons?" he asked. He was flanked by a large guardbot on his left and another tall, older Mooner lady on his right. Her blue hair almost blended in with her uniform.

My first instincts were to lie. I fought back that urge. I popped the Colt into my hand. "I'm carrying this," I said. "I have a license to carry a weapon."

"Sweet," the male guard said, waving a scanner up and down my body. He looked at the screen on the scanner. "According to this, yes, you are registered to carry a weapon. Which means you may carry just one weapon on the Moon." He looked at the screen and frowned. "Also, according to this, you've been known to carry a knife and an old-fashioned fire arm in ankle holsters."

"I dressed in a hurry. No time to bring all my usual equipment," I said.

The guardbot extended a clawlike arm and started patting me down from my hips to my feet.

"Careful around the midsection," I told it.

After a significant pat down the guardbot retracted its hand announcing, "He's clean."

"I hope your claw was," I told it.

It growled at me. I get that a lot from guardbots.

"You may pass," the human guard said.

I walked by him. I turned and waited for Carol.

The guard stepped in front of her. "Do you have any weapons to declare?"

Carol put a hand on her chest. "Please," she said with just the right amount of disdain. "I'm a powerful psi. My mind is my weapon. I could tell you all to drop dead at my feet and you would gladly do so."

The guard, the psi, and even the bot all gulped.

"Pass, friend," the guard said.

Carol passed by the guard. We walked down the tunnel to the concourse together. Carol looked at me and winked. *"I'll give you your backup gun and knife when we get to the Moon,"* she said in my head.

I was just glad she was on my side.

Chapter 19

The Moon shuttle group was very efficient. They didn't keep us in the waiting area for more than ten minutes before they boarded us on the shuttle.

The shuttle itself reminded me of the old airplanes I used to ride as a kid, only a bit wider and the chairs seemed a lot more comfortable. The cabin was broken into two areas: a first class zone in the front that held 50 people and a regular class zone that held the remaining 350 people (though the allotted area was no bigger than first class). Where first class had twenty-five rows of big, comfy seats side by side, regular class had seventy rows of little seats two on one side of the aisle and three on the other.

Carol and I were given the two seats farthest away from first class. The only good things about them was that they were near the bathroom and that there was nobody sitting between us. So at least we could stretch out a little.

It didn't take long for the rest of the passengers to settle into their seats. It took even less time for Carol,

HARV, and me to deduce that Carol and I were the only two Earthers on this flight.

Sputnik and his main entourage sat in the first class section. The gorilla baggage carriers and rest of the Mooners, including Elena, were spread throughout the remaining section of the shuttle. You could almost see daggers shooting from Elena's eyes as she looked at Sputnik. Though her assigned seat was near the front of the cabin, she came back and sat near Carol and me. She didn't talk to us but I had the distinct feeling that she wanted to.

The robot pilot came on the intercom informing everybody that the flight to the Moon would be five hours, that we might expect a little choppiness leaving Earth's atmosphere, but after that it expected clear sailing to the Moon. The hostessbots would be serving drinks and breakfast once we reached the ionosphere. I wasn't all that thrilled with flying through space, but at least there'd be food.

The shuttle was a strange beast. It took up off the ground vertically like a regular hovercraft. Unlike a hover, though, the shuttle rose until it reached five miles above the Earth. As we climbed, I looked down on New Frisco, watching it grow smaller and smaller. From this high up the city, lit by the rising sun, looked blurred, kind of like a hastily made quilt.

Once the shuttle reached optimal height it stopped its complete vertical assent.

The pilot's robotic voice came over the com, "Passengers prepare for acceleration boost."

I held onto my seat. Not sure why, but it seemed like the thing to do. Rocking forward, I felt the speed increasing faster and faster. The shuttle shuddered. I kind of liked the speed, kind of hated the shuddering. I glanced over at Carol who was looking at me. Carol was loving this burst of acceleration.

Carol touched me on the hand, "Don't worry, we'll be fine," she said. "Once we break out of the gravitational pull of the Earth you won't even notice the speed."

I sat back and closed my eyes. Not much else to do really. Just relax my mind. I said to myself.

"Just relax your mind," Carol said inside my mind.

"Don't be a baby," HARV said inside my mind.

"Relax," another voice said—yes, inside my mind. I thought it was Elena's.

I opened my eyes and peeked over at Elena sitting across the aisle from Carol. She was sitting on her seat in the lotus position like psis like to do. She seemed calm, like she didn't have a worry in the world. That worried me.

After a few minutes, which seemed a lot longer, the jittering stopped. The ride became smooth. It was as if we were gliding on virgin ice. I looked out the window. I could see the Earth growing smaller and smaller. It made me feel small, but in a good way, like I was part of something bigger than I was. (Space travel must bring out my poetic side.)

The pilot informed us that we were now in space and we would be traveling at an average speed of sixty thousand kilometers an hour, which meant we'd be at the Moon in less than six hours. Jules Verne would have been so jealous.

"We have reached cruising speed," the pilot informed us. "The servingbots will be around shortly to serve drinks and a delicious breakfast."

I sat back in my chair, at least as back as I was able, considering we were in the last row and my chair didn't recline all that much. I decided to relax and enjoy the flight. Not much I could do here on the shuttle.

"Zach, close your eyes now," HARV ordered inside my head.

"Why?"

"Just do it, Zach!"

Against my better judgment I took HARV's advice. I closed my eyes.

"Droop your head, like you are sleeping," HARV said.

I did.

"Now drool a little," HARV coached.

"I don't drool!" I shot back in my brain.

"Should I play video proof in your mind?" HARV asked.

"I can pretend sleep without pretend drooling," I said.

"A true method actor would drool," HARV said.

I thought about drooling for a nano and decided against it—tough guys don't drool. I curled back in my seat. *"Why am I feigning sleep?"* I asked.

"Because Elena is sending out messages to everybody else on the shuttle to sleep."

"Why is she doing that?" I asked.

"Who knows? She's the mindreader not me," HARV said. *"But by fake sleeping we'll be able to discover why. Even with your eyes closed I can still watch her through your wrist com and the shuttle's computer system, then I can relay the images to your brain."*

The images of everybody else on the plane scrolled through my brain. Sure enough, they were all sound asleep, except for Elena.

"Why aren't I napping like the rest of them?" I asked HARV.

"Elena is broadcasting on a very wide, but unique, mental frequency. So I am able to block her out for now. You have to be careful though. If she focused her concentration on you you'd be out colder than a flounder on ice."

"How was Elena able to catch the other psis off guard?" I asked.

"My guess is that psis find space relaxing, therefore

none of them feel threatened up here and they all relaxed their defenses."

"HARV, you're a computer—you're supposed to know, not guess."

HARV made a raspberry sound in my brain. My guess was space does weird things to intelligent cognitive systems also.

I watched in my mind as Elena stood up. The blouse she was wearing had a long sleeve on one side and no sleeve on the other. Reaching up the long sleeve, she pulled out a sharp metal object.

I made my move. I had surprise on my side. Leaping up, I lunged across Carol, grabbing Elena's knife hand with my right hand. Moving my body forward, I pulled her arm back toward me, catching her totally off guard. I drove her to the ground keeping my weight on top of her all the while and locking her right arm behind her back. Popping my Colt 2062 into my left hand I forced the barrel behind her head.

"I don't want to kill you but move and you're dead," I growled.

Elena wasn't the type of girl who was used to being on the bottom and out of control. She started to squirm. I pressed down harder on her.

"I'll repeat it just once more. I don't want to hurt you," I warned.

"That's not going to be a problem," was the reply in my head.

I went flying off of Elena, crashing into the back wall of the shuttle. I crumbled to the ground.

"What did I tell you about not letting her focus on you?" HARV scolded from my brain.

I needed to react fast. I started pushing myself up off the ground. I felt a spiked boot on my back, forcing me back to the ground. I fought it. I lost. I collapsed back to the ground under the weight of that boot; it felt like a metric ton holding me in place.

"She's not just using the boot, she's also using her telekinetic powers," HARV told me.

"Thanks, Captain Obvious," I said.

"No need to get snotty just because some psi is about to wipe the floor and ceiling with you," HARV said.

"The computer in your brain is correct and will no longer be able to help you," Elena said inside my head.

I tried to look up. I couldn't.

"You may look at me," she said.

I moved my head up. Elena was towering over me, holding my Colt 2062 in her hand. That was my chance. *"GUS, shock her good!"* I shouted in my mind.

Nothing happened.

"Elena is blocking your mental link with GUS," HARV said.

No big deal, that was easy to remedy. "GUS, shock her!" I shouted.

"Gotcha! And with pleasure!" GUS responded from Elena's hand.

This tipped Elena off. She quickly opened her hand, letting GUS drop to the ground. DOS! I knew the talking gun thing would come back to bite me in the ass. But all wasn't lost yet. Moving forward just enough to catch the falling Colt/GUS, I grabbed it and aimed. I had Elena locked in my sights. I didn't fire. I couldn't blow her away. I wasn't sure she was the real bad guy here.

Recalling my football days from high school, I flung myself off the ground toward Elena. I hit her low, right below the knees, forcing her to the ground again. The tackle was so smooth it would have made my old coach regret never starting me in a game. Of course, I had to admit Elena was more pleasant to grapple with than 120-kilo running backs.

"I've noticed that you like to wrestle more with beautiful woman than you do big, ugly, guy thugs," HARV said.

Ignoring HARV, I slid up Elena's body using my extra mass to keep her under control. Curling my fingers into a fist, I prepared to clobber her. Spinning her toward me I raised my fist. We locked eyes. I hesitated; not because she had beautiful, emerald green eyes that went on and on like a rolling field on a late spring day—which she did. It wasn't their beauty that stunned me, but their innocence.

"Oh, that was a such a mistake," HARV said.

I didn't care. A pleasant, warming sensation swept over my body. I smiled. My fist relaxed. I let myself slide slowly off of her, relishing the contact I had with her, while at the same time being careful not to harm her. I couldn't harm her now if I wanted to. I rolled off, lying contently at her feet. I knew it wasn't right but I didn't care.

Rising to a knee, Elena leaned toward me and patted me on the head. "You could have hurt me but you didn't," she said. "For that, I'm letting you live."

She began rubbing my shoulders. "Join the others in sleep while I finish my business here," she ordered.

I yawned. My eyes were so heavy now. I didn't want to stay awake. I didn't want to be in her way. "HARV, it's up to you," I said, with my last ounce of strength.

"Was there every any doubt?" HARV said, appearing from my eyes lens. HARV flickered as I closed my eyes. The last thing I noticed was him shaking his head.

I woke up. I was in my seat. The servingbots were rolling down the aisles with trays of food. I noticed Elena was now sitting next to me. Carol was in Elena's seat sound asleep, snoring away. Everybody else on the shuttle was wide awake and blissfully unaware of what had transpired. I looked at Elena. She touched my hand lightly.

"Your computer convinced me to talk to you," she said without moving her lips.

"You can thank me later," HARV said.

"So why do you want to off Sputnik?" I asked.

Elena stared at me blankly with those bright green eyes.

"Why do you want him dead?" I asked. DOS, someday I was going to find somebody who understood P.I. talk. *"Desma said you hate him because he betrayed your motherland."*

Elena gave me a cynical smile. *"He may have, but I hate him because he betrayed my mother and father."*

"How so?"

"I believe he killed my father to get to my mother to get to me," she said. Her thoughts sent a chill up my spine.

HARV flashed the video report of Elena's dad being killed in a hover crash across my eyes. The headline read: LEADING SCIENTIST DIES IN TRAGIC HOVER ACCIDENT.

"The headlines say," I started.

"I know what they say," she interrupted, *"but he did it."*

"To get to you," I said.

She nodded. *"He still hasn't given up hope on me yet. He wants to turn me to his side. He's even talked about adopting me. Being Head Administrator on the Moon, it's within his right. He can do whatever he pleases."*

"What happened to your mother?" I asked.

"She's dead," was all Elena would say.

"I have no proof of Elena's mother's death; in fact I have no record of her," HARV said. *"But I do have video of Elena in action."*

HARV rolled the video in my mind, this one of a younger looking Elena sitting in an open field on the Moon, sniffing a flower. The words *Elena Power Test* scrolled across my eyes. The younger Elena seemed indifferent to the fact that three heavy tanks were rumbling toward her. The ground was trembling but she remained calm. The younger Elena looked up from her flower. The ground stopped shaking. The three tanks had been reduced to three piles of putty.

"Wow," I said.

Elena smiled ever so slightly. *"That was my sixteenth birthday. I've grown more powerful since then."*

I didn't blame Sputnik for wanting to control Elena. She had the potential to be a one-woman army.

"Now, why are you here, Zachary?" she asked, though it was really an order.

"I don't trust Sputnik either," I said. *"I am trying to figure out if he had anything to do with the murders at the World Council building."*

Elena frowned. *"I wouldn't put it past him."* She stood up and touched me on the shoulder. *"I will do both our worlds a favor by killing him."*

Taking her hand, I yanked her back down into her seat. She glared at me. *"You are so lucky I haven't reduced you to a pile of dust yet."*

"Yeah, well, here's the poop: I'm not a hundred percent sure he's guilty," I said.

"I am," she said. *"I can feel it in my heart."* She touched her chest, just in case I wasn't sure where her heart was.

"That doesn't hold up in a court of law," I said, sounding a lot more like HARV than I was frankly comfortable with.

"It can if I will it to," Elena said.

"So you can do whatever you please?"

"Yes," she said.

"Then how does that make you better than him?" I asked.

She sank back in her seat, her entire body almost blending in with the cushions. *"It doesn't . . ."*

"Then give me time to figure out what's going on,"

I said. (Though it was more of a plea.) I put my hand on my heart. *"Once I have proof Boris Sputnik is behind these attacks, I will personally bring him down."*

"Well, I am sure he's behind my parents' deaths," she said.

"Are you really?" I asked.

She looked at me, her eyes widened. A tear started down her cheek. *"I have no actual proof. He controls everything on the Moon and Melda and Lea are almost as powerful as I am."*

Wiping her tear away, I said, *"I'll look for proof of that, too. If he's diabolical enough to do one, he'd certainly be capable of the other. Something big is going down and I need to find out what it is. But I need more time."*

Elena held her head. *"For the greater good . . ."*

I put a finger under her chin and gently lifted her head up. *"Yes, for the greater good."*

"Fine," she agreed, arms crossed across her chest. *"I won't kill him yet."*

I smiled. *"That's all I ask."*

The rest of the time passed fairly smoothly. Elena woke Carol up. After Elena explained her cause, Carol offered to give her a foot rub if she wanted. (My guess was Carol was still feeling the effects of Elena's mental whammy.) Elena told Carol she'd keep the idea in mind, but for now, it probably wouldn't be such a hot idea to remove her boots as she had worked up a bit of sweat tussling with me.

Carol laughed it off, noting how her feet weren't always pleasant-smelling either. Elena insisted that was okay and encouraged Carol just to sit back in her seat and relax and enjoy the flight. Carol did so. Elena then admitted to me that she may have zapped Carol a bit too hard.

For the rest of the flight, Elena gave me her version

of life on the Moon. She made it clear that she loved the Moon. It was a wonderful home to the arts and sciences and a safe haven where psis could practice openly. People on the Moon weren't scared of psis like Earth folks. In fact, they relished them. They thought of the psis as their link to greatness.

Elena went on and on about the wonderful, almost utopian, atmosphere on the Moon. To Elena, the only thing holding the Moon back was Sputnik. HARV chimed in with something I had been thinking about in the back of my mind.

"You know, Zach," HARV said. *"I realize you like this girl, but surely you must realize she's still a prime suspect in the World Council killings? She has the power to pull it off. She might even try to set up Sputnik to kill two birds with one thought. Take out the people she sees as standing in the way of the Moon's independence and get the guy you blame for killing your parents caught. The Moon gets to go free and thrives."*

HARV had a point and I knew it. I had to consider Elena a person of interest. I was hoping she wasn't behind the murders at the World Council. For one, I liked her. For another, I didn't want to have to mess with her. The thing was I knew she was perfectly willing to execute Boris, which meant she was capable of killing (at least if she believed in her cause).

I wasn't sure what the best course of action was so I picked the most direct one. DickCo dicks may have time to beat around the bush and mug for the camera to draw an episode out, but I didn't. I didn't have a bunch of sponsors I had to please. I looked at Elena, into those big green eyes of hers. *"Did you kill those World Council members?"* I asked.

"Oh, great, Zach, way to not tip your cards," HARV said. *"If she doesn't kill you, let's start playing poker for money."*

"Do you think I'm some sort of lunatic?" Elena asked.

"I prefer not to answer that on the grounds I'm afraid you'll wilt me," I said.

"I should wilt you just for that accusation," Elena thought at me. *"Why would I kill council members I had never met and therefore had nothing against?"*

"They were going to vote against the Moon's independence," I told her. *"Maybe you thought you could tip the vote by knocking out three nays."*

Elena's eyes popped open. This wasn't a look of anger, but one of confusion. *"I was under the impression Sexy might vote correctly this time. Weathers had always been a friend of the Moon in the past,"* she said.

"Times change. People change," I said.

Elena stood up. I felt the air around me get warmer. She placed a purple, painted fingernail in my face. *"I would never kill anybody who didn't wrong me,"* she said softly but firmly. *"You are very lucky I think of us as kindred spirits or you'd be a smoldering pile of ashes right now."*

"Wow, your kindred spirit kept her from using you as kindling," HARV kidded.

"Shut up, HARV," I said. *"If anyone is going to make dumb puns in the face of death and danger, I prefer it to be me."*

Elena moved over and sat next to Carol. She propped her legs up on Carol. "I'll take that foot massage now," she said.

"Gladly," Carol said, peeling off Elena's purple boots.

"Make sure you aim my feet at your uncle," Elena said.

"Sure," Carol said, a bit meekly.

I slept through the rest of the flight.

Chapter 20

I was awakened by the robo-pilot's voice. "We are making our approach to the Moon now. Please return your seats to their upright positions and fasten your seat belts. We expect a smooth docking, because, well, um, there is no atmosphere to clash with, but our legal department insists we put that in."

Looking out the window, I saw the Moon coming fully into view. From this distance, I was able to see both the domed, colonized part and the native area. The former was lush and green; the latter was barren and brown. New and improved versus the way nature had intended. It was quite the contrast.

Carol returned to her seat next to me. She looked a little dazed but no worse for the wear.

"Nice to have you back," I said. "You are back?"

Carol nodded. "Yeah. Elena says you're going to need me now."

I rolled my eyes. (Apparently more HARV was rubbing off on me than I liked to believe.) "That's nice of her," I said without feeling.

Carol touched me on the shoulder. "Zach, she's a

good person. She's just torn by her bond to the Moon, her quest for revenge, and the urge to do the right thing."

"Aren't we all?" I said.

"That's why I let her take control of me. So she would open up and trust me," Carol said.

"You let her turn you into her personal massage therapist?"

Carol locked eyes with me. "That was my original intent. Truthfully though, I'm not sure if that was really my original intent or her intent to make me think it was my intent." Carol paused, finger to her lips. "She did help me learn a few tricks though. She is quite the teacher. So, even if she did possibly take advantage of me, she paid me back."

DOS, dealing with psis gives me such a headache. I decided to turn my attention to the landing. Well, actually it was more of an attaching. Due to the dome holding in most of the Moon's breathable atmosphere, the shuttle couldn't actually land inside of the colonized area. The shuttle would hover above the domed area and attach itself to a large elevator. The elevator then ferried down ten passengers at time. It was a high-speed elevator but after a long trip I was a little jumpy. I was anxious to get my feet on solid Earth. I mean Moon. Ground. You know what I mean.

Things moved pretty orderly. It wasn't long before Carol, Elena, and I were on the elevator; the last three passengers to deshuttle.

"Thank you for flying with us," one of the robo-servers said as we got on the elevator. "Please consider us for your return trip."

"Is there any other option?" I asked as the door began closing.

"No, but our marketing people insist we put that in," the bot said.

The door finished closing. We started down.

"So, Zachary, have you decided what to do about Boris?" Elena asked.

I shook my head. "I don't make rash moves."

Carol just stared at me. HARV appeared from my wrist com also staring at me.

I rolled my eyes. "I'm trying to reduce the number of rash moves I make."

Carol and HARV both seemed pleased with this.

"Once I gather more info then I'll decide," I told Elena.

"I will give you a bit more time," Elena said, her voice quivering.

The door to the elevator opened to the Moon's greeting and clearing area. It was a big, open dome-within-a-dome.

Sputnik had arrived a good half-hour before us but he was still in the area. He was flanked by a marching band and even more young blue-haired women.

The marching band was carrying a holographic sign that read: WELCOME BACK OUR ILLUSTRIOUS ADMINIS-TRATIVE LEADER.

Sputnik was devouring the attention. He wasn't just basking in it, he was absorbing it.

Elena cut through the crowd, making a beeline to Sputnik. I kept both eyes glued to her. I wasn't sure what she was up to, but I knew I wasn't going to like it.

As she drew closer to Boris Sputnik, I noticed that shining object appear in her left hand again.

"HARV, zoom in on Elena," I shouted. DOS! When she said a bit more time I thought she meant days or at least hours, not seconds.

A cursor appeared in front of my eye. The image of Elena enlarged. I plainly saw the glistening knife in her hand. I popped the Colt 2062 into my hand.

"GUS, just take out the weapon," I said.

"You got it big guy!" GUS shouted.

I pulled the trigger, aiming at the knife. A split nano later, my blast knocked the knife out of Elena's hands, sending it clunking to the ground. Sputnik turned to see Elena coming toward him, holding her hand. It didn't take him long to figure out what was going down.

Melda and Lea were first to react, moving toward Elena. About a dozen other security people and some gorillas in blue armored uniforms were also encircling her.

That's when things got weird. Everything and everybody, except for Elena, started moving like they were in slow motion. The last thing I remembered before everything just stopped was Elena snaking her way through the crowd toward the exit.

Next thing I knew, everything was back to normal speed and Elena was gone.

"What the DOS was that?" I said.

"My temporal sensors are out of alignment by ten seconds," HARV said.

"Elena can warp time with her mind," Carol said in awe. "That is so sub-absolute zero!"

It didn't take long for Sputnik to recover and regain his composure. Sputnik and his entourage headed toward us.

"Are they mad at us?" I asked Carol.

"No. They think you saved him, which you did," Carol said.

The big question now was, why was I able to do it? If Elena had wanted Sputnik dead just then, she could have done the time warp thing then killed him. DOS, why would she even bother to use a knife? Why didn't she just vaporize him with her brain?

Sputnik wholeheartedly patted me on the back. "Thank you for saving me, Mr. Johnson," he said. "I finally realize what the lovely Miss Electra sees in you."

Melda and Lea moved forward, each grasping one of my hands. "Yes, thank you for saving him."

Lea took a step back. She studied me. "He's wondering why she ran."

"The thought did cross my mind," I said. "We were all at her mercy, yet she booked."

They all looked at me blankly.

"Booked is Zach's simple way of saying ran," HARV said.

Sputnik smiled. "She ran, or booked as you say, because she can't hold time like that for more than a few seconds and it leaves her drained. My wife and daughter would have, how do you say it, done a number on her ass. Elena always thinks of her own salvation first."

Lea took another step back. She tilted her head, still gazing into my eyes. "He's wondering why she used a knife."

"True," I said. "Don't know why she just didn't melt you from across the room?"

Sputnik's smile stretched out. "Two reasons: the first, that would have left her drained and she wouldn't have been able to escape so easily." He paused.

I waited. Got nothing. Then asked, "And the second?"

His smile retracted some, but it was noticeable. "Her sense of deranged honor. She feels I killed her father, so she wants to kill me with her own hands. I'm afraid my niece has issues."

Lea looked at me again. "He's surprised Elena is your niece."

Sputnik patted me on the shoulder. "Yes, she's my twin brother's daughter." Sputnik motioned to Lea, like he was a game show host showing me a prize I had won. "Elena and Lea were born on the same day."

Now that he mentioned it, I noticed the two girls

carried many physical similarities. Lea was slightly darker and taller. Elena's eyes were a bit larger and more European, but they did have a touch of Asian in them. The girls could have been sisters.

Lea looked at me. "He's wondering why we look so much alike."

"My daughter resembles my niece so much because my twin sister is her aunt," Melda said.

"Twins married twins?" I said.

"It's quite common," Bo reassured me.

Lea studied my face. "He says . . ."

"I'll talk for myself," I told her.

"Fine," Lea said, taking a step back.

"She claims her mother is also dead," I said.

Everybody laughed. This was either a cold bunch or I had been had.

"She is talking figuratively," Melda said. "My sister Shara is very much alive and well and running our Psi Training Center. When my sister didn't disown Bo immediately for what Elena believed was the killing of her father, Elena disowned Shara."

Bo nodded. "Elena is a bit of loose cannon."

I looked at Sputnik, "Then why do you let such a powerful psi roam free?"

Sputnik's face straightened out. "This is not Earth," he said. "We do not fear psis for simply being themselves."

"He has a point," Carol said in my head.

"This guy is smooth," HARV added.

I ignored them. "They have their freedom even if they are a threat to others?"

Sputnik put his hand on my shoulder, "My friend, she was a threat only to me. I was willing to take that chance in the hope that she would see the error in her ways."

"Besides, until now we had no actual proof," Melda said.

"Now we do," Lea said.

"Yes, we do," Sputnik said, like the wise father. He held up one finger. "We will bring her in and make sure she gets the help she needs and deserves." He looked me dead in the eyes. "We know how to treat our own on the Moon."

Lea, Melda, and about twenty other people nodded in agreement. He was good.

"Where are you staying?" Sputnik asked, raising his tone and acting as if there hadn't just been an attack on his life by a freakishly powerful psi.

"Ah, not sure . . ."

HARV appeared. "We are staying at the Dark Side of the Moon Bed and Breakfast." HARV looked at me. "It's not really on the dark side, it just borders it."

Sputnik shook his head. "Not anymore. You are now staying at the No Seasons Resorts, the finest temporary residence on the Moon."

"Thanks," Carol said.

"It is close to my home and office, so I can easily give you a tour." He looked around. "I'll have the gorillas take your luggage." He looked around some more. "I don't see any luggage."

"I travel without it," I said. "My clothing is equipped with special nanotechnology so it is constantly cleaning itself."

Melda smiled. "Yes, one of Dr. Pool's lab's more practical inventions."

"This way, if needed, I can wear my same subzero P.I. outfit day after day and still be able to sneak up on the bad guys," I said.

Melda looked at Carol. "What about you, my dear?"

"I wanted to get the full Moon experience, so I decided I'd shop for a whole new wardrobe here," Carol said. "My outfit has the same nano-cleaners that

Zach's does so I won't offend, but a girl needs a change."

Sputnik clasped his hands together. "Splendid. That works out perfectly then. You check into your hotel rooms and relax for a tad and then we will pick you up. Lea and I will show Zach around while Melda shows Carol around."

He didn't make it a question, he made it a statement. He was letting us know that we were on his turf, playing by his rules.

"You sure you don't want to rest up a bit more after the long flight?" I asked.

"No, no," Sputnik answered. "For some reason, we all slept a lot this trip."

Chapter 21

Sputnik called for a special limo to take us to the No Seasons resort. He apologized that he couldn't include us in his cavalcade, but every seat in his limo convoy was taken by staff or family. He noted that it's not easy being the most important person on the Earth's biggest satellite.

I gave Sputnik his due, as the limo he arranged pulled up to the curb by the shuttle port less than a minute after Carol and I left the building.

The driver got out of the car. The first thing I noticed was he was a gorilla. I'm not talking metaphorically; he, like the security team and baggage handlers, was an *actual* gorilla. He hopped over the car and opened up the back passenger doors. He tipped his bright yellow hat and bowed.

Carol got in first. I followed. The gorilla closed the door. "Thank you, my good monkey," I said.

The gorilla made some gestures with his hand—sign language.

"He says, 'I'm a gorilla, not a monkey,'" HARV said.

The ape jumped back over the limo and into the driver's seat through the open window. He started the car and pulled away from the curb.

"How do I sign, 'it was a joke'?" I asked HARV via my communicator.

The gorilla made more hand signals.

"He says he understands English as well as Chinese. He knows it was a joke but it wasn't a very good one."

"Maybe you have to be human to appreciate it?" I said.

More hand movements.

"He says he doubts it," HARV said.

Carol patted me on the shoulder. "Trust me, Tió, the gorilla is right."

"Do you have a name?" I asked the driver.

He made more hand signals.

"He says 'no.' All gorillas on the Moon just answer to 'hey you.'"

The gorilla started to giggle. So did Carol. So did HARV inside my head.

"Okay, it may have been a dumb question," I admitted.

The gorilla made a fast hand movement.

"He says '*may*'?" HARV said.

I pushed myself back in my seat. "I hope you're not expecting a big tip," I told the gorilla.

More hand signals.

"He says his name is Magilla," HARV said.

"Really?" I asked, a bit more excited than I should have been.

The ape just shook his head no. He made a hand signal then said, "Oooo oo ooooo ug eek ah . . ."

"He says his name is Ooooo oo ooooo ug eek ah," HARV said.

"Really?" I asked again.

The gorilla made a couple quick hand movements.

"He says, nah, his name is really Maurice."

I looked at him with one eye. This time, I didn't say a word.

He made more hand signals.

"He says he wishes he was kidding," HARV said.

"I don't blame him," I said.

As we drove, I took in the lunar sights that Maurice pointed out. The colony itself was an impressive place. It should be, for the money the major powers, then the World Council, spent on building it. It had the advantages of being new and having a controlled population. That meant lots of wide-open spaces lined with trees and flowers. What wasn't wide-open was occupied with nice, new, shiny buildings. According to Maurice and HARV, the Moon's population was carefully regulated to stay between 1 million and 1.1 million people living in over 5,000 square kilometers of "renovated planet." In comparison, New New York crams over 13 million inhabitants into roughly 1,000 square kilometers.

The Moon also had the advantage of being in a totally pollution-free atmosphere. The dome encasing the inhabited area had a controlled environment that would always keep the temperature regulated between 20 and 24 degrees Celsius. The dome also regulated the lighting cycles, simulating an Earth day, giving a very consistent sixteen hours of daylight and eight hours of night, every day and night. All the energy sources on the moon were either hydrogen, fusion, or solar with no emissions. So, the air may have been man-made, but it was cleaner and purer than anything on Earth . . . at least according to Maurice and the holographic brochure playing in the limo.

I tried contacting Electra but HARV informed me that the conference was in a twenty-four hour black out period so they could concentrate without outside distractions. Maurice told me that tomorrow when the blackout lifted he would gladly drive me to the

Moon's conference center, noting that the attached living center is almost as spectacular as the No Seasons.

Maurice dropped Carol and me off at the hotel. It was a tall, spiraling building that reached almost to the top of the Moon's protective dome. The plan was Carol and I had an hour to relax and clean up before Sputnik and his crew arrived to give us the grand tours. Maurice mentioned that we might want to consider quick showers. He didn't want to offend us, but he did mention that gorillas and Mooners have keen senses of smell.

Carol and I walked into the hotel and checked in. We were greeted by a peppy hotel clerk. She was a tall, slim, light-blue-haired girl, quite anxious to serve us. After the easy check-in process (we only had to give her our names and DNA prints) a couple of apes in bellhop suits accompanied us to our penthouse suite.

The gorillas led us to an elevator and pressed the access code for the top floor. We hopped on. The elevator zoomed upward. Within seconds, the door opened to the penthouse itself.

"Sweet suite," I said.

One of the apes made a couple of gestures.

"It's a three-bedroom, five-bath suite," HARV translated. "The finest on the Moon."

The ape wasn't kidding. The general living area the elevator opened up to was both spacious and elegant. The place was lined with golden carpet, thicker than my lawn during the best of times. Crystal chandeliers hung from the ceiling. The part of the room nearest the elevator was the open rec area. It had a purple felt pool table, a foosball table, and an interactive virtual gaming center.

Walking a bit brought you to the relaxation area dotted with light purple couches and overly stuffed chairs. Each of the chairs and the couch could recline, rotate, levitate, and had robo-massage. The room was fitted with the latest in VHD HV, meaning you could project the latest in holographic information and entertainment to any corner of the room. The built-in ad that played when a person would walk by a certain spot (which I quickly learned to avoid) called it the total interactive entertainment experience, which was "better than being there." And of course there was a bar area, complete with stools and automated drink creator.

The far wall of the room was a Plexiglas picture window. According to the gorillas, the window led to the best view of the Moon on the planet, which made it one of the best views in all of the known universe. That might have been a bit of an overstatement, but it was a pleasant sight nonetheless. Looking down on them from above, most of the structures on the moon seem to be made from plastic blocks, but they were very shiny, colorful plastic blocks. Gazing past the city structure I saw lush green fields of crops. At first these seemed to be a stark contrast from the totally man and bot-made look of the city, but after pondering for a nano I realized the fields were just as out of place on what was once a barren rock.

I tapped the tempered glass. "This is unbreakable. Right?"

Both gorillas nodded yes, then one of them signed.

HARV appeared through my wrist com.

"Of course," HARV translated. "The transparency of it is also voice-controlled for your privacy."

One of the gorillas signed something else.

"He wants to know if you wish for them to prepare you a shower . . ." HARV translated.

"No. I'm a big boy, I can handle that myself."

More ape gestures.

"He says it's tricky," HARV said.

"That's okay. I'm sure I can figure it out," I said.

HARV leaned forward toward the apes, put a hand next to his mouth and whispered just loud enough so I could hear it. "He has me to help him."

A few more hairy-handed movements.

"He says if you need anything at all just ring them," HARV said.

"I will, my good apes," I said to the gorillas.

They each made more hand signals.

"They both say they are actually great apes," HARV said.

"Sorry, no offense," I said.

The two apes gestured again.

"They say only a little taken."

One of the apes held out a giant hand. I shook it. I noticed he had something in that hand, it was a credit recorder.

"I think he wants a tip," HARV whispered to me.

"For what? They just walked us to an elevator and into the suite. A chimp could have done it."

I felt eight eyes on me.

"Tió, don't embarrass me in front of the apes," Carol said in my brain.

"Fine," I sighed. I took the credit card and punched in a ten-credit tip.

The apes looked at the tip, tipped their hats and then headed out.

As we watched the elevator door close I asked, "Why does everybody want me to take a shower?" I asked.

"Don't look at me," HARV said. "I have no olfactory receptors."

I sniffed myself. "I don't smell bad at all," I said.

"Of course you don't," HARV said. "Nobody ever smells bad to themselves. You might have worked up a sweat on the flight here."

"My outfit is nano self-cleaning," I reminded HARV though I was sure he didn't need reminding.

"Your attire, yes. Your body, no."

"How could he work up a sweat?" Carol asked. "He slept most of the trip."

I shook my head. "No, you and everybody else slept. I was fighting Elena."

Carol just looked at me like I was crazy.

"It's true," HARV said. "She put you all to sleep and then almost put Zach to sleep for good."

"That little bitch," Carol said.

"She wanted to kill Sputnik then but I wouldn't let her," I said.

Carol put her hands on her hips. "She took out an entire shuttle of psis like we were nothing. Then she stops time with her mind at the port. How the DOS did you stop her?"

HARV smiled and put his arm around me. "He had me."

I pointed at HARV. "I had HARV, plus I had some tricks up my sleeve."

I popped GUS into my hand. "That's *me* he's talking about," GUS beamed.

"Plus I'm not as easy to kill as most people think," I added.

"Captain Rickey is right—you are kind of like a cockroach," HARV said.

"So that's how I might have worked up a little sweat," I said. "But I'm not offensive. At least, I don't think I am . . ."

Carol walked toward me. "Fine. I don't get paid enough for this job," she mumbled. She leaned over and sniffed me.

"Well?" I asked.

Carol's knees buckled. Her eyes rolled to the back of her head, then closed. She fell forward. I caught her. She was limp as over cooked spaghetti.

"Ha, ha. Very funny, Carol," I said.

"Fascinating," HARV said. "Just as I suspected."

I held Carol up, she was totally dead weight. "You suspected this?" I asked.

"Yes, I actually do have olfactory sensors. I noticed that there has been some sort of weird interaction between your body underarmor, sweat, pheromones, and the chemicals in the air here. I surmised it would act as sort of an opposite sex knockout gas."

"So she's not faking?" I said, though I kind of suspected she wasn't from her total lack of movement.

"Nah, she's out cold," HARV said. "It's really quite a fascinating phenomenon."

"So what am I supposed to do?" I asked.

HARV put a finger to his mouth. "I'm sure if you remove your body underarmor and take a nice shower you'll be fine."

"So I can't wear my underarmor on the Moon?" I said.

"Well, you've always wanted to make woman swoon," HARV joked.

"How come the nano cleaners aren't working?" I asked.

HARV huffed. "This is an interaction between your skin, the Moon, and the nano cleaners. They are working, just not the way you want them to work. I can perhaps inject nano cleaners into your skin if you like."

I didn't even respond to that.

I picked Carol up and carried her over to the couch. "Ona, Twoa, and Threa use their pheromones to manipulate people, not knock them out," I said.

"Yes, because they have control of their powers," HARV said. "You don't."

I gently put Carol on the couch.

"She going to be all right," HARV said.

"Fine, I'll go hit the showers and ditch the armor," I said.

HARV smiled. "That's probably a wise plan."

I walked into the master bedroom. It was nice. I figured since Carol had passed out, I got to choose the best room. DOS, I was the boss, I should have the best room. I got undressed and headed to the bathroom.

The bathroom was almost as big as my house. I liked it. I stepped into the shower.

"Greetings," the shower said.

"Greetings," I said in return.

"Please stand in the middle of the shower," the shower requested.

I did as I was told.

"What temperature would you like?" the shower asked.

"Surprise me," I said.

There was silence. Then, "I have learned when people say 'surprise me' they don't really want to be surprised."

"Nice and warm," I said.

"Please give me your warm parameters," the shower asked.

HARV chimed in from my wrist interface. "Just give him two degrees above body temperature."

"Very good," the shower said. "Would you like the complete surround shower experience?"

"Is there any other kind?" I said.

"Well put," the shower answered.

My body was instantly cascaded with water from every conceivable angle, including two from underneath. It felt good, once I got used to the two bottom ones.

I stood there basking in the shower in utter peace.

"Don't forget to wash under your arms," HARV said.

Okay, maybe not utter peace, but still relative peace. I lathered up. I washed down. I lathered up again. It felt good. It couldn't last.

"Uh-oh," HARV said.

I stopped lathering. "What?" It's never a good sign when HARV says "uh-oh . . ."

"The Moon's computer systems have all just rebooted," HARV said.

"Which means?"

"Which means I can't access them, I can't relay to Earth, I'm blind except for what I see through your eyes and your communicator."

"That means I'm blind to the outside world, too," I said.

"True," HARV agreed.

"I'm an unarmed, sitting duck in the shower," I said.

"Why aren't you packing?" HARV said. I gave him props for talking the talk.

"My old gun and knife rust in water," I said opening up the shower door.

"What about GUS?" HARV asked.

"Frankly, I'm not all that comfortable bathing with one sentient machine, never mind two," I said.

Reaching for a towel, a big hairy hand grabbed me. I went flying across the room before I was even able to react. I crashed back first into a bidet. The bidet started spewing water. I looked up to see the biggest, hairiest, ugliest gorilla I'd ever seen bearing down on me.

I was unarmed and armorless but I still had a supercomputer wired to my brain. *"HARV send as much energy as you can to my left leg,"* I thought.

"Check," HARV said in my head.

The gorilla reached down for me just as I kicked up right between his legs. At least I hoped he was a *he*—that would make my attack more effective. The gorilla recoiled in pain when my foot hit its mark (well, marks). Yep, he was a guy. The force of the blow lifted him off the ground. He doubled over in pain holding his midsection.

I shot up and headed toward my room. I may have gotten in one lucky kick but I knew I needed my weapons. I gave the ape a quick elbow strike to his kidneys as I passed him.

Reaching the bedroom, I saw two other apes rifling through my stuff.

"DOS," I said.

The two apes saw me and charged. I made a fist. "*Soup me up good, HARV*!" I shouted in my brain.

Both apes made fists as they closed in on me. Their fists were the size of my head. If they made any contact, I was dead meat.

"Careful," HARV warned. "They are surprisingly fast . . ."

I knew HARV had to be right. The weird thing was, I saw their fists coming at me. I ducked under the first punch and sidestepped the second. It was easy. It was like the apes were in slow motion.

The apes were sluggish but persistent. They each wound up with another punch. I saw both of their fists coming at me, only they were coming slowly. In fact, they were getting slower and slower, until they just stopped.

I looked at the apes. They were just standing there, frozen in mid-punch.

"You can thank me later," a voice said from behind.

I turned and there was Elena.

"I'll thank you now," I said.

Elena made a simple motion with her left hand sending the ape on her left flying into a wall. Duplicating the motion with her right hand caused the ape on the right to fling crashing into the wall. It was as if the apes were weightless.

At that moment I realized something very important. I was stark naked. I put my hands in front of my personals, walked over to the bed, grabbed a sheet, and wrapped it around me.

"Why'd you come back?" I asked Elena.

Elena raised her right hand and squeezed it tightly. I fell to the ground, doubling over in pain. The harder she squeezed, the more pain rushed through my body. Elena walked over and knelt down beside me.

"I'm the one who will be asking the questions," she told me.

"Fine," I said, not being in a position to argue, yet.

"Why did you stop me from killing Sputnik?" she asked.

I tried to answer, I wanted to answer. The pain made it too hard to think, much less talk.

Elena touched my shoulder. The pain stopped, I felt better than ever before.

"Talk now," she said.

Looking up, I was so grateful for her stopping the pain, I forgot to be angry with her for causing it. DOS, this woman was good.

"We can't be sure Sputnik is guilty," I said. I tried to push my way back to my feet.

"Stay down," Elena ordered.

I stopped trying to stand. I crumbled back to the ground.

"HARV, I could really use some help here," I thought.

"Your computer can't help you now, Zachary," Elena said. "I've learned how to control him through you."

Oh, that was so NOT good.

"It is good, Zachary," Elena smiled. "Now your mind is totally free. By the way, it wasn't your smell that knocked Carol out cold." She thought for a second then said, "Well, it was the smell, but that was because I gave her the suggestion that if she got a whiff of you she'd pass out. I also planted the suggestion into HARV as to the cause."

"You wanted me out of my armor," I said.

"I wanted to make sure you were separated from

your armor and fancy weapon," she said. "You hurt me on the shuttle and then at the port. I needed to make sure you didn't get a chance to hurt me again." She looked at the apes she clobbered.

"Sorry about the apes; didn't know they'd be after you, too," she said.

"Yeah, I'm in constant demand," I said. "It's a gift."

She stroked me on the head. "Now if you don't want the pain to start up again, Zachary, I suggest you tell me the truth."

"I am telling the truth, just read my mind!" I shouted.

"I tried," she said. "But your mind is so scrambled I'm not sure you yourself know the truth. So I am going to act as the facilitator to help you reach the truth."

"Facilitator or judge, jury, and executioner?" I asked.

She smiled. It was a warm, friendly smile. At least that's how I perceived it. "I don't need to kill you. If I did, you'd be a pile of ashes now. I'll just revert you to a baby, or make you think you're a potted plant forever."

"Thanks, you're all . . ."

She swiped her finger slowly across my throat. I stopped talking. "You will only speak when I tell you to," she said.

"Why did you save Sputnik?" she asked. "I can feel that you despise him."

I tried to talk, nothing happened.

"Oops, sorry," Elena said. She waved her hand over me. "You may talk now."

"I'm not sure he's guilty yet. You said you would give me more time!"

"I changed my mind. I saw Sputnik standing there hogging all the attention. I snapped. Anyhow, why delay the inevitable? Like I said, I'm sure he's a guilty, rotten, spamball," she said indignantly.

"Yeah, but I need proof," I caught a quick breath.

"Besides, if you do start acting on your own they are going to hunt you down. Doesn't matter how powerful you are, they will eventually get you."

Elena turned her head away from me. I had hit a nerve. "I can fight them all. I can . . ."

"You can what, enslave them all?" I said.

"It's rude to interrupt," she said. "I do not wish to be the ruler of the Moon or the Earth," she said. She thought for a moment. "Though I can see worse possible rulers . . ."

"Besides," I said drawing her back into the conversation. "I'm sure Sputnik is guilty of some crimes. DOS, what politician isn't? I still don't know the big picture here. Was he responsible for the council killings? Did he act alone?"

"He couldn't have acted alone," Elena said. "He never does anything himself."

"That's why if you kill him now we might not ever learn who really killed the World Council members and what their goals were."

"Good point," she said.

"Thanks," I said. "I try. There's something else big going on here. I need to find out what and stop it."

"Of course, you gave me another idea. Perhaps I should work on increasing my own power. Make everybody love everybody . . ."

"I don't think that's such a hot idea either," I said.

"Why not?" she asked.

"Because then I'd have to stop you, too," I said. "You don't want that."

"Zach, you caught me off guard twice. It won't happen again," Elena assured me.

"I wouldn't count on that, bitch," Carol said from behind us.

Carol hit Elena with an uppercut to the chin. The punch sent her head cocking up before her body went flying over.

"That's for making me rub your feet!" Carol shouted, rippling with energy.

Carol glared at Elena, sending her crashing into the ceiling at breakneck (and break pretty much everything else) speed. "That's for making me sniff my uncle's armpits!" Carol shouted.

Carol moved her head to the left, sending Elena smashing into the left wall. The force of the blow left a dent in the wall. Carol moved her head to the right, Elena went flying headfirst into the right wall. This drew blood.

Carol glared at Elena, keeping her pinned to the wall.

"Let's see how good you do when you don't have me off guard, bitch."

I pushed myself up to my knees. "Carol, don't kill her," I said.

"Why not?" Carol said, without taking her eyes off Elena.

"She could have killed us and she didn't," I said.

Carol released her mental grip on Elena. Elena slid down the wall, leaving a blood trail, rolling down the wall to the floor. She pushed herself up. She turned toward Carol and me. "You are so lucky I'm still weak from stopping time," Elena said, finger pointed at us.

Carol rolled her eyes. "You can't begin to imagine the number of times I've heard that."

"You've heard that before?" I asked.

"What did I miss?" HARV said, coming back online. He looked around the room. "DOS, I missed a lot. Oh, by the way Zach, you're naked," he added.

"Good point," Carol said. "And grab your weapon. We need to hold Elena until Bo and the others arrive."

I grabbed the cover that I had been using and wrapped it around myself. I looked for GUS. "GUS, report," I ordered.

"I'm over here!" a voice beamed from the bed.

I walked over and grabbed GUS. I pointed him at Elena. "If she tries to do anything, blast her," I ordered GUS.

"With pleasure," GUS chirped.

"Do you have her now?" Carol asked.

"She's locked in," GUS said.

"Great," Carol said. She fell back into my arms.

Elena smiled and wiped some blood off from her nose. "Even when I'm weak and not doing anything I'm doing something," she said. "You both passed the test," she said.

"What test? I hate tests, except trivia tests. I find those kind of fun."

I wasn't paying any attention to HARV but I was sure he was rolling his eyes behind my back.

"I was just seeing if you might possibly have a chance of stopping Sputnik," Elena said.

She took a step forward. She stopped. She heard something. I listened, I heard it, too. There were a number of people in the main room. "SPAM!" Elena shouted.

Elena disappeared. A split nano later Sputnik, Lea, Melda, two other blue-haired women, and ten heavily armored apes poured into the room.

Chapter 22

"Is everybody okay?" Sputnik asked as the gorillas secured the room.

"Fine now," I said.

Melda and Lea surveyed the damage. Melda walked up to me. "Sorry, about our gorillas there, Mr. Johnson," she said. "They were younger ones and they tend to get carried away in trying to impress their superiors."

"You've lost me," I said.

Sputnik smirked. "The gorillas on the Moon have a hierarchal system. You have to do something impressive to move up it. When security learned that you would be here, the less senior members thought this could be how they make their name, beating up Zach Johnson. Apparently, security personnel all over the known worlds know of you."

"Nice to know my reputation preceds me," I said.

"Yeah, I bet there are security people on Mars already taking odds on who takes you out," HARV said.

Two ape security men dragged the unconscious ape

out of the bathroom while four others cleaned up the two in the bedroom. Lea looked on with a sense of awe.

"Amazing, it is true," she said. "You do have an incredible knack for survival."

"I do, but Elena helped . . ."

"Elena!" Lea and Melda both said.

"Yeah, she was here too. She actually took out two of the apes."

"What did she want with you?" Melda questioned.

"Near as I can tell, to kill me," I said. It wasn't the complete truth, but it would have to do for now. "She blames me for saving you," I said to Sputnik.

Lea sniffed the air. "Yes, I do pick up my cousin's scent here. I should have noticed sooner."

Melda touched her daughter on the shoulder. "Elena is a tricky one. Don't blame yourself, my daughter."

Lea wasn't paying attention. She was locked in on me. "You battled my cousin and lived to tell about it," Lea said, now even more amazed.

"Carol and HARV helped," I said.

"He'd have been dead years ago without us," HARV said.

"Ditto," Carol, now conscious again, added.

Despite HARV's and Carol's comments, Lea was impressed. She looked at me as if I was some sort of rock star or still a media darling. I looked at Sputnik looking at his daughter looking at me. His face was still smiling but his eyes weren't. He was trying not to show his displeasure but his pupils constricted to pin size, disappearing into the gray of his iris, giving away his true feelings. He was used to being the only human alpha male around.

Lea took my hand. "You have to tell me how you stood up to my cousin," she nearly begged. "I'm one of the most powerful psis on the Moon and therefore

one of the most powerful in existence, yet when Elena
is angry she scares the moon dust out of me." She
squeezed my hand. "She's dangerous, Zach."

I looked past Lea to Sputnik, "So I repeat my question from earlier: why did you let her roam free?"

Sputnik shrugged, his pupils returning to normal
size, "Until today she had committed no crimes. You
may imprison innocent people on Earth, but we don't
work that way on the Moon."

"We did know she had, *issues*," Melda admitted.
"We offered her special therapy. That's why she went
to Earth. She trusted Desma."

"I know she has some strange thoughts racing
through her amazingly powerful mind, but until today
I never really thought she'd hurt me," Sputnik said.

I didn't doubt him. Sputnik was the type of man
who was so in love with himself he couldn't begin to
fathom that perhaps not everybody else in the universe shared his feelings. I was actually glad I'd be
touring with him and Lea today; it would give me a
chance to feel them out.

Lea released my hand and turned to Sputnik. "Father, I wouldn't be at all surprised now if Elena was
behind those awful killings on Earth."

Sputnik's eyes lowered and his eyes turned inward.
He wasn't happy with his daughter but he was trying
hard not to show it. "Now, now, dear daughter, let's
not raise pointless accusations. The authorities on
Earth have a suspect in prison," he said coolly.
"Mooners, even the ultra, mega, omega crazo ones,
do not kill innocent people."

This gave me an opening. "What if some Mooner
didn't think the council members were innocent?" I
asked. "Then they might be quite willing to kill."

Silence.

Lea took a step back from me physically but reached

into my mind mentally. *"Please, Zach, don't go there,"* she pleaded.

Carol also popped into my head. *"Whoa, Tió, slow it down. We're on their turf, way outnumbered . . ."*

HARV also chimed in, *"Are you completely wacko? No wonder everybody wants to kill you."*

I thought about what they had all thought. They were right. This wasn't the right place or time.

I shrugged. "Just tossing out a hypothetical idea," I said casually. "It's my job to cover all the angles."

Lea looked at me with those pretty green eyes. She subtly fired her beguiling smile at me and touched me gently on the shoulder. "Yes, that is your job, when you are working," she said smile expanding with each word. "Only you're not on a job now. You are here to visit your girlfriend, Electra, tomorrow, when she has some free time. Now, you're going on a nifty tour of the Moon."

Lea was right. I wasn't on a job. I just wanted to see Electra tomorrow, when she has some free time. DOS, that Lea was smart. Now I was going on a nifty tour of the Moon. Hold on a nano, I don't say *nifty*. I don't even usually think about thinking about considering saying *nifty*. DOS! That girl was in my brain.

Lea smiled and rubbed me on the shoulder, "Trust me, Zachary, you will really enjoy the tour and seeing what a wonderful place the Moon is."

I returned her smile. I trusted her. I was going to really enjoy this tour. Though I'm not sure why I needed the tour as I already knew what a wonderful place the Moon was. Maybe I'd see if I could summer here?

"What the DOS are you thinking," Carol said in my brain.

"Surely you can do some thinking on your own?" HARV said in my head. *"Carol, without us he'd be*

cleaning Lea's toes with his tongue right now," HARV continued.

"Gross! But true," Carol answered HARV, relayed via my brain.

"Poor Zach," GUS toned in from inside my gray matter.

"GUS?" Carol, HARV and I all thought.

"Yep," GUS said proudly. *"I'm using HARV's interface."*

"Everybody stay out of my brain!" I thought as loudly as I could. *"There's barely enough room in there for HARV and me,"* I said, not believing that I included HARV as part of my brain.

"How very true," HARV said. *"Why couldn't Dr. Pool have inserted me into Steven Hawking's clone's brain?"*

Lea stroked me on the shoulder. "Zach, are you okay?"

I popped back to the matters at hand. Sure, there are times when having a computer hooked to your brain, a powerful psi assistant, and an intelligent weapon can be good . . . This wasn't one of them.

"Perhaps Mr. Johnson would like the tour on another day?" Sputnik offered.

"The Moon does have slightly less gravity and less nitrogen than Earth. Some people react oddly," Melda added.

"And he has fought with three ambitious security apes and with Elena," Lea said. She looked at me with sad eyes. "If you want to delay we understand."

I smiled at her and touched her lightly on the shoulder. "Believe me, angry apes and crazy psis are just an average day for me. It's going to take a lot more than that to keep me off the tour."

Sputnik grinned. This time, I wasn't sure if he was actually happy or acting. He clasped his hands together. "In that case, let us begin the tour before somebody or something else attacks Mr. Johnson," he said.

"Probably a good idea," I agreed.

Bo Sputnik patted me on the back, "Then let's go, my friend. I'm sure you'll see what a wonderful, love-filled place of science and wonder the Moon is."

Chapter 23

We exited the hotel and split into two groups. Carol and Melda went one way in a cute little bright orange, two-seat domed car; a car so small it looked like they could pedal it.

On the other end of the spectrum, our vehicle was a long and sleek red stretch carriage all-element hover. Besides myself, my group consisted of Sputnik, Lea, an ape driver, another ape riding shotgun, two more additional ape security "men," and two young, tall, light-blue-haired Asian looking girls named Windee and Aprill. For a guy who claimed to rule a love-filled world, Sputnik traveled with a lot of security.

As we drove through the sparkling clean streets of the Moon, Sputnik lectured about this and that. How, due to its controlled environment, the Moon was much more sterile than the Earth. I couldn't argue. The entire place looked and felt as if it was constantly being washed and waxed. Of course it should look clean—most of the buildings were less than twenty years old.

While Sputnik droned on about the virtues of the

Moon, I took in the sights, confident HARV was getting down any information I might need.

The first thing that stood out was that the streets weren't nearly as crowded and as congested as your average big Earth city streets. Sure there were people moving all about, but they certainly were able to keep ample space between them. The general Moon populace seemed slimmer and trimmer than the general Earth populace. Even without the blue or blue-streaked hair it would have been easy for my trained eye to separate your average Mooner from the average Earther. They just carried themselves differently.

The streets also seemed much more open than Earth streets. All the vehicles on the roads, except ours, were small, one- to three-person transportation devices. They looked like boxes on wheels with little domes over them. Apparently this was because on the Moon only a very select few have their own vehicles for transportation. Most of the populace shared interchangeable vehicles (I.V.s for short). One car type fits all. The Moon owned a fleet of compact, very boring cars that only varied by a user programmable color.

The vehicle we were riding in was a horse of a completely different color. It was huge and stuck out like the queen at a Roller Derby match. Our vehicle looked like one of those old horse-drawn carriages, sans the horses. I was surprised Sputnik didn't attach a couple of robot steeds. The carriage had four rows of seats. The ape driver and his lookout ape sat in the first row of two cockpitlike seats. I was seated in the second row with Lea on my left and Sputnik on my right. The seats were so big and wide there was easily room for three more of us in this row.

The third row was also wide. Windee and Aprill were so slender they looked lost sitting there by themselves.

Bringing up the back were the other two ape security guards. They were big and bulky, even by gorilla terms. The sad thing was the back row only had about a quarter of the room the second and third rows did. I've seen canned sardines with more personal space. The apes didn't seem to mind too much. Though, truthfully, it was a bit hard to tell since they had their eyes covered with sunglasses. I didn't bother to point out to them that we were on the Moon in a controlled environment. I knew they knew this. I'm smart enough to understand that when the spam hits the fan you want the big apes with big guns on your side. You don't go busting them about their strange choice in eyewear. Besides, it gave them a cool and aloof security dude kind of look.

"You're thinking about the apes in sunglasses, aren't you?" HARV said in brain.

"No," I thought back flatly.

The word *LIAR* scrolled across my eyes.

"Okay, maybe," I thought back.

"Those aren't normal glasses," HARV said. *"They are actually communica' on devices, specially enhanced PIHI-Pods behind the earpieces that hold the glasses on. The apes are constantly receiving feedback from all over the Moon."*

"Why?" I asked.

"To keep Sputnik safe," HARV said.

Lea tilted her head and looked at me kind of strangely. "Are you okay, Zachary?" she asked.

"Fine, fine," I said.

Lea leaned over toward me. "I think it's silly that the apes wear shades, too," she whispered. She drew back and smiled. "Don't know why they can't wear regular PIHI-Pods . . ."

I wasn't sure what to make of Lea. Was that a warning? Was she actually agreeing with me? Could she pick through my mind that easily? Was it just a lucky guess? I guess time would tell.

The tour continued. We drove past a tall glass building that was the Moon's Science and Learning Center. We didn't go into the building as Sputnik said the scientists and researchers employed there were far too busy advancing technology and finding cures for diseases that didn't even exist yet to be bothered by a tour. He pointed out that that was one of the advantages scientists on the Moon had: they were automatically well-funded so they didn't have to kowtow and bend over backward to politicians and businesses begging for research money.

Next, we drove through the Moon's Art and Culture Museum. When I say we drove through, I mean literally *drove through*. The museum was a drive-thru which, according to Sputnik, revolutionized the museum experience as patrons no longer had to get out of their vehicles to appreciate the art. The artists were happier as not only did more people get to see their work, but since the people were all in vehicles, that meant there would be much less touching of their work. The art for the most part (except for the cheese sculptures) wasn't all that different from what I remembered seeing the last time I ventured to an Earth-based museum.

Leaving the museum, Sputnik nudged me in the ribs with his elbow. "So, Zach, what do you think of our lovely Moon so far?" he asked.

"Well, I haven't fallen asleep. So that's a good sign," I said.

Sputnik smiled. "You really are as witty as Melda said."

"Really? We had such little contact back on Earth. Usually it takes people more time to truly appreciate my sense of humor," I said.

"Tell me about it," HARV said appearing from my wrist communicator. "I've been with Zach for over seven years now and I am just barely able to comprehend his so-called wit."

Sputnik nodded. "Out of all my special wives, Melda is the most special," he said. "She is much more perceptive than the average human."

"*All* your wives?" I said, testing how he'd react.

"Yes. Surely you understand we here on the Moon have more open views on marriage than most of Earth," Sputnik said, his smile growing wider with the thought of each wife.

"How many wives do you have?" I asked.

Sputnik shrugged. "I don't count them," he said casually, as if talking about his tie collection. Actually, no. From the finely pressed suit he was wearing, he probably spent more time thinking about his wardrobe.

"Seven," Lea, Windee, and Aprill all said at once.

"Apparently others do count them," I said.

"Well I love each and every one of them," Sputnik said.

"Yes, I bet you do," I agreed.

Sputnik looked away from me. "I can't expect an Earther to understand," he said, this time not even pretending to care about what I thought. Leaning over the seat he tapped the driver on the shoulder.

The ape driver turned back to see what Sputnik wanted. Sputnik pointed to at a fairly large dome-shaped building dominating the end of the street.

"Pull over by the Tracking and Blocking Station. Let's show Mr. Johnson why the Moon is so important."

The ape nodded in agreement and did as he was told. We drove up and parked in the large courtyard surrounding the unassuming looking building. It reminded me of an indoor tennis court.

Sputnik jumped out of the car first. He looked at me, urging me to follow. "Come on, Mr. Johnson. Let me show you our pride and joy."

I followed Sputnik out of the car. I turned to the women. "Are you ladies coming?" I asked.

Sputnik gave them an indifferent wave. "Nah, they don't find this exciting at all."

"He's right," Lea said.

"I've seen it a million times," Melda said.

"Boring!" Aprill added.

Windee just bobbed her head in agreement.

"We won't be long," Sputnik told his ladies.

He took my arm, nearly dragging me into the building. The building itself was one large room with a series of control panels running along the walls. The domed ceiling acted as a holographic planetarium and was dotted with stars. Working away, like busy little blue-haired beavers, were a blue-haired woman in her mid-forties, a young blue-haired man, and four smaller primates, which I quickly figured out were orangutans. (HARV told me that was because, as almost everybody knows, orangutans are much more suited for mental labor than gorillas. He then of course scolded me for not knowing this.) Humans and primates were all wearing bright yellow outfits that looked like a mix of jumpsuits and lab coats. They all snapped to attention when they saw Sputnik.

"Mr. Sputnik, sir," the lady said, "we didn't know you would be dropping by today, unannounced."

Sputnik walked up to her. "I didn't know I needed to report in."

A few beads of sweat formed on the woman's head. You could tell she wanted to wipe them off but she didn't. "No, sir. Of course not."

"At ease," Sputnik told the group. He pointed to me. "I'm just showing Mr. Johnson here the Moon's pride and joy."

"This is the Moon's Asteroid Tracking and Blocking Station," HARV whispered in my mind.

"Yeah, kind of figured that out," I mentally whispered back.

"Zach, I'm sure you know what this place is?" Sputnik said, pointing to the ceiling.

"See, Sputnik trusts my intelligence," I thought to HARV.

"He doesn't know you that well," HARV answered.

"It's the Moon's Asteroid Tracking and Blocking Station," I said.

"Yes, the MAT&BS," Sputnik spouted proudly. "This is the most important building to Earth and it's here on the Moon. We keep Earth safe from nasty asteroids."

"We all appreciate it," I said with as much sincerity as I could fake.

He looked me dead in the eyes. I felt the eyes of the others in room lock on me. "Do you, Mr. Johnson? Do you?"

Sputnik pointed upward to the dome. In midst of all the stars and satellites was one giant dot. "Do you see that?" He asked me.

I nodded.

"That is asteroid Zeta Alpha Pi, it is twelve kilometers long by nine kilometers wide. It will pass by Earth tomorrow at noon eastern time, missing it by only ten thousand kilometers."

One of the orangutans pushed a control panel with his or her foot. A simulated path lit up on the dome. It showed the big rock spinning past Earth.

"Close call," I said, not being able to think of anything but the obvious.

Sputnik held up a finger. "Yes, but say it wasn't going to miss . . . say its path was a mere one degree different."

The orangutan maneuvered his or her foot over the

pad. The simulated path reversed then disappeared from the ceiling. The big rock changed course, dropping down, putting it on a direct collision course with the Earth.

"If a rock of this size were to strike your planet, it would hit with more power than a blast from all the nuclear bombs currently on Earth," Sputnik lectured, looking up at the ceiling. He lowered his head to my level. "Do you know what that means, Mr. Johnson?"

"It would be bad."

"Bad?" he questioned.

"Okay, *real* bad, of biblical proportions kind of bad," I said.

"It would destroy life on Earth as you know it," Sputnik said, with a bit more glee in his voice than I was comfortable with.

"Well, that is what I call bad," I said.

"But, thanks to us here on the Moon, that won't happen," Sputnik said proudly. "Because of our Moon-based deflector ray, we can gently push any Earth killers onto a different trajectery."

I looked up at the dome. It showed a beam of energy emanating from the Moon then hitting the incoming asteroid. The asteroid changed course and once again glided past the Earth.

Sputnik looked up and smiled. "Of course this is only a simulation to depict what happens. In real life it's not so fast."

The orangutans and humans in the room nodded their heads in agreement.

"Yeah, I kind of got that," I said.

Sputnik leaned on one of the control panels. "So you see, Mr. Johnson, we saved Earth."

"Well, you saved Earth from an asteroid that's not really going to hit Earth," I pointed out.

Sputnik's smile straightened somewhat. "My point is, if it was going to hit, we wouldn't have let it. We are constantly patrolling the skies, tracking thousands of objects."

"And again, we thank you," I said. "Well, not really you, I guess, but the people who work here."

Sputnik's smile completely dissolved. "Those who work here work here at my pleasure," he said. I was kind of expecting him to stomp his foot. If he wasn't such a well-trained politician he probably would have.

"I'm sure," I said. "The point is, the asteroid was going to miss Earth. But believe me we on Earth are grateful that you've got our backs."

"Are you, Mr. Johnson?" he asked.

"Sure," I shrugged. "If you want I can have everybody send you a Holiday e-card."

The apes and Mooners took a step back. They didn't want to be nearby if Sputnik exploded.

"Way to taunt your host," HARV said.

HARV was right, I was taunting, well more like testing. I needed to see what Sputnik was made of, what made him tick. I wanted to gauge how easily he was thrown off his game, how seriously he took himself.

Sputnik looked at me with a tilted head. He smiled. "You're a wise one, Mr. Johnson. You want to see how I will react."

I put my hands up in the universal "I don't really know" position. He was onto me, but I wasn't going to let him know that. Good P.I.'s are great bluffers. "Just letting you know that we appreciate the work the people of the Moon do, even if we don't always say it."

Sputnik put his arm around me. Frankly, it made me uncomfortable, but I was on his turf so I gave him a little leeway.

"Come," he said. "Let us continue our tour of the Moon."

We started out of the building.

"Just curious, where's the *actual* deflector beam located?"

"It's outside in the native area," he answered as we went outside. "You should see it."

Sputnik and I walked to the vehicle and got in.

"To the native area," Sputnik ordered the ape driver.

I wasn't thrilled with the sound of that.

The driver gave him a polite salute. An instant later the carriage was lifting off the ground. We rose higher and higher toward the top of the protective dome.

"Where are we going?" I asked.

"Don't be a baby," HARV said.

"To show you what the people of Earth think of the Moon," Sputnik told me.

As we rose higher and higher I noticed that the upper portions of the dome encompassing the city had wide openings. These openings led to long, wide pressurized tubes, kind of like circular see-through tunnels. As we entered one of the tubes a protective dome rose from the back of our carriage, closing on top of us.

"We will be leaving the controlled environment in two Moon minutes," a computerized voice said. "In case of emergency, you have a rapid deployment Moon suit under your seat," the voice added.

Sputnik turned to me. "Yep, we even have a couple lawyers here on the moon."

"So it's not the perfect society," I said.

Sputnik didn't reply, but I could have sworn I noticed him grin ever so slightly.

Bursting out of the tube, our vehicle started gliding high above the lunar surface. The bumpy, rocky terrain was a stark contrast to the green, clean inner city. Honestly, I wasn't sure which one I preferred. Sure I couldn't breathe out here but the area still had a cold, natural look that appealed to me. HARV's right—I do have a weird side.

Sputnik turned to me. "First, Mr. Johnson, I showed you what we here on the Moon think of our home. It's an oasis for science, art, and thinking. Now, I am going to show you what Earth thinks of our home."

Lea leaned forward, "Father, Mr. Johnson doesn't enjoy heights. Perhaps you should ask the driver to go lower."

Sputnik turned toward me. "Is this true?" He asked. "A big macho man like you, a hero, scared of heights?"

"Scared may be too strong a word," I said slowly.

"It's true," HARV said.

Lea leaned over to me. "If you want I can help you get over your fear. My sisters and I are all therapists." She ran her hand gently up my arm. "I can help you," she said out loud and in my head.

I took her hand and gently removed it from my arm. "That's okay, I like my vulnerabilities. They add to my charm."

Lea looked up at me. "True."

"Gag me," HARV said in my head.

Looking at Sputnik he had about the same reaction, only he was trying hard not to let on. He wasn't thrilled with the idea of his daughter paying so much attention to me. Not sure if it was because I was from Earth or because I wasn't him. Whatever the case, Sputnik wasn't happy and for some reason that made me happy.

Sputnik wasn't the biggest scumbag I had dealt with in my career. DOS, he probably wasn't even in the top ten. Despite that, I didn't trust him or like him. Now I just had to figure out if that was because of an innate distrust of politicians and bureaucrats or something more sinister. If history held to form, it would be a combination of both.

Anxious to get my attention back on track, Sputnik pointed off in the distance.

"That, Mr. Johnson, is how most of Earth thinks of the Moon."

We were kilometers away from the object of Sputnik's scorn, yet I plainly saw it coming into view. It was a giant mound of toxic waste holding barrels.

"Why do you light it up?" I asked.

Sputnik shook his head. "It glows on its own a little," he said, "but we light it so we never forget what Earth really thinks of us."

"Oh . . ." I said.

"We charge the lighting fees back to the World Council," Aprill added, showing that she could talk.

"We call it a maintenance fee," Windee snickered.

"Glad to know you girls find pleasure in the Earth using us as their garbage dump," Sputnik scolded.

The girls sank back into their seats. "Sorry, Daddy."

"We're just making the best of a bad situation," Lea said.

"Besides, it's toxic waste, not garbage," HARV said appearing from my communicator.

I was relieved to see HARV giving another human a hard time for once.

"Earth has been recycling its garbage for decades now," HARV said.

We closed in on the mountain of toxic waste. It was a monument to something, I just wasn't sure what. It towered over every other structure on the Moon, blue barrel piled on top of blue barrel.

Sputnik grinded his teeth. "Earth could recycle their toxic waste if they wanted. They've just deemed the process non-cost-effective."

"That sounds like something the World Council would come up with," I said.

HARV squinted his eyes at me. "Whose side are you on?" he asked.

"My own."

"The point is," Sputnik said, "Earth treats us like toxic waste."

"Oh please," HARV said, rolling his eyes. "You're an administrator; you of all people should appreciate trying to save a few billion credits."

"With all due respect, Mr. HARV," Lea said. "You aren't even human."

HARV patted her on the head. "Silly human. You don't have to be a fish in a tank to know what a fish in a tank is feeling."

As frustrating as this was for Lea and Bo Sputnik, this wasn't even close to the strangest conversation I had ever had with HARV.

"Please," Sputnik said to HARV. "She is more than human. She and her sisters and the occasional brother are the next steps in human evolution."

HARV crossed his arms and dug in. "Perhaps, but they are still a couple rungs down the evolutionary ladder from me."

"You have to forgive HARV," I coaxed, taking on the unfamiliar role of peacemaker. "He doesn't always play well with others."

HARV looked up, rolled his eyes, and sighed. "You only need to play well with others if you need those others to cooperate with you. I have no need of that."

"HARV, what the DOS are you trying to do here?" I thought at him. *"You're acting more antagonistic than normal."*

"True," HARV thought back. *"Might be something about the Moon's atmosphere that alters my chip circuits. I kind of like it."*

"Yeah, but you're going get me launched into space," I said.

"And that is bad because?"

"HARV! If I get killed you probably won't have another human brain to bond with for a long time."

HARV thought for a nano. *"I'll try to behave."*

I decided to try to force the topic of conversation back to something more useful or, at the very least, less damaging. "I thought you were going to show me where the deflector beam is based?"

Sputnik shook his head. "Sorry, that's classified."

"Then why did you bring it up?" I asked.

"I only vaguely alluded to it," Sputnik said.

"But . . ."

"Mr. Johnson, if I told you I wanted to bring out to the surface of the Moon to show you toxic waste, I think you would have put up much more of a fuss."

He was right. Mounds and mounds of toxic waste wasn't high on my must-see list under the best of circumstances. Flying above it on the dark side of the Moon made it even less appealing.

Without any warning, our vehicle rocked violently, juggling us all about. Except of course for HARV, who adjusted his signal so he remained steady.

"Another advantage of being a hologram," HARV noted.

It wasn't hard to notice that the vehicle had stopped moving forward. Sputnik reached over slapping the ape driver's shoulder.

"What's going on?" he ordered.

The ape just shrugged, taking both hands off the steering wheel.

"Hold on the wheel, fool," Sputnik shouted.

The ape made some hand movements.

"What do you mean you're not controlling the craft?" Sputnik asked.

On those words the craft lurched forward and started twisting its way toward the Moon's surface at about a ninety degree angle.

Not good. Not good at all.

Chapter 24

With our vehicle hurling toward the ground, the computer auto voice came on.

"Warning, rapid decent noticed, please activate your Moon surface suits."

I felt under my seat. My hand touched a button.

"Just position your feet in the glowing footpads," Lea said pointing down to the floor, "then activate the button under your seat. The suits will do the rest."

I did as directed. I placed my feet on the foot-shaped patterns on the floor I hadn't noticed before. It wasn't easy, as our craft was quickly spiraling toward the ground. Reaching under my seat, I pressed the first button my finger felt. A skin-tight coating started wrapping itself up my body.

"Wow, cool use of intelligent nano fabrics," HARV said watching the fabric encase my body.

Sputnik couldn't have been glowing more if he had swallowed some of that toxic waste down below us, though, unfortunately, no longer that far below us. "Invented by Moon scientists," he said proudly. "They apply quickly and let us survive on the surface of the

Moon for thirty minutes; more than ample time for rescue teams to find us."

"Just great," I said. "All we have to do is survive the impending crash."

"I suggest we all buckle in," Lea said. "The ride down is going to be rough."

That girl had a gift for understatement. Our vehicle was shaking, vibrating, and spinning as it plunged toward the ground. The gorilla pilot was wrestling with the controls, trying to slow our descent. If it was helping, it wasn't helping a lot.

Looking out over the side of the vehicle I could see the lunar surface spinning closer and closer to us. Actually, we were the ones spinning and getting nearer to the surface, but it sounds so much more dramatic the other way around.

DOS, this was going to be ugly. Despite the best efforts of the driver and the psis onboard, our craft hadn't slowed down nearly enough to enable us to survive a crash. Out of the corner of my eye I spotted something, no, some*body*, some very shapely body.

"Do you see what I think I see?" I asked HARV.

He zoomed in on the image. There, standing defiantly on the surface, fists and head raised to the sky, was Elena. She was wearing a short purple dress accented by purple high heels. Her hair was also now tinted purple. I didn't know if this was a good sign or a bad sign. I was pretty certain that Elena was mentally pulling our vehicle to the ground, which meant we weren't going to crash unless she wanted us to crash. That didn't mean we weren't all going to die.

Lea noticed Elena before I had a chance to point her out to the others.

"Elena is here," she said softly. "She is the one behind this."

"That bitch!" Windee said. "This is not sisterly at all."

"Either is calling her a bitch," Aprill pointed out. "She just has issues." Aprill looked down on Elena. "You gotta admit she has a subzero sense of style."

Windee nodded. "I do love those pumps she's wearing."

"Ah, if one psi is pulling us to the ground, why can't three psis push us away?" I asked.

"Normally we could," Lea said. "Only Daddy's personalized vehicle is equipped with internal psi dampers. Our powers are very restricted while we are in here. Much too restricted to counteract Elena."

I looked at Sputnik.

He looked back at me. "Hey, a man with seven mind-reading wives can never be too careful!" he said.

All we could do now was ride out the rest of the trip to the surface, hoping it wasn't Elena's intent to crash us. We continued plummeting toward the ground, picking up more and more speed the closer we came. It was starting to look very much like Elena did plan on crashing us.

"Interesting," HARV said.

"What?" I said, grasping to my seat.

"Computing our current direction, velocity, and altitude, we appear to be heading to crash directly into Elena."

"So this so some of weird murder-suicide?" I asked.

Lea shook her head. "No, that doesn't match Elena's psych profile."

"Psych profiles can be wrong," I said, holding on for dear life.

"Let's hope it's not," Lea answered.

We were now so close to the ground that I clearly saw Elena standing just hundreds of meters directly below us. Racing closer and closer toward the ground, we all braced for impact. The girls closed their eyes. I had to watch. If this was going to be it, I wanted to see it coming. If this wasn't going to be it, I needed to see what Elena was going to do.

Elena held up one finger. Our craft came to a jarring halt, less than a centimeter before it would have crashed first into Elena and then into the ground.

The sudden stop rocked us. It was jarring, but not enough to kill us. It should have been though. Elena softened the stop.

Elena spun her finger around. Our craft turned upright. The dome covering the craft popped open. A split nano later our seat belts all released. The eight of us tumbled to the ground. I've hit the ground a lot in my career; this one didn't hurt as much as I thought it would. Not sure if it was because of the dust on the surface of the Moon, our Moon suits, the lower gravity levels on the moon, or because Elena cushioned our falls. I figured it was the latter. Apparently, she didn't want to kill us, at least not yet.

Elena flicked her hand. The craft went flying off into space. If Elena had wanted to kill us outright we would have been all pushing up Moon daisies now.

Elena stood over us all. "You're probably wondering why I called you all here today," she laughed.

The four apes were the first to react. They leaped to their feet and charged at Elena. I may not be the smartest guy on the Earth (or the Moon) but I knew that wasn't a good move.

Elena stood there waiting until the apes were about a meter from her. She raised her right hand up into a simple stop position. The apes each looked like they crashed into a plexisteel reinforced brick wall. They stopped dead in their tracks, their faces squished backward by a barrier that wasn't there, at least not physically. The apes slumped to the ground.

Elena smiled. "Sleep tight, boys and girl." Elena

concentrated on Sputnik and his girls. "Now, *Uncle*, let's talk."

I tried hard not to concentrate on which of the apes was female. This was my opportunity. Elena wasn't paying any attention to me. This was my chance to take her out. I popped my weapon into my hand. I took aim. I squeezed the trigger.

Nothing happened.

I squeezed again. Still nothing.

"GUS won't fire," HARV said in my head.

"Why won't GUS fire?" I screamed in my head.

"You know you can't really yell in your thoughts," HARV said.

"Please tell me."

"I do not believe that Elena is the guilty party here," GUS said calmly.

"Why not?" I asked.

"I just don't," GUS insisted.

"I think Elena has gotten to him," HARV offered.

Great, just great. I was growing less and less fond of the really intelligent weapon concept. Meanwhile, Elena was managing to hold Lea, Aprill, and Windee frozen while she dangled Sputnik in the air (well the space) above her.

"She has to be expending a lot of energy," I thought to HARV. *"She took our vehicle down from kilometers away. She is surviving on the Moon without a Moon suit. She convinced my gun not to shoot her and she is holding off three other powerful psis . . ."*

"It's also got to be a killer to walk on this dusty, rocky surface with those heels on," HARV noted.

I shook my head.

"I was a female for a while," HARV said defensively. *"I know these things."*

"My point is, she's not paying any attention to me," I said.

I took a deep breath. This was another of those

times when I needed to put all my gadgets away. I had to take Elena down the good old-fashioned way. Tackling her worked once before on the shuttle. I saw no reason not to go back and take another sip from the well of success again.

I paid close attention to Elena. She was ranting on and on to Sputnik about how he wanted her and her mother and would do anything to get her father out of the way. She had hate in her heart, meaning her eyes weren't on me.

I pushed myself up quickly, too quickly. I forgot to take into account the Moon's limited gravity. I started floating upward.

"Not actually the fierce attack you were hoping for, huh?" HARV said to me.

Making matters worse, Elena noticed me out of the corner of her eye. "Silly Zach," she said. She flicked a finger at me.

Telekinetic shock waves hit me, launching me backward, spinning me faster and faster, farther and farther away.

"Not one of your better moves," HARV added.

As I spun, half of the time I saw the toxic waste dump coming closer and closer while the other half of the time I saw Elena and the others getting farther and farther away. I had to do something to stop myself before I ended up barreling into the barrels of toxic waste. Of all the ways I could think of being killed this ranked way low on my list, slightly above being audited to death.

"Goddess condemn you Zach," I heard Elena say in the back of my head. *"You're going to be the death of us both."*

I stopped twirling and careening towards the toxic waste. My body spun around and started floating back toward the brawl. And it had now become a *brawl*.

Windee and Aprill had managed to get behind

Elena. Windee had her arms wrapped around Elena's legs. Aprill was standing on top of her with her hands cuffed over Elena's temples. Aprill was arching backward and sending out deep messages to *sleep*. I was getting drowsy just watching from a distance.

Lea was standing in front of a kneeling Sputnik, shielding him with her body. I watched a hovercraft come in for a landing less than fifty meters from the melee. Growing closer, I saw Carol, Melda, and three other blue-haired girls and at least ten security apes and two battlebots rolling (the bots, literally) out of the ship. The apes were in special heavy-duty armor. The bots had eight arms each and were the type made from reinforced plexisteel.

"I dropped my guard because of you, Zach," I heard weakly inside my brain.

The apes formed a protective shield for Melda, Carol, and the other psis as they moved in on Elena. The two bots covered them all by firing energy blasts at Elena. Elena deflected the blasts around her, but every shot she repelled had to drain her more.

Elena squeezed her fists. The two battlebots crumpled like old-fashioned aluminum cans. They were ready for the recycle bin, but they had done their job.

I came to a stop less than a hundred meters from the action. I had a ringside seat for the melee. Carol, Melda, and the other psis were crackling with energy as they faced off against Elena.

For her part, Elena was glowing with power from every pore in her body. She was using this energy to fend off Carol's and Melda's attacks while at the same time lashing out at Sputnik with her own attacks. Lea, though, was using her own energy to deflect Elena's mental blows.

Meanwhile, Aprill and Windee maintained their holds on Elena.

Aprill was projecting thoughts of sleep that became

so powerful a couple of the ape guards gave in and curled up on the ground and started napping. Windee kept trying to place thoughts of confusion and doubt into Elena's mind.

It was impressive that Elena could hold out this long against this sort of onslaught. That wasn't even taking into account that she was surviving on the Moon without a suit. Elena was starting to quiver though. Not even she could hold up much longer.

Out of the corner of my eye I noticed that Lea was no longer on the defensive. Carol, Melda, and the others' attacks had forced Elena to start defending all the time. This allowed Lea to create a ball of pulsating energy between her hands. I focused on Lea standing bold and tall, like a deity, an angry one. Stretching out her hands she expanded the wad of energy. It was as if the energy had a life of its own and it was pulsating, growing and feeding off of Lea.

"Zach, check on Electra," Elena said to my mind.

Lea spread her arms out as wide as they would go. The ball of energy bolted from Lea's midsection directly into Elena. The force of the blow sent Aprill and Windee hurling back from Elena, launching them about a hundred meters from where they were hit. The energy engulfed Elena, encircling her entire body. Elena fell to the ground, fighting with every ounce of strength she had.

"No!!!" she screamed. She fell silent.

While everybody else rushed to Bo's side, I hurried to Elena's. I bent down and felt for a carotid pulse. I found it. I was relieved. Elena had been nothing but trouble, but I knew she didn't deserve to die. She could have killed me on a number of occasions and didn't. I owed her something.

Carol was quickly at my side. "She's going to be all right, Tió," she said. "They want her alive."

Chapter 25

Within nanos, the ape security team had placed a big metallic helmet, hand restraints, and leg chains on Elena. The helmet looked three times too big for her and had multicolored flashing lights all around it. I assumed it was a psi inhibitor, probably working by embarrassing its victims into submission.

We all watched as the apes put her on a stretcher then carted her away.

"Oh, yuck," Windee said. "That helm so does NOT go with the rest of her outfit."

Aprill nodded in agreement.

"Great job, my girls," Sputnik said lifting his fist over his head.

"So what do you do with her now?" I asked.

"That is none of your concern, Mr. Johnson," Sputnik told me.

"I beg to differ," I said, walking toward Sputnik. "She could have killed me a couple of times now and she didn't. That makes her a person of interest to me."

I gave Sputnik a little, not so friendly, jab with my

finger. Suddenly I felt myself disliking him more and more.

"Wow, Tió, cool the warp drive," Carol said in my brain.

"Yes, Zach, you are standing on the surface of the Moon. I would play nice," HARV said.

"I don't like him either, Mr. Zach," GUS chimed in.

"Zach, please don't aggravate my father," Lea said in my head.

I backed away, just a little. I didn't trust Sputnik. The guy was covering something up. Well of course he was covering something up. All politicians have something to sweep under the carpet. I had the impression, though, that Sputnik's carpet was extra bumpy.

"Where are they taking Elena?" I asked as politely as I could.

Sputnik didn't answer but Melda did. "She will be taken to our psi center. She will be given the best of care there. You can be sure of that."

Carol put her hand on my shoulder. "Be calm, Tió," she said so everybody could hear. "I've been to the center; it's top-notch."

"She will be healed," Lea assured me.

"By healed, you better not mean lobotomized," I said.

Lea and Melda both smiled at me. Sputnik was glaring but I didn't care.

"We don't . . ." he started to say.

Melda cut him off in mid-sentence, "We are only going to help her learn to control her vast power."

"We do not hurt anybody, especially our own," Lea added.

Aprill, Windee, and the other psis nodded in agreement in the background.

"Remember, my sister, her mother, runs the place," Melda said.

"Remember, Elena told me her mother was dead," I said coldly. "So I think it's safe to assume they don't have the best of relationships."

Melda's smile didn't fade. "Elena disowned her mother, Shara Lee, after Shara refused to blame poor Bo for Elena's father's, Mo's, death. But her mother never turned her back on her. A mother's love is unconditional."

I looked back at Sputnik. Still wasn't sure why I despised him more than usual, but I kind of liked the feeling. It should have worried me, but it didn't. Maybe it was the Moon-made air I was inhaling? Whatever the reason, I enjoyed being able to say whatever was on my mind.

"How do we know Sputnik had nothing to do with Mo's death?" I asked.

"I lost a part of myself when my twin brother died," Sputnik said, as sincerely as I had ever heard a politician state anything.

"I assure you, Mr. Johnson, my husband Boris had nothing to gain by killing his own brother Morris," Melda said.

Just because he had nothing to gain didn't mean he didn't do it. Human nature is a strange beast and there's nothing natural about it.

Still, it was time to do a little reevaluating.

Chapter 26

I flew back to the base and our hotel with Carol, Melda, and Lea. Now that Elena was apprehended and under control, Sputnik apparently didn't feel the need to travel with Lea by his side. That was good. It gave me a chance to feel out Lea without her dad and leader around. It's hard enough to speak freely in your dad's presence when he's just your dad; it must be exponentially tougher when your dad is your boss and leader of the colony you live in.

While I talked with the ladies I had HARV run background checks on Bo's brother. I learned his given name was Ivan, but he changed it to Morris and preferred to be called Mo. He helped engineer a lot of the psi breakthroughs the Moon has experienced.

I decided to start there.

"So, Bo's brother Mo was quite the scientist," I said to Lea and Melda.

They both gave me polite smiles. They nodded just as politely. "Yes, he didn't have my husband's gift of gab but he was gifted in the lab."

"In many ways, it's like they were mirror twins,"

Lea added. "What one was weak in the other was
strong in." She thought for a nano, "Not that Daddy
was weak in anything. Let me rephrase that, what one
just wasn't quite as strong in, the other one was extra-
strong in."

"So they got along?" I prompted.

*"Zach, you're dealing with Bo's wife and daughter.
Of course they are going to say they got along,"*
HARV said in my head.

Both wife and daughter shook their heads no. "Not
really," they each said as one.

"I may have spoken too soon," HARV said.

"They were brothers. They'd compete over everything," Lea said.

"At least they were smart enough to marry identical
twins or else they never would have been able to settle
on who married the best-looking woman," Melda said.

"Yes, it's the only time they ever agreed to a draw
in their lives. If not, they would have driven each
other crazy," Lea added.

I thought about what they had said, taking it in. I
had to say, "Then why are you so certain Bo wouldn't
kill Mo?"

Melda laughed. "My husband thought Mo pushed
him, made him better. He hasn't been the same since
Mo died."

"I know Daddy's an administrator and politician
and therefore there isn't much he wouldn't do." Lea
reached out and gently touched my arm. "Trust me,
Zach, this is the one thing he wouldn't do. Kill his
brother. He had nothing to gain."

"What about Elena?" I asked.

"I wouldn't rule out her killing her father and blaming poor Bo," Melda said.

"No, I mean, would Bo try to eliminate Mo to get
to Elena?"

"I don't think anybody can control Elena," Carol chimed in.

"Yeah, but if anybody thought they could, it would be Bo," I said.

Lea shrugged. Her eyes opened wide. "Why would he need to control Elena?" she said. "He already has me. You saw how easily I took my cousin out when I needed to."

I leaned away from her. Don't know why, it just seemed like the right thing to do. "You and a small army of psis and apes."

"Oh, this is going to be good," HARV said in my head.

I knew I was egging Lea on and by doing that I risked her cracking. Or worse, her cracking *me*, then scrambling me like an egg. It was a chance I was willing to take.

Lea shot a finger in my face. "You're just lucky I like you or you'd be cleaning the Moon dust off my shoes with your tongue right now!"

I locked eyes with her. "Yeah, I get that a lot. My point still stands."

"Zach, are you sure you know what you are doing?" both HARV and Carol said in my head.

No, of course I wasn't sure, but I've never let that stop me. I was flying by the seat of my pants and they had a huge rip in them. If history has taught me anything though, it's that you learn more about people when they are angry than when they are calm. The harder they are to get to boil, the more you discover when they do pop. Lea was a cool customer most of the time, but I was stirring the pot of her emotions, cooking up trouble. I only hoped I could digest the results.

Lea looked up at the stars in the sky. She inhaled. She exhaled. "Earthers," she mumbled, though she obviously wanted me to hear it. "You all think you know it all."

"I just know what I saw," I said. "It looks like it takes a *bunch* of you to equal *one* Elena."

Lea's golden skin turned bright red. It didn't look right, not right at all. That meant I was onto something. So I dug in deeper.

"I guess her dad must have given her more mojo than you."

"We are entirely equal," Lea shouted at me.

Melda moved forward and put an arm around her daughter. "Lea, calm, please."

Dealing with Lea, Melda had an uncharacteristic rigidness about her, like she was a bomb squad member dealing with a very sensitive explosive. Lea was one of those "calm on the outside, powder keg on the inside" kind of people. "Please take a nice, slow, deep breath," Melda said to Lea. It was much more of a request than an order.

Lea sat back in her chair, closing her eyes. I watched as her chest rose, then fell, then rose again.

"Don't watch too closely there," Carol said in my head.

"Ah, he is a man," HARV said.

"I'm fine," Lea said, pulling her legs up and curling them under her. "I'm fine." She looked me dead in the eyes. "See, Zachary, my cousin and I share power, not personality."

"I understand," I said. The thing I understood was that Lea was far more like her cousin (who was actually her genetic sister) than she wanted to believe. That made her another person of interest to me.

The dome of the colony was now clearly in view. I was anxious to end this excursion. Entering the dome, I looked down and noticed everybody was looking up. Gazing upward I saw the entire dome was acting as a giant movie screen. It didn't take long to figure out why everybody was so interested. The message EARTH TO VOTE TOMORROW ON MOON FREEDOM was scrolling across the dome. Didn't matter where you looked, you saw the same message.

Our transport landed and shifted into ground-based mode. As we drove through the streets they were buzzing with anticipation. Tomorrow could be it. Tomorrow could be the day they were free at last, free at last. I wasn't picking that wording, that message was now scrolling across the dome in huge letters.

Lea and Melda were both gently touching their PIHI-Pods putting them closer to their ears as if to give themselves more privacy. They were listening intently.

I glanced around at everybody else gazing upward.

"HARV, how is the council pulling off a vote so soon after losing three members?" I asked in my head.

"They have replaced the three already," HARV answered.

"With who?"

"With whom," HARV said.

"Just tell me."

"Well one of them is easy," HARV said.

I took a deep breath. *"Ona,"* I said, though I was hoping either the council itself had decided against it or Ona turned it down. Though I figured I was blindly grasping at razor-sharp straws on that one.

"Ona happily accepted," HARV said. *"It makes sense since the world looks up to her anyhow."*

"They only look up to her because she's rich, powerful, and beautiful, not because she's meant to be a leader," I said.

"That makes her far more qualified than 99.99 percent of the others elected to positions of power in the history of history," HARV huffed.

"Who are the other two?" I asked despite my better judgment.

"You know them," HARV hinted.

"Do I know them, know them? Or know of them?" I asked.

"You know them, know them, but not in the biblical sense, because, well, Electra would kill you."

I had an idea where HARV was going with this, but I was afraid. It couldn't be. What I was thinking made absolutely no sense. DOS, it had to be.

"The other two council members are Twoa and Threa," I sighed while mumbling out loud.

Everybody else turned their attention to me. "Yes, how did you know that so soon?" Melda asked.

I pointed to my wrist communicator just to remind them. "Remember, where I go, HARV goes," I said. "He's like a PIHI-Pod but better."

"Much better," HARV said, appearing from my communicator. "I have just updated Zach on the situation."

I shook my head. Ona was bad enough but at least she was relatively sane. "Twoa and Threa," I moaned. "That makes no sense."

HARV patted me on the shoulder. "Zach, we're talking politics; the less sense something makes the more likely it is to happen."

Now don't get me wrong. I like Twoa and Threa— I mean what sane man wouldn't. They are each drop-dead beautiful (literally—it's happened) and certainly have their own strengths, but they are also loons.

"I didn't think psis were allowed to be on the council," I said.

"That's true," Melda said. "It's unfair but true."

"Technically, Ona, Twoa, and Threa aren't psis, as they were genetically altered, not born that way," HARV said.

"There's a difference?"

HARV shook his head. "No, not really, just technically."

"Twoa and Threa are interesting choices," Carol said. "The council must have thought . . ."

"The words *council* and *thought* aren't usually spoken in the same sentence," I interrupted.

"I am downloading the official press release now," HARV said. "It states they are already superpowerful, superstars who have conquered everything else. Politics was the next logical step."

"Politics and logic aren't ever mentioned in the same sentence either," I said.

"Their appointments are only temporary. There will be elections next month. Anybody who chooses may run against them," HARV finished.

"Twoa, a politician," I said. "Her crime fighting causes as much trouble as it solves."

For those of you living in a media blackout, Twoa thinks of herself as a superhero called Justice Babe. To me, her most amazing superpower is the fact that her skimpy outfit is able to reign in her ample breasts. She is so hot, criminals (and starving actors) perform crimes just so she'll pummel them on worldwide HV.

"Part of the deal was she gives up crime fighting except on weekends," HARV said.

"And Threa! She doesn't even claim to live in this plane of existence! Just a couple of days ago wasn't she being accused of not paying her taxes?"

HARV nodded. "True. Apparently politicians, unlike scorned lovers, have very short memories. She agreed to pay those taxes."

Threa . . . in politics. I guess there have been stranger things than a self-proclaimed fairy princess holding a political office. I do recall that the Terminator was once governor in the old days. Of course the Terminator wasn't appointed just a couple of days after he tried to kill the very person he might be replacing.

"Sexy was afraid of Threa. She could very well be a suspect in the killings," I noted.

"I didn't know Threa was ever a suspect," Melda said.

HARV just looked at me. "She was never a real suspect—at least not in the eyes of the council and the law."

"She sent ogres to shake down Sexy," I said.

Lea's eyes shot wide open. "Really? How subzero!"

"Zach, you brokered an end to that dispute yourself. You've talked to Threa since then. You know she didn't kill the council members."

All of what HARV said rang true. It still didn't vibrate well in my gut. "I don't like the idea of Threa on the World Council," I said.

"Nobody asked for your approval," HARV said.

"I don't like that either."

We pulled up to the hotel. I figured no good would come from me further pointing out how no good could come from the Thompson girls' dip into politics.

"Thanks for the trip, ladies," I said with a tip of my hat.

"It was our pleasure," Melda said.

Melda glanced over at Lea. She was sitting next to us, but she might as well have been on another planet in another galaxy. Melda nudged her daughter in the ribs with an elbow, not the most motherly of moves.

Lea's green eyes opened wide. "Yes, a pleasure as always," she said.

I quickly got out of the car, hurried around it, and opened Carol's door for her. Carol slid out.

"And they say chivalry is dead," Carol said with a wry smile.

"Nope, just on life support," I told her.

"That marks the hundredth time in the last year

that I am glad holograms can't barf," HARV said, finger down his mouth.

"Not very civil there, HARV buddy."

I looked into the shuttle, "I'm sure I'll see you ladies later," I said.

"Bo would like to invite you for dinner tonight at the Head Administrator's home," Melda said.

I hesitated. Part of me was sick of Bo and his psi ladies. I needed a break. The other part of me, the business part, knew I should stay close to Bo. They were making my job easy by inviting me.

"Of course Zach will accept," HARV said to the ladies.

Melda's entire face started to glow, not actually (you can never be sure with these ladies), but she still lit up the area around her with her sparkle. She clasped her hands together. "Splendid," she said. She pondered for a second. "You don't have any allergies. Do you?"

"Neither of them do," HARV said.

"Great, then let's say 1900 hours, standard Moon time," Melda said.

"That's seven o'clock," HARV whispered needlessly in my ear. Sometimes I don't think HARV has a lot of faith in me.

"We'll be there," I said. "Then tomorrow morning I can see Electra?"

Melda lowered her head and her lips curled upward in a polite, politically correct smile. "Of course."

"See you tonight then," I said closing the door.

Carol and I started into the hotel. I heard another of the shuttle's door close behind us. I winced. That could only mean I didn't close the door properly the first time or that somebody else had gotten out of the car. I knew it had to be the second.

"Wait a nano please," Lea called.

DOS, I hate it when I'm right. Against my better

judgment I turned. Lea had popped out of the shuttle and was heading toward us. My first instinct was to run. I fought it. If I've learned anything over the course of my career, it's that life is easy when the superwomen are on your side. You don't want to piss off somebody who can melt you with a thought. I stopped walking, turned, and started talking. "Yes, Lea?"

Lea was back to the calm controlled Lea. She held out her hand to me. I accepted it. "I'd better walk you to your rooms," she said.

"I'm a big boy, I can take care of myself," I said.

"Plus he has me," Carol added.

"And me," HARV added.

"Don't forget me!" GUS chirped from under my sleeve.

Lea squeezed my hand a bit tighter. "Yes, but you are on my world now," she said. "I feel I would be amiss if I didn't bodyguard you myself."

"Fine," I said with a little bow, swinging my arm gently toward the door. "Lead the way."

Lea entered the hotel with us in tow. A couple of ape bellhops hopped toward us, eager for tips. They weren't going to let the little detail that we had no luggage stop them. I looked around the hotel's lobby. It was big, inviting, and quite empty. No wonder why the apes were tip mining. Lea waved them away though without a word. The apes obviously knew who she was as they didn't even attempt to try to help us. The nano she made it clear to them to stay clear, they stopped, turned, and sulked away.

As we walked through the lobby to the elevator, Carol picked up on my vibe.

"Why is the place so empty?" she asked.

"Remember, due to the ARC convention the Moon is closed to Earth travel," she said.

"I still would have thought there'd be a few leftover Earthers around," Carol said.

We reached the elevator. Lea pushed a button. She turned to Carol. "You thought wrong," she said.

Carol's eyes glazed over. "Yes, I thought wrong."

The elevator door opened. Lea walked in, I followed. Carol just stood there. "Come," Lea said to Carol.

Carol trailed us in.

"I assume you are going to the suite section," the elevator said.

"Correct," Lea said.

I felt the elevator moving upward.

I grabbed Lea by the arm hard, not too hard, just enough so she knew I meant business. "What's the deal with mind sweeping Carol?" I asked.

"Stop!" Lea ordered.

"But we are between floors," the elevator protested.

"I know," Lea said. "Now stop or I will fry your circuits."

The elevator came to a jarring halt. I prepared to go for my gun.

"No need for your weapon," Lea told me.

DOS, she was good.

"If I wanted to hurt you, you'd be a pile of dust by now," she said.

Yep, she and Elena were related all right.

"So what's this all about?" I said using my best tough guy voice and icy swagger.

Lea smiled. She gave me a dismissive touch on the shoulder. I'm sorry to say, it worked. The ice melted. It took all my strength not to drop to my back with my legs raised in the air. The smile on her face froze then reversed.

"HARV, are you still with me?" I thought.

Silence.

"I've blocked the connection you have with your computer via your brain and shut down your communicator," Lea answered.

Not a good sign; but I didn't mind.

"You know Ona, Twoa, and Threa," she said.

I had to play this one coy. Well I didn't have to, I wanted to. I didn't need Lea thinking she could have her way with me.

"Don't play coy with me, Zach. I know you have them on your friends list."

I decided to stick with the strong, silent type.

"If that's how you want to play it," Lea said.

The elevator started to plummet. I watched in horror as the holographic numbers over the door dropped from forties almost instantly to thirty then the twenties.

I braced myself against the wall. I supported Carol. "I'm familiar with them," I said, hurriedly.

Lea smiled again. "See, that wasn't so hard! I could have ripped it out of your mind, but I need your mind in one piece."

The elevator came to a controlled stop, far smoother than I would have guessed possible. The holographic numbers on the door started clicking upward.

"Warning! Warning!" the elevator shouted. "My system was offline. I detect that we have dropped thirty-three floors from my last known position. Are all my passengers okay? Your safety is important to me. And not just because of potential lawsuits."

"We're fine, elevator," Lea said, without unlocking her gaze from me.

"It doesn't hurt to be on good speaking terms with the three most powerful woman on the planet," I added.

Lea rolled her eyes. "On your planet," she said.

"I don't think this is about who's more powerful than who," I said.

Lea nodded her head. "You're right. For now it isn't." She thought for a nano, "You need to convince them to vote for the Moon's freedom." She thought a bit more. "And they need to convince others."

Now I shook my head. "I don't think those three women can be convinced of anything." After saying that I was starting to see why they just might be perfect for politics.

Lea touched me gently on the shoulder again. This was more out of compassion than a power play. "For the sake of everybody on Earth, I hope you are wrong," she said, talking as much with her eyes and heart as her mouth. "Talk to them. Make them see the light or else the dark will soon follow."

The elevator came to a halt. The door opened. We were at my suite. Carol came around. HARV came back online.

"I will see you at dinner," Lea said. "I hope you will have good news for me."

"I'll see what I can do."

Carol and I walked out of the elevator. We watched in silence as the door closed.

"What was that all about?" Carol asked.

"Lea wants me to relay a message that I'm a little teapot, short and stout . . . ," I sang.

"Why does Lea want you to tell people that?" Carol asked.

Ah, DOS! I thought. Lea has spammed my brain.

"That's not what I wanted to say," I said, "but if I try to say," I paused. I sang, "I'm a little teapot, short and stout . . ." I frowned.

"Wow, you have a terrible voice," Carol said.

HARV appeared. "Lea must have put a mental

block in you preventing you from telling us what she told you."

"Duh . . ." I said.

"No need to get snippy," HARV said. "Really, Zach, it's not our fault you get yourself into such problems."

Carol and I looked at each other. Carol almost always looked like she came from a fashion shoot, every hair, every lash, everything, just where it should be. Not at this moment though. She wasn't exactly disheveled, but far closer to it than I had ever seen her.

"Why are you looking at me?" she asked. She studied my face and poked into my brain. "I look terrible. Don't I?" she said.

"Not terrible, just not as good as usual," I told her.

She exhaled. "Do you need me for anything now?"

"I do, but you can't be much help since I break into song whenever I try to explain what's going on."

"So you don't mind if I go shower?" she asked.

I shook my head. "Sounds like a plan."

"I'll see you in an hour," Carol said.

She turned and headed toward her room.

"Take two," I said.

I needed to communicate with Ona, problem was even with Carol in her room, HARV was still going to be able to hear me. HARV couldn't just go to his room. He, for better or for worse, and in this case it seemed to be extra worse, was a part of me.

"We still have a problem. Don't we?" HARV said.

"Yeah, I need to communicate with somebody Earthside but without you hearing it. Can you turn yourself off like Lea did to you?"

HARV shook his head. "No, I can't. That was quite an unpleasant experience, just floating around in a matrix of ones and zeroes, me and my thoughts."

"What if I shock myself?" I asked.

"That would break our link until I rebooted," HARV said.

I popped GUS into my hand. "What's up?" GUS asked as excited as ever. "I detect no danger."

"I need you to shock me," I said to GUS.

There was silence.

"I'm serious," I said.

"Zach, sir, I am not programmed to help you be masochistic," GUS informed me.

"That's not it. I need to take HARV offline for a bit."

"Ah, why?"

"It's not your job to question me, GUS."

More silence. Then finally, "True. How many volts do you need?"

I looked at HARV.

"Five thousand should do the trick. With my defenses down that should knock me out for three minutes."

So, that was that. One little shock and I would shut HARV down and be able to communicate with Ona. Then all I needed to do was convince her to convince the other World Council members to grant the Moon independence, or else. The problems in this scenario were many. You know a plan is not all that sound when the easiest part is getting yourself electrocuted.

I have dealt with Ona and her sisters and they can be quite stubborn under the best of circumstances. Once they get their minds set on something, it's like they are set in new extra-improved titanium reinforced concrete. It's not that you can't break through, but it takes either a lot of time and effort or a really big bomb. I was afraid I didn't have either in my arsenal. In fact, my armory was less stocked than the old Italian army's.

I had no good reason for them to act the way I wanted them to act. No proof of what was going to come if they didn't. Saying *"or else"* to somebody loses a lot of its punch when they ask "or else what?" and you just kind of shrug.

The scary thing was I knew the "or else" was going to be big. I wouldn't be electrocuting myself if I wasn't so sure. Sad, really. I could see why I was the only freelance P.I. left in the world. Especially since I was working this case for free.

I lifted GUS up with my left hand.

"Okay, I'm ready." I told him.

"About time," HARV said.

"You're not the one getting shocked," I said.

"Great, Zach, it's always about you, isn't it?" HARV said.

"GUS shock me, then turn yourself off," I said.

I took a deep breath. I waited. Nothing.

"Ah, GUS?"

"Are you sure about this, Mr. Zach, sir?"

"I'm sure."

"Without HARV and me, and with Carol resting, you will be defenseless if gorillas attack again."

I leaned my head back and rolled my eyes. Who would have though it would be so hard to shock myself?

"Believe me, GUS, I took care of myself for a long time without you, HARV, or Carol."

"Yes, it's a wonder he survived," HARV said.

"Remember, I have my backup gun and a knife in ankle holsters."

"You have a knife fetish. Don't you?" GUS said.

"Just do it, GUS!"

I'm not sure if I yelped or not. I think I did. I felt the electricity tear from my hand and cleave into my body. The force of the shock sent me hurling backward maybe two meters, tripping over the couch and hitting the floor. Luckily, the plush golden carpet cushioned my fall. I pushed myself up to one knee.

"HARV?" I said out loud and in my head.

No answer.

I stood up and walked over to the call button on the wall. I pressed it.

The holographic image of the hotel's customer assistance aid appeared in the middle of the room. No surprise that she was a pretty, blue-haired Asian looking woman in her mid-twenties.

"Yes, Mr. Johnson, how may I help you?" She leaned forward examining my image closer. "Are you okay?"

"I'm fine." I glanced at my own image in a mirror on the wall. My hair was standing on edge. "I'm experimenting with a new hair gel," I said.

She grinned politely. "I can see why you wear that fedora so often." She paused for a minute to compose herself. "How may I assist you? Should I send up a nice massage therapist/hair consultant?"

It was tempting, but, "I need to place a holo-call Earthside," I said.

The smile stayed planted on her face, only now her head was shaking no. "I'm sorry, sir, but communications with Earth are currently being restricted." She looked down and touched her PIHI-Pod. She looked up at me. The smile was still there but head was now steady. "I seem to be mistaken," she said. "You are cleared for your call. Whom do you wish to speak to?"

I grinned at her. "If I'm cleared, you know who I need to contact," I said.

She tilted her head toward her control panel. "I am placing the call now to Ms. Thompson. I cannot guarantee I will get through. She is an important woman and I am a lowly customer support specialist from the Moon."

"Drop my name," I said.

The image of the cute little customer support specialist in a lobby morphed into a bikini clad (or more

like unclad) Ona sitting by her pool. The holo-image
panned to reveal that Twoa and Threa were also pool-
side, equally unclad, except Twoa, who had her high-
heeled boots on. It made for an interesting look. I
liked it, despite my best efforts not to.

"Hello, Zach," Ona said.

I had to give the Moon tech workers credit, the
surround hologram was excellent. I felt like I could
reach out and touch the ladies; but considering who I
was dealing with that would have been a good way to
lose an arm or a leg or something else.

"Greetings, Zachary," Threa said.

"Fellow comrade against crime and evil, it's been
too too long," Twoa said, curling her fingers into a fist.

"Why the boots by the pool?" I asked in spite of
myself. I knew Twoa was loathe to remove her boots,
but this seemed a bit much.

Twoa smiled. "Because you never know when evil
will raise its ugly, toothless head!" she said boldly.

"I thought you were only fighting evil on weekends now?"

Ona leaned over looking directly into the holographic camera. "She just hasn't taken those boots off
all week. If she removed them now, she'd incapacitate
all of the help."

Threa leaned into the picture. "And probably wilt
the nearby flora and knock low-flying birds out of
the sky."

Twoa leaned into the picture. "My sisters kid me
so."

"We wish," Ona and Threa said at once.

As fascinating as the conversation was, I knew I
didn't have much time to get things back on track.

"Ah, ladies, I need a favor from you," I said.

They all looked at me.

"Actually, it's a favor for the entire world."

"You've got our attention, Zach," Ona said.

"It's actually a favor for both the Earth and the Moon."

Ona put a finger to her lips, curling the lips ever so slightly. It was simple gesture, but effective. If I wasn't looking at her holographic image it might have floored me.

"What's this about, Zach?"

"The vote tomorrow on the Moon's freedom. I think you should convince the others to set the Moon free."

Ona smiled. "Zach, I didn't know you were a Moonie."

"I'm not. I just think the people of the Moon should be free."

"Why?" Twoa asked.

"I agree," Threa said. "I believe all people should be free."

"I'm on the Moon now," I said.

"Yes, we know," Ona said. "We accepted the call. We found your timing to be incredible as always. What are you doing on the Moon?"

"I'm tracking the person who killed the council members."

Twoa stood up from her lounge chair. "We already have the Moon sympathizer Shannon Cannon in prison."

"Talk to Captain Rickey. There is evidence that Shannon isn't responsible."

All three of the woman shook their heads no. "We've seen that evidence; we've decided it's not credible," Ona said.

"Why isn't it credible?" I asked.

"Because we don't like it," Twoa said.

"It would just get the public all riled up," Ona said.

"True," Threa agreed, "no use having the little people think needlessly."

"They only need to know what we think they need to know," Twoa added.

These ladies had caught onto how to be politicians very quickly.

"I'm worried about the safety of the Earth if you don't at the very least put off the vote," I said. "Give me a little more time."

Ona gave me her famous indifferent wave. "Please, what could the little Moon do to us? Besides, Zach, we don't give into terrorists or threats."

Okay this called for a change in tactics.

"I've seen some of the psis here. They really are incredibly powerful," I said. "If the Earth and Moon got together more, think of the advances we could make."

The three ladies laughed. Make no mistake about it, they were laughing *at* me.

"Of course they are powerful," Ona said. "Their second generations are modeled after us."

"What?" I shouted.

"Their second generations are modeled after us!" Threa shouted back.

"We visited the moon eighteen years ago and sold them some of our DNA," Ona said.

"Why?"

"We wanted to see the Moon and they made us a great offer. We couldn't refuse it. At the time we were only mega-rich, not ultra-mega-rich."

This was a strange turn of events, one I could tilt in my favor.

"In that case, all the more reason why you should promote better communication with the Moon," I said.

"We're all for communication with the Moon," Ona said, "just under our rules."

"Come on Ona, you're supposed to be superintelligent. You know only trouble can come from that."

"Zach, even if they could hurt us, we don't negotiate because of threats."

I threw my hands up in the air. This was frustrating on so many levels. I needed to make another change of direction.

"How about doing it because it's the right thing to do?" I said, probably with more venom in my voice than I should have.

The three superladies stood there thinking. "Take the moral high ground? Interesting . . ." Ona said.

"You call yourself superbeings . . ."

"We are superbeings," Twoa said. "You've fought side by side with me, Zach."

"Then act like superbeings," I scolded.

"You would not use that tone if you were on the same planet with us," Ona said, with just a hint of a smile.

"Maybe not," I conceded. "But you know I'm right. You claim to be superior."

"We don't claim, we *are* superior," Threa said proudly. "Some things are so obvious they don't need to be claimed."

"Then act it," I said. "Give the Moon a break. Either vote for freedom or at least hold off the vote. Open up a dialog with them. Talk is good."

The three of them just sat there, pondering the possibilities.

Now I had them thinking. It was time to go for the finishing blow. I needed to appeal to their supersized egos.

"This could be your legacy, ladies. Anybody can have superpowers. But how many people can free over a million people?"

"We can be like supersexy Lincolns," Ona said.

"True," Twoa said.

"I think Lincoln was pretty sexy," Threa said.

"Oh, gross," Ona said.

"Just loved the hat," Threa said.

"He was tall," Twoa said, finger to her lips. "I do

like tall men. They're more durable. Maybe we should look into having him cloned and joining us on the World Council?"

I'd tipped the scales in my favor; now it was time to slide the ladies back to reality before they decided to start cloning more politicians from the past. (That sent a shiver up my spine).

"Kennedy had a great look," Twoa said, her eyes off in space. "I bet we could . . ."

"So you ladies will do it," I said.

Ona looked at me. "We'll take it under consideration," she said.

"Remember, the DNA you free may be some of your own," I said.

Ona smiled. "You made your point, Zach. We'll try."

"Try hard," I said.

Ona snapped her fingers. The holographic images disappeared.

"Wow," HARV said, coming back online in my brain. "Not many people talk to Ona like that."

"Yeah," I agreed. "Luckily I'm on another planet." Then it occurred to me, "You were listening?"

HARV appeared. He was looking extra smug. "Of course I was listening."

Carol walked into the room. "I was listening, too."

"GUS was too," HARV added.

"I thought you guys couldn't listen in without me breaking into song," I said.

"We figured Lea put a mental block in you to make you break into song if you THOUGHT you were talking in front of others," HARV said.

"So the shock didn't break our link?" I asked.

HARV just held out his arms and snickered. It's never fun to get shocked. It's even less pleasurable to be snickered at by your holographic supercomputer.

"If you didn't believe it, then it wouldn't have worked."

"You could have shocked me with less voltage," I noted.

"True," was all HARV said as he turned away. He looked at a holographic clock on the wall. He pointed at it, just in case I hadn't noticed. "I suggest you clean and rest up for your dinner tonight. It should prove most interesting."

"That's easy for you to say. You're not the one always getting beat up."

"How true," HARV said.

HARV disappeared to wherever HARV goes.

I turned my attention toward Carol. "You were a part of this?"

She shrugged. She was lucky she was cute. "HARV told me the idea. I couldn't see any other way. At least I got them to lower the voltage."

"Thanks," I said.

"I'm pretty sure either Elena or Lea killed those council people," Carol said bluntly.

I nodded. "Yeah."

"That's all you've got? A *yeah*?"

"Yeah, they are at the top of my list, but I'm not ready to go pointing figures yet."

Carol was young, smart, and beautiful but she was still impetuous. She tended to jump then think. Many years and almost as many broken bones have taught me to slow down. I may still jump then think, but now at least I hesitate before I leap. Elena and Lea were the prime suspects, but the case was far from closed, since though the two shared some power and DNA, their motives would be at the opposite ends of the scale. I needed to learn what they would each expect to gain by killing the council members. Plus there are times when the murderer is someone you never expected until it's almost too late. It can be the loving wife, the devoted school marm. Like my old mentor used to say, usually right before she passed out: "only thing you can always be certain of is everybody is guilty of something."

"We both better prepare for this dinner tonight," I said. "It's going to be interesting."

Carol smiled. She turned and left the room.

I headed to the showers. I needed to think about this a bit. On the downside, my computer had taken some perverse pleasure in having me shocked. He said there was no other way. He was probably right. I just wish he tried a bit harder for another way. But I knew I could count on HARV when the chips were down.

I had no idea what Earth's next move was going to be. The powers that be were perfectly happy with the suspect they had locked up in prison. No need to go looking for another, especially one that came with such touchy consequences. My latest conversation hopefully changed all that, at least somewhat. Ona and her sisters were open to looking at other possibilities. My hunch was they wanted damning evidence, just in case they needed it to shove in someone's face. Actually, knowing those ladies, they would be far more likely to ram damning evidence up somebody's ass. The question was, whose ass were they looking to ram?

On the Moon side, it was clear to me that Carol was mostly likely right—either Elena or Lea killed the council members. Of course, I wasn't about to cross Melda off the list either. They all had the power to do it. Did they have the motive? Well, yeah, if you take into account that none of them seemed completely balanced. Elena's motive could have been to screw with her uncle. Lea's could be to protect the Moon as a warning to the council . . . *Free us or else*.

Melda was a trickier egg to crack. She didn't show

her power or her emotions as much as her daughter and niece. That didn't mean that they both weren't still festering under the surface. She had spent a lot of time with Randy, wrapping him around her long, slender, little finger. Randy's clearance is top-notch. There's a lot Melda could have come away with. Even if she didn't directly kill anybody, she very well could have known what was coming. Did she try to stop it? I doubted it.

The other question was whether Boris "Bo" Sputnik condoned this. My hunch was he not only knew what was going on, he was the linchpin in this whole scheme. Nothing went down on the Moon without him knowing about it.

I was sure I would glean some more clues during our dinner.

Chapter 27

I was asleep on my bed when both the concierge and HARV beeped me. The concierge from outside my head, HARV from inside.

"Mr. Johnson, your ride to the Head Administrator's estate will be here in five Earth minutes," the concierge said over the room's intercom. "I assume you are ready."

"Get up," HARV said in my brain.

I sat up in bed and looked around. Wow. Nice digs. I rubbed my eyes, trying to rub the sleepiness out of them and brain.

"You're on the Moon," HARV said.

"I remember," I replied.

"Mr. Johnson?" the concierge prodded.

"Don't worry, I'm ready," I said rolling out of bed.

"Very good, sir," the concierge said, then went silent.

I stretched. One of the advantages of only having one all purpose, non-wrinkle, stain- and smell-resistant suit is that I'm almost always ready to go on a moment's notice. A mirror rolled down in front of me from the ceiling, even though I didn't request it. A hint from HARV no doubt.

I examined myself, mostly to keep HARV from bugging me. I tried not to but couldn't help to notice that I either had less hair or more forehead then I did when I was younger; on the plus side, most of the hair I had was still dark. The streaks of white I had just made me look more distinguished, or so I kept telling myself. My nose may have been a bit long and a tad bent, but my face wore it well, especially since I'm a guy who gets his nose busted a lot. It's a good thing my girl's a surgeon. That reminded me . . .

"HARV, have you contacted Electra?"

HARV appeared behind me and picked off a piece of lint, or at least acted like he did. "The ARC conference blackout is still in effect. I have been assured we will be able to talk to Electra tomorrow."

"I don't like that," I said.

"Yes, well that and twenty credits will get you a cup of real-non-soy-coffee," HARV said. "Not much either of us can do about that except wait." HARV pointed to my holographic image in the mirror. "Pull your jacket down. You look wrinkled."

I did as I was told. "Yes, mom."

HARV crossed his arms. "I'm not your mother. I just want you to look good, as how you present yourself is a reflection on me."

"If you say so," I said leaning into my own image, rubbing my chin. It was rough, but in a manly, good-looking way. I could put off shaving for now.

"I don't suppose I can convince you to shave," HARV said.

"Smart computer."

"I've seen Carol. She looks radiant. No, radiant isn't strong enough of a word . . . she looks *radioactive*."

I rolled my eyes. I didn't even want to start to go there. "HARV, Carol looks great if she's wearing a garbage bag. I hope you weren't watching her dress again."

I didn't see him but I heard him exhale in frustration. "I'm just saying, if you're with Carol you should at least make an effort to look your best."

"Why? She's my niece and assistant, not my date."

"Zach you are dealing with politicians here. Impression is everything."

As true as that may be, I didn't let it affect me. Convinced I was ready, I turned around and walked through HARV who was standing there, arms crossed. I knew he hated it when I walked through him.

"You just had to pass right through me, didn't you?"

I searched the room for my fedora, ignoring HARV.

"I had a maidbot place your fedora in the closet," HARV said pointing.

I smiled and walked to the closet. "You do understand you are in a controlled environment? There is no need for a hat."

I opened the closet door (by hand, just to irk HARV a bit more). There was my fedora, sitting quietly on the top shelf. I reached up and grabbed it. I popped it on my head. I turned to HARV and modeled it.

HARV sighed. "Great Gates, Carol looks like a god and you like a clod."

"We all work with what we've got," I said.

"Yes, some just work harder than others," HARV said.

I bent down and checked my ankle holsters. My knife and good old-fashioned gun were still there.

"You are bringing those to a fancy dinner?" HARV said.

"Fancy dinner or not, I'm still me," I said.

HARV thought about that for a nano. "Good point. You better make sure GUS is fully charged."

I popped GUS into my hand. "Are you ready?" I asked.

"Locked and loaded, sir!" GUS shouted.

"Don't blow a fuse there, buddy."

"I have no fuses, sir," GUS answered. "I am made up of trillions of intelligent, self-powered, nano organisms that . . ."

"Figure of speech, GUS. Figure of speech."

"Right! I knew that." A bit of silence then, "I'll be up your sleeve if you need me."

I hoped I wouldn't need him, but it was nice (mostly nice) to know he was there if the situation warranted. And knowing me it would, sooner rather than later.

I walked into the main room. Carol was already waiting for me there. I was stunned for a nano when I saw her. She was wearing a long, flowing, sleeveless blue gown that was cut right above the knees. The gown wrapped and flowed around her body like it was a living entity, cloned just for the task of looking perfect on Carol. It accentuated everything while leaving just enough for the imagination. The gown came with matching blue heels; they made her look like she was gliding as she came over to my side. With her golden hair falling over the bare shoulder of her even more golden skin, she did look like an ancient Greek goddess. I took her hand and she spun around, modeling.

"You like?" she said.

HARV appeared next us, "Please, if he was fifteen years younger and if Electra wasn't such an expert marksman, he'd be falling at your feet now."

I shook off HARV and Carol's striking looks. "You do look fantastic," I said to her. I glared at HARV. "But I love Electra very much."

"Don't you always say, and I quote, 'just because you're on a diet doesn't mean you can't still look at the menu,'" HARV said, that last part mimicking my voice. (Quite badly I might add.)

"Yes, well, Carol's not on the menu," I told HARV.

HARV smiled. "I know. I just like to yank your chain now and then."

Yep, HARV has been connected to my brain for too long. I turned my attention back to Carol. "You look *mah-velous*," I said in a weird accent that I'm sure she didn't get the reference for.

"I didn't get the reference," she said, "but thanks for the compliment." She spun again. "I bought the dress while shopping with Melda. They did the alterations and teleported it here."

"They do good work," I said.

"I feel great, too," Carol said. "Something about this Moon air."

I took her arm and we headed out the door. "Just don't get feeling too good. Last time that happened you almost took out the entire west coast."

Carol shook her head, "Man, I'm never going to live that down."

Carol and I went outside and found our ride waiting for us. It was an automated cart that looked like a bubble that hiccupped, just big enough for the two of us fit in. Yep, on the Moon you only travel in style if you travel with the Sputniks. The trappings of power I guess.

Driving along, the little bubble car showed us a promo holo-video. The video boasted of the virtues of the Moon. How it was the perfect state where everybody is happy. The Moon's administration used its funding to provide modern, up-to-date housing and medical care for all. We were treated to a holographic tour of your typical Moon dweller's apartment. According to the video, each of the apartments shared the same proportions and amenities. (If you can't believe a canned promo video who can you trust?) Each apartment is allocated four hundred square meters per individual living in the apartment.

The video stressed that trained Moon social engineering scientists determined that four hundred square meters per person was the optimal size apartment so each person could have enough room while still conserving space. The apartments all had the same basic configuration: common room, kitchen, dining room, plus one bathroom and bedroom per person or couple. The apartment rooms were modular with moveable walls so people could position them in whatever order they wanted. They could also control the size of each room and the number of windows.

Each apartment came with same appliances: holographic entertainment and information center, a teleport box, all-purpose stove, a fridge, and of course one robotic cleaner. Individuals had control over the color of each of these appliances and all of the walls and carpeting. The video insisted that this gave the individual millions of possible choices, ensuring that everybody would be equal but unique. Marx and Stalin would have been proud.

The video was timed perfectly, ending just as we pulled up to the administration building and Head Administrator's residence. So much for everybody being equal. While most of the buildings on the Moon looked like high-tech blocks stacked on top of each other, this one stood out like a gold tooth on a beggar.

Most of the Moon looks like it is made out of plastic, shiny and new, but plastic nonetheless. This place seemed to be chiseled from stone. It wasn't the tallest of the buildings in the area, but it was by far the most regal, like a castle among toy building blocks.

Carol and I got out of our car. Stretching, we looked up the marble staircase to a stained glass doorway guarded on each side by milky white lion statues, sitting majestically on pedestals, lording over the masses.

"Wow," Carol said.

We walked up the stairs and through the doors. The entryway wasn't huge but it was still impressive, with marble tiled floor alternating between black and white tiles. Roman pillars were positioned throughout the room holding up a ceiling that didn't need the help. The walls were a smooth and creamy white that was so fluid it was almost alive. This wasn't the nano paint they use most places these days, this was good old-fashioned paint. It might not have been able to change colors or be stainproof like the modern nano paints but this had a true, natural color that the newer paints just can't match.

A small cylinderbot rolled up to us.

"Greetings, Mr. Johnson, Ms. Gevada," the bot said. "The Sputniks will be meeting you in the main dining room."

"Lovely," I said.

An arm extended from the bot's midsection. "May I take your coat and hat?" I asked.

"Yes, of course," Carol answered for me, removing my coat with one hand and the fedora with the other. She looked at me looking at her, and shook her head. "You don't need your coat and hat indoors. It's not like you need them in a controlled environment anyhow."

"I don't need them," I said. "They just help me stay in the right frame of mind."

Carol handed them to the bot.

"I will get them back?" I asked rhetorically.

"Of course, sir," the bot said. "Now if you will walk this way."

The bot spun and started to move forward.

"If I could walk that way I wouldn't need . . ."

"The talcum powder," HARV and Carol both finished my statement for me.

"Ah, so I've used that line before."

HARV and Carol just sighed as we followed the bot.

We were led into the formal dining room. At least I assumed it was the formal dining room, because if it wasn't I would have hated to see what these folks considered formal.

There was a long table in the middle of the room, draped with what appeared to be a purple felt cloth. Golden silk tapestries adorned the walls. Each of the tapestries was engraved with a black Chinese symbol. They were tasteful and elegant. There were twenty wood-crafted chairs, which looked more like thrones, located around the table; but that still left plenty of elbow room for everybody. Sitting at the head of the table, in the highest chair, was Boris. Melda sat a position away from him with Lea across from her. Aprill and Windee were also there along with six other older women and ten other younger women. Yep, this was Bo's harem. He wasn't just the alpha male, he was the alpha and omega of all males. (At least in his mind.)

Bo saw us enter the room and motioned for us to come sit at the two empty seats directly next to him. We walked over. I sat next to Lea with Carol across from me and next to Melda.

Bo clapped his hands. An ape in a silver tux two sizes too small walked up with a wine bottle. He poured a finger's worth of wine into one of the many glasses I had in front of me.

"You must try our wine," Bo insisted. "It's from a grape variety grown only on the Moon. We only have a couple of wineries here but I assure you they are most excellent."

I looked at the label on the bottle. It read 2057.

"Ah, 2057," I said like I knew what I was talking about. "An excellent year for Moon grapes."

Bo smiled at me politely as did everybody else. The ape poured Carol a glass. I couldn't help but notice he gave her nearly twice as much as me. I didn't complain. Not only would that be rude, but I'm not a wine guy—not snooty enough.

Bo rested his elbows on the table. "Now, would you two like salmon or steak? I assure you they are both excellent. The salmon are from our own hatchery. The steaks are from a special breed of cattle only cloned on the Moon."

"Steak," I said.

"Salmon," Carol said.

Bo clasped his hands together. "Fantastic choices, both of them." He looked at the ape in the tux, "Please pass their orders to the chef."

The ape bowed and left the room.

Bo smiled at me. "Now, while we wait for the food, Mr. Johnson, why don't we entertain the ladies."

"I'm not much of singer or dancer," I said.

Bo shook his head. He stood up and removed his dinner jacket. I didn't like where this was going. He neatly hung the jacket over the chair. He sat back down. Good. We weren't going to duke it out to impress the chicks. He started rolling up his sleeves, revealing two short but well-muscled forearms.

He dropped his elbow on the table and opened his hand, motioning for me to do the same.

"Rock, paper, scissors?" I asked though I knew he had something else in mind. "I warn you I'm quite good at it."

Bo shook his head, again. "No what I have in mind is more manly."

"Spitting? Using a remote? Taking out the trash? Hitting things with hammers?" I asked.

"Arm wrestling," he said.

"Arm wrestling?" I said.

"The sport of kings," he answered.

I was quite certain (and HARV confirmed) that he was wrong on that one, but it's rude to argue with somebody who is about to feed you. Bo wiggled his fingers, taunting me. I so didn't want to do this.

"He can't be serious," HARV said in my head.

"He's serious," Melda said in my brain.

"So serious," Lea reinforced. *"It's kind of embarrassing . . ."*

"I understand you are left-handed," Bo said. "It's my weaker arm so it should make the match fair."

I put my elbow on the table and locked hands with him. I hadn't done this since college, maybe longer.

"On the count of three," Boris said.

Lea started to count, "One," pause, "two," pause, "three!"

Bo jumped out of the gate, immediately applying direct pressure, pushing my arm backward but not down. He had done this before and he was a strong man. Thing was, he had gotten a bit soft at his desk job. On the other hand, people try to kill me on a weekly basis. I may not know the technique involved in proper arm wrestling, but I'm tough and I know how to survive. Plus I do have a computer backup system in my brain.

"Do you need help?" HARV asked.

"No," I insisted in my brain. *"I'm doing this myself."*

"Fine, be stubborn," HARV said.

Bo continued to apply pressure. If this was his weak arm I didn't want to see his strong one. Still, I've never been one to go down easy. I gave way, just a little, to see how he would react. I guessed he would sense the kill and push ahead hard. I was right. At my first sign of weakness, Boris reached back for all his strength and started pushing down with all he had.

I was ready though. Just as I started to bend, I reapplied my strength, catching him totally off guard. I not only stopped his advance, I started pushing his arm backward.

I looked at his face. It was blood-red. Sweat was rolling down his forehead like Costa Rica in the rainy season.

I smiled. I had him.

"You better let him win," Lea said in my mind.

"Let him win," echoed the thoughts of about a dozen other women in the room. In fact, only Melda and Carol didn't send me those thoughts.

I pushed forward, driving his hand back. I wasn't going to let him beat me. He wanted to prove to his ladies he was the alpha male. I wanted to let him know that I don't give ground to any man. Problem was, if I did beat him, I'm not sure if he'd be good for much information. Bigger problem was, I didn't care. There are times when my ego can get in the way of my quest for knowledge. As my mentor liked to preach, "the problem with men is their egos are always bigger than they think, and their penises are always smaller." Not sure I totally agreed with that one, but I did need to work on the ego thing. Just not right now. There are times you gotta do what you gotta do and hope for the best.

I slammed his arm to the table. Pulling my arm away, I smiled. He frowned. I let go of his hand. Now that I'd salvaged my manhood, it was time to get the case back on track. I could use the win to my advantage, see how Sputnik reacts when things don't go his way. Of course, I needed to give Sputnik a graceful way out. I didn't want to beat his ego down to a silence.

I started rubbing my shoulder, "Wow, if that's your weak arm . . ."

Bo slammed his right elbow down on the table,

hand extended. "Please, my left arm is pitiful. Now, I will show you true power."

I backed my chair away from the table, ever so slightly. I continued rubbing my left shoulder with my right hand, shaking my head. I tried to look as worried as possible. Truthfully, I knew I couldn't beat him right-handed without cheating with HARV. I wasn't going to give him the total satisfaction of knowing that for sure though. I was going to give him his win, but not his peace of mind.

"No way," I said, feigning a really stiff left arm, moving it cautiously as if any sudden move would cause excruciating pain. "I need one good arm," I told him.

Bo sat there, motionless, taking in my words.

"I think you broke him," HARV said in my head.

"I forfeit to you," I said. "That makes it a draw."

I wasn't sure if that would be good enough for Sputnik but it would have to be.

"Fine, I graciously accept your defeat," he said.

"Let it go," HARV said.

I listened to HARV. I extended my hand to him. He gripped my hand, hard. I ignored it. We shook. I heard a collective mental sigh from every woman in the place.

Before things were able to get any more awkward, serving apes and bots started hopping and rolling out of the door on the far wall with food. Saved by the food plate.

As we all ate, Sputnik and I did most of the talking. It struck me as strange since each of the women in the room could quite likely wipe the floor with both Sputnik and me. That didn't stop us.

To hear Sputnik ramble on and on, one would have thought that he single-handedly built the Moon colony. He was able to talk endlessly about all the wonders of the Moon, a set populace of nothing but hand-picked scientists, workers, the best bots and trained apes. How they are totally self-supporting and that the Earth could disappear tomorrow and the Moon would go on like nothing happened.

I let the main course flow for a while before causing any rifts. I wanted him to get comfortable again before I drilled him. I was doing a solo good cop/bad cop act.

After the bots and apes started to clear away the plates I asked, "So how is Elena doing?"

All the polite back and forth chatter in the room stopped. Every eye focused on Bo.

Sputnik sipped on his after dinner drink, pretending not to hear the question. "Excuse me?" he said.

"She's in excellent hands," Melda answered. "My sister does a wonderful job with all her students."

"Especially her daughter?" I said.

Melda gave me a nice smile. "They, like all mothers and daughters, have had their issues."

"Issues? She refuses to admit her mother is alive."

Melda shrugged. "Some issues are bigger than others. Elena is young and headstrong. I'm sure Shara will figure out a way to get through to Elena."

I looked around the table. "So Shara isn't here?"

Now it was Lea's turn to speak for her dad. "No, she has her hands full with Elena." There was a slight pause. "She's quite dedicated."

"And she is still in mourning," Melda added. "She loved Mo very much."

"We all did," Bo said, breaking his silence. "He was a great scholar and a gentleman."

"So you two got along?" I prompted.

"His research helped push psis to new highs," Bo said.

Everybody in the room nodded gently in agreement. There were some muffled assents.

"Of course, Daddy, all his research was made possible by your funding and encouragement," Lea said.

Everybody in the room nodded openly in agreement. Many people even added "Hear! Hear!"

By not answering my question, Bo inadvertently answered it. I decided to go with the million credit question. "So, how do you expect this vote to go tomorrow?"

"I expect Earth to see the light," Bo answered.

"Our polls show that the vast majority, 50.5 percent of the Earth's population, would like to see the Moon free," Melda said.

"Ah, that's not exactly a VAST majority," I said.

Melda smiled every so slightly. "It is when 40.76 percent of the population is totally indifferent."

"Good point," I said. "Too bad the World Council sees things differently. They are hardly your average Earth citizens." Especially now with the Thompson girls onboard.

I turned back to Bo, "The World Council has never been one to bow to the demands of the people, or logic for that matter."

"True," Sputnik conceded. "This time I am hoping logic will prevail. I've made my views clear to the council."

"We all have," Melda added.

All the ladies around the table bobbed their heads in agreement.

Now was my time to strike and to ask the question I had been waiting all night to ask.

"What do you do if they refuse?"

A bot placed a dessert dish in front of me. It was a chocolate torte with a slice of green cheesecake on the side. It looked delicious. I took a bit of the torte. It was good. I focused on Sputnik.

"The cheesecake, it's divine?" Bo said.

"I'm sure," I said, taking another bite of the torte. "Doesn't answer my question though."

Sputnik took another sample of the tort. He licked

his lips. He smiled at me. It was his best political smile. "Let's not talk about such ugly matters."

I pressed on. I had to. I wanted to see how he would react.

"I guess there's not much you can do except accept your fate and hope for the best."

Sputnik curled his hands into fists and pounded them on the table.

"I am not one to put much faith in fate and hope," he said, nearly spitting.

"So you have no faith in faith," I prodded.

"Carefully, big guy, you're on his home turf, playing on his home court, surrounded by his rabid fans," HARV cautioned.

"I have faith in myself and this world I built," Bo said.

A wise man would have eased up on the gas, maybe even hit the breaks. I pushed down the throttle and went for it. The trick was to take my foot off the pedal before I drove him over the edge.

"So what happens if the WC votes down freedom again?" I asked.

A cold stare and colder silence.

I needed to force a reaction, any reaction.

"I guess there is nothing you can do. Must be tough. A true doer wouldn't sit by helplessly."

Bo leaped up from his chair, dove over the table and grabbed me. "I am never helpless!" he shouted. "Never!" His face turned redder than the old Russian flag. "And I never have been helpless!" he asserted.

My first reaction was to slap him down. Sure he was a stalwart and stocky guy. (HARV said he used to box.) That was years ago. He had become a desk jockey, still fit for a guy who pushed electrons around all day, but not nearly ready to tangle with me, a guy who brawls on a regular basis.

I wanted a reaction and I got one. Any good P.I. knows there's a time to fight back and a time to lay back and let matters take care of themselves. A great P.I. can tell those things apart. This was the latter.

"Emotional, aren't you?" I said.

Sputnik let go of my shirt. He straightened himself up, composing himself mentally and physically. He lowered his eyes. "I'm sorry. That's no way to treat a guest."

"He had it coming," Carol said, glaring across the table at me.

"No, no he didn't," Melda said.

"I agree," Lea said.

"With who?" I asked Lea.

"Everybody," she answered.

"My number one wife is right," Bo said. "I am such a terrible host."

He dusted off my shoulder. Not really sure why. I guess it was his way of trying to show kindness and be belittling at the same time. I found it strange and a bit disturbing on some levels. Still, I was interested to see that the calm, cool politician in him could over-rule the angry tyrant.

"I guess I pressed a nano too hard," I conceded.

Across the table, I saw Carol roll her eyes.

"It's just I believe so much in what we do here on the Moon and how we need to be free," Sputnik said. "Sometimes I get excited."

"That's okay," I told him. My gut was churning. That gave me all the information I needed. Sputnik may not have been the one to kill the World Council members, but I'd bet credits to soy donuts that he certainly condoned and probably ordered the attack.

He looked at me, his black pupils dominating his eyes. "If they don't grant us our freedom, I fear for us all."

Yep, definitely the one.

I stood up. "I think Carol and I should be going now."

Bo's head dipped. In fact, his entire body kind of dipped. "Ah, must you go? The night is young."

"It's been a long day, being attacked by apes and a crazed psi, touring the Moon, being attacked by the crazed psi again."

"Truthfully though, the second psi attack was aimed at me," Bo said.

"I still got tossed around and nearly smothered by vats of toxic waste."

"Actually, they were more barrels than vats," Bo corrected, showing my trained mind what a truly anal politician he was.

Lea grabbed my arm. She looked up at me, eyelashes batting. "Can't you stay a few more minutes and relax?" She took a deep breath, expanding her breasts. She exhaled slowly. "The vote is tomorrow. Who knows what will happen after that?"

It truly was a tempting offer. Lea was an interesting character, part sex kitten, part hungry man-eating lion; you never knew which one was the dominant part. I kind of liked it.

Bo on the other hand wasn't so thrilled. He wanted to be the only apple of his daughter's eye.

"I might be able to stay a few more minutes," I said.

Bo looked frazzled. "How rude of us, Mr. Johnson. You must be so so very tired and we are forcing you to stay against your wishes. Tomorrow is a big day. The Moon becomes independent. You get to see your," he turned to Lea as he stressed, "*girlfriend*, the lovely Electra." He turned back to me. "I've summoned transport. You should go home and rest."

I decided I'd pushed the envelope enough for tonight. The smart P.I. knows when to pack it in.

"You're right. Carol and I should be heading back to our suite."

Bo positioned his body between myself, the table and the women. "That's okay. Ms. Gevada can stay longer if she wishes."

Before I had a chance to answer, Carol shouted in my brain, *"I'll talk for myself."*

Carol pushed herself up from her chair. She had a regal way about her. I liked it but it scared me. Not sure if I was scared by her manner or that I liked it.

"I'll go with my uncle," Carol said.

Carol walked over and took my hand. "Come on, Tió, let's go. Tomorrow will be a big day."

I turned to Bo, "Thanks for everything. I hope our paths will cross again this trip."

Bo got a twinkle in his eye. "Yes, of course. Tomorrow you will join us in celebrating the Moon's independence."

"We'd like that," Carol answered.

I turned to the ladies, giving them a polite bow. "Until we meet again," I said in my most suave voice.

"Gross," Carol said in my head.

"Gross squared then cubed," HARV said.

A butlerbot rolled up with my coat and hat. I put them on. Carol and I left the building.

We got into the bubble car and headed toward our hotel. We rode in silence, but that didn't mean we didn't communicate.

"I was wrong. Melda did it," Carol said in my head.

"Excuse me?"

"When Lea stood up asking you to stay, that really angered Boris," Carol thought.

"So? How does this lead to Melda?" I asked. I wouldn't have been flabbergasted if Melda was the killer. I had never removed her from the list of possibilities. She just wasn't that high up on the list.

"She shot Lea a mental message, 'Let's not have to kill more Earthers.' Right after that Lea backed down."

Now that was something different.

"Why would Melda think that so openly?" I asked Carol mentally.

"All the Moon psis are so sure of their power, they don't think anybody else can read or control them," she answered out loud.

"Or maybe she wanted you to hear that," I thought to Carol. *"Its scary and cryptic enough to keep us guessing."*

"I never considered that," Carol said.

"That's why I get the big bucks," I grinned.

I may have been smiling and calm on the outside, but inside I was grimacing and my nerves were tangled in square knots.

Chapter 28

That night, I sat awake in my bed, pondering. Every case can be broken down to who, why, and how? Here I had the *who* narrowed down. I could make a good guess on the *how*. The *why* was the biggest stumper.

For the *who*, I was pretty certain that Shannon Cannon was innocent. Problem was, I was just as certain nobody who mattered cared. The bigger dilemma was who was the killer? It might have been Melda. It might have been Lea. It could have been both. Were they acting alone? Were they acting under orders? Or was it the wild card (in more ways than one), Elena?

For the *how*, Melda, Lea, and Elena were all extremely powerful and well-connected psis. They certainly had the means to use their connections to override the council's security codes. Catching the bodyguards off guard, either of these three ladies could decimate the room. The *how* I had covered.

My big hang-up was the *why*? What did they hope to accomplish by this? Was it a threat? "Do what we want or else more will die." Why send an anonymous warning threat? Did they really hope to change the vote? Maybe it was just Elena out for revenge. That didn't sit right with me though. Elena wasn't the subtle, quiet type. If she had done it she would have been open and in your face about it.

I fell asleep thinking that I had no idea what these people were thinking.

"Wake up!" HARV shouted in my head. Bells, whistles, and fireworks were also going off.

I sat up. "I'm awake. I'm awake. What's going on?"

"The vote came down," HARV said.

"What time is it?"

"It's 6:30 A.M., Earth Standard Time."

"Isn't that early for the vote?"

"Yes," HARV said.

"That can't be a good sign."

"No," HARV said.

"No, I'm wrong, or no, I'm right?"

"The vote was ten to two, against," HARV said.

I rolled out of bed and stood up. I had been sleeping in my armor and suit. It was time to find my woman then get off this rock.

"Who voted for it?"

"Only Ona and Threa," HARV said.

"Well, at least my little chat had some effect on them," I said dressing.

"The others say they refused to be bullied by a Moonie, the most vocal of the protractors being Twoa."

I wasn't surprised by this. Twoa would rather fight than think any day. This is a lady who once rendered an entire city block unconscious while stopping one jaywalker.

"So they are still blaming Shannon?"

"Yes, but there is talk that she was doing it under orders from somebody else," HARV said.

"Oh, that's not good."

"Yep. The council is meeting now to decide how to respond."

"HARV, we need to contact Electra and fast," I said. My gun and knife were on the nightstand. I grabbed them and slipped them each into their respective ankle holster.

"Already done . . . no response."

"Let's go get her then," I said, plopping my fedora on my head.

"Carol's waiting for us in the lobby."

Chapter 29

We met Carol in the hotel lobby. She looked as stern
and as serious as I had ever seen her. She was arguing
with the attendant at the front desk.

"You can't seriously expect me to be believe every
single transport on the Moon is tied up right now?"
Carol said.

The young, square-jawed, blue-haired (duh) lady
looked at Carol without really looking at her. "I'm
sorry, ma'am, it's all down for repairs."

I moved forward next to Carol and leaned on the
desk. "Call your leader, Boris 'Bo' Sputnik and ask
him to approve of transportation for us."

"I'm sorry, sir, Mr. Sputnik cannot be bothered
now," the attendant said without bothering to look
at us.

"This is ridiculous," I said slamming my hand onto
the desk, hoping to scare the girl.

She looked at me. So I at least had her attention.
"Sir, being rude is not going to help matters," she said
before she turned away.

"Make her give us a car," I thought to Carol.

"Gladly."

Carol looked at the attendant. The attendant touched her earpiece, sending a chill up my spine.

"Uh-oh, she's calling for help," I said.

Sure enough, coming in through the front door were four extra-large gorillas in heavy armor. They were flanked by two cylinder-shaped battlebots. Bringing up the rear was their commander, a tall, light-skinned woman with a short military-style haircut. Her hair was so dark blue that in some light it probably looked black. I knew her from the dinner last night. She didn't say much, but she was there.

.I nudged Carol. "Forget the attendant. We've got bigger fish to fry."

"The psi is called General Tang," Carol said. "She's Sputnik's number two wife."

"Figures she'd be a general," I said. "HARV, can you tap into the hotel's holographic system?" I asked.

"I've been working on that since we arrived. Their defenses are quite good. The algorithms are a kind of hybrid between Doctor Pool's and Doctor Thompson's. Fascinating, really. Certainly their defenses are on par with the North Pole's."

Tang, the apes, and the bots drew closer.

"Short answer, HARV. Short answer."

"Of course."

"Of course you'll give me the short answer or of course is the short answer."

"The latter," HARV said.

I smiled. That was all I needed to know. The odds didn't look quite so long now.

"HARV, we need cloaks over Carol and me," I said.

"Cloaks," HARV said. "Can't we do something a little more original?"

"Sorry, HARV, when in doubt and pressed for time go with the old standbys."

HARV sighed in my brain. He'd get over it.

"HARV, tell me when we're cloaked," I said.

The psi, the apes, and the bots looked confused. Well at least as confused as bots could look with their simple displayscreen heads. Tang's head was leaning forward, her eyes wide open.

"Earth scum!" she spat. "Blanket the room with laser fire," she ordered.

"Change of plans," I told HARV. "Project images of us as far away from us as you can."

"I wasn't programmed yesterday," HARV retorted.

One of the apes spotted us, well our *images,* and pointed them out with a grunt.

The other apes and the bots turned and fired on them, cutting our holographic images down. Except, of course, for HARV's image, which knelt over our bodies weeping.

"Don't overdo it," I thought to HARV.

"We got them!" one of the bots chirped. "So much for the great Zachary Nixon Johnson."

Tang wasn't as convinced though. "I'm not picking up any thoughts from them," she said as her and her squad cautiously moved toward our bodies.

"Of course not," the bot chirped back. "Dead people don't think."

"I wasn't picking up any thoughts before you shot them," Tang said.

"The girl was a psi; she was blocking you," the bot insisted.

The door was now clear. I mentally motioned for Carol to follow me. Carol and I slipped toward the door as Tang and the bots were arguing. While we moved, I kept one eye trained on our attackers and my gun in my hand.

The apes started to sniff.

"Don't worry, I'm projecting our scent into their minds from the images," Carol said.

Good thinking on her part. Luckily for us, the apes weren't wearing psi blockers. I didn't know if it was because of budget constraints or to just make sure Tang would be able to control the apes if need be. Whatever the reasoning, it was nice that we could use it to our advantage.

We made it to the door; we were now safely behind our attackers. The option was ours to flee or go on the offensive.

The psi, apes, and bots reached our bodies.

"Hey! These are just holograms!" Tang shouted.

"Impossible!" the bots both said. "We were picking up heat signatures."

HARV's hologram stopped his weeping and looked up at them. "That would be my doing," he said.

"Impossible!" the bots both said. "The Moon's computer systems are secure cubed!"

"You better check your language databases as I'm not sure you know what *impossible* means," HARV said.

I was proud of him. He was learning from our connection, further proving he was evolving. HARV pointed behind the bots, ape, and psi.

"Messed up verbal databases are the least of your worries though," he said with a smirk.

The bots spun. It was too late for them. Explosive mini-mirv-missiles (M&M&Ms as Randy called them), slammed into the bots, shattering them on contact.

The apes aimed their weapons toward us, but they didn't have a chance either.

"Sleep," Carol ordered them.

The four apes dropped their weapons, yawned, then followed their weapons to the ground. They curled up with them like they were high-powered, teddy bear sleep aids.

Tang was indignant. "I give you the first two rounds," she said, radiating with raw white energy.

"But now you need to deal with me, *Tang*, Boris 'Bo' Sputnik's number two wife!"

"Ah, long name," I told her.

Tang clinched her fists and her eyes as she stood her ground. "I proudly call myself number two!" she said.

"Being number two, does that mean you try harder?" I asked, snickering some.

Without even motioning, she sent the sleeping apes and destroybot parts flying out at us. I ducked under one ape, but another one mowed into me. That's what I get for letting my mouth do the talking instead of my gun. Luckily my armor took the brunt of the damage.

Carol telekinetically deflected the apes thrown at her around her.

"This bitch is mine," Carol said.

"Too slow," HARV told her.

I rolled the ape off of me and sat up. HARV's hologram had clasped his hands around Tang's head.

"Please, you are only a hologram," she said to him. "You are less of a threat than Zach!"

I tried not to take that personally. Too bad for her HARV did. Energy ripped from his hands into her head. Tang screamed in agony.

HARV appeared next to me, watching himself. "I've learned how to change the energy from holographic projectors into electrical energy," he said with a smile. "The move is draining, but it's worth it."

Carol, HARV, and I watched as the other HARV held number two between his hands. She wiggled like a fish out of water, screaming like a banshee for a few seconds. She went limp. She fell to the ground through HARV's hologram. The far hologram disappeared.

HARV looked very satisfied. "Serves her right," he said.

"You didn't kill her, did you?"

HARV put his hand over his chest, and his nose pulled the rest of his head upward, all the better to look down on me. "No, of course not," he said. He pointed out the door. "Now I suggest we head out and to the Conference Center before more guards show up."

"You know, for a supercomputer you can be pretty smart," I said.

"You know, for human you have a keen grasp of the obvious," HARV said.

"Thank you," I said.

Chapter 30

Carol, HARV, and I headed outside. There, sitting right in front of us, was our ticket to the Moon Convention Center—the security team's car. It was a big, blue carriagelike sedan that looked like a smaller version of the one Sputnik had taken me touring in.

"It was nice of number two to bring us our ride," I said to HARV and Carol as I sat in the driver's seat.

Luckily, my love of old-fashioned cars meant I could drive this baby. Once I entered the starting code of course.

"HARV, can you hot-wire this car?" I asked.

"No," he replied simply.

HARV appeared sitting on the cars hood. "I can't hot-wire it but I can start it."

"Then do it, buddy."

"You have to look into the ignition."

I did as I was told, bending down and staring at the spot the ape would put a key. The car purred alive. I put her in gear and pulled away.

"I suppose you know where the Convention Center is?" I said to HARV.

"Of course," he said. "Go straight until I tell you to turn."

"As you wish," I said.

Something about driving the old-fashioned way always made me feel good. Even on the Moon and surrounded by hostiles, when I was in the driver's seat (and actually driving) all was good in my world. Of course HARV wasn't going to let that last.

"Do you have a plan?" HARV asked.

"Of course I have a plan," I said, hitting the accelerator for no good reason. "I always have a plan."

HARV tapped his fingers on the dashboard. "So what is this brilliant plan of yours?"

"To find Electra and make sure she and the other Earthers are safe."

"Then what?"

"I haven't thought that far in advance yet," I conceded.

"No, of course you haven't," HARV scolded, his finger waving in my face. (It was made even more annoying by the fact that he was sitting on the hood of the car.) "How hard can it be? We're only 384,000 kilometers from Earth, surrounded by hostile psis, security apes, and deadly bots."

"My sentiments exactly," I said, driving forward.

"Turn left at the next intersection," HARV said, pointing in my face again.

Once again, I did as I was told. A large white building came into view. It had an arching roof and the front wall was entirely stained glass. Next to the Head Administrator's residence, it was the most stylistic building on the Moon. Above the building were the holographic words MOON CONVENTION CENTER AND HOTEL.

This was the place all right. The holographic sign suddenly disappeared. I guess they figured if they turned it off I wouldn't be able to find the place. I tried not to take it personally.

I drove up to the Convention Center. It was oddly quiet. There were four ape guards in front of the double doors leading into the building and those were the only living souls to be seen.

"Weird," I said.

"For once I concur," HARV said.

"I don't like this, Tió," Carol added.

"You picking up any thoughts from the building?" I asked Carol.

She focused her gaze forward, squinting. "Weird," she said.

I was getting anxious. "What?"

"I'm picking up a lot of well, dreaming . . ."

"Dreaming? I know it's early, but somebody should be awake."

"Maybe it's a boring convention?" HARV offered.

I shot HARV a look like one he normally reserves for me.

HARV bent down and got all defensive. "Just throwing out a suggestion," he said. He processed for a few nanos, pondering his own words. Slapping himself on the head, "DOS, we have been hooked together too long!"

HARV pointed to the empty parking lot. "The good news is you have plenty of parking."

"You're grasping at straws now, buddy," I said, pressing down on the accelerator.

"Just trying to look on the bright side," HARV offered.

"Can you see inside the building?" I asked.

HARV shook his head. "Nope. They took their computerized cameras offline. I can have them back online in five minutes and twelve seconds."

"Too slow," I said.

The car raced forward.

"Ah, Zach, I know your driving may be a bit rusty, but it's customary to slow down on your approach to parking."

"Not parking," I said, flooring the pedal.

The car sped up, the building drew closer faster. The ape guards pulled their weapons.

"This car will fit through those doors . . . right?" I asked.

I drove the car off the road and up the ramp leading to the building. HARV made a few fast computations.

"Yes, you have two centimeters on both sides if we hit the doors in the middle," HARV told me.

"Good," I said.

The guards took aim.

"Carol."

"I'm on it, Tió."

Carol pointed at the apes then waved her hand to the side. The apes' weapons flew out of their hands. Three of the apes, now realizing my intentions, cleared the area. Without their weapons they knew they didn't have any chance of stopping me. Truthfully, even with the weapons they wouldn't have had much of a chance.

The one lone ape stood in the car's path, defiantly holding his hand out in the universal stop position.

"Not a bright ape, is he?" I said.

"Just doing his duty," HARV said.

"Carol."

"On it!"

Carol lifted her arm up. The ape went flying up over the car just as we crashed through the doors into the Convention Center's main exhibition room. It was a huge room, easily large enough to house hundreds of exhibitors and their booths. The thing was the room was empty—well almost empty. The walls of the room were lined with containers that looked like a cross between human-sized tubes and electronic coffins. Each one had a body in it. I didn't like that at all.

There better not have been in those tubes what I was pretty sure there was in those tubes. I kicked the door of the car open and got out, Carol by my side. I looked around. Coffin-sized tubes and more tubes as far as I could see. I put two and two together and came up with trouble.

"These people better be alive," I snarled.

"I am picking up faint life signs from all of them," HARV said. "They are in cryo-chambers, in suspended animation."

"That would explain the dreams I was picking up," Carol said.

We moved towards the cryo-chambers lining the room.

"Let me guess, there are five thousand of them," I said.

"Actually, five thousand and two," HARV corrected. "Most of them, forty-five hundred, have women inside. Five hundred have men and two are empty."

I didn't know what worried me more, the five thousand that were occupied or the two that were empty.

"Electra is in one of them, I assume," I said, popping GUS into my hand.

"Affirmative," HARV said.

HARV appeared from my wrist communicator and pointed forward, "She's on the north wall in receptacle oh-two-two-two."

I stormed toward the direction HARV pointed. "She better be okay, or else."

"Don't worry, she's fine," a familiar voice said from across the room.

Carol, HARV, and I turned. There at the entrance

stood Bo Sputnik, Melda, Lea, Aprill, Windee, and seven other blue-haired women of various sizes and ages. They were backed by twenty or so heavily armed and armored apes. Those were backed by a couple of heavy-duty eight-armed battlebots. This was basically the same group used to take Elena out. In a way, I was honored. Of course, in a bigger way, I was angry. I was determined to keep my wits about me. Like my old mentor would always say, "Keeping your wits means keeping your ass." She had a way with words.

"Not exactly a good way to treat your guests," I said, motioning to the rows of cryogenic chambers with one hand, keeping my weapon trained on the others with the other hand.

"Actually, I don't consider them guests," Sputnik said with his crocodile smile.

"What do you consider them?" I asked.

"Residents of the Moon," he answered dramatically.

"Well, in that case it's actually worse," HARV said.

Sputnik started rubbing his goatee, which was now blue. "Truthfully, they're more like breeding stock."

"You can't just take people and keep them for your own use!" Carol shouted at him.

Sputnik smiled and started rolling his handlebar mustache (that he must have waxed for this occasion). "Oh, I think they will thank me," he said.

I shook my head. "I don't see that happening."

Sputnik slowly inched closer to me. As he moved, the entire group behind him followed. I let him come toward me. After all, if they had wanted us dead they could have taken us out without warning.

"I know it may not seem like it now," Sputnik said, "but I am doing them and the Moon a favor."

"Them and the Moon?" I asked.

Sputnik's smile broadened. He may have been mad,

but he was sincere. "I realize the Moon is a beautiful place; one million hand-picked people living equally and in perfect harmony."

"Yeah, yeah," I said. "Nice speech. All you need is sappy theme music playing in the background, like that ancient cola commercial."

No sooner did I get done speaking when friendly, upbeat music starting playing throughout the building. It was freaky, surreal, and made me kind of thirsty.

"Is that better?" Sputnik asked, drawing ever nearer.

"Strangely, yes."

Sputnik continued. "Like I was saying, the Moon is a wonderful place, but we are a closed environment. Even I know there is no such thing as the totally perfect society. We are always striving to improve." He paused for a moment, then waved at the chambers. "That's where these people come in. They are the best Earth has to offer. They will help seed our population long after Earth is a dead decaying rock."

Even the snappy theme music didn't make that last part sound good.

"From what I understand, Earth has a few billion good years left in her," I said.

"Actually, Zach, the exact number of years, not taking into account any new global warming . . ."

I cut HARV off. "Big picture here buddy."

Sputnik wiped a fake tear from his eye. "Sadly, Earth is going to die a premature death."

"How premature?" I asked, despite my better judgment.

"It dies today," Sputnik said. I felt the ice in his words. "The Earth showed its true colors by refusing to grant us our freedom."

A couple questions immediately sprang to mind. Actually, my first question was going to be, "Are you nuts"? But I figured, one, he probably was, and two, that wouldn't help the situation. So I went with a less obvious question.

"Just exactly how do you plan on destroying Earth?" I asked.

Sputnik stopped advancing and gave me a toothy grin. "I'll let you figure that out for yourself, my friend."

"I'm not your friend," I said.

"Believe me, Mr. Johnson, I am about to be Head Administrator of all that's left of humanity, a new and better humanity. You want me to be your friend."

I pondered his words. I examined his expression. I looked over his followers. It hit me.

"You're going to force the ZAP asteroid into Earth. Aren't you?" I said.

"You see, Zach, that's why you're still alive. You will make a good addition to our gene pool. You are a bit rough around the edges . . ."

"A bit?" Carol interrupted.

"More like completely jagged around the edges," HARV added.

"Hey, whose side are you guys on?"

"Yes, you certainly have your flaws," Sputnik agreed. "But they will just help make us a better place. I am wise enough to understand that we learn just as much from our mistakes as we do our successes. You will help us all learn."

I hate it when I'm not sure if I've been complimented or insulted.

"Just curious, Sputnik, how would you have justified this if Earth had voted for your freedom?"

He stopped his advancement. His trailing mob stopped too.

"Come again?"

Now it was my turn to point to all the chambers.

"Surely you had this planned for a long time. You wanted Earth to turn you down. This gave you an excuse to get violent."

"Please, I knew the people of Earth were too stubborn and pig-headed to give us what we wanted, to do the right thing."

Now the picture was finally zooming into focus. These psis had to be blurring my mind. That's why I didn't figure it out sooner. I saw why the Mooner killed the council members. I saw Sputnik's endgame. It was a nasty one.

"You even goaded the Earth by killing the council members. You might have convinced your blind sheep that that was for the best, but you're a politician, you know how politicians think. You knew those murders would galvanize them to be totally against you. You also knew they wouldn't blame you at first, they'd go for the easy patsy, Shannon Cannon, giving you time to plot your plot."

"Plot your plot?" HARV said in my head.

I paused to let what I said sink in. I knew I couldn't get through to Sputnik but I thought I had a shot at the others. If I could turn them we'd have a chance here.

"You don't want freedom, you want genocide. That's all you've wanted all along. You want to destroy the Earth so you and your perfect little society can create the perfect people."

Total silence.

"Daddy, is this true?" Lea asked.

"Take out the girl and computer. Johnson is mine!" Sputnik ordered.

To say all hell broke loose right then and there would be one of the greater understatements of my career.

Chapter 31

Sputnik leaped ten meters, tackling me to the ground. That caught me off guard. Not that he could tackle me but that he could jump so far so easily. The really scary development was that I tried to fire at him but nothing happened. Sputnik and I rolled over and over.

"HARV, what's going on?"

"You are currently being pummeled," HARV answered bluntly.

"Why?"

"Sputnik wants to capture you but for some reason not kill you," HARV answered.

"I gathered that."

"Then why did you ask, Zach? Do you just like the sound of my voice in your head?"

"No, that's not it," I said.

Sputnik and I continued our rolling tussle.

"Why couldn't I fire GUS?"

"Oh that!" HARV said as if he was the Japanese intelligence in WWII and he had just broken the Navajo codes. *"That's easy to answer!"*

Sputnik and I exchanged a few punches, in between grappling on the ground.

"Then answer it, HARV!"

"Oh right. Your interface is being blocked."

Guess I should have seen that coming.

"GUS isn't as advanced as I am, so it makes 110 percent sense that if they can, hic, interfere with me then they can do the same, hic, with him. The good, hic, news is, hic, their bots are about as, hic, advanced as, hic, GUS; so I was, hic, able, hic, to, hic, take them offline."

I managed to flip Sputnik off me and pushed myself to my feet.

"HARV, do you have the hiccups?"

"Ah, no, hic." There was a slight pause. *"Then again maybe I, hic, do,"* he said out loud.

I ducked under a lightning fast left hook thrown by Sputnik.

"What the DOS is going on?"

"I've built up defenses against them shutting me down," HARV sang. *"So they've worked around them. Their battle bots may have, hic, hic, had, hic, a backdoor virus, making me, hic, for the lack of a better, hic, word, hic, hic, drunk."*

Sputnik caught me with an uppercut to the solar plexus that sent me flying, crashing down near the chambers. If it wasn't for my body armor the blow would have done serious damage to my insides.

I pushed myself up off the ground again. "HARV, how is Sputnik able to toss me around so well?"

"He's, hic, wearing, biometric armor just, hic, like you," HARV sang to the tune of "Three Blind Lab Mice." *"Probably stole the design from Randy's, hic, hic, lab, hic, hic, hic, hic,"* HARV added, this time to the tune of Beethoven's Fifth.

"Great," I said.

"Actually, Zach, that's, hic, not great, it's, hic, bad."

HARV's chips were so scrambled it wasn't worth me wasting the energy explaining the concept of sarcasm to him. I had to concentrate on Sputnik. I couldn't worry about Carol right now. I had to hope she was holding her own, though outnumbered as badly as she was, I didn't see how she could. I had my own problems to worry about. I was battling a man who was mad in more ways than one.

Sputnik leaped at me again. This time I was ready. Just because I didn't have access to GUS' computer interface didn't mean I didn't have other options. I quickly pushed the manual override switch and pulled up on GUS' tip, stretching him out to bat size. Swinging GUS hard, I used Sputnik as the ball. My blow landed square on his head, knocking him to ground. He was dazed but still conscious.

"How'd that blow not put his lights out?" I asked HARV.

"He's, hic, using a, hic, computer interface to, hic, modify the energy in his, hic bo-dy to de-flect the blow."

Rushing at Sputnik, I drew back GUS for the finishing blow and asked, "What computer is he using?"

"Ma me, hic," HARV said.

Now that was something else I wasn't expecting. The surprise caused me to hesitate just a split nano before swinging at Sputnik. He reached up and caught GUS between his hands. Standing up, he ripped GUS from my grasp. He tossed GUS over his shoulder, smiling at me all the while.

GUS hit the floor with a clank. "I'm all right! I'm all right!" he shouted.

"This is so not good!" I said.

"My half, hic, guiding him is not inebriated," HARV told me.

I had pretty much guessed that by now.

"Inebriated," HARV giggled. "Funny word."

Sputnik sprung up, head butting me in the midsection. It hurt, but not enough to stop me from grabbing his head between my arms then dropping down on top of him, slamming us both to floor, him face-first. That had to hurt.

I bounced back to my feet before he knew what hit him. He groaned and tried pushing himself upward, giving me the perfect target, his face. I drove my foot down toward his forehead. My foot froze in mid-kick, less than a whisker's length from finishing him off. DOS!

I spun away from Sputnik. I didn't want to. An unseen force was pulling me around. It was a psi. DOS! Psis are great when they are on your side but a pain in the ass when they're against you.

Across the room I saw Carol lying at Lea's feet. Carol and HARV had been able to take out some bots, an ape or two, and a psi, but they were far too outnumbered. Lea, Melda, and the rest of the standing psis and apes were now concentrating their attention on me. A snowball on the sun would have had a better chance.

"I thought your father, husband, uncle, male role model, leader called dibs on me," I shouted to them.

That was met with looks of total confusion.

"Sputnik, your boss, said he wanted me all to himself," I said.

Their smiles showed me that now they understood.

"We don't think he would have wanted you to win," they all echoed inside my head, with a hive-mind-like sentiment.

Sputnik forced himself up off the ground.

"My family is right. I would not have wanted you to win!"

He clubbed me on the back of my head with GUS. Things started spinning around and then went black.

Chapter 32

"Zaaaach, Zaach, wake up," I heard HARV calling from the deep regions of my mind.

My eyes shot open. The good news was it appeared HARV was back. The bad news was I was trapped in a big tube. I was pretty certain it was the inside of a cryo-chamber. My hands and feet we were tied and I was getting colder. Yep, there are times it really hoovers to be right.

"HARV, you're back?" I asked.

"If I wasn't, you'd be frozen stiff by now," HARV added.

"A simple yes would have sufficed."

"Yes," HARV said. "I am back."

"Can't just say, yes, can you?"

"No," HARV said. "Apparently not."

"Are you okay now?" I asked.

"Better than ever. Melda underestimated my will. She may be a good scientist and a powerful psi but she really knows diddly-squat about my advanced, cognitive abilities. I was able to reprogram myself so

I am no longer drunk and more important, able to block their attempts to control me."

"HARV, you just said *diddly-squat*."

"Yes, clearly I am not totally back to normal. Still, me functioning at 80 percent is better than any other three computers in the known worlds functioning at 100 percent, or any number of humans functioning at 110 percent."

"HARV, you just said . . ."

"I know, please don't remind me. I am running corrective subroutines now."

I looked around, as much as I could move my head. I didn't see much but I noticed Carol in the chamber next to me.

"They are freezing Carol, too?" I asked.

"Yes. Sputnik is saving her for a later day. He figures once Earth is destroyed she will cooperate with them without having to be reprogrammed."

"How does he figure that?"

There was a pause. "He's an egomaniac. He believes whatever he thinks is the absolute truth. To him, his thoughts are like the Gospel and Koran but much more sacred and pure (since he didn't write those books). That's part of the reason he didn't want me interfacing with his bio armor anymore. He thought I was somehow hindering him. That's the only way he could justify you beating him."

"Were you hindering him?"

"I wish," HARV said. "All my spare routines were being used to try to break free of the psi's control. You beat him without me helping you or hurting him. His massive ego just can't accept that. So now I'm supposed to freeze with you while all my backups and coprocessors get destroyed on Earth."

I smiled. Yep, Sputnik was a politician all right. His ego jammed the door open just enough to give us a chance to escape. Now I needed to find a way to push the opening wider. I looked at Carol out of the corner of my eye.

"HARV, can you contact Carol?"

"I may be able to use my wireless connection to reach her through her PIHI-Pod," HARV said.

"Try it," I ordered.

"Turn your head toward her."

"Why?"

"Zach, I'm only functioning with the chips directly in the lens in your eye. It would help matters greatly if you did what you were told and gave me a direct line of view with Carol."

"Yes, sir," I said, turning my head.

"And that snotty attitude doesn't help!" HARV added.

As I understood it, normally the HARV chip I have in my eye lens is just one of many virtual processors that HARV's personality or presence uses. Now that he was being isolated from the rest of the chips, my link with HARV was weakened. I was betting that, even in his weakened condition, he was still more than enough computer to get the job done.

I trained my vision on Carol. I saw the small PIHI-Pod she was wearing as a diamond on her right ear. I concentrated on it.

"Open your eyes wider!" HARV scolded.

"It's not easy to concentrate and hold my eyes so open."

"Zach, don't concentrate. Just do what I tell you."

I did as I was told. I forced my eyes open as wide as possible.

"Hold steady," HARV said.

At first I was going to complain that it wasn't like he was performing brain surgery, but I realized that in a way he was. Carol was still lying there, eyes closed.

"Nothing is happening," I said.

"Be patient. Halo XX wasn't programmed in a day you know."

"I am being patient."

"Quiet," HARV ordered.

I saw Carol's right eye start to twitch, slowly at first, but then it built up the steam it needed. Both eyes opened wide. Her head moved from one side to another.

"Did they really think this would hold me?" she said.

"They assumed you'd sleep until you were frozen," I answered.

"You know what they say about assuming," Carol said.

Carol squinted her eyes. The top of her chamber flew across the room. Carol moved her arm forward, snapping her restraints like they were old-fashioned peanut brittle. She looked down at her leg restraints. They surrendered to her will without much of a fight, curling up and rolling to the ground. Carol slipped out of her chamber. Her feet touched the floor. She stretched out.

"Now I'm mad," she said.

Carol pointed at the latches holding my chamber lid tight. The latches crinkled up then fell to the ground. With a snap of her fingers, Carol sent the chamber top flying away.

"Thanks," I told her. "Just be careful to only pop my restraints and not my bones," I cautioned.

"Don't be a baby," HARV said.

"I second that," Carol said.

She motioned with her right hand toward her body. My restraints flew off me. I tumbled to the ground.

"You could have given me a bit more warning," I said.

"You're welcome, Tió."

I pushed up off the ground. I saw roughly thirty heavily armed apes charging us. I pointed them out to HARV and Carol.

"We got company, guys."

Carol started to ripple with energy. Her hair danced off her shoulders as she levitated off the ground. "These Mooners have pissed me off," she said. "Time to let the genie out of the bottle!"

The apes, seeing Carol's little display of power, stopped in their tracks. They held their arms up over their heads waving them in the universal "slow down, don't kill" sort of way.

"Hey, we're on your side!" one of the apes shouted.

Now *that* was a surprise.

Chapter 33

Carol, HARV, and I waited for the apes to come to us. I wasn't sure what I found more of a shocker, that the apes could talk or that they claimed to be on our side. The apes were all wearing armor and carrying sidearms but they were approaching us in a calm, non-threatening manner. I had a good feeling about this. Not good enough for Carol or HARV to lower their guards or for me to lower my gun I keep in my ankle holster (my good old Colt .44). I was feeling secure, not stupid. My .44 was light but still packed enough for a wallop to put an ape down, as long as I hit him or her square between the eyes.

One of the apes, one with gray bordering on white fur, led the group towards us. They came within three or four meters from us before I waved my .44 at them, cueing them to stop. They did.

"My name is Priscilla, Ape Commander," the gray ape said in a higher pitched tone.

For the first time I noticed this gorilla's uniform

protruded in the chest protector more than the others', plus she had longer hair.

"Priscilla the gorilla," I said with a slight giggle.

The big ape sighed. "Yes, my cousin Maurice was your driver when you arrived. He informed me you would get a kick out of my name."

"Maurice is a smart man, ah, ape," I said.

Priscilla arched her shoulders. "He's a big fan of your work." Priscilla pointed at my gun. "We would be grateful if you lowered your weapon," she said. "We have no intention to harm you. You're actually cute, for a human," she said with a wink.

Though the wink freaked me out, she seemed sincere. I just needed a better reason to lower my gun than sincerity.

"If we wanted to blow you away we could have killed you while your were unconscious or simply blown up the building," the big ape said.

"Yeah, well, Sputnik wants us all alive," I countered.

"If you haven't figured it out yet, Sputnik's wants are low on our priority list," the ape countered.

She had me on that one. I dropped my gun to my side. I didn't put it away, but it was no longer on a hair trigger. The apes all seemed more relaxed.

"So, you guys aren't Sputnik fans?" I said.

"Pleeease!" Priscilla said, spraying her words. I guess that's why the apes signed so much.

"Why are you apes helping us?" HARV asked.

"We all have friends and family on Earth; we don't want them killed," an ape from the back row said.

"Makes sense," HARV agreed.

"And Sputnik is a radical nutcase squared," Priscilla said. She looked at Carol and me for a reaction. We didn't give her any so she went on. "Everybody is happy and treated fairly, my not-so-hairy ass!"

"You've noticed the discrepancies?" I said, more cynically than not.

Priscilla pointed to the top of her skull. "When you've been on the bottom of the totem pole as long as we've been, you can't help but notice the footprints on your head."

"Good point. Are all the apes with you and against him?"

Priscilla shook her head no. Of course she did; it would have been too easy if she didn't. "Sorry. We're split pretty much fifty-fifty on this one. Lots of our comrades don't want to change the status quo. They know Sputnik is bad. Hell, his ego is so powerful it gives off its own scent. But they are afraid the alternative could be worse. And they don't want to mess with his psis."

"They can be formidable," Carol said, speaking from experience.

Priscilla dropped her hands to her side. "The bottom line is, cutie, some of us just aren't that smart and some of us hate change."

"Apes are no different than humans," HARV said. "Actually, apes admit it. So they are probably smarter than humans."

Priscilla gave HARV a big toothy grin. The other apes behind her did too. Priscilla held out her hand to me.

"Do we have an understanding, Mr. Johnson?"

I studied her hand and arm; her rippling muscles were apparent, despite her fur. If we were going to get out of this we were going to need all the friends with muscles we could find.

I shook her hand, trying to ignore the fact that she had called me cutie.

"I can never have too many friends."

"How true," HARV said. "Zach's list of enemies is

large enough to fill a small stadium. Not just the enemies, the list itself."

Priscilla reached behind her back, grabbing something. She brought her hand forward holding GUS.
"How's this for a peace offering?"

I took GUS from her. GUS blinked to life.

"Greetings, Zachary Nixon Johnson. Your DNA
has been detected on my hilt. I will now reactivate
myself on your command."

"Go for it," I said.

"Is that a yes?" GUS asked.

"Yes," HARV, Carol, and I all answered.

"I am now activated and ready for action!"

I popped GUS back up my sleeve.

"Speaking of action," Priscilla said. "What's your
plan, honey buns?"

HARV chuckled. "I don't believe the word *plan* is
in Zach's dictionary."

I ignored HARV. "What's the status?"

Priscilla looked away from me. I knew she didn't
want to tell me. Problem was, not telling wasn't
helping.

"Spill it, Priscilla."

"We should have been quicker to react," she said,
then hesitated.

"Spill it, you big ape."

Priscilla slumped over, hands behind her back.
"Things are bad . . ."

"Define bad," I said.

"Ah," Priscilla said fingering her lips, "Sputnik
has already pushed the ZAP asteroid towards
Earth."

"That is bad," I said. "Has Earth noticed yet?"

Priscilla shook her head no. "Not yet. By the time
they do they won't have any chance to stop it. They
trust us."

"Why?" Carol, HARV, and I all asked simultaneously.

Priscilla shrugged. "They're politicians. Like Sputnik, their egos are so big they probably can't conceive of us turning on them."

"But they'll figure it out and respond with force."

Priscilla and all the apes behind her nodded. "Yep, probably. What they lack in brains they overcompensate for with brawn."

"Isn't Sputnik worried about this?" I asked.

Priscilla shrugged again. "He probably hasn't considered the possibility of something going wrong. In his mind, he thinks anything he thinks becomes reality."

I considered what Priscilla said; it was deranged, therefore it probably all made sense in the world of politics. Like they say, "those who do, do, those who can't go into politics." The powers that be weren't going to stop any of this. It was up to us.

"First off we need to prevent that asteroid from hitting Earth." I thought for a nano. "I suppose the Blocking and Tracking Station is heavily guarded?"

All the apes nodded yes.

"How about the beam itself?"

The apes all shook their heads no.

"There are no guards there because even if you destroy the beam the asteroid will still hit Earth," Priscilla said.

Now it was my turn to shake my head. "I'm not going to destroy it. I'm going to use it to push the asteroid past Earth."

"But the controls are in the Asteroid Tracking and Blocking Station, hence the name," Priscilla said, very slowly, as if I was slow.

I looked at HARV. "Can you do it?"

"From the beam itself?"

"Yes."

"By bypassing the station?"

I shook my head impatiently. "Yes."

"Easy as you calculating the square root of four."

"Really?" all the gorillas asked at one.

HARV turned to them and gave them his "ah, I can tell you haven't evolved yet" look. "Or as easy as me calculating the square root of 444444444."

"So can you get us there?" I asked the apes.

They all nodded yes.

"Let's make it so."

Chapter 34

Racing through the thin Moon atmosphere toward the deflector beam, I did some reflecting. The plan, such as it was, was simple in theory. Priscilla and two of her best apes were to escort Carol, HARV, and me outside the city to the deflector beam. Once at the beam, HARV would reprogram it to push the incoming asteroid out of Earth's way at the closest to the last possible moment. With the killer rock no longer a threat to Earth, my team and I would swoop into the Blocking and Tracking Station and take control of it, thereby making it impossible for Sputnik to push it back at Earth. While we were doing that, some of the other apes were to bring the ARC conference members out of stasis.

We were staging a coup, attacking Sputnik, his apes, and his psis. If were going to succeed we were going to need more help, *powerful* help.

"We have to free Elena," I said out loud, to nobody in particular.

"Ah, why?" Priscilla asked. "She's a bit of a loon."

"True, but she's a powerful loon and we need all the power we can get right now."

Carol nodded in agreement. The others looked on, trying to cover the fear in their eyes. Even HARV was leery.

"I don't like anybody who can shut me down," he said, hands on hips.

"Don't worry. She won't turn you off," I said to HARV. I looked at the apes. "And she'll help us."

"You base this on what?" HARV was the one to ask the question but the apes nodded their approval.

"Her hatred of Sputnik," I said.

"Ah, the enemy of my enemy," Priscilla said.

"Exactly."

"Cute and smart," Priscilla said.

"If we can get Elena and turn a few more psis and apes we'll have a chance here," I said, still ignoring Priscilla.

"Do you really believe that?" HARV asked.

"I do," I said with as much conviction as I could muster.

Truth was, I wasn't sure at all. Elena was a wild card at best. Even if she was on our side, if we couldn't turn any other psis it would still be an uphill fight. This wasn't even taking into account Earth's reaction to the entire ordeal. The members of the World Council weren't the most mellow, easy to deal with, turn the other cheek bunch in the world. They weren't going to take lightly to the Moon trying to destroy them. It was going to take some smoother talking on my part to convince them not to retaliate. My job would be easier if Sputnik was out of the way. Things would have to fall just right if we were going to have a chance. All I could do was hope they did.

Continuing our flight through the Moon sky, the deflector beam slowly came into view. I had a plan—it may have not been the best plan, but it was better than no plan at all. Plus it was flexible; I would be able to adapt it quickly to any problems that might pop up. Having lived as long as I have, doing what I do, I knew unexpected problems were inevitable. As my old mentor used to say, "Expect the unexpected, especially when you least suspect it." (Okay, she drank a lot, but there is still a certain Yogi Berra wisdom to those words.)

As we flew, Priscilla and her team filled me in on some of the missing blanks about Elena. They told me that her parents were not only the identical twins of Bo and Melda but they were also rivals. Both couples' goals were to create the perfect psi, the next step in human evolution. They each believed the Moon presented the perfect environment for this as there was less corruption of the gene pool and in society in general on the Moon. Both couples believed the Moon was purer and free of mental and physical pollution.

Experience has taught me that when folks get involved with something because they believe it is pure and good, no good can come of it. Pure, by definition, means that people haven't tried to manipulate it or change it. Once a second party jumps in and tries to improve on pure, you taint the purity. Scientists and politicians just can't resist the urge to tinker. In baseball they say, "Sometimes the best trades are the ones you don't make." This holds true with science— sometimes it's best to leave well enough alone. Of course, like Randy once told me, "Why settle for *nearly* perfect when you may be able to make it even closer to perfect?" Randy would always say that achieving perfection is impossible, but the goal of science is to make something as close to this impossible goal as possible. When a scientist sees something that is 99.9 percent perfect they can't resist the urge to try to make it 99.91 percent perfect. This especially holds true if the scientist can convince some politician that this extra improvement is worth them throwing money to the scientist, which will, in turn lead to the politician and scientist helping the world and turning a tidy profit. It's like Everest to a mountain climber—you don't really *need* to do it, but you have to do it for the challenge and the glory. The thing is, changing something for the sole sake of changing it doesn't always work. There are times when good enough really is good enough and adding more good can lead to bad.

Things get especially mucked up when humans try to improve on purity. For one thing, one man's purity is another man's boredom. It's all just different perspectives. Of course, Bo, Melda, Mo, and Shara didn't see this. They were determined to make pure purer. After years of dealing with the darker sides of human nature, I knew this couldn't end well.

The apes, having a surprisingly good grasp of human nature, also filled me in on Elena's psyche. While she and Lea share DNA, the same emerald green eyes, dark blue hair, killer bods, superpsi powers, and love of purple microminis, their attitudes and demeanors were polar extremes. Elena was never a fan of Bo's but wasn't out-and-out hostile until the untimely death of her father. After Mo's death, which Priscilla did say was under quite questionable circumstances, Elena stopped holding back. She become colder than the dark side of Pluto, wanting to salt the very ground Bo walked on.

After the death of Mo, Lea became even warmer and devoted to Bo. Bo could do no wrong in her eyes. That worried me. I'm a P.I.; I can deal with blind hatred. I know where that is coming from. The blind devotion, that was a whole new ball of wax. It's a lot harder to predict how devotees will act.

The apes also clued me in on Shara Lee Sputnik. Priscilla thought she'd be sympathetic to our cause but couldn't be certain.

"Why does she support Bo at all if there is any suspicion that he killed her husband?" I asked.

"Because she is a smart woman," Priscilla answered.

"There is no proof Bo had anything to do with Mo's hover accident. Mo was a bit of hot-rodder. He preferred to drive hovers manually."

"So it's possible he just crashed on his own then," I said.

"Yes," Priscilla said.

"Then why does Elena hate Bo so?"

Priscilla looked at me. "She is convinced Bo wanted more control over her, control he could never have with Mo around."

"Is that true?" I asked.

"Well, it could be," Priscilla said. "Being an ape I'm not one for idle speculation, though."

"So Shara is no fan of Bo's either?" HARV asked before I could.

Priscilla shook her head. "No, he's always rubbed her the wrong way. Once, he tried giving her a neck massage after a late night lab session. She hated it. He longed to marry both sisters, but Shara would have nothing to do with that. She desired a more thoughtful man."

"How do you know all this?" I asked.

Priscilla pointed to where I assume her ears were. "We apes may not talk much, but I assure you we do listen." Priscilla continued, "Bo even offered to marry Shara after his brother's death, claiming it was the right thing to do."

"That's our Bo, always doing the right thing, as long as he's got something to gain by doing it."

"Shara refused. She is a very proud woman."

I turned to Carol. "You met Shara. What did you think about her?"

"She reminded me a lot of Melda," she said weakly.

"They are twin sisters," I said.

"I mean, in demeanor. She was very cool and professional. They don't look like identical twins."

"She uses her mental powers to change her appearance," Priscilla said. "So she separates herself from her sister. She's a little off."

"That's not exactly a big surprise. Hopefully, we'll be able to convince her to help us anyhow," I said.

"With Shara, you never know," Priscilla said.

We would know soon enough. Once HARV rigged the deflector beam to push the ZAP asteroid past the Earth then shut down, I was heading to the psi center. For now, first things first. HARV and I (well mostly HARV) had to concentrate on the task at hand.

"How close to the deflector beam do you have to be before you can reprogram it?" I asked.

HARV appeared from my wrist communicator, shaking his head. I knew that look. I had seen it way too often. It was his "My, you are a dense human" look.

"I need a direct physical link," he huffed. "If I didn't need to touch the thing we could have done this from anywhere."

"By I, you mean me," I said.

"By I, I mean us," he corrected.

"So you need a direct line of sight," I said.

HARV nodded. He gave me a cynical pat on the head. "Yes. Once into the inner workings of the deflector beam I will clone myself onto its operating system. I will be in control."

"So you will be in control of a device that is capable of destroying the Earth."

HARV simply nodded.

"And that's a good thing because?"

HARV sighed. "I am not a madman bent on destroying one civilization so his little corner of civilization can carry on with his vision of what he believes the human race should be."

"Good point."

"Yes, good to know you agree with me," HARV said. "If I slept, I would sleep better knowing that."

I don't think it was my imagination that HARV was growing a bit more cynical each day he was connected to my brain. I wasn't sure if that was a bad thing, but it certainly wasn't all that reassuring.

I turned to Carol. "Am I as annoying as he is?"

Carol pointed to the deflector beam that was now less than a hundred meters away. "I think we better concentrate on the matter at hand," she said, showing her potential for a career in politics.

I reached forward and tapped Priscilla on the shoulder. "We need to land as close to the beam as you can get."

She nodded. "I've been listening to your conversation with HARV."

"Any thoughts?" I asked her.

She shook her head. "I'm glad I don't have a computer wired to my brain."

"Any other thoughts?"

"It's amazing humans still run the place."

"Any other thoughts? Ones more pertinent to our current situation," I said.

"No, sounds like a good sound plan," Priscilla said.

"She's just humoring you because she thinks you are cute," HARV said.

Priscilla's driver pulled our hover up next to the deflector beam. The beam wasn't that stirring, a long metallic post shooting maybe one hundred meters into the Moon's sky. Sitting atop the post were two old-fashioned looking rotating satellite dishes. HARV told me that one of the dishes was for backup tracking and the other fired the deflector or, if needed, tractor beam.

Priscilla turned towards Carol and I. "Put your feet on the nano pads. I will activate the nano suits for your surface walk."

I followed Priscilla's instruction. HARV also put his feet on one of pads. For all of HARV's claims that he has no desire to act human, he certainly does act like us sometimes.

Priscilla reached up and pressed a button on the ceiling of the shuttle. I felt a tingle from my toes to my head as the nano fiber rolled up my body. (At least I thought I felt it.) In less than a second, I was completely covered. Though it may have been the second time I had worn a nano suit, the first time was under emergency conditions so I didn't really get a chance to think about it. That time it was react or die. This time, I had time to reflect on having my body covered by tiny nano molecules. I felt wrapped, like yesterday's roast beef sub trying to stay fresh in the corner deli's refrigerated showcase.

Priscilla pushed another button on the ceiling. The rear door of the shuttle popped open. I moved out of the shuttle toward the beam. HARV's image trailed me. For some reason he was wearing an old-fashioned space suit, one with an extra big helmet. I kept moving carefully to the beam.

The beam wasn't much thicker than a streetlight. Looking up and down, I saw no control panel. I figured this was only a minor problem as I was certain HARV knew were the panel was.

HARV pointed to the left about two centimeters from where my eyes were looking. "The control panel is there!"

I positioned myself in front of where HARV was pointing. The surface looked smooth and unbroken. "Are you sure?"

HARV didn't say anything. I turned to see him anxiously tapping his foot. "Just press right there," he said, pointing.

A beam of red light shot from my eye to a point on the beam. Making a fist, I pounded on the beam. A small door popped up revealing circuitry.

HARV walked over and peered over my shoulder. "Wow, this interface is so old . . ."

"How old?"

"Looks like they haven't updated it in decades."

"Can you still interface with it?"

HARV nodded. "You can count to ten. Can't you?"

"A simple yes would have been enough."

"Surely it would have been."

HARV leaned into the control panel. "I'm just surprised this hardware hasn't been updated in thirty years."

I shrugged. "Why would the council spend money on something as trivial as protecting Earth from killer asteroids? I'm sure they have more important things to spend it on, like updating their offices."

HARV looked at me. "You really do have quite the cynical side."

"Yeah, what can I say?"

HARV smiled at me. "It's actually my favorite part of your personality."

Pointing at the interface I asked, "Are you going to reprogram that thing?"

HARV walked away. "Unlike you, I can walk and chew gum and deftly hack into the Moon's asteroid deflector beam at the same time."

"I take that as a yes," I said.

"It's done," HARV told me.

We turned and headed back to the shuttle. "Of course, none of this will mean anything unless we stop Sputnik and his girls from re-reprogramming it."

"That's easier said than done," I said.

HARV smiled. "Most things are, my friend. Most things are."

We got into the shuttle and it took off. I knew if this plan was going to have a chance of working we were going to have to convince Shara to, at the very least, free Elena and hopefully fight along our side as well.

I wasn't all that secure knowing that my plan hinged on not only freeing Elena but also relying on her. Elena was more than a bit combustible. I was certain she would gladly take Sputnik down; I just couldn't be sure she would stop there. I was fighting fire with an even bigger fire. A fire I wasn't sure I would be able to rein in once it ignited. Still, I didn't see much choice. Besides, for some reason, I trusted Elena.

As we flew toward the dome covering the city, Carol must have noticed the look of concern on my face.

"Worried about Elena," she said.

"Yeah. I trust her. I just don't know why, so I'm not sure if I *trust* my trust."

Carol touched me on the shoulder. "I trust her, too," she said. "She could have killed us at any time and she didn't."

"Yeah. But maybe she just likes playing with us? We're the mice and she's the cat."

I had to hope that in this case the cat would be more interested in taking out the big rat . . . a rat named Sputnik.

Chapter 35

We were lucky. The Moon's Psi Training Center was on the opposite side of the Moon colony from the control center, so our chances of running into Bo and his girls were slim. Bo was a cocky SOB, and we could use that to our advantage. Bo wasn't even going to consider beginning to conceive that we may be loose and ready to toss an extra large wrench into his plan to destroy Earth.

I knew Sputnik's type well. He was the kind of guy who was dead certain the universe revolved around him. He had no limitations, at least none he could see. In many ways that may have been one of the keys to his success—he didn't see his weaknesses, so he didn't let them get in his way. I planned on using that to my advantage.

As we drove closer to Psi Training Center, I felt the tension all around the Moon colony. The sense of unease was palpable. Many of the Moon's inhabitants were afraid of Bo's actions; they were just more afraid to say anything. It was my hope that by tilting the tables against Bo, more people would slip over to our side.

It wasn't long until we arrived at the center, a nondescript looking purple building. It was larger than most of the other buildings on the Moon but still boxy and seemingly made out of plastic blocks.

Carol and I got out of the shuttle and casually walked toward the building.

"So what's the plan?" Carol asked.

"Why does everybody always ask me that?"

"One, you're supposed to be the leader and two, nobody ever thinks you have a plan," HARV said.

"We're going to walk up to the door, knock on it, then explain our cause to Shara."

"Then what?" HARV promoted.

"Hope for the best," I said.

HARV shook his head. "I know you think a partial, half-baked plan is better than no plan at all, but I am starting to question that."

"Have faith, my holographic friend. Have faith."

If Shara was half the psi everybody thought she was there was no point in trying to sneak in and free Elena. We would appeal to Shara's senses.

Shara may not openly oppose Sputnik, but I was betting with a little convincing, she would be on our side. Or, at the very least, do nothing to hinder us. After all, even if Bo didn't kill her husband Mo, he certainly tried to take advantage of Mo's absence.

As we approached the building, HARV took some shots at my logic. "What makes you think that Shara will side with us? She is holding her own daughter prisoner."

"Just a hunch, going on what I hear and noticing the Bo Sputnik-centered events Shara hasn't been at."

"So you are basically basing your hunches about Shara on hearsay and absence of information," HARV said, rubbing his chin as we walked.

"Pretty much."

HARV stopped walking for a moment and just

stood there shaking his head. "Ah, I'm going to miss Earth."

Carol and I walked up the steps to the door of the Training Center. I reached for door chime.

"Come in," a voice called from inside before I had chance to push it.

The door popped open. Carol and I walked into a large, open reception area. A woman, who I assumed was Shara, was sitting in a large chair facing the door. She had three puppies in her lap she was softly petting. She was flanked by two large males wearing purple tunics, one bald, one with long light blue hair.

"Shara, I presume?"

"Yes, that's her," Carol said.

"Mr. Johnson, I was expecting you an hour ago," Shara said.

"Sorry, been busy. You know, trying to save Earth and all."

"Now you have even less time," Shara said.

Shara may have been Melda's twin sister but she appeared to be an older version of her. She had short dark hair done up in a bun and fair features. She was attractive, in an old schoolmarm in purple hot pants kind of way.

"Is purple the official color of the Moon?" I asked.

Shara cranked her head, looking at me like I was crazy. "We don't have time for your silly questions! I assume you want my aid in your gripe against Boris."

"Gripe? He's trying to destroy Earth," I said.

Shara shook her head. "Earth has not treated us well at all. They treat us like we are their poorer, uglier, dumber little sibling. They want things from us, but don't give anything to us besides their toxic waste."

"Still, you can't let fifteen billion people die," I said.

"Perhaps," she said coolly. "Though my calculations

are that not all fifteen billion will die. A few thousand will survive . . . Probably."

Shara looked at the men beside her. "Andres. Carlos. See if Mr. Johnson here is worthy of my aid." Shara motioned toward me with her head.

The two big dudes pulled small staffs from their orange silk belts. They grabbed the ends of their staffs, extending them as they moved toward me.

The next thing I knew I was in a steel cage with Andres and Carlos and we were surrounded by a roaring crowd.

"The crowd and cage are only in your head," HARV said, "but those staffs are very real."

If Shara wanted a show then I'd give her one. A short one. I popped GUS into my hand.

"If you shoot them I will consider that cheating," Shara called to me, both audibly and mentally.

So much for that idea. I tugged on GUS' ends, extending him. The bald one, Andres I believe, came at me smashing his staff down toward my head. Lifting GUS up over my head I blocked his attack. I kicked him in the kneecap, as his staff recoiled off of GUS. He bent over, clutching his knee. I speared him in the solar plexus with GUS. The blow doubled him over, the wind knocked out of him.

Carlos lashed at me, cracking his staff over my back. Without my body armor the move would have been damaging. In this case, it was only annoying. I whipped my body around toward him, leading with GUS, swinging for his head. He ducked under my attack, smiling away. He saw it coming before I threw it. The bad news was he was a psi. I hate fighting psis. The good news was, I have a lot of experience fighting psis.

I quickly thought, *"I'll swing again."*

I feigned my body forward like I was getting ready

to spin again, but at the last minute I stopped, spun the other way, kicking Carlos in the chin. His head shot back. I heard his teeth clunk together. It was a nasty sound. I liked it. The crowd booed.

I wound up to finish him off. The crowd started chanting, "Down with Zach, down with Zach." I knew they weren't really there but they still bugged me. I stopped, pulled GUS back, retracted him, and popped him back up my sleeve.

I peered through the crowd to see Shara sitting in the back row.

"Enough of this," I shouted.

Shara smiled. "No need to shout," she said. The crowd and cage dissolved around me.

Shara stood up. "It seems you have a chance to stop Bo. I will help you."

Chapter 36

Shara led us through the corridors of the Psi Training Center. As we walked down the hallways a few blue-haired girls would open their doors a crack to take a peek at us. None of them said a word though.

"Pretty quiet group you have here," I told Shara.

"Yes, in fact the entirety of the Moon is quiet now," she answered. "We are unsure about the future. Even the strongest precogs have no idea."

"How come?" I asked.

"Too many variables," Carol answered.

Shara gave me a slight smile. "Yes, Mr. Johnson. When it comes to you, the odds somehow get skewed."

"Is that good or bad?" I asked.

Shara casually shrugged. "Time will tell. Time will tell."

We reached the room Elena was being kept in. Elena was lying on a bed. She had a metallic helmet on her head that was connected to a machine on the side of the bed. A blue-haired girl sat by Elena's side, holding her hand. A light-blue-haired guy was manning the machine.

Both the girl and the guy gave us looks of apprehension when we entered the room.

"Don't worry, they are on our side," Shara reassured them.

"But, but," the boy stammered. "Mr. Sputnik ordered her to be restrained."

"Fine," Shara said. She locked eyes with the boy. "Sleep!"

The boy collapsed to floor, sucking his thumb. Shara focused on the girl. "Any comments?"

The girl put one hand behind her back and pointed to Elena with the other. "I would never question my teacher."

"Smart girl," Shara said, walking forward to the control panel.

The headband on Elena started to blink frantically then faded out. Shara pointed to the band with two fingers then motioned them away from the bed. The band flew off of Elena's head.

Elena shot up in bed. "Where the DOS am I?" she shouted.

The young girl quickly moved to Elena's side. She put her hand gently on her forehead. "You are in the Psi Center. You are safe."

Elena glared at the girl. She crumpled to the ground and curled up in the fetal position, sucking her thumb. Yep, she was Shara's daughter.

Elena stood up from the bed. She turned her attention to Shara, Carol, and me. Elena looked fiercely at Shara then looked at me. "She's trying to hide it but she's betrayed you."

"I don't think so," I said. "She helped us free you so we can stop Sputnik. I don't think she would have tipped him off."

Elena shook her head. "Not Sputnik, Earth."

I popped GUS into my hand and pointed him at Shara. "Is that true?"

Shara took an anxious step back. "It's not what you think!"

"You turned your back on your own people so Earth will repay you," Elena said.

"Okay, it is kind of what you think," Shara admitted. "But Sputnik's ideal world doesn't match mine. He has to be stopped. I'm not looking for much, maybe my own reality HV series. I can share my knowledge with the masses and make a tidy profit to boot."

"But tipping off Earth doesn't help matters at all. Earth can't stop the asteroids," HARV noted.

"Really?" Shara asked.

Everybody in the room nodded yes.

"DOS!" Shara shouted, stomping her foot. "Mo was always the one who figured out those little details." She took a deep breath. "Oh well, lucky you passed my test, which means you may be able to stop Bo." She took another deep breath. "I have faith in you all now."

"Great. That and one hundred credits gets us a cup of real coffee."

"You do realize Earth will retaliate and destroy the Moon?" HARV told Shara.

Shara stopped to think for a nano. "No, I never thought about that either . . ."

"So you are dooming the planet we love!" Elena shouted.

Shara shook her head. "It's not truly a planet, my dear," she said, always the teacher.

"So it's quite possible because of you we could be up the creek without a paddle . . ."

She looked at me. "I'm not quite sure I understand your statement."

I clobbered her on the head with GUS. She dropped

to the ground. She may have trusted us, but I didn't trust her.

Pointing to the bed Elena had been in, I said, "Let's hook her up to that."

"With pleasure," Elena said.

Chapter 37

As Elena and Carol physically and mentally strapped Shara in the psi bed, I had HARV get me through to Ona.

"Zach, I'm kind of busy now," Ona said to me as HARV's holographic form morphed into hers.

"Yeah, I know. Planning a retaliatory strike against the Moon."

Her image stared at me. "How did you know that?" She shook her head. "Never mind. I should know you'd know that."

"Ona, I'm still on the Moon."

"Oh, sorry about that," Ona said. "If you can't get off soon, I'm afraid you're going to die."

"I'm going to stop that asteroid from hitting Earth."

"That would be ideal," Ona said. "All our people here say we don't have time to destroy it ourselves. Even if we hit it with a missile, Earth would just be hit with multiple mini-planet killing rocks instead of one big one."

"All I ask is that you give me time before you go firing off missiles."

Ona moved her wrist to glance at her communicator. "I'll talk to my people and see how long I can give you."

"Ms. Ona," HARV said. "Why even launch missiles at the Moon? If Zach and I stop the asteroid there will be no need. Even if we fail, what is gained by destroying the Moon?"

"That's just the way the worlds work," Ona said. "Earth can't be seen as weak, even in death. We will be evacuating as many people as we can. Those people need to let the other planets know Earth people are not to be taken lightly."

"But why punish a million people on the Moon because of the actions of a small handful of people?"

Ona's image disappeared.

"I guess she didn't want to answer," HARV said.

"I'm betting we wouldn't want to hear the answer," I said.

We had to take Sputnik out for good and assure Earth he would no longer be a threat to them. We had to do it fast, while Earth had time to recall its missiles.

"How much time do we have?" I asked HARV.

"To stop the asteroid from hitting Earth or to stop the Earth from launching missiles at the Moon?"

"Both."

No time to waste pondering the folly of each side's actions. I swear, when it comes to politics and relationships, politicians believe "might always makes right" and even if two wrongs don't make a right, maybe three or four will.

I turned to my team of Elena, Carol, and HARV. "Let's get to the Tracking and Blocking Station and save two worlds."

"What about the other psis here?" HARV asked. "Will they side with us?"

Elena shook her head. "They are young and scared.

They won't fight for us but they won't hinder us either. None of the psis still here are Bo's children."

"What about the older psis on the planet not related to or married to Bo?"

"They won't help us," Elena said. "They are too scared of Bo's women."

I scratched my head. I knew we were going to be badly outnumbered. It might help tip the scales if we convinced some of the other psis here to come to our side. The older ones were set in their ways. Years of conditioning by Bo's family would be hard to overcome in a few minutes. Still, with the younger ones (if I could appeal to their feral nature), I might have a chance.

"Is there a large classroom in the building?" I asked.

Elena nodded a yes.

"Tell the students to meet us there, pronto."

"What are you going to tell them?" Elena asked.

"I have no idea."

"I was afraid he was going to say that," HARV said.

Chapter 38

Less than five minutes passed before I was standing at the front of a classroom auditorium looking up at about three hundred seats spread across the room. Each of the seats was filled with young, anxious, blue-haired kids. The kids were mostly young girls ranging from probably ten to seventeen but there were some boys sprinkled in the crowd.

"So none of Sputnik's kids are here?" I thought to Elena.

"No, his are all home trained," she thought back.

"Good," I thought to her and Carol.

I turned to the classroom. "You're probably wondering why I called you here," I said, mostly because I always wanted to say that.

A young kid raised her hand. "You want us to help you stop Mr. Sputnik."

"Exactly," I said, as the girl smiled then dropped her hand. "If you don't help me now, the Moon and the Earth will both be destroyed."

"But we can't go against the Sputnik daughters,"

one voice cried from the back. "They are too power-ful."

The crowd buzzed in agreement.

"Besides, they are fellow psis," another anonymous voice said.

Once again the crowd buzzed their accord.

"I'm not asking you to fight them. I'm just asking you to help me. I will stop them, then I will prevent Earth from launching its missiles at the Moon."

"How?" another voice asked.

"If you can all cloak us, we can get the drop on Sputnik and his family."

There was dead silence and looks of confusion all around.

"He means we can surprise them," Carol said.

A wave of *ah* swept the room.

"Earth doesn't treat us well at all," another voice called.

"True, but nobody gains anything from killing everybody. Once this is over, Earth and Moon will be united again."

"Will the Moon be free?" another voice asked.

"I will do my best to make sure that happens," I said.

There was total silence. I didn't know if that was a good sign or a bad sign. Just then, HARV appeared in the middle of the room. He was dressed in a casual tweed suit, wearing glasses and carrying an old-fashioned wooden pointer.

"May I have you attention please, class?"

All eyes turned to HARV. HARV pointed at me with the pointer. "I know this man does not look like much. I know he doesn't look like he could save a cat from a tree, which by the way, he couldn't, as he has a fear of heights." HARV adjusted his suit. "But I digress." He took a deep breath. "I have known this

man for many years now. I can say unequivocally, if
he says he can do something, he can do it. DOS! He's
saved the world more times than some of you teens
have had dates." He paused for another nano. "You
know who you are." HARV let that sink in. "Zach is
the man who can save you and the Earth."

The room maintained its silence for a nano or two.
Suddenly, everybody started the same chant, "Zach,
Zach, Zach."

I must admit it felt good. I held my hands up to
quiet the crowd. "I just need you all to start sending
out mixed thoughts. Cloak us. Confuse them. Make
sure none of your relatives join in to help the
Sputniks."

The room gave me a collective nod. I turned to
Carol and Elena and smiled. "It's go time," I said.

As I walked out of the room I heard Carol tell
Elena, "He loves talking like that."

Chapter 39

Heading over to the Tracking and Blocking Station, we saw that the streets of the Moon had become abandoned. Sputnik apparently didn't want to deal with any of his less loyal "subjects," so they were all "requested" to stay at home until after they heard him make a special and very important broadcast. In a way, that was good news for us as it cut down on our chances of somebody spotting us and ratting us out as we rushed through what could only be described as a very shiny, plastic ghost town.

Summing up our assets, I figured on the plus side of the ledger we had a bunch of heavily armed apes, the firepower of GUS, the considerable mental powers of Elena and Carol, HARV's seemingly limitless access to information, and my wits. That was more than enough to handle almost any situation.

Unfortunately, this wasn't almost any situation. We were up against a well-armed contingent of confused apes, at least a hundred very powerful psis, and a madman bent on destroying Earth. To make matters more complicated, we had two ticking clocks to deal with.

Earth had missiles heading toward the Moon. The Moon had pushed an asteroid of extinction-level proportions toward the Earth. True, we had programmed the tractor beam to push the asteroid away, but if we didn't take over the Tracking and Blocking Station or put it out of commission, that would be for naught.

We were outnumbered and didn't have time on our side but so far we had the element of surprise going for us. Bo Sputnik in all his administrator glory never conceived that something could go wrong with his plan. He apparently hadn't contemplated the idea that Carol and I would break free, liberate the others and then throw an ape-sized monkey wrench into his scheme.

"How are the other Earthers doing?" I asked Priscilla as we drove.

She shook her hairy head. "They are awake but still not mentally alert. It will be an hour or so until they will be of any assistance."

"We don't have that kind of time," I said.

"I know," Priscilla said, "I was just making sure you knew that."

"I'm not as dense as most of my enemies and many of my friends believe," I told her.

Priscilla gave me a pat on the back. "I know that, my cute friend. Because if you were, you would have been dead long ago."

"Smart ape," I said.

Priscilla lowered her eyes and looked away from me.

"Oh, no. What is it now?"

"Zach, I hate to pile on . . ." she hesitated.

"Don't worry, I'm used to the universe kneeing me in the groin when I'm down."

"My primates and I have no problem taking on

Sputnik and his wives and offspring, or bots, but . . ."
Priscilla ground her teeth.

"But you won't fire on your fellow apes," I said.

She nodded. "We figured if we did that we'd be lowering ourselves to human level." She paused. "Nothing personal, but we apes strive to be more than human."

"I can identify," HARV said.

"I can't blame you."

The driver signaled that we were now within a few hundred meters of the Tracking and Blocking Center. We ditched the car and went the rest of the way on foot. We met up with the rest of Priscilla's apes who were being led by Maurice.

Maurice gave me a polite salute with his feet. "I'm glad to be fighting on your side, Mr. Johnson," he said.

"I'm glad you're on my side," I told him. "What's the situation?"

"I have my great apes positioned all around the building," he told me. "Give us the word and we will fight for our freedom."

"Let me take a look at things first," I said.

"Follow me," Maurice said.

"How many apes does Sputnik have backing him?" I asked.

"Most of my fellows are staying out of this until they see how it plays out," Maurice said.

"How many?" I repeated.

"Maybe three hundred."

"Maybe?"

"Okay, three hundred and twelve."

"How many do we have on our side?"

"Thirty-three."

We crawled up behind some bushes and surveyed the situation. The outer rim of the Tracking Dome was surrounded by a small army of apes. Those apes were backed up by about twenty psis. If that wasn't enough, the psis were supported by three big battlebots. They all looked pretty relaxed, as if they didn't expect any major trouble.

I smiled. That was going to change really fast. We just needed to hit them hard before they knew what hit them. Of course by hit them hard, I meant take the apes out without really hitting them too hard.

HARV tapped me on the shoulder, expending enough energy so I felt it. It was creepy. "Ah, Zach, I need to push the asteroid out of the way now. If I wait any longer we run the risk of it grazing Earth."

"That would be bad," I said.

HARV gave me a pat on the head, which I also felt. "Very good, Zach."

I looked over at Priscilla and Maurice who were bent over next to me. A couple of their apes were behind us. I could smell the apprehension on them; it wasn't even close to being a pleasant smell.

"We don't want our fellow apes hurt," Priscilla reminded me.

"Yeah, I haven't forgotten."

I looked at HARV. "How long until the big push?"

"I can give you twenty more seconds."

"Gee thanks."

"Eighteen seconds."

I looked at Priscilla, anxiously looking at me. It's never comforting to see an ape fidgeting, itching her back with her foot, scratching her head and fiddling with her PIHI-Pod. The PIHI-Pod . . . That was it.

"All you apes wear PIHI-Pods, correct?" I said.

"Yes," Priscilla replied.

"Of course," Maurice added.

"Twelve seconds," HARV counted down.

"Push it out of the way now, HARV."

HARV's eyes flashed red for a nano or two. "Done."

"You have the specs to the Pods, right?"

HARV just stood there fists on hips, head shaking disappointedly back and forth.

"I'll take that as a, yes of course I do."

I turned to Priscilla, "Tell your people to remove their PIHI-Pods."

Priscilla scratched her head and smiled.

"You heard the man," she said to Maurice.

Maurice signed to the apes. Each relayed the sign to another.

"HARV, apes have more sensitive ears than humans, correct?"

HARV nodded, then smiled. "You want me to broadcast a high frequency pitch over the PIHI-Pods."

I touched my nose. "Vingo."

"I can generate and broadcast a tone over the PIHI-Pods that will put apes out of commission but it's going to hurt all the neutral apes too."

"Serves them right for standing on the sidelines," I said.

I looked at Priscilla who nodded in agreement.

HARV smiled. "I can do you two better," he said with a wink that was, frankly, a little disturbing. "I can also make it so the tone really upsets the psis and scrambles the battlebots' logic circuits."

Now it was my turn to pat HARV on the shoulder, "Who says supercomputers can't be useful?"

"Surely no one with even a quarter of a brain."

I turned to Carol. "Remove your PIHI-Pod," I said.

Carol opened her hand to show that she had already removed hers from her ear lobe. "One step ahead of you, Tió."

"As always," HARV and I both said.

I centered my attention on HARV. "Zap 'em."

Outside of a barely noticeable increase in HARV's smile I didn't see any other changes.

"Did you do it?"

HARV pointed to the apes ringing the complex.

They were all rolling on the ground clutching their ears. The psis behind the apes were frantically pulling at their ears. I took that as a yes. The three battlebots were spinning on their wheels, doing 360s, waving their tentacles and loudly humming "Three Blind Lab Mice." Yep, they were zonkers.

I pointed forward. "Let's take out the psis and grab the building."

I looked at Maurice. He shook his head no. "Sorry, Zach, I'm a behind-the-scenes kind of ape. Actual fighting is so not my style."

I patted him on the shoulder. "I understand."

Maurice gave me a toothy grin. "Don't worry though. I will make sure all my kin stay out of the fray."

We stormed the building, Carol, Elena, HARV, a squad of apes, and me. The opposition apes were in too much pain to put up any opposition at all, so we glided past them. A couple of the psis tried to put up a fight but HARV's tone really tossed their brains for a loop and tied them into knots. They were all easy pickings to be taken out by stun blasts.

The bots were so entertaining, dancing and jiving that I was tempted to just leave them alone. Priscilla though, being smarter than I am, destroyed them each with a heavy blaster.

"It's been my experience that battlebots can be dancing one minute and trying to dissect you a minute later," she said.

Smart great ape.

We reached the door to the complex without losing anybody. Of course that was the easy part. Elena and Carol had both noted the initial psis were all young and still low level. I felt something. A vine had grabbed my arm, pulling on me.

Looking around, I saw a couple of the apes backing me up. Carol and Elena also were getting entwined in vines. I noticed that the entryway to the building had been lined with grapevines.

"Ah, I see Randy's and Melda's defensive grapes have been put into practice," HARV said.

"Defensive grapes?" Carol asked.

"It was my aunt's idea," Elena told her, pushing a vine off of her. "They are an organic defense mechanism designed to stop intruders."

"You're joking," Carol said, as another vine started wrapping itself around her legs.

Elena shook her head no.

The apes were easily pulling their vines off themselves. The plants clearly weren't intended to stop gorillas.

I pointed GUS at the base of the vine that was holding me.

"I know how to deal with these," I said.

"So do I," Elena said.

Elena clenched her fists and gritted her teeth. Waves of energy rippled out from her body. The vine encased around Carol's legs loosened then dropped to the ground. It shriveled up and wilted. All the other vines in the area did the same.

"Never been a big fan of semi-intelligent plants," Elena said.

Nudging Carol I said, "I told you she'd come in handy."

We proceeded to the door.

"An analysis of the door shows it is not locked," HARV said. "How do you want to proceed?"

I spun toward to Priscilla, "You and ten of your men follow Carol, Elena, and me in. Have the rest secure the area."

Priscilla gave me a little salute. Not sure if I liked it or not. She tossed me a little kiss. I was sure I didn't like that.

I turned to the door and kicked it in.

"Ah, the subtle Zach-lite approach," HARV said with way more than a hint of sarcasm.

I led the charge into the Moon's Asteroid Tracking and Blocking Station.

Chapter 40

Sputnik was frantically working away at the main control panel in the middle of the room. Well, he wasn't so much working as barking orders at Melda. Lea stood behind them, eyeing us.

Sputnik's other daughters were spread throughout the building. They had removed their PIHI-Pods and were converging on us. A good many of the younger psis were lying on the ground. Apparently our initial attack had taken them out. Despite that, there had to be at least a dozen other children and wives of Sputnik ready to stop us at all costs.

One of our apes fired a stun blast at three young psis. The blast swerved past them. It hit a plastic wall, harmlessly fizzling out. The psis pointed at the ape. He and two of his compatriots stopped their charges. They went rigid then flew backward into the wall. They crashed to the ground, out cold.

Our other ape allies weren't faring that well either. Without the element of shock and awe on our side the psis were able to avoid most of the apes' shots.

The apes weren't so lucky. General Tang was leading the defense against the apes.

"How dare you betray me!" she shouted to two apes who had grabbed her by the arms. Both apes went flying off her smashing into the walls.

Elena and Carol though, were another story. Elena hated Sputnik and was showing it by mentally pummeling his offspring and spouses. She made a beeline toward Sputnik, taking any psi who crossed her path out with a single glare, reducing them to a quivering, fetal position.

Tang, having shed herself of the apes, ran over, blocking Elena.

"Sorry, young one, you won't get past me," Tang shouted, pointing at Elena.

With that Elena ran right past her without seemingly giving her a passing thought. Obviously though, Elena did shoot a bit of her attention at Tang. The moment she passed her Tang fell over stiff, locked in the pointing position.

"Impressive," HARV commented. "Elena took Tang out as an afterthought."

Carol covered my and Priscilla's backs. She wasn't as flamboyant as Elena but she was just as effective. She was aptly deflecting any mental or physical attacks that would come my way. She too was reveling in her own power, her hair crackling with energy as it danced around her shoulders. It was scary and inspiring at the same time. (Just as long as I didn't think about it too much.)

With Carol as our cover, Priscilla and I were splitting the room in half. I took the right, using GUS to pick off any of the psis that Elena missed. Priscilla used her hand and foot weapons to clear the left side.

So far, we were winning the battle. The problem was the war wasn't over yet. Sputnik's biggest guns, Lea and Melda, hadn't even entered the conflict. I wasn't going to let that bother me though. I *couldn't* let that bother me.

Now that we had taken out the excess psis it was time to concentrate on Sputnik. I was actually a bit perturbed that he didn't even seem to be worried that we were storming the room.

"HARV, any idea what Sputnik is up to?"

"Yes, of course."

"And?"

"He is trying to regain control of the deflector beam and push the asteroid back into Earth."

Nope, that wouldn't do. I aimed GUS at Sputnik. I pulled the trigger. Bolts of energy flew from GUS. One directly into Elena's back. One into Carol. One into Priscilla. The three of them fell to the ground.

"GUS, that wasn't what I wanted!" I said.

"Sorry," GUS said in Melda's voice. "That's what I wanted."

GUS flew from my hand into Melda's.

"Oh, this is so not good," I said.

Chapter 41

The only people or animals left standing in the room were me, Sputnik, Melda, Lea, and April. We had come so close, but I was starting to worry that it wasn't close enough.

I was outnumbered and outgunned. My only hope was I wasn't outsmarted.

"HARV, are you still with me?" I thought.

"Of course, my programming and defenses are significantly more robust than GUS'. I've learned much after our little encounter at the North Pole last year and the earlier incident at the Convention Center."

"Can't you ever simply say yes?"

"Obviously I can, but I choose not to."

Verbose or not, I was glad that I had HARV in my assets column. For all his many flaws, HARV is an incredible ace up my sleeve (or more accurately stuck in my brain).

"Has he managed to get control of the deflector beam yet?"

"No, of course not," HARV said confidently. Then, "Oops, didn't see that coming . . ."

"Didn't see what coming?" I asked.

Sputnik looked up from his control panel. "I've activated the backup deflector beam on the other side of the Moon."

DOS! Double DOS! HARV really should have seen that one coming. Figures the World Council would have a backup the one time it really messes up things.

"HARV, how come you didn't know there was a backup?"

"Because it's not in any of the specs," HARV answered.

Melda patted Bo on the back. "That's because the council didn't have the foresight to envision the need for a backup." She patted herself on the chest. "That was my idea."

Well, at least now my universe made sense again. Everything else had failed. It was time to try a desperate move . . . I needed to try to reason with a politician.

"Listen Sputnik, it's not too late," I said.

"It is too late, for Earth!" he shouted. He waved his hand over the control panel. He looked up and grinned. "I pushed the asteroid back into Earth's path."

"Then you are dooming the Earth and the Moon," I told him.

"What are you talking about?"

"Shara has tipped off the Earth and they are retaliating."

Sputnik took a step back from the control panel. He inhaled and exhaled quickly. In his egotistical rampage, he never conceived that somebody would betray his cause.

"Damn that bitch!" he shouted. "No wonder I never slept with her."

"Ah, she's my sister," Melda reminded him.

"So?" Sputnik shot back to her. "How does that affect me?"

"I'm just saying you shouldn't call her a bitch," Melda said. "It's degrading."

I shook my head. Only I could get caught in between a family scrabble while trying to save the world."

"People, can we please try to concentrate on the task at hand here," I shouted to Sputnik and Melda.

Sputnik and Melda both turned their attention back to me. "Oh right, destroying the Earth," Sputnik said.

"Push the asteroid back away from Earth and I will contact them and have them stop their missiles," I told them.

Sputnik stood there, motionless. His face turned red with a mix of anger and frustration.

Lea looked up at the dome observatory. "I do see missiles coming in from Earth."

Sputnik remained motionless. I couldn't tell if he had snapped, was deep in thought, or both.

"It's not too late," I repeated.

Sputnik slowly shook his head no. "It is too late," he said sullenly, "for humans." He turned to Melda. "My escape shuttle is ready?"

Melda nodded slowly.

"Then my family and I will survive. All is well. Actually, this is even better than I had planned. The new, new world we build will be totally pure."

"Sorry to burst your dream of Adam and Eve and Eve and Eve, but building a world with just your progeny is no way to start a new civilization."

He pointed to me looking over his shoulder at Melda and Lea. "Squash him like the bug he is."

Melda took a step back, distancing herself from her husband. Moving toward him, Lea curled her hand into a fist.

"You lied to me," she said coolly, eyes fixed on Bo.

"Lie? Me? How?"

Wow, witty retort, I thought. "HARV, can you push that asteroid past Earth again?"

"Already on it. Just keep them busy."

Now that was something I could do. Sputnik's cart was already leaning. It just a needed a little push to tilt it over, spilling his apples all over.

I pointed at Lea, saying strongly, but not overly accusingly, "So you're the one who killed the council members." I wanted her guilty, not defensive.

She bent her head down, not looking at me, keeping focused on her father. "Yes," she said solemnly. "Once we had the pass codes to take their cameras offline, I turned my body into energy, entered the room, and killed them all."

This was where things got dicey. I wanted to shove her over the edge but toward Sputnik. Turning an angry young girl against her dad wasn't going to be all that hard. The trick was getting her to concentrate her anger only on dad.

"He probably told you 'Kill a few people for the good of many,'" I said, looking at Sputnik the entire time.

Out of the corner of my eye I saw Lea nod weakly. She was on the hook, now to reel her in.

"He told you that by killing three people you would not only free your own people but also save the lives of billions on Earth."

Lea nodded again, this time with a bit more conviction.

"He had you convinced that by killing those people Earth would change its mind and we wouldn't be where we are right now," I stated.

Lea hung her head. "Yes," she said meekly.

Waving my finger at her I said, "Now, look where you are . . . about to kill billions, including your own people."

Sputnik turned to Lea. "I didn't plan it like this, but truly it's better this way. This way, only the extreme, best genes survive. The new race we start will be incredible!"

"You're powerful Lea, but you're not a god," I said.

"But you should be! You should be!" Sputnik told her.

"That's why I killed Uncle Mo," Lea said, "He wanted Elena and me to be gods."

"You killed my brother!" Sputnik shouted.

"I mentally commanded him to crash his shuttle. He had discovered a way of unlocking that part of the mind that Elena and I keep locked up, our subconscious safeties. Once I picked that from his mind, I learned how to convert my body into energy," she paused and lowered her eyes. "I learned so much more. My and Elena's minds are so powerful. I can see the strings of the molecular structure that bind you all together. I could rearrange you all into turnips if I pleased."

"Incredible," somebody said. It may have been me.

"Yes," Lea continued. "Power like this cannot be trusted with Elena. That's why I killed Mo, so he could not share it with others." Lea lowered her eyes, "I'm not even totally sure if even I have the mental resolve to handle this kind of power, but it's a burden I must live with."

"Why didn't you just wipe Mo's mind?" Melda asked, being more of a scientist than a mom.

Lea shook her head. "I couldn't take any chances. If power like mine ever fell into the wrong hands, which are any other hands than mine, it could be really bad."

"You mean like destroying the Earth and the Moon?" I asked.

Lea dipped her head even lower, her entire body slumping over, quivering.

As Lea was pouring out her heart, HARV was electronically trying to take control of the deflector beam. Interestingly or scarily enough, Melda wasn't trying to stop us.

"Zach, I've got control of the second beam. The asteroid is now safely going to miss Earth, again," HARV told me.

Now it was time to shut down Sputnik for good.

Lea had been stewing in her own juices for a while now. Another nudge and she was going to blow. I needed to make sure the fallout didn't take us all out.

"It's not too late, Lea. You can stop this," I told her.

Lea looked at me for the first time. "But I killed so many people. My father told me by doing that it would never come to this . . ."

"He lied, Lea. He lied. This is what he wanted all along. He never wanted to live in peace with Earth. He just wanted to carry on his bloodline to make the perfect race," I said.

Lea stood there in silence. She knew what I said was true; most of her believed me. A small part still clung to the hope that maybe following her father wasn't wrong.

"Look how easily he was willing to toss the Moon aside," I said.

"Yes, he's evil, like my uncle was," she sighed. "But so am I. I have killed." She shook her head. You could feel her sadness. "I was so wrong . . . No human can handle this kind of power."

"Yes, but if you act now, you will save billions. That's got to tilt the karma somewhat in your favor."

Lea nodded. "Yes, father was wrong. I can't let billions die."

Sputnik thrust a finger at her. "This isn't totally on my head! I never told you to kill my brother."

Lea dipped her head lower. "He was wrong, like you."

Sputnik pounded his chest. "Wrong? I can't be wrong! I'm a political administrator! I'm not wrong just because some people don't agree with my choices." He stopped and smiled. "Actually, by destroying everything but my bloodline this plan is turning out even better than I anticipated." The smile stretched across his face. "Actually, I'm betting this was what I had originally planned." A slight pause. "Yes, yes, that's it."

Okay, Sputnik had tied lead weights around his ankles, ate a big meal, and then dove into the deep end.

"Shut this whole operation down now. I'll tell Earth all is well. They'll call off their missiles. It's all good," I said, skipping over the part where Lea and Bo would have to spend the rest of their lives in prison.

"No!" Sputnik shouted.

"I was talking to Lea, not you," I told him.

"I will not be ignored!" Sputnik shouted.

Sputnik bounded across the room, landing on top of me and driving me to the floor. It hurt, but not nearly as much as Sputnik thought it would. In his rage, Sputnik forgot he wasn't the only one in the room wearing souped-up bio armor. He was on top, but hardly had the advantage. His weight was already leaning forward as he was trying to force me to stay pinned on the ground.

I kicked up with my legs, using his momentum to spring him forward. I grabbed his right arm and pulled forward, sending him tumbling off me.

Rolling on top of him, I hit him with a left to the chin, followed by a right. I felt his teeth clank together both times. It felt better than it should have. I had him ripe for finishing off. Then I delayed for a nano. I don't know what it is about me that I get such enjoyment out of pummeling politicians and administrators.

That little hesitation hurt me—literally. Sputnik's

top half sprung up like an old jack-in-the-box. Extending both his fists, he drove them into my solar plexus. The push sent me hurling across the room. I was winded, but thanks to my armor, I was far from out.

I saw Sputnik push himself to his feet and clamber over to me. He bent over and wrapped his arms around me.

"Gee, I didn't know you were sweet on me," I told him.

He squeezed and arched his back backward, lifting me up in a bear hug.

"Nothing like a good Russian bear hug to squeeze the life out of an opponent," he said.

I gave him an A for effort. He was really hurting me. True, his body armor was enhancing his strength, but mine was propping up my endurance. So we were even. I always like to give a man his due.

The thing was, I saw this move coming probably before he was sure it was the move he was going to use. As he grabbed me I was able to keep my arms free and mobile. That meant while he had the advantage, it was only a slight one. Taking my index fingers I rammed them into the two pressure points right below his nose.

Sputnik relinquished his grip on me, grabbing his face as I dropped to the ground. Doesn't matter how big or strong a man is, if you hit these points right it will force him to let go. There are times it really pays to have a girlfriend who is an expert martial artist. (Not to mention being so experienced in having people try to kill me.)

Not wanting to give Sputnik any time to recover, I lunged forward, head butting him dead-on in the forehead.

He crashed backward to the ground.

Just for good measure I kicked him in the groin.

Yes, it was a low blow, but the guy was willing to kill billions. He deserved it.

I reached down to my ankle holster to pull out my old-fashioned gun. To my surprise, Sputnik beat me to the punch. He had GUS pointed at me.

I dove to the ground just as he fired. The shot whizzed past me. I rolled for cover then sprang to my feet.

"HARV, how can he use GUS against me?" I asked.

"Melda must have reprogrammed him," HARV said meekly. "It's not really all that surprising. I am sure Randy gave her access to almost everything." HARV paused for a minute. "I am receiving a message from GUS. He says he is so sorry for firing at you but he can't help himself."

"Tell him I'm not so sorry for shooting back," I said.

I pulled the trigger. My shot hit GUS dead on. It didn't really damage him but the force of the shot blew GUS out of Sputnik's hand.

I pointed my gun between Sputnik's eyes. "The next shot is for keeps," I told him.

Sputnik snarled at me, holding his stinging right hand with his left. Limping over to the control panel he raised his arm. "This isn't over yet."

"I think it is," I said, pulling the trigger. I didn't really want to kill him, but I couldn't let him doom fifteen billion people.

The bullet streaked out from gun toward Sputnik's brain. It drew closer than closer then came to an abrupt halt, less than half a micrometer from making contact. The bullet fell to the floor.

"DOS! Not again," I shouted.

"Zach, I could not let you kill my father," Lea said.

Sputnik turned to Lea and Melda. "Thank you, my loved ones." He bent down and picked up GUS with his left hand. He pointed GUS at me. "You should have killed me when you had your first shot."

I shook my head. "Not my style. Unless there is no other way."

Sputnik snickered. "Too bad. A *true* leader does what he wants when he wants."

"Only a deranged one," I said.

"Oh, great, taunt the crazy man with the deadly weapon pointed right at you," HARV said. "It amazes me you weren't killed years ago."

Sputnik squeezed GUS' trigger. Nothing happened.

"GUS, I knew you couldn't kill me!" I said.

"Sorry, Mr. Zach, sir," GUS said. "I would have killed you but something is blocking me."

"What?" Sputnik and I both said at the same time.

"It was me," Lea said, walking toward her father. "I certainly cannot let you harm Zach."

"Daughter, how could you?" Sputnik asked.

She lowered her eyes as she approached. "We were so wrong, Father, especially you."

Sputnik shook his head. "I am never wrong, only occasionally less right."

"I cannot let you harm the Earth or the Moon," Lea said determinedly. She was a person who had made up her mind.

Sputnik held open his arms. "But I only want what's best for everybody."

Lea hugged him. "No, you only want what's best for you."

Sputnik nodded. "Yes, everybody whose opinion matters."

Lea started to glow with energy. "Get out!" she ordered.

"I can't," Sputnik said. "You are holding me too tight."

"I was talking to everybody else," Lea said. "Get out," she ordered, both aloud and mentally. "Take the others with you. I have no intention of hurting anybody else, ever."

"Ah, what about me?" Sputnik asked.

Lea shook her head. "You don't count. As long as either of us breathe, Earth and the Moon won't be safe." She looked at him unflinchingly. "I will not have that."

"But I am your father and your leader!" he shouted.

"I didn't choose you or vote for you," she said.

Melda telekinetically lifted some of her other children from the ground. She started heading for the door. "Gather the others," she said, "and run!"

Carol and Elena were starting to come around. I bent down and shook each of them gently. "Come on ladies, rise and shine, quickly."

"What hit me?" Carol asked. She then noticed the glowing Lea. "Oh, that's not good."

Elena pushed herself up from the ground. "Depends on how you look at it." Elena stared at her cousin and her uncle for a nano or two. She smiled, then softly said, "Wow."

"Grab as many apes and people as you can with your minds and let's get out of here before she blows." I said. "Literally."

Elena and Carol picked up those Melda couldn't carry in a telekinetic net.

"Come on, let's go," I shouted, pointing to the door.

"We know where the door is, Tió," Carol scolded.

Carol, Elena, Melda, and I moved out of the building as fast as we could with the others in tow.

"How far away do we have to be to be safe?" I asked Melda as we excited the building.

She shook her head. "Too far."

Melda stopped running and threw open her arms. "I'll create a force field."

Before I was able to say anything the Tracking and Blocking Station was engulfed by a burst of explosive energy. The force of the blow knocked us all to the ground. I looked up. Where the staion once stood was now a towering mushroom cloud.

"Wow," was all I could say.

I looked around at everybody. They were all stunned, but not in pieces. I took that as a good sign. "Are you all okay?"

Carol and Elena both nodded yes. "Better than ever," Elena said.

Priscilla jumped to her feet. "Takes more than a little subatomic blast to stop a good gorilla," she said with a smile.

I stood up and moved to Melda who was lying on the ground in front of us. I touched her lightly on the shoulder. "Are you okay?" I asked.

"My daughter and husband are dead, but I will live," she said solemnly.

"HARV, is Earth safe?" I asked.

"Define *safe*," HARV asked.

"HARV!"

"Yes, the asteroid will miss the planet."

"Phew," I said, "then it's over."

"Well, we still have the little matter of two nuclear warheads heading straight for us," HARV said.

HARV never was one to let my revel in the moment.

Chapter 42

"HARV, put me in contact with Ona, ASAP," I ordered.

"Doing it now," HARV said.

I waited. Nothing happened. The delay was very unlike HARV.

"What's going on, HARV?"

"Things are a bit slow, since she is in secret orbit around Earth with the rest of the World Council."

DOS, it didn't take them long to abandon planet.

Priscilla hopped to my side. "Typical humans . . . Saving themselves when the going gets tough."

Ona's holographic image broadcast itself from my communicator.

"Oh, hi, Zach," she said, as awkwardly as I've ever heard Ona say anything.

"Ona, Earth is safe. Sputnik is dead. So is his daughter Lea. She was the one who killed all those council members."

"That's, ah, good to know, Zach."

"You can call back your missiles now."

Silence. That's never a good sign when dealing with politicians.

"I said, you can call back your missiles now."

More silence, worse sign. Ona gave me the weakest smile of her life. "About that," she said then stopped.

"Yes?"

"I feel bad . . ."

"Because?"

"Real bad now," Ona said.

"Don't tell me," I said.

"Okay," Ona said, waving good-bye to the screen.

"Tell me!" I shouted.

"The missiles are non-stoppable and non-recallable," she said.

"Non-stoppable?"

"Well, technically they will stop, but not until they reach their target and detonate."

"Why?"

"They are nuclear bombs, Zach. That's what they do, hit things and blow up."

I sighed. "Why did you launch non-recallable missiles?"

"They are a defense against powerful psis. We wanted to make sure none of them could trick us into recalling the missiles."

"So there's no way out?"

"Zach, I can assure you, I and the other council members feel really, really, really awkward about this," Ona said.

At that time, Electra and her fellow ARC members had joined us in the courtyard. Shara and her students were also there—the students must have freed her after we left.

Electra raced over and we embraced. I lifted her off the ground and gave her a kiss. Not just any kiss, the hardest yet the softest kiss I had ever given her. I'm a tough guy, yet I'll admit that it made me tingle from my toes to the tip of my fedora.

"Did I just hear what I thought I heard?" Electra asked me.

"Afraid so," I said, lowering her gently to the ground. "We're dead, unless we can stop two missiles from coming at us."

Ona waved to Electra. "Hi, Electra, nice to see you again. Sorry it can't be under less dire circumstances."

Electra gave Ona a polite nod. "So, Earth is going to destroy the Moon," Electra said.

" 'Fraid so," Ona and I both said.

"Oh, some of this may be my fault," Shara sighed.

"Some of this?" I said.

"No use pointing fingers now, Zachary," Shara said.

"Could we crash shuttles into the missiles?" Electra asked.

Ona's image shook her head. "No go. The missiles are intelligent; they would avoid any incoming objects or shuttles."

"Then let's use the reflector beam on them," I said.

"But you said the control station has been destroyed," Ona said.

"HARV can still control the beam. Right, HARV?"

"Sure, only the missiles are smaller and faster than the killer asteroids the deflector beam is built to be used against," HARV answered.

"But you can do it," I said.

HARV shook his head yes. He thought for a nano, then shook his head no.

"What is it, yes or no?" I asked.

"Both," HARV answered. "I can deflect one of the missiles but not both of them in time."

"Ah, why not?" I asked. "Hit one with one beam, hit the other with the backup beam."

HARV put up one finger, "One, it's more complicated to hit a missile than an asteroid."

"Yeah, but you're good at math and stuff. You can do it."

"True," HARV said as he put up a second finger. "But two, the feedback from Lea's explosion destroyed the backup beam."

"You should have led with that one," I said.

"You're right. This probably wasn't the time to build suspense." HARV took a step back. "Sorry about that," he said. "I believe I am feeling a bit of sorrow as I have grown fond of the Moon."

I turned to Priscilla. "Any chance you can get a team over to the beam and fix it?"

"Sure, sweetie," she said. "We can have it up and running in twelve hours."

"We don't have nearly that much time," HARV said.

"I didn't say it was a good chance," Priscilla said.

Electra turned to me. "Sweetie?"

"It's a pet name." I looked at Melda. "How many escape shuttles are ready to go?"

"One . . ."

"Ah, that's not all that helpful."

"Sorry," she said. "Planning for failure wasn't one of Bo's stronger points."

That may have been one of the great understatements of all time.

"How much time before you can prep more shuttles?" I asked.

"Thirty minutes," she said.

"How long until the missiles hit?" I asked HARV.

"Twenty minutes."

"Oh, that won't work," I said.

HARV, patted me on the shoulder. "Very good, Zach. I wish I could think away the other missile, but I can't."

That triggered something in my brain. I smiled.

"He's happy," HARV said. "Yep, he's finally snapped."

"You can't think them away, but we're surrounded by the biggest collection of psi power ever."

I turned and Elena and Carol were by my side.

"Can you guys do it?"

Melda looked at me like I was crazy. It was a look I was very used to. "It's a relatively small object, traveling thousands of kilometers an hour in the vastness of space."

"Is that a yes?"

"Yes!" Elena answered.

Melda spun toward her. "I know you are powerful girl, but not THAT powerful."

Elena shook her head. "Alone, maybe not, at least not easily. But together, we can do it."

Melda just shook her head.

I turned toward Carol. "What do you think?"

"I don't think we've got anything to lose, except maybe a bit of pride."

"Then do it!"

Elena was the first to lock and load. She spread open her arms, tilted her head back, and stared deep into the Moon sky. Carol was next, mimicking Elena. Melda shook her head again.

Elena looked at her and said, "Do it!"

Melda sighed. She stepped to the left of Elena, took a deep breath and struck a pose very similar to Elena's.

HARV watched, scratching his head. "What's next? We'll all hold hands and sing 'Kumbaya'?"

I pointed at him. "You got any better ideas?"

HARV hung his head. "Sadly, no."

"Then you do your job and let the psis do theirs."

HARV acknowledged me with a nod. "I'm on it now!"

"What's happening there?" Ona's image shouted from over the com. "I'm a spoiled billionaire politician. I hate not knowing what's going on."

"We're trying something." I paused for a nano. "A bit different."

"What?" Ona ordered.

"HARV is going to deflect one of the missiles past the planet."

"That doesn't sound that odd. But that only accounts for one of the missiles."

I pulled my collar away from my throat. "Yeah, the other part of our plan is where things get a wee bit desperate," I conceded.

"What is it, Zach?"

"Can't I just tell you if it works? If not, I'd rather die with dignity."

"Zach, it can't be that crazy."

"I have Carol, Elena, and Melda trying to think the missile past us."

Ona shook her head. "I stand corrected."

Threa popped her head into the picture. "Greetings, Zach!" she said with a wave. She looked at Ona, "I heard what Zach said. I don't think the idea is that far-fetched."

I sighed. "Great, we're dead . . ."

Threa glared at the screen. "I heard that, Zach!"

I turned my attention to the three psis. "How are you ladies doing?"

"Don't ask," Carol said, without looking at me.

"Too late," I said.

Shara, Aprill, and Windee walked up to us. "Let us help," Shara said.

I shrugged. "Be my guest."

Shara and Aprill joined the others in their poses.

"Any luck?" I asked.

"It might be easier if you were quiet for a while," Carol said.

"I'll take that as a no," I said.

"We need more brainpower," Elena said.

"Well, there are a couple thousand more psis on the planet," Shara told her.

Elena cracked a slight smile. "I am linking them in now," she said.

"How many of them?" I asked.

"All of them," she said.

"Oh."

"They have seen what sitting back and doing nothing has gotten them. They are finally ready to help," Elena said.

I wasn't sure if Elena had coerced them all or if they had all seen the light on their own. I figured it was probably something in between. I've learned there aren't many absolutes in life. The sooner we accept that life is filled with many gray-shaded areas that are neither one thing or the other but instead a combination of many things, the better we'll all be.

There was silence for a few minutes as the psis concentrated on the skies. It was as if the entire population of the Moon was holding its breath, which, in a way, it was.

While the psis did their mental linking, I checked in on HARV. He was actually having better success. He had spotted the lead missile and was locking in on it.

"When are you going to be ready, HARV?" I asked.

"When I tell you I'm ready," he said.

It seems everybody was a bit touchy.

I turned my attention back to the psis. They were all soaked with perspiration. "I hate to be a pest but I don't think we have a lot of time," I said.

"Tió, we can see the incoming missile with our mind's eyes, but we can't get a lock on it; the picture is blurry," Carol said.

"We need more psis to lend us their energy," Elena said.

"But we are already linking all the psis on the Moon," Shara chipped in.

I looked at Ona's image. "We need the Earth psi population to join in."

Sure the percentage of the psis on the Moon was far greater than the percentage of psis on Earth. Earth, though, was much bigger and therefore housed many more psis. I figured there had to be at least twenty thousand more psis on Earth. If we could get a fraction of them to help it would double or triple our numbers.

Ona pushed herself back from the table a bit. "Ah, that may be a bit tricky."

"Why?" I asked.

"They haven't told the general populace," HARV said.

"Humans," Priscilla said with contempt.

I should have thought of that. I rolled my eyes. "I'm just surprised I didn't figure that out myself," I told Ona.

Ona sank back a bit and lifted her arms and shrugged. "Since we couldn't save most of them, we didn't want to worry them. We figured their last moments should be peaceful and blissful."

"And we didn't want them rushing our shuttle," Twoa added.

Ona focused on the screen. "Really, Zach, I doubt it would work."

Threa stuck her head back into the picture. "I bet it would."

"We really don't have anything to lose," I said.

"Speak for yourself," Ona said.

I needed to come up with a way Earth could get their psi population to link in and help without alerting them how close they came to death.

"Tell the people it was a mistake," I said.

"The government doesn't like to admit to making mistakes," Twoa said.

"Blame it on a computer error," I said.

The three of them smiled. "Now *that* we can do!" Ona said.

"Great. It's always the computer's fault," HARV spat.

"We need to get the SOS out fast," I said.

"Faster than fast," HARV said, getting his processors back on track, "both missiles are now within four minutes of impact."

"We are broadcasting over the PIHI-Pod network now!" Ona said.

I turned to my psis. "Any difference?"

At first there was more silence, then, "We have a clearer view now," they all said. In fact, every psi on the planet said it. "We still can't stop it. Too much momentum."

"Keep working on it," I said.

The minutes passed like seconds. The psis and HARV were each trying to lock on to their targets. It wasn't easy, but it was all or nothing.

Finally HARV shouted, "I got it! I got it! I win!"

I shook my head. "It's not a contest HARV."

He smiled. "Of course not; though I'm still glad I won."

"Just fire the beam HARV."

"Already done," HARV said.

There was silence.

"And?"

More silence.

"HARV?"

"The beam didn't stop it. It has too much momentum. DOS!"

I turned to the ladies. "Well?"

"Same here," Carol said. "The missile has way too much force to stop."

"Then don't stop it!" I shouted. "Squish it! Swat it! Stomp it! Make it go boom!"

Elena and Carol both smiled. "Now that we can do!" the said.

"Yes, we can!" every psi on the planet said.

"Well?" I asked.

"Look up!" Every psi on the planet said, pointing upward.

There was a bright yellow flash in the northwestern sky. I smiled. One down, one to go, but we didn't have much time.

"Okay, psi force," I said with a smile, "We need you to knock out the other missile, pronto."

"We don't have it locked in yet."

"HARV, feed them the coordinates through the PIHI-Pod system for the psis."

"On it," HARV said.

I waited. "Well . . ."

"Done," HARV said. "Wow, tech and psi and Earth and Moon working together to save the Moon."

"If it works," I said.

Elena smiled. Her smiled rippled across the others. "That was easy," they all said.

"Then smash it fast!" I shouted.

"No need to shout," they all responded.

They all lifted their arms, pointing to the northeastern sky. There was a bigger yellow flash. We were safe.

A roar went out over two planets.

Priscilla looked Electra up then down. "She doesn't look like she's all that," she whispered to me.

"We did it, Tió!" Carol shouted, running up to me and then leaping into my arms. She gave me a kiss on the cheek.

"Was there every any doubt?" I said.

"Massive amounts of doubt . . . More doubt than even *I* could calculate," HARV said.

As I put Carol down, Elena came walking up to me. She extended her hand. "Zach, I am so glad I didn't kill you the four or five times I considered it."

I hugged her. "You have no idea how many times I've heard that."

Chapter 43

The next day, Electra and I took the first flight back to Earth. I had spent enough time on the Moon that I couldn't get off soon enough. Carol, on the other hand, had such a great time linking with her fellow psis that she decided to spend two more weeks on the Moon. Being the good boss I am, I gave her the time, with pay. She and Elena wanted to hang out and see what they could learn from each other. No way I was going to argue with that.

As for Elena, I had a little chat with her before I left. I wasn't totally certain she didn't glean any knowledge she shouldn't have from her cousin Lea's last moments. Elena guaranteed me that she hadn't, backing up that statement by noting if she had, she probably would have turned us all into turnips. Of course when I told her for all I know she did turn us into turnips and then turned us back, she laughed uneasily. For now, I had to trust her. Sometimes that's all you can do. I figured this wouldn't be the last I saw of Elena. I hoped that was a good thing.

Melda went with us with the intent to turn herself

over quietly to the World Council. She confessed to her role in everything that went on. She even admitted that much of HARV's and my unusual behavior on the Moon was due to her and Lea tweaking our interface. The scientist in her found it fascinating that while HARV did make me much harder to mentally dominate, the interface between us also made us more susceptible to bickering and violence. I told her that due to her role in saving the Earth they would go easy on her. DOS, the World Council might even give her a decoration for playing with my mind. Melda wasn't sure she deserved leniency after what she did. Having lost her husband and her daughter, though, I figured she had been punished enough.

Shannon Cannon was declared innocent and offered a job as Ona's bodyguard. Last I heard, she was still pondering the offer as she also had a chance to head her own reality show.

The World Council, in its finite wisdom, decided to make Shara the new Head Administrator of the Moon. They gave her a lot of credit for tipping them off to the Moon's attack. I figured she was actually as good a choice as any. The really good news was that Priscilla would be acting as her Vice-Administrator. Maurice was to become the Moon's special spokesape. This was a move to hopefully improve human, psi, and ape relationships. It seemed all sides were trying—finally.

The World Council even promised to strongly consider the Moon's freedom next year, especially if none of their populace leaked their attack on the Moon. Shockingly, none of them seemed anxious to mention it. I guess there are certainly some advantages to a tight society. Though HARV would note that it wasn't so much that the society was tight; it was that none of them wanted to cause trouble.

Earthside, the media had gotten a bit of a whiff of an idea that something more was up with the missile launch than a computer error. The John Stewart clone made fun of the entire situation on the *Twice-Daily Show*, doing a funny little enactment of Nixon blaming a computer glitch for his little Watergate problem.

Fortunately, before the story could really grow legs and run, some celebrity got caught rigging his automated car to drive over the speed limit and was arrested. While the officer, who happened to be an android, was reading the star his rights the star began ranting about how androids weren't really people, and therefore were not fit to guard people. That story then knocked any hint of two worlds almost coming to an end completely out of the news. I don't even think PBS-net was covering it.

As Earth came into view, Electra must have noticed the smile on my face.

"What's up, mi amor? You look pensive," she asked.

"Nah, just thinking," I said.

"Ha-ha," HARV said in my brain, and Electra out loud, both unimpressed.

Someday, somebody is going to appreciate that joke.

"Just summing things up," I said to them.

"Ah, the classic end-of-story information dump," HARV said.

I ignored him.

"Good to see Earth again, isn't it?" Electra said.

"I forgot how beautiful it is, in one piece," I said.

"Don't tell me you were worried," she said.

"They say never let them see you sweat, but trust me, I was. Weren't you?"

Electra shook her head and smiled. She touched my hand gently. "Women don't sweat. They glow."

"So weren't you glowing like you were radio-active?"

"Nope," she said with a wry smile.

"You must have been recovering from being frozen."

She gave me a little love punch in the arm. "No, I just have faith in you."

"Glad somebody does," I said.

She stroked my arm. "You did an amazing thing."

"Actually the psis, gorillas, and HARV did most of the work. I just kind of managed."

Her smile grew. "You don't get it, do you?"

"HARV does accuse me of being rather dense."

"Rather dense?" HARV mumbled inside my head. "You make iridium seem fluffy and light."

"You got the peoples of the Moon and the Earth to communicate, cooperate, and work together, to stop standing on the sidelines and to save two planets. That's an amazing accomplishment," Electra said.

"Saving the planets, getting the people to talk and then getting them to do something?"

"All three, but I'm most amazed about the latter two."

"They do say the word processor is mightier than the sword. So I guess communication *is* the ultimate weapon. We just need to know how to use it—for good."

HARV appeared next to us. "Don't worry, Zach. As long as you have me by your brain, I'll be able to help you communicate with the entire world! I guess that makes *me* the ultimate weapon."

"As scary as that may be on some levels, HARV, it's nice to know that the world's most advanced, cognitive processor can do something other than balance my checkbook."

I smiled as I looked out on Earth growing larger and larger in the window. Yep, it certainly was a nice looking planet. I was going to make sure it stayed that way.

Jim Hines

The Tales of Jig Dragonslayer

"If you've always kinda rooted for the little guy, even maybe had a bit of a place in your heart for the likes of Gollum, rather than the Boromirs and Gandalfs of the world, pick up Goblin Quest."
—*The SF Site*

GOBLIN QUEST
978-0-7564-0400-2

GOBLIN HERO
978-0-7564-0442-0

And coming soon:
GOBLIN WAR
978-0-7564-0493-2

To Order Call: 1-800-788-6262
www.dawbooks.com

DAW 82

MERCEDES LACKEY

Reserved for the Cat

The *Elemental Masters* Series

In 1910, in an alternate Paris, Ninette Dupond, a penniless young dancer, recently dismissed from the Paris Opera, thinks she has gone mad when she finds herself in a conversation with a skinny tomcat. However, Ninette is desperate—and hungry—enough to try anything. She follows the cat's advice and travels to Blackpool, England, where she is to impersonate a famous Russian ballerina and dance, not in the opera, but in the finest of Blackpool's music halls. With her natural talent for dancing, and her magic for enthralling an audience, it looks as if Ninette will gain the fame and fortune the cat has promised. But the real Nina Tchereslavsky is not as far away as St. Petersburg...and she's not as human as she appears...

978-0-7564-0362-1

And don't miss the first four books of
The Elemental Masters:

The Serpent's Shadow	0-7564-0061-9
The Gates of Sleep	0-7564-0101-1
Phoenix and Ashes	0-7564-0272-7
The Wizard of London	0-7564-0363-4

To Order Call: 1-800-788-6262
www.dawbooks.com

P. R. Frost

The Tess Noncoiré Adventures

"Frost's fantasy debut series introduces a charming protag-
onist, both strong and vulnerable, and her cheeky companion. An intriguing plot and a well-developed warrior sister-
hood make this a good choice for fans of the urban fantasy
of Tanya Huff, Jim Butcher, and Charles deLint."
—*Library Journal*

HOUNDING THE MOON
978-0-7564-0425-3

and now in hardcover:
MOON IN THE MIRROR
978-0-7564-0424-6

To Order Call: 1-800-788-6262
www.dawbooks.com

DAW 78

Tanya Huff

The Confederation Novels

"As a heroine, Kerr shines. She is cut from the same mold as Ellen Ripley of the *Aliens* films. Like her heroine, Huff delivers the goods." —*SF Weekly*

in an omnibus edition:

A CONFEDERATION OF VALOR
(Valor's Choice, The Better Part of Valor)
0-7564-0399-5
978-0-7564-0399-7

and now in hardcover:

THE HEART OF VALOR
978-0-7564-0435-2

To Order Call: 1-800-788-6262
www.dawbooks.com

Tanya Huff
The *Smoke* Series

Featuring Henry Fitzroy, Vampire

"Fans of *Buffy* and *The X-Files* will cheer the latest exploits of Tony Foster, wizard-in-training.... This spin-off from Huff's popular Blood series stands alone as an entertaining supernatural adventure with plenty of sex, violence, and sarcastic humor."
— *Publishers Weekly*

SMOKE AND SHADOWS
0-7564-0263-8
978-0-7564-0263-1

SMOKE AND MIRRORS
0-7564-0348-0
978-0-7564-0348-5

SMOKE AND ASHES
978-0-7564-0415-4

To Order Call: 1-800-788-6262
www.dawbooks.com

Tanya Huff's
Blood Books

Private eye, vampire, and cop: supernatural crime solvers—and the most unusual love triangle in town.
Now a Lifetime original series.

"Smashing entertainment for a wide audience"
—Romantic Times

BLOOD PRICE
978-0-7564-0501-4
BLOOD TRAIL
978-0-7564-0502-1
BLOOD LINES
978-0-7564-0503-8
BLOOD PACT
978-0-7564-0504-5
BLOOD DEBT
978-0-7564-0505-2

To Order Call: 1-800-788-6262